ALSO BY REMI ADELEKE

Transformed: A Navy SEAL's Unlikely Journey from the Throne of Africa, to the Streets of the Bronx, to Defying All Odds

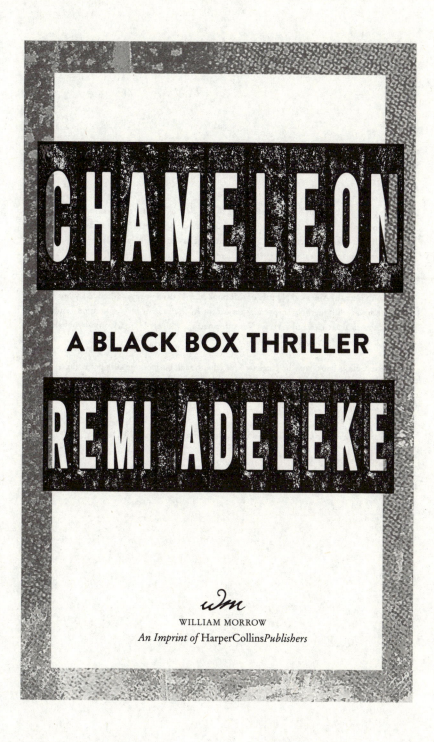

CHAMELEON

A BLACK BOX THRILLER

REMI ADELEKE

WILLIAM MORROW
An Imprint of HarperCollinsPublishers

CHAMELEON. Copyright © 2023 by Remi Adeleke. All rights reserved. Printed in the United States of America. No part of this book may be used or reproduced in any manner whatsoever without written permission except in the case of brief quotations embodied in critical articles and reviews. For information, address HarperCollins Publishers, 195 Broadway, New York, NY 10007.

HarperCollins books may be purchased for educational, business, or sales promotional use. For information, please email the Special Markets Department at SPsales@harpercollins.com.

FIRST EDITION

Library of Congress Cataloging-in-Publication Data has been applied for.

ISBN 978-0-06-323883-1

23 24 25 26 27 LBC 5 4 3 2 1

*To my daughter, Ciana, and my sons, Carter,
Caleb, and Cayden; this book would not be what it
is without the winds of inspiration and motivation
that you four have blown into my creative sails.
Whether consciously or unconsciously I thank you
for the constant push. Remember to always charge
forward with excellence. Never settle. Never quit.*

Love you always,
Daddy/Remi/Kali/Chameleon

THE SETUP

OUTSKIRTS OF ROCINHA, RIO DE JANEIRO, BRAZIL

IN THE STEAMING LUSHNESS OF THE JUNGLE, DRUG smugglers' airstrips appear like vampires between midnight and dawn, then dissolve in gunfire or the rush of monsoons. This particular criminal enterprise was less like a runway, and more like a shaving scar.

It was six hundred feet of flat umber earth, plowed and leveled by sweating cartel slaves after they'd hacked down kapok trees and hauled them aside. It broiled in the morning sun, silent except for the slithers of snakes and the howls of macaws. The only other things there were the carcass of an old Huey helicopter, the abandoned hut of a murdered cocaine boss, and a camouflage net laced with coca leaves that looked like mush from the sky. There was previously a fresh bomb crater in the middle of the strip, made by a Brazilian Tucano strike fighter, but it had just been repaired.

The CIA had asked the Brazilian air force to please not bomb it again. At least for today.

Twelve hard-looking men were standing under the net, surrounding three brown Land Rover Defenders parked nose to nose. They were the Package, operators from a US Army Special Forces Tier One unit, with untrimmed beards, Glock handguns under their bush shirts, and MK18 assault rifles racked in their rides. Off to one side were three CIA agents, two men and a striking woman. They were prepping a RMUS tactical surveillance drone, MBITR communications gear, and a battered white VW Kombi minibus. The woman was donning a long black frock and a pastel scarf to cover her face.

The Package commander, a large captain with Sicilian features called Pacenza, was poring over a map on the hood of one Land Rover with the CIA team leader, a middle-aged, square-jawed blond man called Thane. They all turned their heads as an aircraft engine buzzed over the trees.

A purple-and-white Cessna 180 bounced down on the far end of the strip in a cloud of grit, disgorged a single man from the cockpit, then kept right on going and took off again as if the place was infected with a plague. The man trudged through the sun-flickered dust. He was bronze-skinned, like the darkest of Brazilians, with a straw gaucho hat, a baggy tunic over worn jeans, and sandals. He was hauling a bulging leather satchel on a shoulder strap and slipping what looked like a bracelet of prayer beads into one pocket. He was frail, skinny, and weathered, with the posture and gait of an old train conductor who's seen too many rides. Not the kind of man you'd want standing next to you in a bar fight.

Pacenza straightened up from the map and squinted at the intruder. Two of his men swept their bush shirts open and touched their Glocks.

"Who the hell's this vagrant?" Pacenza said to Thane.

"Take it easy," Thane said. "He's mine."

The man walked under the camouflage net, but he remained outside the Package perimeter, just listening as Pacenza turned back to finish briefing his men.

"Truck One," Pacenza said. "Remember, your only objective is to wrap this guy up. Grab him and get out of Dodge. Two and Three, when we move, head straight for the choke point." His men nodded and a few gave a thumbs-up. "Thane?"

"This target's elusive," Thane said to the men. "He never shows his face." He looked briefly at the stranger, then turned back again. "The asset will lead us right to him, but we'll only get this one shot."

Again the operators nodded, while peering over at the weird interloper.

Pacenza said, "All right, mount up," and they began moving toward the Land Rovers. The man ambled up to Thane. They didn't shake hands, and he ignored the glares of the operators and the smirks of the CIA agents. The expression on his mahogany features was indiscernible, though his deep, dark eyes beneath the floppy brim of his hat seemed to tell tales of pain. Thane made no small talk. There was something in the man's demeanor he didn't want to disturb.

"You ready?" Thane said.

"I am," said the man in a Portuguese accent. He glanced anxiously at the operators. "And are they?"

"Pit bulls are always ready."

The man sighed, almost mournfully, and said, "May I ask about the bad ones?" He had a voice like gravel mixed with honey.

"They're about fourteen kilometers away. I'd say thirty minutes."

The man nodded, then looked over Thane's shoulder at the CIA agents. They had already loaded the drone into an open-topped box that looked like a luggage carrier atop the minibus. They had the doors open, the woman was climbing into the rear cargo compartment, and the two male agents in civilian Brazilian garb were standing by. One of them smiled at the man and swept an inviting arm toward the bus like a chauffeur. The man didn't smile back, but he crossed himself.

He walked past Thane toward the Kombi, his gait still crooked as if one hip ached, and all the operators followed him with suspicious eyes. They were accustomed to working with some strange characters, but having an entire kinetic mission depend on one hobo seemed over the top. The man climbed into the cargo compartment beside the woman and slid the door shut. The other two CIA agents looked at Thane, who twirled a finger in the air, then they jumped in the front and the Kombi took off through the jungle in a tire spray of mud.

Thane turned to the Package and barked, "We're rolling. *Now*."

The operators turned over their Land Rovers and gunned the engines. Pacenza held back for a moment and gripped Thane's arm.

"Okay, Thane, spill it. Who *is* that dude?"

Thane looked down at Pacenza's grip, then up at his face.

"They call him Perdido."

"What's that mean?"

"The Lost One," said Thane.

ONE

THE TRI-BORDER AREA OF SOUTH AMERICA, WHERE the fingers of Paraguay, Argentina, and Brazil reach out to touch, is one of the most dangerous places on earth. And the mischief that flows out of the Tri-Border easily makes its way to Rio.

Cocaine is harvested there by the bushel, drug kingpins rule, and bandits and terrorists ply their trades while paying off policemen and politicians. Hezbollah, the notorious terror proxy of Iran, ships boatloads of mind-altering treats from Rio de Janeiro to Europe, earning their keep for Tehran. The Comando Vermelho, the vicious Brazilian gun-running and drug cartel, rules the streets of Rio with an iron fist.

But there's always room for good business. You can buy and sell nearly anything in the TBA, except for a nuclear warhead. Odds are, however, that's coming soon.

The Kombi minibus rumbled out from the jungle hills, where the muddy track became the broken lane of Rua Tenente Márcio Pinto and crooked mountain huts kissed the road, and it headed downslope for the favela called Rocinha. The CIA driver, a compact, rust-haired man called Spencer, kept his pace modest as he gripped the steering wheel in one hand and with the other used a controller to launch the rooftop drone. The agent in the passenger seat, a former recon marine named Jason, looked out the dirty windshield through a pair of cheap sunglasses and said nothing. The woman in the back, Neveah, twisted a bone mic deep in one ear, but she didn't speak to the disheveled man sitting next to her either.

They'd all been told to leave the man called Perdido alone. He was staring out his window, as if taking a moment to steel his heart.

Spencer picked up speed, skewing left, then right, until he was cruising due west along Estrada da Gávea. Then from the back Perdido muttered, "*Um momento, por favor.*" Spencer stopped the Kombi at an overlook, while Perdido rolled down his window and appeared to be taking in great gulps of air.

From their perch, Rocinha looked as though God had squatted with his butt to the beach, scooped out a muddy trough between two enormous slabs of granite, then spilled pastel Legos all over the bowl. There were thousands of crooked houses piled atop one another, with winding streets and alleys and switchbacks, and every wall and storefront was splashed with some sort of rainbow graffiti. The favela echoed with motorbike engines, coughing old cars, and the wild twangs of samba. Yet despite its carefree daylight rhythms, it was no place to be after dark.

"*Avante,*" Perdido whispered.

Spencer gunned the Kombi and drove into the ruckus, weaving among fruit stalls, garbage bins, motor scooters, prostitutes, drug peddlers, and rough men in loose shirts that barely concealed their guns. Driving due west, he spotted the rendezvous point at last, a hotel called Nossa Senhora da Boa Viagem, which looked strangely like the Texas Alamo, except it was painted azure blue.

"*Aqui,*" Perdido said when they were still three blocks from the hotel square. Spencer pulled over, Perdido unfolded himself from the van as if his old limbs were arthritic, and the Kombi kept on going and disappeared somewhere.

Perdido walked toward the square, muttering to himself as if engaged in a conflict with his soul, the hunch of his back making him appear even shorter than before. As he neared the hotel, he could see the agent called Jason already seated at an outdoor café, sipping *cafezinho* and reading *O Globo*. The Kombi was parked a block farther down, where from inside the agent called Spencer was controlling the drone high in the sky. The woman, Neveah, was nowhere to be seen.

"Dark Horse Two for Overwatch," Jason murmured as he sipped from his coffee cup and glanced at Perdido. "Our guy is moving to contact." A "Roger" from Thane crackled in the bone mic inside his ear.

Across from the blue hotel was the canopy of a carpet shop, with a black-and-silver Moto Guzzi California 1400 motorcycle parked in front, leaning on its kickstand. Perdido trudged past the bike and went inside. The shop was lined with shelves full of finely woven rugs, with the shop owner perched behind his teakwood counter at the far end, and the motorcycle rider standing close by.

The rider was tall, with walnut-colored skin and short black hair. His hazel eyes were watchful, while his mouth was set in a relaxed smile above a square jaw. He wore a leather motorcycle jacket over broad shoulders, black jeans, and steel-tipped boots. He was the sort of man you *would* want next to you in a bar fight. He was slipping a wad of Brazilian reals into the shop owner's hand.

"Please watch the bike, my friend," the rider said in a Portuguese baritone.

"Take your time, *irmão*." The shop owner placed the cash into an inlaid wooden box. Now the rider could leave his motorcycle in peace and it would not be touched.

Perdido hung back, as if reluctant to intrude. The rider turned, grinned at the frail man, and said, *"Bom dia, irmão."* Good morning, brother.

"Bom dia, Senhor Marco," said Perdido, but before he could say anything else, the rider took his elbow and walked him deeper into the rows of carpets. Perdido cringed as if the rider's fingers were claws.

"Do you have the microchip, Perdido?" The rider looked down at the smaller man. He was half a head taller, athletically built.

"Yes, of course, Mr. Marco."

"You are sure?" The rider squeezed his arm a bit tighter. "These men are the Red Commando. They do not play games."

"Y-yes, I have it," Perdido stammered.

"Tell me again how you got it. And please don't lie."

"I told you," Perdido pleaded. "My cousin, Armando, he works for the American drug men in Panama. He is taking a terrible risk, but he badly needs the money, as do I."

"Good." The rider called Marco grinned. "We all like money."

"But . . . but what if they simply decide to kill me?" Perdido seemed panicky now. "And keep their money, and take the chip?"

Marco moved his large hand to Perdido's shoulder and squeezed. "Have no fear, Perdido. Their leader trusts me. That will not happen."

Perdido's knees trembled. Marco glanced at his leather satchel. "What's in that bag, Perdido?"

"Clothes, for my journey." Perdido's eyes gleamed as if he might cry. "And food."

Marco laughed. "Well, after today you will have enough cash to buy a feast for the entire favela. Now come." He slapped the smaller man's back. "It is time to go to church."

He took Perdido's elbow again and walked him out of the shop, and the agents in the square saw them exit and made their moves . . .

The Igreja Santo Pedro was a small Catholic church three blocks south from the hotel square, surprising in its orderly cleanliness given the slum that filled the surrounding air with swill. Its interior walls were plaster white, the pews of rough-hewn candle-wood, and the ceiling of wooden beams that looked like Kit Kat bars. There was a small office behind the church's podium and gleaming crucifix, and the priest was hunkered down inside, reading a passage from James 2:13 about mercy. He'd been ordered by the Comando Vermelho, the Red Command, not to emerge until they were gone.

Marco, the rider, rapped on the church's heavy oak door, then pushed it open and led Perdido inside, gripping his neck as if he were a child. But Perdido saw none of the chapel's quaint decor. He saw only the six frightening men of the Comando. They were spread out among the pews, wearing pricey kicks and slim jeans, their muscular arms bursting through leather vests or cutoff shirts. They had red bandanas over their faces, like bandits of the Old West, and backward ball caps. They gripped short-barreled Russian Krinkov submachine guns and had silver revolvers jammed in their leather belts.

Their leader, known only as Bruto, was a bear of a man with wild black hair like a member of Kiss. Wanted by six international police agencies, Bruto would emerge from hiding only for something of great value, and he now stood in the aisle like the wary captain of a pirate ship.

Perdido froze where he'd entered with Marco. These men thought nothing of taking fortunes and lives. He knew they ran drugs and guns from the TBA and over the southern US border, and even the Mexican cartels gave them full quarter. The previous month, the Comando had captured an American DEA agent and his female partner outside Ciudad Juárez.

Not only had they murdered the pair, but the way they'd done it could not be described.

Perdido had told Marco that his microchip contained a list of all the DEA's undercover agents in the TBA, and Marco had agreed that the Comando would pay a very high price for it. Yet despite Marco's assurance that all would be well, Perdido now looked like he wanted to be anywhere else on earth but there.

"*Cristo sejalouvado.*" Christ be praised, Bruto growled as he dipped his large head. "You have come, Marco."

"Of course." Marco grinned. "I am a man of my word."

"We will see." Bruto pulled his red kerchief down and spat on the church floor. He looked at Perdido. "Who is this scarecrow, Marco?"

"My source," Marco said.

"Your source should eat more," Bruto snarled. "A strong breeze would blow him away." He glared at Perdido. "Show me the microchip."

Perdido reached into his tunic pocket and produced a small black plastic box. He opened it to reveal a micro thumb drive nestled in metallic clips, and held it out with both quivering hands as if it were a scorpion.

"*Muito bom.*" Very good, said Bruto. "Give it to me now."

"And . . . the money, Senhor Bruto?" Marco asked.

Bruto's smile was ugly, with gold-rimmed teeth. He dropped a canvas satchel onto the floor, then touched the butt of a heavy Browning pistol in his belt.

"You can take it, Marco," he said, as if it were a dare. "But I suggest you wait."

Marco didn't move. Sweat was starting to pop on his brow as he suddenly realized that Perdido might have been right. They might not be leaving there alive.

One of Bruto's men stepped up to take the chip from Perdido, but Bruto shoved the man back, walked to Perdido, and snatched the thumb drive himself. He snapped his fingers, another man handed him a small laptop, and he opened it next to Perdido on the back of a pew. He plugged the thumb drive in. Marco and Perdido held their breaths.

After an endless minute, Bruto nodded, unplugged the drive, and dropped it into the pocket of his leather jacket. He tossed the laptop to one of his men, snarled a victorious grin, then reached for his pistol and started turning back to Marco and Perdido.

All at once he was viciously spun around, yanked backward on his heels, barely able to grunt out with a gasp, "*Babaca!*" Bastard!

The man called Perdido, who only seconds before had seemed about to pass out, had Bruto in a headlock. Perdido's eyes were like a shark's; he was choking Bruto with his sinewy left arm, and a .45-caliber Derringer pistol had sprung from his sleeve into his right hand. He was grinding the barrel into Bruto's temple, and his left fist held a gleaming digital detonator. Perdido's leather satchel was now on the floor, and he toed it over toward Bruto's men.

"Open it," Perdido spat.

Bruto's men were cursing and waving their weapons, yet his second-in-command bent to the satchel, opened it, and blinked. It was packed with four bricks of Semtex high explosives, with a digital readout flashing in neon green. He jerked back from the satchel as if it contained a hissing cobra.

"We shall be leaving now with the chip," said Perdido. "And the money."

"I . . . I have nothing to do with this!" Marco blurted.

"Shut up, Marco," said Perdido as he ground the pistol into Bruto's skull and held the detonator up, thumb poised on the trigger. "You all know I have *nothing* to lose."

Bruto was choking in Perdido's powerful armlock. His hands flailed toward his Browning, but it had fallen and skidded across the floor. "*Sabaca!*" he cursed again as he looked at his shocked men, who were training their weapons like a firing squad, but helpless to act.

"*Do it,*" Bruto gasped. One of them kicked the money satchel over.

"Pick it up, Marco," Perdido snapped.

Marco stared at Perdido in shock, but he picked up the money. The man who he'd thought was a submissive weakling was now calling the shots and in complete control.

"Now," said Perdido to the Comando as he backed up with Bruto toward the door, "if any of you move, you'll be breaking bread with the devil tonight. So be wise, stay where you are, and count your blessings."

And then he, Bruto, and Marco were gone . . .

TWO

A BROWN LAND ROVER DEFENDER SCREECHED TO A halt outside the church. Two operators jumped out as Perdido shoved Bruto toward the truck, and they grabbed Bruto by the hair, cranked his wrists up his spine, and slammed him face-first into the back. Then they jumped into the Defender and roared away south.

Perdido grabbed Marco by his leather jacket and dragged him north on the run.

Two minutes later, Perdido and Marco burst back into the carpet shop from the rear as the shopkeeper jolted and spilled his tea. Perdido hauled Marco outside to the Moto Guzzi, gripped the back of his belt, slung him onto the seat like a rag doll, and swung up behind him.

"Drive," Perdido barked as he jammed the money satchel between his thighs.

"But Perdido," Marco pleaded. "I just bought this machine!"

Perdido conked Marco on the side of his skull with his Derringer butt. "Drive the damn bike. If they don't kill you, I *will*."

"All right, all right," Marco moaned, and he gunned the machine to life and they roared into the street, scattering cursing locals.

Perdido could have made Marco drive south toward the beach and they'd have been gone from Rocinha in a flash. But instead he forced him to turn east, where in a few blocks they'd be plunging into the favela's teeming warrens and alleyways. He bent low over Marco's vibrating shoulder as his hat flew off and he barked in English, "Dark Horse Main, with the asset, running for the X."

"Roger, Main," Thane's voice said in his ear. "Make sure you keep him alive."

Back at the church, it had taken only a minute for the Comando Vermelho to understand they'd been had. The accursed bastard with the detonator was gone, and he could not possibly know if they'd moved or not. Bruto's second-in-command peered into the bag of Semtex, saw that the detonators were wired to nothing, yelled, "It's a fake!" and ran from the church with his men on his heels.

They burst out onto Rua Quatro, and as they piled into a maroon Toyota Tundra the second-in-command saw a small boy staring and shouted, "Men running?" The boy stabbed a finger north, and the driver spun the wheel and punched the gas and they roared off as the Tundra's sunroof cranked open. A Comando popped up with his Krinkov and racked a round in its breech.

"There!" The driver jabbed the windshield as the Tundra bounced onto Estrada da Gávea, just as a black-and-silver Moto Guzzi blurred through the intersection from west to east. Marco was perched in front, knees nearly touching his hunched-over chest, and that bastard Perdido was behind, gripping Marco's jacket collar as if he were whipping a racehorse.

"Where's Bruto?" the driver exclaimed.

"Never mind," the second-in-command spat. "We get *them*, we get *him*."

Atop the bouncing Moto Guzzi, Marco also yelled "There!" as he spotted the onrushing Tundra in the bike's side-view mirror. He saw the Comando perched on top with the horrid submachine gun and knew they were going to die. But Perdido only growled *"Perfeito"*—Perfect—and he yelled in Marco's ear, "Faster."

"Why didn't you just blow them up?" Marco cried over his shoulder.

"There was nothing but clay in that bag," Perdido replied.

"God *help* us," Marco keened.

The first bullet cracked the air just beside Marco's face, a pistol round fired from the Tundra's left rear window. Next came a wicked burst from a Krinkov on the other side, and as Perdido yanked Marco's arm and made him jink left, the bullets whipped past his back and pocked up the face of a stucco flat. The Tundra roared down Estrada da Gávea, only one block now behind the Moto Guzzi, and the Comando men fired wildly as Marco slalomed the bike among scattering vehicles and pedestrians. Shopkeepers came out to watch the melee, smoking their Brazilian pipes as if running gun battles in Rocinha were a daily occurrence.

"Dark Horse Main for Dark Horse Two," Perdido barked, hoping his voice would be heard. "Now would be good."

"Dark Two for Main, gun it and trust us," came the reply, and Perdido heard it loud and clear and prodded Marco with the pistol barrel in his back.

The CIA team's VW Kombi suddenly burst from a side street, just behind the bike and fifteen meters in front of the Tundra. The Comando driver slammed on his brakes and the rooftop gunner's chin impacted with the Krinkov, drawing blood. Bruto's second-in-command thrust his head from the front passenger window, waving his pistol and cursing the two men in the Kombi. They flipped him off and cursed back, but then they saw the pistol, raised their hands, and rolled the Kombi backward, stalling the Comando for another ten seconds. Then the Tundra burned rubber and raced onward, with its occupants screaming at the idiots in the car, but now they were two hundred meters behind the motorcycle.

"Dark Two for Main, you got breathing space now," said the Kombi driver through a grin.

It was Jason driving, while beside him Spencer worked the drone. He squinted at its feed on his tablet and spoke to Thane. "Dark Two Bravo for Overwatch. Route looks clear, three more mikes and they're out of the sugar cubes."

"Roger," Thane answered from somewhere else.

Perdido pushed Marco eastward and upward. They weaved among cars and bicycles as behind them vehicles honked madly and he could feel the Tundra closing. He knew Marco couldn't handle the rest of it, so he jammed the Derringer in his belt, leaned hard into Marco's back, kicked his boot off the clutch, swatted his hands from the throttle and brake, and took over as Marco grabbed the headlight to keep from flying off. Perdido took a hard banking right as if he were heading south for the Zuzu Angel Tunnel, then whipped the bike hard to the left as Marco screamed, then straightened up and flew north again on Estrada da Gávea, full throttle.

On the outskirts of the favela, just outside the Café Pingado on da Gávea, the woman Neveah was standing in her black frock and scarf. She watched as Perdido and Marco blurred by and waited until the roaring Tundra appeared and raced after them. She held her position for ten seconds, her jade green eyes scanning the streets from which the bike and the Comando had emerged, then muttered as if to no one.

"Dark Horse Three for Overwatch, no more follows. They're clear."

"Overwatch for Dark Three, good copy," said Thane in her ear.

Perdido jinked right at the hairpin overlook, gunned it flat out where the traffic was clear and quick, and glanced in the bike's rearview mirror to make sure the Tundra was there. It was closing fast, and he cut across traffic as oncoming drivers skidded and he sped north onto Rua Tenente Márcio Pinto, where there was no more urban cover, only the crumbling mountain huts at the foot of the jungle.

The Tundra followed, spitting up mud from its tires, and Perdido knew there was nothing to stop them now from opening fire on full auto. He hunched over Marco's cringing form and ducked as low as he could, and sure enough he heard the Krinkovs behind him, like jackhammers on anvils, and bullets cracked the air on both sides of the bike and kicked up dirt from the shoulders. He felt a blow like an ice pick on his spine and another right after that, but he kept on cranking the throttle to the end of its twist and Marco didn't hear his grunts.

The Moto Guzzi dived into the jungle, running fast on a hard-packed track for half a klick, then its wheels left the earth at the top of a rise. It arced into the air, then crashed down hard on the other side. Marco gasped, because there on both flanks were two brown Land Rover Defenders poking from the trees with bearded, wild-looking men crouching behind them with long black guns. But Perdido kept on driving, right through the Package's ambush and out the other side, as the Comando's Tundra also crested the rise and bounced back down onto the track, with the men inside firing madly from its rooftop and all its windows.

The Package had no other option. The Tundra exploded with the impact of a LAW rocket as the operators opened up on it with everything they had. Its nose rose up as if it had been kicked in its guts, yellow flames burst from the splintering windshield, and the rooftop gunner cartwheeled in the air as the Tundra rolled over on its side, skidded ten feet, and stopped, a smoking wreck full of corpses.

Thane got out of one of the Defenders, walked to the wreck, and stood there with his hands on his hips as an operator put out the flames with a fire extinguisher and some ammunition cooked off. Pacenza walked up beside Thane as he switched the magazine in his MK18 for a fresh one.

"Well, that worked pretty good," Pacenza said, though he didn't seem pleased.

"Yes it did," Thane said as the third Land Rover with Bruto inside rolled out from the jungle on the other side and stopped. "We've got Bruto. The rest of them didn't leave you much choice." He thrust his chin at the smoldering mess. "And we'll still want everything they have."

"Roger." Pacenza called to two of his operators while the rest held security at both ends of the ambush site. From the favela side, the VW Kombi cruised over the rise, pulled to one side, and Neveah, Jason, and Spencer got out. A white drone with four silver propellers appeared over the trees and landed with grace at Spencer's feet, as if the pilot were a falconer.

Perdido returned on the Moto Guzzi with Marco, who was muttering and dripping sweat. Neveah pulled off her scarf, helped Marco to the ground, and walked him over to one of the Land Rovers as he stared at her and blathered nonsensical epithets.

Perdido dismounted the bike, walked to Thane, and gave him the microchip and the satchel full of illicit cash.

"Give me a hand," he said in a normal American accent as he pulled off his tunic. He was wearing a plate carrier, and the rear ceramic had two bullet punctures, one on each side of the center. Thane unstrapped the carrier, lifted it over Perdido's head, dropped it onto the track, and handed him a bottle of water. Pacenza was standing close by, but he simply stared at the man who he'd thought was no more than a CIA asset.

"You were lucky." Thane smiled up at Perdido. "They could have hit you in that thick skull of yours."

"It wasn't luck," Perdido said as he put his tunic back on and remounted the bike.

"Right," said Thane. "See you in Virginia."

Perdido nodded, turned the motorcycle around, and drove off north into the jungle.

Pacenza walked back over to Thane as both men watched Perdido disappear. The Package commander's expression was stormy.

"All right, Thane, so who *is* that dude?" Pacenza demanded. "I thought you said he was an asset!"

"When did I say that?"

"When you briefed my men." Pacenza was fuming. "You looked at him and said he's the asset leading us to the target!"

"Wow, easy, tiger. I admit I looked his way, but that doesn't mean I was talking about him. I was talking about Marco." Thane shrugged. "You assumed. And you know what they say about people who assume."

"Screw you, Thane," Pacenza snapped. "Who the hell is he? Better tell me now, or I'll ensure my men never support another one of your freak shows."

Thane smiled.

"He's the key that turns the lock," he said. "His name's Kali Kent."

THREE

THE COLD CUTS HARD ON THE ATLANTIC OCEAN AT midnight in March, when even a spitting drizzle can feel like ice needles stabbing your skin. The Boston Whaler Dauntless cruiser, a sleek twenty-seven-foot craft, had twin 600 horsepower Mercury outboards driving it west through four-foot waves. But a headwind was making the vessel bounce like a sumo wrestler on a trampoline, and the rain felt like hail.

That didn't bother the pilot much. He was hunkered behind the console's windshield with a Plexiglas roof over his head. A big man, he was thick through the chest and shoulders, warmed by a fisherman's roll-neck sweater, a woolen watch cap, and his bushy beard. Mother Nature didn't faze him, and neither did the threats of men. He had an unlit cigar clamped in his teeth and an MP5K submachine gun clamped in the cockpit.

The other four men and one woman in the Whaler were soaking wet. They'd waded out to the boat through the surf from Hog Island's ugly west beach, where vacationers never appeared and the only beachcombers were wild dogs. A lone agent was there to collect their cell phones, but none of them had grumbled about the lack of marina amenities. These sorts of clandestine pickups were standard procedure in their world.

One of the men was Thane, who sat in the stern on a slick leather bench and was dressed like the pilot, except that his jeans were heavy with seawater and he was packing a Glock 19. The man beside him was Kali Browder Kent, wearing a black Arc'teryx jacket, a backpack, and a balaclava that showed only his eyes. Up forward in the bow, Jason, Spencer, and Neveah, also wearing parkas and balaclavas, hunched with their backs to the wind, grunting as every bounce smacked their spines.

None of them spoke, and the balaclavas were not for disguise. It was going to be a long, cold ride.

At six nautical miles from the beach, the pilot eased back on the throttle and held his azimuth at 94 degrees—you didn't race through this entry control point or you'd get a Javelin missile up your ass. A flash of heat lightning fringed the purple clouds in the starless sky, and he glimpsed the prows of two fast-attack craft off his port and starboard, a hundred meters ahead. They were heavily armed boats manned by members of Navy's Special Warfare Combatant-Craft Crewmen, SBT-2. He knew they were watching him with night-vision goggles. You didn't play with those dudes.

The pilot pressed a console button and above his head a trio of amber, green, and blue beacons flashed in a pattern that was preset each night. He received a double flash from each boat in return and passed through the cordon.

Half a mile later a large ship appeared, seemingly out of nowhere. It was six hundred feet from bow to stern, an old World War II—era oiler-refueler that had long been retired, then quietly revived. It had a three-story superstructure topped by the bridge near the stern, and a long steel catwalk shot forward above the main deck and its eight sunken fuel-storage tanks. The catwalk ended at a hulking box bristling with antennas just aft of the bow. The ship was an ugly old scow, painted charcoal black, with rust dripping from the gunwales and the name *Saugatuck* stenciled on its flank. It flew no flag.

The Whaler pilot eased his boat alongside. A rope-and-plank gangway winched down from the gunwale above, its bottom sinking into the roiling waves. Thane got up, nodded at the pilot, and he and his team leaped from the rocking Whaler to the gangway and climbed. They all got soaked to their knees again, while the pilot backed off and dropped anchor.

Two armed men slinging M4 rifles were waiting topside. Thane showed them his CIA CAC card, and they nodded and said, "Welcome aboard, sir." They hauled on a heavy steel hatch and Thane led his team into the superstructure.

Once inside, everything changed. It was as if the *Saugatuck* were a crusty old oyster concealing a pearl. The bulkheads were painted cream white, heat blew gently from stainless steel vents, and recessed lighting spread a comfortable glow. They tramped down a steel gangway to a three-hundred-foot corridor that lanced forward between the silo-size fuel storage tanks, four on each side.

The tanks had been emptied, detoxified, insulated, and also painted cream white, each with a heavy steel doorway above which a green light would signal "Come on in," or a red light would warn "Stay the hell out." One tank was the TOC, the ship's tactical operations center; another was the communications cell. A third tank served as the armory, and another was the intel shop. The rest were a documentation center; a gym; a tank for co-ed quarters, where sixty-two personnel bunked in shifts; and a brig for prisoners, pending their transfer to a maximum-security, ultrasecret black site. The whole ship buzzed with low-frequency vibrations because the hull was lined with an electronic countermeasures shield. The vessel was a floating sensitive compartmentalized information facility, or SCIF, through which nothing could penetrate. Not even the most sophisticated Russian or Chinese satellites could hear what was going on inside.

If you'd ever served on a nuclear sub, the *Saugatuck* was like home. If you hadn't, it was a claustrophobic's bad dream.

Thane and his crew walked down the corridor on their squishy soles, nodding at a few young folks passing from tank to tank with classified folders under their arms and steaming coffee mugs in their hands. They were all dressed casually, in jeans, rubber-soled deck shoes, and various sweaters, but each carried a SIG Sauer P220 in a waistband holster. This wasn't Langley, where heavily armed federal agents guarded the perimeter and grounds. At Black Box headquarters in the middle of the ocean, they were on their own.

At the end of the corridor a young man seated behind a metal desk logged Thane and his people in and asked for sidearms. Thane turned over his Glock. Then the team walked up another steel stairwell, where a sentry wearing a Kevlar vest and slinging an MP5 was guarding an armored door. He rapped on it twice, then hauled on the latch and waved them inside.

In the course of the *Saugatuck*'s seaborne history, many old salts had captained the ship from the wood-paneled cabin filled with nautical charts, brass sextants, and collections of liquor, pipes, and cigars. But it was nothing like that anymore. The director of Black Box, a handsome, fiftyish Asian American man called Ando, sat behind a semicircular Steelcase desk with two Asus desktop PCs, in front of a ninety-inch flat-screen on the wall. The cabin's paint scheme was azure blue with recessed pale yellow lighting, and besides the array of thick leather chairs that faced Ando's workstation, there were no paintings, family photographs, diplomas, government trophies, or anything else.

Ando was all business. He didn't even miss home. If he had one.

"Evening, boss," Thane said as the guard locked the door from outside.

Ando just grunted. He was reading a file in a red folder with Q CLEARANCE ONLY stamped on its face. Behind his head a digital map on the flat-screen showed animated Russian troops and armored columns lining what was once the entire Ukraine border. In the center of the land border lay the text "New Russia." Ando turned and looked at the flat-screen for a moment. He sighed, shook his head in frustration, then returned to reading the file.

There were only four guest chairs, so Thane had his people sit and stood behind them with his arms folded while they pulled off their damp balaclavas. Kali Kent, placid and unreadable, sat there patiently waiting. Jason, the six-foot former Force Recon marine, rubbed his scruffy beard. Neveah, always the poised professional, pulled a waterproof notebook and pen from a pocket. Spencer, the smaller man with reddish curls whose favorite cocktail was Red Bull, looked around at the *Star Trek* decor. It was his first time inside Ando's recently renovated lair.

None of them spoke, and they wouldn't until Ando spoke first. As the director of Black Box, he held a rank equivalent to brigadier general, while they were mere first lieutenants and Thane the equivalent of a field-grade major.

The CIA's Black Box initiative was one of the most highly classified special access programs, or SAPs, in the entire intel community. Devised by a forward thinker in Clandestine Services, each BB team was composed of carefully selected special operators, trained for their particular tasks for a minimum of two years. Small in terms of personnel, yet large in terms of talents, each team had a commander, or Overwatch, like Thane. The operators consisted of Chameleons, like Kali Kent and Jason, who were multilingual, tactically trained, and able to become whomever they needed to be, depending on the mission. In support were Ghosts, like Neveah, essentially surveillance and breaking-and-entry experts, and Wind agents like Spencer, who were hotshot pilots, NASCAR-level drivers, motorcyclists, and drone jockeys, who could operate any machine that moved. Each team was also linked to Aberration agents, deep-cover operators who could infiltrate a target area and remain undercover for extended periods, but they never appeared at HQ.

None of them were "volunteers" who'd walked into the CIA looking to serve. They'd all been recruited by talent spotters. Thane had been an Off-Broadway theater director in Manhattan when the twin towers came down on 9/11, killing his beloved wife, who was working that day for Cantor Fitzgerald. Desperate for revenge, he'd turned to the CIA, which had occasionally contracted his services to train clandestine agents in Method acting. While serving as a full-time instructor, he had impressed Ando's spotters, and he'd been recruited as a Chameleon. From there he'd excelled in his tradecraft and tactics training to become a deep-cover Aberration agent, serving overseas for seven years, until Ando had pulled him back in, assigned him to train other Chameleons, and eventually promoted him to Overwatch status.

Aside from Ando and the Overwatch team leaders like Thane, no one in the agency was privy to the files or faces of Black Box agents, except for those personnel who served aboard the *Saugatuck*. Most of those folks were young, big fans of Tony Stark, and loved keeping secrets.

"All right," said Ando as he dropped the red file onto his desk and tapped it with a CIA fountain pen from the Langley gift shop. "You people did a respectable job on the Rio affair." Ando had a PhD in strategic studies from Yale, still spoke in those nasal Yalie tones, and was stingy with compliments. "The Package boys relayed the results to USASOC at Bragg, and the DEA is pleased. Of course they'll deny any knowledge of our actions, but those Comando animals won't be bleeding us anymore." He glanced at the file again, then looked up from under his brows at Kali Kent. "You actually picked up Portuguese in four weeks at Monterey?" He meant the DoD's intensive language school. "And dropped thirty pounds?"

Kali Kent just said, "Yes, sir," as if such efforts were unexceptional.

Thane said, "I've got him on protein shakes, sir. He'll be back to normal soon."

Ando grunted and leaned back in his chair.

"There's an interesting issue here, Thane. After you people withdrew from the Rio hit, a Package forensics specialist did a complete SSE." He meant a sensitive site exploration conducted by a Tier One support technician, which consisted of gleaning intelligence from devices, vehicles, abodes, or corpses left behind. "Apparently, even as the Package were still emptying their guns, all of the bad guys' cell phones and comms devices, *including* the computer engine module on their Tundra, were remotely wiped clean by some outside source. And when I say wiped, I mean even Apple wouldn't be able to recover the material . . . not that they'd help if we asked."

Kali Kent looked over at Thane and raised an eyebrow, then leaned forward over his knees.

"We're talking substantial funds, sir, for something like that," Kali said.

"That's right," said Ando. "Big tech support and probably access to a satellite array of some sort. Plus, one of those Comandos, though deceased, was thrown clear of the vehicle, and another one wasn't totally immolated. The faces of those men rang no bells on any facial recognition software, anywhere, including all our databases and INTERPOL, which is odd because DEA had images of them from ops in Mexico. They also had no fingerprints. Surgically removed."

Jason whistled softly. "Somebody pulled their biometrics, *and* their fingertips?"

Thane said, "You sure about that, boss? Might have happened in the vehicle fire."

"It didn't burn long enough to melt their fingers, Thane. I watched it all on a Predator feed." Ando folded his arms. "Your source in Rio . . . this fellow Marco . . . is currently having a conversation with the DEA in Panama. Bruto, however, is right here in the brig." He looked at Kali. "Think you can get something out of him?"

"I'll do my best, sir," Kali said.

"Have at it." Ando pressed a button on a desktop audio feed. "I'll be recording here for later review."

Kali took his backpack, left Ando's office, and went down the gangway to the ship's centerline corridor. The brig was located close to the forward superstructure, with a standard barred cell door and a hefty guard standing by. Kali slipped into a latrine marked MALES.

Inside the small bathroom, he opened the backpack and switched his Arc'teryx jacket for the same baggy tunic he'd worn as Perdido. He changed his damp jeans for Perdido's worn ones as well, though he dispensed with the sandals or anything further. Bruto would certainly recognize the withered man who had violently snatched him from the church.

Kali left the backpack on the floor as he slipped his bracelet of prayer beads from his pocket. This was a Chameleon's amulet of transition, something all of them had learned from Thane, a technique for getting into character. As he focused on his image in the bathroom mirror, he wrapped the bracelet around his hand, as though the beads were a timer, and used his thumb to cycle through each one. His voice emerged and began shifting in tone, as he recited in Portuguese the words of the Brazilian poet Manuel Bandeira.

"When the undesirable of the people comes, I do not know if tough or gentle, maybe I will be scared. Maybe I will smile, or say, 'Hello, uncheatable.'"

More of the beads clicked across his palm, and his voice once again became honey mixed with gravel.

"My day was good, the night can fall, the night with its maledictions. It will find the field plowed, the house cleaned, the table ready. With everything in its place."

And gradually, as he recited this secret mantra, he became Perdido. He pocketed the beads and walked back out into the corridor, still murmuring the stanzas that fueled his disguise, and nodded at the guard. The man turned an old-style key in the door lock and pulled it open on creaking hinges. Kali entered the cell.

Bruto was dressed in oversize flannel pajamas patterned in small blue flowers. He was barefoot and the front of his top was missing some buttons. It was a technique to make him feel small and unmanly. His left wrist was manacled to the upright of a steel bed that was bolted to the floor, and he sat on the worn mattress. His long black hair was oily and unwashed and he had a few days' growth of beard. He looked up at Kali and squinted as the guard closed the door behind him.

"It is you, *sabaca*," Bruto snarled in Portuguese.

"Yes, Bruto, it is I, Perdido . . . the man who has changed your life."

"I should have shot you as soon as I saw you. You and that bastard, Marco."

"Perhaps, but you didn't," Kali said. "We grow careless with age."

Bruto leaned back on the bunk, an arrogant posture against the concrete wall.

"Careless, Perdido?" he said. "It is *you* who was careless. I had done nothing to you when you and those American criminals kidnapped me. You have nothing on me."

Kali leaned against the cell door and laced his fingers together in front of his waist, as if he had all the time in the world.

"Yes, nothing, Bruto," Kali stated. "Nothing more than the killing of two American agents in Ciudad Juárez."

Bruto flicked his free hand in the air as if swatting a fly.

"I was not there, Perdido. You are bluffing."

Kali looked up at the cell's ceiling, as if summoning a memory.

"And nothing more than the murders of attorney Juan Ortega," he said, "and his wife and four-year-old daughter, in Mexico City. Isn't that right, Bruto?"

"*Besteiro!*" Bullshit, Bruto exclaimed. "I had nothing to do with that!"

Kali looked down again, examining his fingernails.

"November 7, 2015, Bruto. We have bloody fingerprints from all over their house. And now, we have yours. Will they match?" He shrugged. "We shall see."

Bruto's defiant expression collapsed and his thick cheeks paled. He lurched forward from the wall and his manacles rattled.

"What do you want?" the Comando leader snapped. "First you are my kidnapper, and now you are to be my tormentor?" He tried to snarl, but the corners of his mouth trembled. "Or perhaps my bloodsucking attorney?"

"I am the man who will decide your fate, Bruto," Kali said. "All of your men are dead. All of them, and you, were being controlled by someone else. Shall we call that someone a higher power?"

Bruto waved his free hand again as if Perdido's claim was nonsense.

"I know nothing more."

"Well, I *do* know more," Kali said. "I know that you and your men murdered American agents and innocents in Mexico. I know that you can hang for that. I know that you can speak to me here and now, or speak to other men in a prison in Cuba, where you are also wanted, and no one will hear you scream, for the rest of your life."

Bruto considered this. He hunched over his knees, and at last looked up at Kali.

"I do not know much. There were always cutouts. If I tell you what I do know, what will happen?"

"You will still be our guest, but in a much more pleasant place. And perhaps, someday, you will walk the streets of Rio again."

Bruto sighed. "You are a bad man, Perdido."

"More than you know, Bruto," Kali said. "But if a man is truthful with me, it makes me gentler."

"All right," Bruto said. "All right." And he began to talk . . .

Kali left the cell after a few minutes. The guard locked the door again as he returned to the latrine and emerged once more as himself. He climbed the gangway, went back into Ando's office, and sat down.

"Well?" Ando said as he switched off the recording. "My Portuguese is primitive, but that sounded rather civilized."

"It didn't require much pressure, sir," Kali said. "He's already been broken inside his own head. Just needed a nudge."

"What does he know?"

"Not very much. These Comando operators have been working as side contractors for someone else. A cutout schedules them for a job, they pull it off as ordered, and collect a percentage of whatever the take is. It appears they had some sort of project scheduled for a week from now, but hadn't yet been briefed on the details. It might be nothing more than a drug deal, but Bruto has no idea. It also might be something kinetic, like a hit."

"And where is this supposed to take place?" Thane asked.

"At a private celebration," Kali said, "being held at a very large mansion and estate in northern Italy, on the shores of Lake Como. Belongs to a wealthy businessman named Vittorio Sietto."

Thane turned to Ando. "Okay, boss, what would you like us to do?"

"Get yourselves invited." Ando raised a black eyebrow. "But try not to ruin the party."

FOUR

GENESIS

Kali Kent did not feel the damp or the cold on the thundering boat ride back to Hog Island. The purple clouds had been swept by the wind from the postmidnight sky, but he did not see the jeweled stars above, or the gleam of the moon on the waves.

He was seeing a different kind of social gathering than the one Ando had just assigned him to, and he remembered . . .

He was seven years old, walking down to the beach in Lagos, Nigeria, his small hand grasped in that of his best friend, Adejare, whom everyone called Jare. On either side of the boys, Kali's father, George Adeyemi, and his mother, Yvonne, also grasped the boys' hands. It was a pleasant day in the spring, with the towering palm fronds waving like great birds' wings in the warm breeze and Kali's bare toes curling in the sand. He was always happy whenever his parents surprised him with a family outing.

There were so many people at the shore, tall men in colorful shirts, pretty ladies all wearing headscarves as if they were going to the church, though it was Saturday, not Sunday. They all had such stern expressions, and although the sea was gentle and blue and pretty, and the waves were softly kissing the beach, no one seemed to be swimming or enjoying the party.

Why are there so many policemen in their light blue uniform shirts and peaked caps? Kali wondered. *Why are there so many soldiers in their thick green uniforms and orange berets?*

Some of the mounted policemen pulled on the reins to hold back their snorting horses, and many of them had fierce-looking guns.

Kali looked at Jare curiously, but Jare only shrugged. The little boy had a tribal marking on his cheek below his right eye. Usually those double-slash markings were beneath both eyes, but Jare had wailed such bloodcurdling screams during the ritual that the witch doctor had refused to go on.

Will there be fireworks? Kali thought. *No, it is daytime. But maybe a sailing regatta?* Kali's father liked big boats.

They stopped at the edge of the large, murmuring crowd, facing the beach, where down near the water a great pyramid of blue and white oil drums was piled, and before that was some sort of wooden stage with stairs leading up to the cone of drums. There was also a large truck parked down there, with a stencil that said LAGOS STATE GOVERNMENT FREE CINEMA UNIT on its side. Kali was proud that he could read that and smiled.

"Is there going to be ice cream, Mum?" he asked his stunningly beautiful mother. With a smile, she arced her elegant neck toward him, stroked his short hair, but didn't answer.

"No, my son," his father said. "But there will be a lesson." He was holding a bracelet of prayer beads in his palm and moving them with his thumb. The beads made a soft clicking sound. They had once belonged to Kali's grandfather. Someday they would be Kali's.

It was then that Kali saw the wooden coffin. It lay to one side in the sand, a shape like one of those Egyptian mummies he'd seen in books, but its cover was off and there was no one inside.

That part is good, Kali thought. *I don't like funerals, because the adults always cry. Maybe it's a tribal ritual of some kind. Maybe there will be ice cream afterward.*

A group of policemen appeared, leading a man by his elbows. His hands were tied in front of his waist with rope. He was a portly man with a kind, full face and a soft mustache. Kali frowned because the man looked familiar, but he did not seem frightened.

Maybe the celebration is some sort of game?

The policemen walked the man up the wooden stairs, then turned him around to face the crowd. Kali looked on intently as they started to tie him with long white ropes to the oil drum tower behind him. The ropes looked very tight and made bulges in his loose gray shirt. A lady in the crowd wailed something and almost fell to her knees, but two other men who looked like officials held her up.

Someone held a silver microphone to the man's mouth. He smiled and spoke, though with the breeze and the licking of the waves Kali could barely hear him. He said something about God. He said something about judgment. He said something about forgiveness.

That sounds familiar. Dad always says that forgiveness is very important, because no one is without sin in this world.

The policemen left the man alone now. A priest in flowing white robes walked up the stairs and spoke to him. Their foreheads were nearly touching, and still the man smiled.

This is not going to be a bad thing, is it? Kali hoped, but he squeezed Jare's hand tighter.

There was a very large circle of sand between Kali's bare toes and the man and the oil drums, and all at once it was empty. Except someone, a soldier officer, was barking something, and three other soldiers marched into the circle with big, shiny rifles. They stopped and stomped in the sand, like the British soldiers of old, then turned toward the man, raised their rifles, and aimed.

Bang!

The gunshots made Kali and Jare flinch in unison. Kali's mouth fell open. His eyes went wide. The man jerked there where he was tied, but he could not fall, because of the ropes, and after a moment his hands twitched and started to rise.

Bang! Bang! Bang!

There were more horrible gunshots. Kali turned to his father, burying his small face in George's belly, and Jare did the same thing from the other side. His father petted both their heads.

"There is a price for doing bad things, Kalief," he whispered as the echoes of the rifles faded, and there were no other sounds but the waves. "A heavy price, my son."

Kali's mother was weeping . . .

FIVE

KALI KENT STEPPED FROM A BLACK BMW M5, WHILE slipping a bracelet of prayer beads into his suit pocket. He seemed to have gained more weight as he filled out his Brunello Cucinelli charcoal suit with a white silk shirt, no tie, and Christian Louboutin black oxford shoes. The shoes were expensive, but also suitable for running—if you had to.

And the man who was driving the luxury car also seemed to be different in his persona. It was Spencer, but he now appeared to be a faithful chauffeur. An Italian parking attendant motioned to where he should park the vehicle among a row of Mercedes and Ferraris, and said, "*Attenzione, per favore.*" Carefully, please. Spencer would be staying with the car.

Kali strode toward the lakeside villa, joining a throng of other arriving guests, all dressed in bespoke suits and gowns. The evening was warm, with breezes drifting off the water and the lights of Varenna across the lake making the tree leaves sparkle like jewels. He paid no mind to the arriving royal blue Mercedes-Benz S-Class sedan that contained Jason and Neveah. They were posing as a couple, James and Maggie Corse, the American heirs to an Italian publishing magnate.

"Dark Horse Two, on the X."

It was Jason's voice and it sounded to Kent like it was inside his head. He was wearing a subminiature receiver buried deep in his ear, as well as a miniature mic disguised as a lapel button.

Vittorio Sietto's villa was an enormous multistory rectangle of pink Pompeii granite with cornice towers and archers' battlements like a medieval castle. There were too many windows to count, with vines and flowers dripping from balcony boxes, and the faux Corinthian columns on the wide entrance portico all had bolted iron arms gripping torches like the Statue of Liberty. The strains of a classical string quartet wafted from the grand entrance, and as Kali walked up one of two curving marble stairways, he could see past the villa's southern corner to the rear of the estate.

There was a wide, semicircular veranda jutting out above an Olympic-size heated swimming pool—the water was steaming like an Icelandic hot spring. Two stone staircases led from either side of the veranda down to the pool, where Kali spotted two large men in dark suits—armed security, no doubt—patrolling the grounds. He assumed there were more of them, inside and out.

Vittorio Sietto was a man of means, the founder and CEO of a publicly traded business advisory corporation, Franco International, based in Milan. His friends and associates were international bankers, movie stars, and politicians. Tonight's celebration was for the fiftieth birthday of his beloved wife, Sophia. Kali guessed that with her kind of wealth and a no-stress life, she probably looked forty.

Still, none of those personal details about the Siettos hinted at why Bruto and the Comando Vermelho had been given a "warning order" about the event. Maybe Kali and his Black Box team would find out, or maybe they'd all just go back to their safe house at midnight, call it a dry hole, and get drunk.

Thane was over at the safe house now, an Airbnb rented in Menaggio just a few hundred meters up the coast. He'd be sitting somewhere on the top floor, using a Micom single-sideband transceiver to monitor the transmissions of his team. He wouldn't interfere, and he didn't really expect much to happen at the party. It was more of a recon mission, and certainly Bruto's Comando faction couldn't cause any problems here. Bruto was still locked aboard ship in the Black Box brig, and the rest of them were dead.

Kali was surprised to see that at the top of the entrance stairs,

Vittorio Sietto and his wife were greeting the arriving guests them-selves. He'd expected a pair of stern-faced butlers, so this said something about their gracious characters.

Sietto was tall, with a full head of thick gray hair like an Italian film star, an impeccable powder blue suit, and a perpetual tan. He looked to be somewhere in his sixties, and his wife, a raven-haired beauty in a magnificent red Portia and Scarlett cocktail gown, looked considerably younger, just as Kali had predicted. As he ar-rived at the head of the line, he bowed to Signora Sietto, kissed her hand, then offered his business card to Vittorio.

"Ah! Signor Goodson, what an absolute pleasure," Vittorio said as he shook Kali's hand. Kali had become Chester Cecil Good-son III, a handsome and rather arrogant British banker, managing director of mergers and acquisitions at Barclays on Artillery Row in London. That's what his ivory business card said, as well as his pro-file on the bank's website, which was why Vittorio referred to him as such. "The ambassador insisted we should meet, that we might have interests in common."

"Well, Ambassador Pennright is terribly kind," Kent said in a pure British Cambridge accent. "I'm only dismayed we didn't meet *prior* to your recommendations to Avio aerospace and all that busi-ness with Virgin Galactic."

Sietto cocked his head. "Do you think that might not have been a good bet for Avio?"

"Frankly, I think it's a lark," Kali said. "Galactic's market cap is hovering around two-point-five billion, with a seventy-five percent share loss over the past twelve months, and only a recent uptick of five-point-four-five percent for a paltry share price of less than ten dollars. Seems to me Richard Branson's selling fantasies, wouldn't you say?"

Sietto laughed, impressed. "I think he's selling bucket-list rides on rocket ships, and Avio believes he'll make a healthy profit and wants in on the bottom."

"I agree, sir," Kali said, "if that bottom doesn't fall out! However,

I shan't worry too much about Avio. Their revenue's at nine hundred and seventy-four million. They'll be just fine." Kali touched his own chest. "I trust I haven't offended?"

"Not at *all*," Sietto said. "It's always a pleasure to chat with a man of knowledge. And how do you know the ambassador, Signore Goodson?"

"He invites me to hunt on occasion, although I frankly prefer to take my nourishment from Hawksmoor." Kali's mention of the high-end steak restaurant in London wasn't off the cuff. He knew that Sietto favored the place, because he'd been researching him for days, nonstop.

Sietto smiled. "We should dine there together on a mutually convenient occasion. In the meantime, I hope you will enjoy my little soiree."

"I certainly shall." Kent then charmed Signora Sietto with a smile. "I trust you shall have a memorable thirtieth, signora. And please know that my firm has made a donation to your favorite charitable cause."

"*Grazie!*" Signora Sietto laughed at the age compliment, squeezed Kent's arm, and then he was off and dived into the throng.

There were already more than a hundred people milling about the ground-floor salon, with waistcoated waiters carrying silver trays of hors d'oeuvres and champagne. Streamers, balloons, and birthday tinsel were hanging from crystal chandeliers, and the classical quartet in their tuxes and gowns were sitting off to one side in a recessed music alcove that included a grand piano.

Directly across the crowd, at the west side of the villa, a four-door exit opened onto the rear veranda. Lace curtains lining the frame were fluttering in the evening breeze and Kent could see that the Siettos' only child—a beautiful blond twenty-year-old named Daniella, whom he recognized from Black Box's files—had retreated with her friends from the boring adults. She was leaning back against a stone balustrade, wearing a silver tube top and a black pencil skirt with a slit. Spiky-haired Italian boys were adoring her from either side, and she was kicking back vodka tonics and loving the attention as if it were her birthday party rather than Mamma's.

Kali swiped a champagne glass from a waiter's tray, took a sip, and mimed a cough into his fist.

"I've got bloody nothing thus far," he grunted. He wasn't going to be using his call sign inside the party. None of them were.

"It's a big boring ball here too," Jason said into Kali's ear.

Kali glanced over to one of a pair of enormous winding staircases with red center carpet runners that led up to God-knew-where. Jason and Neveah were halfway up to the first landing, holding hands and both cradling wineglasses, leaning into one another and seemingly enjoying the bash. She was wearing an off-the-shoulder jade gown and looked absolutely smashing, as "Goodson" might have remarked. Jason looked like a cleaned-up version of Chris Pratt in a tux. The snobbish but approving glances from attendees confirmed their display of a perfect power couple, deeply in love.

"Be patient," Neveah murmured to both of them, while she appeared to be nibbling on Jason's ear. "I'm going to drag this brute around and see if I can get some faces." She had a digital recording device in her cocktail purse and a minicam in a small brooch above her left breast. She was going to capture images for facial recognition analysis later.

"Good show," Kent said. He felt fingers touching his arm and spun to find a stunning petite woman smiling up at him. She had long red tresses, sparkling green eyes, and a dancer's figure in a black tube dress.

"*Buonasera, bell'uomo,*" she said. "*Mi compri da bere?*"

Kent knew she was calling him handsome and asking him to buy her a drink, but he pretended otherwise and shrugged.

"I'm awfully sorry . . ."

"Ah!" She switched to English. "I was asking if you would like to buy me a drink, handsome man. I am Federica."

He took her small hand in his. "I'm Chester, and it's an absolute pleasure, my beauty. But I do think the drinks here are all gratis."

She took his elbow and pulled his arm into her chest. "Buy me one anyway."

"Of course."

Then Spencer's low voice banged in his head.

"Heads up, Dark Horses, something's going down out here."

There wasn't much Kent could do but listen and escort Federica over to the bar. The quartet had stopped playing. Outside on the veranda, Daniella had taken over the ambience and a DJ was starting to scratch Rico Nasty rapping "Money."

Spencer was standing outside the BMW in a temporary parking area on the south lawn. He'd been leaning back on the flank of the car, finishing up a cigarette, when something along the wood line in the dark caught his eye. The blue halo from the steaming pool made it hard to see clearly, but he was sure that figures were emerging from the trees fifty meters away.

He straightened up, squinted hard, threw his butt to the grass, and took three steps forward. He'd seen the security men too, just as Kent had, and assumed these guys were the dressed-down version of Sietto's team. But they weren't moving like that. They were moving like men with bad intentions.

That's when he'd alerted his teammates via his bone mic.

But it was too late.

There were four of them, all members of the Italian extreme-left terrorist organization called Nuove Brigate Rosse, the New Red Brigades. They were dressed in all black, wearing balaclavas and carrying Glock 17 handguns. The pistols had no suppressors. That was by design.

The four men advanced around the pool's perimeter. Sietto's two security men on the back side of the house were standing beneath the veranda, but they'd both been watching the party and turned to face the gunmen only on instinct. The terrorists were moving smoothly, elbows unlocked, with two-handed grips on their pistols, and before the security men could sweep their jackets aside and go for their guns the NRB men opened fire.

It was loud. Very loud. The gunshots carried even above the

pounding rap of Rico Nasty, and the two security men slammed backward into the stone veranda walls and went down.

Kali pushed Federica over a divan. It wasn't very graceful or gentle, but she might thank him later. Jason broke away from Neveah and leaped right over the staircase balcony, while she turned and ran down the stairs. It had taken a moment for the inebriated guests to understand that something bad was going down, but when Daniella Sietto screamed from the veranda, they scattered like fleeing pedestrians in a Godzilla movie.

Kali charged toward the veranda, Jason close on his heels. They weren't fast enough. Two men in black had already rushed up the veranda stairs. They grabbed Daniella as she screeched, shot one of her boyfriends, threw her right over one man's shoulder, and pounded back down the stairs before Kali and Jason made it halfway there.

The four men in black hauled Daniella's flailing body past the pool, then crashed through the wood line and disappeared.

SIX

I CEBERG, ICEBERG, ICEBERG!" SPENCER BARKED AND jumped into the BMW M5.

His callout was the Black Box version of "Mayday," selected by some young operator in Codes and Ciphers who was a fan of the movie *Titanic* and thought it perfect for events that could become catastrophic. At any rate, it worked, and Thane heard it loud and clear at the safe house, while Kali, Jason, and Neveah were already on the run.

Spencer burned mud in the grass, the BMW leaped in reverse, and its front bumper raked a priceless silver Maserati, but he figured these one-percenters were all insured up the ass and kept on going. "Front entrance," he barked again as he screeched it around the hardtop driving circle, nearly killing the same parking attendant who'd cautioned him about this very thing, and then Kali came flying down the marble stairs. Kali tore the passenger door open and dived inside as Spencer slammed the gas pedal and Jason and Neveah blew past them, sprinting for their Mercedes. Neveah had already torn off the below-the-knee half of her jade green gown, which had been designed with a breakaway Velcro strip for just such occasions.

"Overwatch for Dark Horse Main," Thane called to Kali over comms.

"*Busy,*" Kali spat back as he locked his seat belt and Spencer popped out onto the lakeside main street in Menaggio and skidded hard to the left. "Assessment," Kali said to Spencer.

"Vehicles, probably two, back side of those woods. They're not gonna hike with her on foot."

"Agreed." Kali turned around to make sure Jason was on his tail.

He saw the Mercedes in the dark fishtailing onto the road from the villa, and it screamed forward to catch up.

"Dammit, Main! Sitrep!" Thane roared so loud inside Kali's head that it actually hurt. Jason answered for him while Kali pulled out his cell to turn the volume down.

"Dark Horse Two for Overwatch," Jason said on the net. "Somebody snatched Vittorio Sietto's girl."

"His girl?" Thane said.

"Affirmative, his daughter," Kali reported.

"Dark Horse Bravo here," Spencer said as he cranked the BMW hard to the left around the corner of a square yellow stucco café and a young couple leaped backward to prevent being smeared like butter. "They also killed two security guys on the back lawn."

"And a guest up top," Neveah jumped in.

"Roger," Thane said. "Get 'em."

It was very dark in Menaggio. The town had a population of roughly three thousand souls, but it was "sleepy" despite the vast wealth all around, and its streets were cobblestoned, narrow, and braced by thick nineteenth-century buildings, quaint shops, cafés, and pricey flats. Spencer, as always before any job, had studied the town's layout, in particular the streets that branched off from Sietto's villa. The way the villa's rear property was arranged, the kidnappers could have parked their vehicles only somewhere on the road just west of the town. He gunned it, roared the BMW up over a cobblestone road, broke out onto the coast road that ran due west, away from Lake Como, and stabbed a finger at the windshield.

"There!"

Two vehicles were rapidly receding along that road, going way too fast for tourists or even some jacked-up Italian kids. He could see their red rear lamps but not what types of cars and was just about to slam it into fifth and catch up, when a pair of blue-and-white Italian National Police Alfa Romeo 159s came screaming out from a side street next to the Hotel Adler and went careering after the kidnappers.

"Guess somebody called the cops," Spencer said.

"Vittorio Sietto's my guess," said Jason from his car.

"He didn't call them," Kali said. "With money like his they were already sitting around here somewhere."

"Overwatch here," said Thane. "I'm tracking you all on Blue Force. They're heading for the Swiss border."

"What's the range?" Kali asked.

"Fifteen klicks, and I think I know where," Thane said.

"Where?" Neveah asked.

"Lugano. There's an airport."

"What're they gonna do?" Jason scoffed. "Shove her on a Swissair flight and hope nobody'll notice?"

"It's mostly private jets," Thane said.

"Shit," Spencer said and drove faster.

They broke away from Menaggio on Via Italia where it stopped curving and ran straight and true, but still it was only a two-lane blacktop with a white stripe down the middle and braced by old stone walls and high fences, no shoulders. Up ahead the kidnappers' two vehicles, which Spencer was now convinced were Mercedes SL 73 AMGs—throwbacks, yes, but with 518 horses—were pulling away from the cops' Alfa Romeos, which now had their cherries spinning and sirens hee-hawing in that weird European scream.

"You're going to have to pass the cops," Kali said to Spencer.

"If I can get a clear hundred meters, I will."

Steady traffic kept dribbling toward them from the opposite direction, Vespa scooters and Smart cars in no hurry to get anywhere. He was already doing 90 miles per hour on the right side of the road, with intermittent jerks as vehicles tried to pop out onto it from the flanks, then heard and saw the cops flying by and pulled back their noses.

Kali popped open the BMW's glove box, pulled out a Glock 19, press-checked the action, and slipped it back in. He looked up and snapped at Spencer, "Watch it!"

A young woman had appeared from the right in the dark, with

only the weak headlight glowing on her bicycle basket as she emerged onto the road. Spencer swung hard to the left, nearly skidded into an oncoming Fiat Panda, then regained control.

"Overwatch here." It was Thane. "I've got Swiss Polizei from the local canton heading for the airport. Our snatchers won't get past the terminal."

"If that's where they're going," Neveah said.

"Why don't the Italians just call for a roadblock?" Spencer asked.

"They're arguing with the Swiss over jurisdiction," Thane said.

"No effing way," Jason said. He sounded breathless behind the wheel of his SL.

"Way," Thane confirmed.

All six vehicles had to slow in Porlezza, where the streets were narrow, quaint, and claustrophobic just like Menaggio. But in a short two klicks they were out again on Via Fontanella, running full throated with all carburetors sucking air and engines screaming. Lake Lugano was off to the left, indigo waters gleaming with the sparkles of stars in the sky and village lanterns from all around its skirt, but none of the occupants of the racing vehicles noticed the beauty.

Daniella Sietto, pushed down on her face in the rear floor of the first New Red Brigades Mercedes, was shaking and weeping, with a boot on her back and a fist gripping her blond hair. In the kidnappers' second vehicle, the two men who'd shot Vittorio Sietto's bodyguards were locking their Glock 17s into FAB Defense full-auto-conversion stocks, effectively turning them into submachine guns. The two pairs of Italian cops in the Alfas just behind them were calling everyone they could think of on the net, hoping that by some miracle the Swiss Army would blockade the road ahead. And in the Black Box vehicles picking up the rear, all four agents knew that no one was coming to the rescue. It was up to them.

They blew past the Swiss border crossing just south of Monte Boglia. What had once been a controlled entry point of steel booths, drop-down striped poles, passport inspectors, and guards with white gloves was now no more than a welcome sign. Kali didn't think the whole European Union open-borders thing was a great idea, because it made hunting bad guys that much harder, but such socioeconomic policies were way above his pay grade. Anyway, it would have been nice if the old "tiger teeth" that could pop up from the road were still there, but they weren't.

Five hundred meters past that down the road, Spencer suddenly shot his right hand out, slammed his palm into Kali's chest, yelled *"Hang on!"* and regripped the wheel. Kali saw the police car fifty meters in front of them swerving as the first police car did a full, screeching, gravel-spitting 360-degree spin, went careening off to the left, tore through a metal guardrail with a sound like a twisting beer can, and disappeared down the lakeshore. Then he saw why. Up ahead, the rear kidnappers' Mercedes was parked broadside right in the middle of the road and its occupants were standing outside, firing their Glocks on full auto.

The second police Alfa had nowhere to go. There wasn't time. The driver hit the brakes, just as the shooters turned and sprinted off into the woods and straight up a hill, and the Alfa Romeo impacted head-on with their abandoned Mercedes.

Spencer, who was fast enough to catch a fly with a pair of chopsticks, jinked hard to the left, ran one tire so close to the lake that Kali was sure they were going to go over, pulled it back around the rumpled two vehicles that were still sparking and skidding from the high-impact crash, and kept going.

"Remind me to compliment you for that," Kali said.

"You're welcome."

"Sitrep," Thane snapped from his safe house. "What the hell was that?"

"They just took out the cops," Kali answered.

Thane said nothing else.

The kidnappers' car raced on toward Lugano proper, with Spencer closing the distance but holding at fifty meters. Even with the girl in the car, they might pull the same gambit their partners had, and he needed the brake room. They zipped past Gandria and up ahead the lights of the town of Lugano grew into clusters of sparkles, like a Christmas tree lying on its side.

"Looks like they're heading right for that mess," Jason said from the follow car.

"Once they're inside," said Kali, "they could go anywhere."

"No," Thane said from the safe house. "It's the airport."

"Why?" Neveah said.

"I'm a pessimist," Thane snapped.

Sure enough, the kidnappers kept racing due west, bouncing through the narrow streets of the tourist town, running red lights and scattering cursing pedestrians. They tried no evasive maneuvers, perhaps sensing that the crazy man on their tail was tethered to their bumper by skill, and that jinking off into some side street to lose him wasn't going to work.

The three vehicles roared under the Number 2 highway and past the Continental Parkhotel, and the kidnappers gunned it straight into the district of Sorengo, past the fat lake called Lago di Muzzano, and kept on going under the E35. And then they were crossing the Vedeggio, a manmade canal, and right past that they could see the airport strip running south to north, with its runway lights blazing and its tower looming on the far side.

"Dammit, he's right," Spencer said about Thane. "Why's he always right?"

"Experience," Thane answered.

"Old age," Jason quipped.

"What are they going to do?" Neveah said. "Check in?"

"Hold tight," Kali warned.

Sure enough, the kidnappers had no intention of heading for the west side terminal. The runway was surrounded by a high chain-link fence, and just as Kali spotted a double-hinged gate locked with a padlock, the kidnappers' Mercedes turned 45 degrees to the right, bounced off the road, dipped its nose, and burst right through it, sending the gate sides whipping open and curling the steel. Spencer raced through the hole right after them, but Jason spun out as Neveah's head banged against her doorjamb; he then regained control to pursue but was now behind Spencer by two hundred meters.

The kidnappers' Mercedes sped north alongside the runway. In Spencer's BMW, Kali pulled the Glock from the glove box, got his suit coat off, leaned forward, and jammed the pistol into his rear waistband.

"See it?" Spencer was leaning into the steering wheel, eyes wide and staring straight onward. At the far end of the runway, a Dassault Falcon jet was facing their way, its rear engine nacelles glowing.

"I see it," Kali said, but he was staring at the front of the aircraft as it grew in his vision. It had a strange sort of silver mustache mounted just below its nose, like some kind of radar antenna array that he'd never seen before on a private jet.

"I can stop them," Spencer said.

Kali knew what he meant. He could broadside the BMW into the plane's forward nose gear and that would be that.

"You can," he said, "but that bird's got a full fuel load, which would mean death for all of us. Try for the car."

"Roger."

The Falcon was starting to roll forward. The kidnappers' Mercedes screeched into a tire-burning side slide just aft of the tail on the right. Kali saw the rear doors fly open. A man jumped from the back seat, dragging Daniella Sietto by the hair, one arm cranked behind her back. He hauled her to the jet, which had its aft passenger door open but no stairway extended. Someone inside grabbed her and hauled her up as she screamed with her legs flailing. Her escort jumped up inside just as a second man came around the Mercedes, spraying bullets at Spencer's car. The windshield spidered but Kali and Spencer didn't flinch one bit. Seeing how ineffective his weapon was against the ballistic glass of Spencer's car, he tossed his subgun Glock, sprinted for the Falcon, and dived inside.

Spencer braked in a wailing tire burn ten feet from the kidnappers' car. The driver was slow and just exiting the car when Kali leaped from the BMW and ran full speed at him like a linebacker, leveling him to the ground, and subsequently causing his face to smash against the tarmac.

Kali jammed a knee into the moaning man's back, drew his Glock, and aimed at the plane. But he knew he couldn't use it. One bullet in the wrong spot could kill Daniella. He didn't have a shot.

He watched as it picked up speed, roared down the runway, and took off into the black Swiss sky.

SEVEN

THE BLACK BOX SAFE HOUSE IN MENAGGIO WAS A stand-alone three-story flat on the northern outskirts of the town, selected and equipped by an Aberration agent based in Milan. Maintaining such facilities for Black Box teams was one of the essential tasks of these deep-cover Aberration agents.

It had taken Spencer and Jason an hour and a half to drive their cars back to Menaggio. With Kali's fresh captive locked in the BMW's trunk and the havoc they'd left on the highways, Spencer had to use back roads. Kali had dragged the man to his feet off the tarmac at gunpoint, wrapped his head in his suit jacket, secured it with Spencer's necktie, and zip-tied his hands. The man mumbled protests in Italian, but he hadn't struggled much. He wasn't going to mess with a crazy, large British Black man with a gun. Kali never broke character, but he was frightening in any disguise.

The four Black Box agents had parked their vehicles in front of the flat, checked their surroundings for any observers, then hauled their prisoner inside and up the stairs to the second floor. Back in a rear bedroom, they'd frisked him again, shoved him into a wooden chair, and roped his wrists to the chair back. Kali had briefly removed his hood to take a photo of his face, replaced it, and gone out, locking the door.

Thane made a fresh pot of coffee in the ground-floor kitchen and brought it up to the second-floor salon, where his agents had sunk into a purple chintz couch and chairs surrounding a long coffee table. He had a stereo pumping out Beethoven's Ninth so the prisoner couldn't hear their conversation, and also in case he decided to wail.

"Bourbon would've been better," Jason complained as he sipped the brew. His voice had a touch of California-boy accent, unless he was going Chameleon, when it would disappear.

"I want you awake, not happy," Thane said as he sat down next to Spencer and opened a secure laptop.

"No worries there," Spencer said.

Thane reached out and squeezed his shoulder. "Nice piece of driving, kid," he said, and Spencer grinned.

Thane knew all the details of what had transpired. The team had back-briefed him during their return ride.

"Is Ando up to speed?" Kali asked Thane as he transmitted the fresh photo of the prisoner from his cell phone to Black Box's seaborne headquarters.

"Affirmative, and he's interested."

Everyone knew what that meant. There were code words about Ando's moods. "Interested" meant he was satisfied with their performance thus far. "Concerned" would have meant he was pissed.

"He also relayed some comms from the Swiss," Thane said. "They scrambled a pair of PC-21 pursuit aircraft to go after that Falcon."

"Where's it headed?" Kali asked.

"No one knows. It disappeared off of radar."

"Disappeared?" Neveah scrunched her nose. She'd released her frosted tresses from her piled-up hairdo, was holding a baggie with ice cubes to the bump on her head, and looked like a model who'd partied too hard.

"That's right," Thane said. "Like a UFO. *Gone*."

"Weird," Spencer said.

Kali pulled his Glock from his rear waistband and laid it on the table. Jason jerked a thumb toward the bedroom.

"What's the plan with this dude?"

"Wait one." Thane raised a finger and bent to his laptop, squinting. "We've got incoming from HQ. Looks like facial recognition on your trunk passenger, Kali . . . Name's Fabio DeCarlo, age thirty-two, member of the New Red Brigades. They're the bastard children of the old Red Brigade terror group from back in the day . . . Looks like he's got multiple arrests and an outstanding warrant from the

Carabinieri in Milan." He scrolled through the file, stopped, and said, "Oooh, and would you look at *that*." Thane jabbed a finger at the screen. "Guess who the New Red Brigades has bad blood with."

Jason leaned in to look. "That might be our way in."

"You think?" Thane asked sarcastically as he leaned back with both hands on the back of his head. "Softballs. I keep throwing you guys softballs."

Jason looked over at Kali. Jason clearly wanted to handle it, but Kent was senior and more experienced, so it would be his call. Yet Kali surprised him.

"He's already seen me," Kali said. "Which means that he's expecting to see me again, and has been working that out in his mind—how to handle me, what to say, how to appeal to the guy who hurt him." He smiled at Jason. "You do it."

"Agreed," Thane said and turned to Jason. "Go prepare."

"Okay," Jason said. He slapped his hands on his knees, got up, and went into the master suite, where he opened a double-door french closet and pressed a recessed button on the inside frame. The closet's false bottom clicked open and he extracted a black Pelican case. He brought it over to the kitchen table and opened the Pelican. Inside were a Bluetooth printer, fully charged, and an array of different types of paper products. If required, Black Box agents could create high-quality business cards, stationery, or even wedding invitations.

He stood there for a few minutes perusing the internet on his cell phone—no one else in the room spoke to him or disturbed him. Then he loaded the printer with a small square of specialized tattoo paper, clicked his phone, and pocketed the square as the printer spit it out. He walked to the coffee table, picked up Kali's pistol, jammed it into his front waistband, and went into the bathroom.

Inside, he took off his tie, left his suit jacket on, and opened all the buttons of his white silk dress shirt. He turned on the sink spigot, pulled the paper square from his pants pockets, passed it under the water, pressed it to the skin above his right hip bone, peeled it off, and threw the paper away. He patted the spot dry with a hand towel, buttoned the shirt up, and tucked it back in.

He leaned on the porcelain sink and looked in the mirror. His beard was neat and trim, but he wanted more sheen for his hair. He found a comb in the medicine cabinet, wet it, and slicked his hair back. Then he removed a small rabbit's foot from his pocket. He turned it in his hand and murmured a mantra over and over. The rabbit's foot was much like Kali's prayer beads, an amulet used to get into character. It was a technique adopted from Thane, who'd learned it in turn while studying Method acting at the Lee Strasberg studio in New York.

When Jason emerged from the bathroom, his appearance and demeanor seemed cool and relaxed, as if he'd just taken a long, smooth pull from a cigarette. His dark eyes were focused, but on only the images inside his head, and it was as if he didn't even see his teammates anymore. He walked past them with a different gait and posture that were certainly not Jason's, took out his cell phone, clicked on an app to record, put it back into his pocket, turned the knob on the bedroom door, went inside, and closed it quietly.

Thane and his remaining three agents sat back to wait for Jason's results. They couldn't hear much above Beethoven's Ninth and said nothing. Finally, Thane got up and said, "I'll get that bourbon."

Inside the bedroom, Jason removed the suit jacket from the prisoner's head. The Italian had thick black hair, all mussed from his struggle, and a small, neat mustache. His dark eyes were angry and his nose was oozing and bloody from being slammed by Kali on the tarmac. He looked up at Jason, who walked over to a writing desk, pulled out an office-type swivel stool, placed it in front of the prisoner, and perched above him like a placid hawk.

"*Buonasera, compagno.*" Good evening, comrade, Jason said in dead-fluent Italian, with the northern accent he'd acquired while studying the language in Florence.

"*Fanculo.*" Screw you, the man said, and spat on the floor. "*Non sono il tuo compagno.*" I am not your comrade.

"*Vero.*" True, Jason said, and nodded. Then he examined his fingernails as if he were bored. "You are Fabio DeCarlo, a member of the New Red Brigades."

The prisoner's eyes widened for a fleeting second, but he raised his chin in defiance.

"So, you know who I am," he sneered. "Then you *also* know you'd be wise to let me go, and fast."

"Perhaps." Jason shrugged. "But I think it would be wiser for you to tell me everything you know."

The prisoner laughed. "Why the hell should I?"

Jason slowly shook his head. It was a mournful gesture, as if he felt sorry for the man. He laced his fingers together over his thighs and leaned closer.

"My *padrone* is very good friends with Vittorio Sietto," Jason said. "I and my men were at the Siettos' party to provide protection, and you embarrassed us greatly."

"Too bad for you and your *padrone*," the prisoner spat.

Jason kept his eyes locked on the prisoner's as he rose from the stool, pulled his shirt from his trousers, and showed him the tattoo. It was a small black skull with a red stiletto piercing one eye.

Fabio DeCarlo's face went pale white and his shoulders slumped. He glanced at the butt of Jason's Glock, then up at his placid eyes. He was trying not to shiver now.

"That is the mark of the Giordano family," he whispered.

"Correct," Jason said as he tucked his shirt back in.

"And . . . your *padrone* is . . ."

"Don Giordano." Jason cocked his head slightly, and waited. The Giordanos were a brutal Mafia family that controlled the underworld of Milan.

"Do as you please with me, but if . . . if I talk to you," Fabio pleaded, "can you please not hurt my loved ones?"

Jason smiled.

"There is nothing so precious as family, Fabio . . ."

Five minutes later, Jason emerged from the bedroom, closing the door quietly again on the way out. He stood still for a moment, allowing his Chameleon character to wash from his system. Then he nodded at his teammates. He was once more Jason.

"What did he give you?" Neveah asked.

"Everything he had," Jason said.

"How do you know?" Thane asked.

"I know," Jason replied and sat down on the couch. "He might be a killer and kidnapper, but he doesn't want to face the Giordanos."

Thane smiled and handed him a tumbler of bourbon. He swigged half of it down.

"Well?" Kali Kent said.

"He's a boot." The word was Marine Corps slang for a new grunt. "Doesn't know much, except for the cover name of one man."

"Which is?" Neveah asked.

"Somebody they call Orca."

Thane sat back and sipped his bourbon.

"Ahh," he whispered. "A killer whale."

EIGHT

ZIMBABWE, AFRICA

HE WAS A YOUNG MAN STUMBLING, ALONE, THROUGH a triple-canopy jungle. His three-hundred-dollar bespoke skinny jeans were split and frayed. One sleeve of his silk Pierre Cardin chartreuse shirt was torn away. His bare feet and slim arms were scratched and bloody from pounding through the acorn jackal-berry and three-thorn acacia. He had filthy curly blond hair and red-rimmed green eyes.

He was screaming for help. No one was coming.

His name was Alfred Tizer. It was an odd first name for a Gen Z kid, but with the kind of wealth his family had it didn't matter. He was the youngest son of a Seattle-based billionaire who owned a controlling share of one of the world's largest pharmaceutical firms. Alfred had been cruising the Philippine Sea on a modest yacht with only a chef, a three-man crew, and his Swedish model girlfriend on board. Filipino pirates—or at least that's who he thought they were—had snatched him right off the stern deck from a lounge chair while he was sipping a blueberry mojito and reading Paul Krugman's *Arguing with Zombies.*

But this wasn't the Philippines. This was someplace else, a dark, humid, horrifically hot jungle, not some barren desert wasteland full of street beggars and famine. His captors were muscular, well-fed monsters, not starving, desperate, or skinny. He didn't care where it was. He would run and run until he reached the sea. Except that he was already pouring sweat and slinging drool, and he was gasping for each breath now and his lungs were on fire. He had no weapons with which to protect himself from man or beast. He was lost.

"Somebody help me . . . please."

It didn't emerge as a shout or scream. At this point, it was barely audible.

Then the jungle's density seemed to clear. Up ahead there was more light and a path. He lurched forward over the matted leaves, thinking villagers probably tramped here back and forth, and that gave him a sliver of hope. He saw something gleaming on the jungle floor and his eyes grew wide as he realized it was a whispering stream, and his energy surged as he already tasted the glory of that quench.

A man flew out of the trees on his right and smashed Alfred down on his face in the mud as he screamed. Another man flew from the left and joined the first assailant, their knees buried in his clenching buttocks. He could see only their muscular black arms and rolled-up sleeves of South African camouflage as they pinned his flailing hands down. He was only a foot from the stream and trying to cup a handful of water and slosh it into his parched lips. One of them slapped his hand away and wrenched it behind his back.

"No," he boomed. "It is full of baboon piss and lion shit. It will kill you."

"What does it matter?" Alfred wept as they dragged him to his feet and turned him around.

They marched him back to the clearing. It was almost a kilometer, and one of the mercenaries complimented Alfred that he'd gotten that far. They broke out of the jungle and into the clearing, a large oval the size of a baseball diamond surrounded by Inodzi gums, the tallest trees in Zimbabwe. A cooking fire burned on the far side, smelling like hardwood and vervet meat. There were two large gray troop tents along the far perimeter, one smaller staff tent, and two camouflaged armored Spook vehicles that looked like fat frogs sitting on four giant truck tires. There were more men in the clearing too—some Black, some white, some neither—all wearing Selous Scout jungle camouflage and carrying FN FAL rifles or AK-47s. None of them looked over at Alfred.

His two captors marched him to the center of the clearing and shoved him down to his knees. He hung his head as his bony back shuddered from sobs. The first man who'd knocked him to the ground in the jungle pulled a 1911 pistol from his holster, cocked it, and pointed it down at Alfred's head.

"Do you hear that, Alfred?" he asked.

Alfred nodded.

"Do not try to run anymore," the man said.

Alfred nodded again and whispered, "Please. My father will pay you whatever you want."

"Yes, we know."

Alfred wept.

The front flap of the staff tent opened and a man emerged. The walls of the tent were rolled up and fixed, and he could have simply ducked underneath, but he didn't. Inside four men were sitting at folding tables, working at laptop computers. They were wearing loose cargo trousers and short-sleeved shirts and looked like misplaced stockbrokers. There was a large solar-powered fan to cool the computers, and wires led from the laptops to an array of SATCOM antennas outside that looked like something from the International Space Station. The man walked toward Alfred and the two men guarding him.

He was not tall, not short, but also not average in any aspect of his looks. He had short blondish hair but its texture was wiry like a hyena's coat, and his brows were wide and bushy above his blue eyes. His nose was flat, but one couldn't say if by genes or a boxer's glove, and the thickness and strength of his neck hinted at similar musculature throughout his body. He wore mesh and rubber commando boots, combat cargo trousers, and a matching bush jacket, all pristine, as if he'd just arrived from a five-star hotel via helicopter. He looked clean. He looked deadly. He had very white teeth and no hint of a window to his soul.

He pulled a silver cigarette case from his bush jacket pocket, selected a black Balkan Sobranie, lit up with a gold-plated lighter, and put the case back. He smoked with his left hand—he was the kind of man who always kept his dominant hand free. He walked to the spot where the boy was on his knees and his two men were guarding him. He crossed his hands behind his back and looked at the boy with the dispassion of a hunter regarding freshly trapped prey. The boy didn't look up at him.

Another man emerged from the staff tent and strode across the pitch. He was Congolese, tall and broad, with wide lips, one earlobe missing from a bullet, and panther eyes. He also wore Selous Scout camouflage and carried a small spiral notebook. His cover name was Nabuto. It was not his real name.

"Well, Colonel," Nabuto said to the smoking man, "it looks like your plan worked fine."

"Tell me, Nabuto," the blond man said. He had a Boer accent. Nabuto consulted his notebook.

"The moment that word of Daniella's kidnapping broke in the news," Nabuto said, "Vittorio Sietto's company stock dropped seven percent in value per share."

The Colonel nodded. "That's even more than I thought it would. I predicted only five percent. Go on."

"Well, as you also predicted, sir, Vittorio was still reluctant to pay the New Red Brigades' ransom."

"He is a businessman first," the Colonel said with a cynical smirk, "and only a father second."

"Exactly, sir," Nabuto agreed. "So, we had Sorento call Vittorio and make his pitch, as you instructed."

Sorento was a corrupt business reporter for the Italian newspaper *La Repubblica*, and the Colonel had Sorento in his pocket. Sorento had called Vittorio, ostensibly to glean details about the business mogul's kidnapped daughter, but then he'd offered some financial advice. Sorento had suggested that if—heaven forbid—something bad happened to Daniella, the public would be so outraged at Vittorio's failure to act, that his company's stock might crash. "It might be wiser, Signore Sietto," he'd said, "for you to pay the ransom, emerge as a fatherly hero, and see your stock value soar. After all, the ransom will be considered a write-off."

Vittorio Sietto knew what that meant: *Pay the kidnappers. Take the loss.*

"And?" The Colonel raised an eyebrow at Nabuto, who grinned in triumph.

"Sietto has just paid off, Colonel. The New Red Brigades have received five million euros in their account in Barbados." Nabuto cocked his head toward the staff tent. "The finance boys inside are leaving them ten percent and wiring the rest to us." The big Congolese consulted his notebook again. "The news is already breaking in *La Repubblica.* Vittorio Sietto's stock has spiked eleven percent, and since we purchased a million in options when the price dropped, we're now walking away with another fat cut."

The man called the Colonel nodded and looked at the tip of his burning Sobranie.

"What about the Red Brigades' man who was captured?" he asked. "Who took him?"

"We're not sure yet, sir," said Nabuto. "But even if he talks, he knows nothing but what we want him to know."

"Very good," the Colonel said. "Tell the Italians to free the girl."

"Yes, sir." Nabuto then looked down at Alfred, who had calmed somewhat during the conversation, but was still staring at the ground as his nose tip dripped with tears. "What about him?"

"His father's a bastard," the Colonel said. "He's not going to pay off. How's *their* stock doing today in the market?"

"Tizer's stock is doing very well, sir. It's actually up a point."

"Well, it's about to crash," the Colonel said as he walked to the man who was holding Alfred at gunpoint. He took the 1911 from his hand and pointed it at Alfred. "It's a good thing we're selling short."

And he shot Alfred in the back of the skull.

NINE

NOTHING EVER HAPPENED IN VALENSOLE, FRANCE. It was a sleepy provincial town in the Côte d'Azur, at the foot of the French Alps, halfway between Monaco and Avignon. If you were a cop with the Police Nationale patrolling in Valensole, you were probably bored to death.

But the two policemen parked in their white Peugeot 504 on the shoulder of the D6, beside a vast, open field, didn't mind. After all, they had fresh chocolate croissants, aluminum mugs of steaming coffee, and the overtime pay was good. It was a breezy cool midnight, and the open windows of the car delivered wafts of perfume that nearly made them dizzy. Valensole was famous for one thing: the endless rows of purple lavender that carpeted the fields and were marketed for bath beads, eaux de toilette, and magnificent bouquets. Their wives also didn't mind that they both smelled like garlanded church girls after a shift, rather than sweat.

Fontaine, the patrol car's driver, had just made a lurid remark about a barista in one of Valensole's midtown cafés, and his partner, Didier, was laughing. Then Fontaine forgot about the barista's figure as he stared at something on the horizon. It was a light, just above the distant trees at the far edge of the lavender field, and it was moving from east to west. He stopped chewing his croissant and pointed.

"*Qu'est-ce que c'est, Didier?*" he wondered.

"No idea," Didier said as he squinted too. "OVNI?" The acronym meant "UFO."

The light was growing brighter as whatever the object was headed toward them. Fontaine turned off the engine and punched the AM radio button. They'd been listening to bawdy French folk songs. Now it was eerily quiet, except for the unmistakable beating of rotor blades.

"It's a helo," Didier said.

"A Gazelle, I think," said Fontaine. "It looks like it's got that weird rear rotor fan thing."

There was no mistaking it now. It was a French helicopter, but as the policemen leaned forward toward the Peugeot's windshield they could discern no markings.

"It's all black, no numbers, and it's moving fast," Didier said. "Hit it with the radar."

Fontaine laughed. "What are we going to do? Give him a ticket for speeding?" But he turned and picked up the radar gun from the back seat and clicked it on. Didier wasn't laughing.

"What's a helo doing out here in the middle of the night? And look at the nose."

Fontaine leaned out his window with the gun. Indeed, as the helo came onward and was now only a hundred meters straight out in the lavender field, he could see a strange sort of antenna affixed to its nose under the cockpit. It looked like a silver mustache. He pulled the radar gun trigger and looked at the amber readout.

"*Rien de tout, mon ami,*" Fontaine said. Nothing at all, my friend. "It's like it's not there."

The helicopter slowed, its rotors bit the air harder, the lavender field fluttered and whipped as it hovered. Then it turned broadside, pitched nose up, settled just a meter or so from the ground, and all at once its side cargo door slid open. It looked like a young woman was being manhandled from inside and lowered so her bare feet would touch the long black skid. She had wild blond hair whipping in the rotor wash, a mussed white blouse, and a black pencil skirt torn right up to her hips.

Someone shoved her and she fell to the ground.

"*Mon dieu!*" Fontaine shouted.

The helicopter immediately pulled pitch, rose straight up, banked hard to the right, and roared off into the night.

Fontaine and Didier were already out of the car and sprinting through the lavender field, their black boots pounding along the furrows between the long, magnificent feathers of lavender under the midnight moon. The girl had struggled up to her feet and was staggering toward them. They had their hands on their pistols on instinct, though they knew she was in no shape to do any harm. Her face was twisted, with black lines of makeup coursing down from her tear-brimmed eyes, and her full lips looked bruised, but less as though from a beating and more like she'd chewed them in utter terror.

"Who are you, mademoiselle?" Fontaine cried as he and Didier reached her.

"I am Daniella Sietto," she moaned, and then she took one more step toward them and her eyes rolled back in her head and she passed out into their arms.

Once in a while, something *did* happen in Valensole.

TEN

THE BRAND-NEW HEADQUARTERS OF THE NORTH AT-lantic Treaty Organization was an ugly monstrosity. It was eight long buildings of glass and steel, each shaped like a drooping talon, arranged in two quartets that faced away from each other and were joined at the knuckles. The billion-euro structure hulked on ten acres of mowed grass and vast parking lots in the middle of Belgium's capital city.

Kali thought it looked like a target, sitting out there in the open so that Russian satellites could easily take aim. All you had to do was take an aerial photo of it, feed it into a tactical ICBM, and game over for Europe. But what really bothered him was the postmodern architecture blaspheming the beauty of the continent's old world. It was like what they'd done to the Louvre in Paris, dropping an unsightly glass pyramid at the entrance to the world's greatest museum and pretending it was art.

Thane and Kali were sitting in a rented Audi A6 on the other side of Leopold III, in front of the old NATO headquarters. That assemblage looked like a block of 1970s university dorms, but it still had the circular array of international flags and that rusty iron NATO sculpture in the middle that resembled the Death Star. Frank Gibson, one of the president's chief of staff and national security adviser, had told Thane to meet him there.

Thane and Kali were both wearing suits. Everyone in the NATO enclave wore either business attire or a uniform full of medals. They'd flown into Brussels from Milan, while their prisoner, Fabio, was still being temporarily housed in the safe house at Lake

Como, being watched by the rest of the team. Ando hadn't decided what to do with him yet, but he'd ordered the Black Box ship to pull anchor and steam for the Mediterranean. Apparently Ando thought that Europe was the spot where this unknown entity called Orca was going to make his or her next move. So did Thane and Kali.

"Run this down for me again," Thane said. "The way you think it all ties together." He was sipping black coffee and looking at the flags whipping in the breeze. The sky was goose gray and it was starting to drizzle. Kali was at the wheel.

"Okay, so I took a deep look at the market trends during the relevant time," Kali said. "First, Daniella Sietto is kidnapped, and when the news of that breaks, Vittorio's company stock takes a dive. During that downturn, a number of anonymous purchasers buy in . . . Then, Daniella's set free, the company's stock value spikes again, and there's a sell-off, of almost the *exact* same number of shares, give or take a few thousand . . . And finally, almost immediately after Daniella's return to her family, Alfred Tizer turns up dead in Africa. His father's firm, Tizer Pharmaceuticals, suffers a big dip in share value, and a big chunk of their stock sells short."

Thane looked over at Kent. "Maybe you should have been a stockbroker."

"I'm sure my mother would have been happier." Kali lifted his own Starbucks cup and took a sip.

Thane turned to Kali in the car. "But that's only two incidents," he said.

"Think about it, Thane," Kali said. "It might seem coincidental, but to me it seems carefully planned. Whoever arranged for Daniella's kidnapping was prepared to take profitable positions in the market. And, that person, or entity, took a sell-short position on Tizer stock, well in advance of Alfred Tizer's death. They knew they were going to kill him, and that his death would pay off."

"That's pretty dark," Thane said, "and I'd like to refute your logic, but I don't think I can."

"Well, I'm fairly certain there will be more such events," said

Kali. "Whoever or whatever this Orca is, my guess is he's running some sort of Hostage Inc. He takes a wealthy victim, plays the market on both ends, and cleans up. We just need Mr. Gibson to allocate federal access."

"That'll be fun," Thane said as he turned and looked out his side window again. "He's hard as lizard lips."

Frank Gibson had that sort of reputation. He'd worked his way up from congressional aide to a seat on the Senate Intelligence Committee, and then a presidential-level campaign boss. He'd left scores of political opponents in the dust and was a cold, calculating man who never suffered fools gladly. But Gibson and Ando had known each other for years, which was why the national security adviser had agreed to see Thane.

"There he is," Thane said.

A tall, wiry man wearing glasses, a tattered golf hat, and a black raincoat was walking across the NATO green. His face was pale, as if he never spent time in the sun. He was using a handkerchief to swipe the fog from his glasses and already looked impatient. Thane opened his car door.

"Let's go," he said. "I think we'll need our raincoats."

Kali nodded and both got out of the car.

Gibson had parked himself at the foot of the German flagpole, hands in his coat pockets. Thane and Kali walked through the drizzle. Thane offered Gibson his hand but the national security adviser didn't take it.

"It's too wet," Gibson said. He had a voice like a baritone who'd tried to sing too many high notes.

"I'm Thane, sir," Thane said. "This is Kent."

"I know who you guys are. Look, I'm here with POTUS and I'm the only one in there that's kept him from fumbling a response about New Russia. So, unless you want red, white, and blue to look even more passively weak, I suggest you make this snappy."

"Well, sir," Thane said, "there's a player out there with assets, taking hostages and manipulating the markets."

"What we'd like to ask for, sir," Kali said, "is approval from the council to do a wide-reaching forensic financial investigation. We'll need the IRS, SEC, and Federal Reserve."

Gibson squinted at the Black Box agents as if they'd asked him to spin up an aircraft carrier.

"That's all?" he scoffed. "You want me to recruit the most powerful financial bodies in the Fed to confirm your hunch?"

"Yes, sir," Thane said. "But it's more than a hunch." He turned to Kali. "Mr. Kent?"

Kali took a minute to lay out all the facts he'd just relayed to Thane in the car. When he was done, Gibson cocked his head and almost smiled, but not quite.

"Where'd you go to school, Kent?"

Kali was about to answer, but Thane cut him off.

"We just need a green light from you, sir," Thane said to Gibson. "We think this entity's running some sort of hostage ring, and it's going to expand."

"I'll think it over," Gibson said, but he was staring past Thane at the new NATO headquarters, not engaging his eyes. Thane had begun his career with Black Box as a Chameleon himself and knew all the tells and signs. Gibson was holding something back.

"If we're off the mark, sir," he said, "then it can't hurt to find out."

"Look, Thane," Gibson said, "I've got respect for Ando, and I don't ask him exactly what sort of ops he's running, 'cause it's all secret squirrel and I only approve the black budget. But frankly, this sounds a bit far-fetched, don't you think?"

Thane just looked up at the taller man, then smiled.

"Sir, with all due respect, you seem reluctant to say what you're really thinking."

Gibson glared down at Thane like a wolf about to devour a rabbit, but then his expression broke and he pulled a hand from his coat and waved it.

"All right, gentlemen, listen up. We already know about all of this. It's been boiling up for a while and, let's just say, folks on Wall

Street are *concerned*. There were three other similar incidents in the recent past, like the Sietto thing, but now the Tizer crash has people sweating up a rainstorm."

Thane smiled and nodded. "I thought you might know more."

"That is a privilege of my position," Gibson declared, as if angry at having been caught. He pulled a hand from his pocket and looked at his watch. The rain was really starting to come down. "I'll give you your assets. But tell Ando anything that's found out stays within your unit and anything more that he knows has to come straight to me. Not even to the director at Langley. To *me*. Are we clear?"

"Clear. Thank you, sir," Thane said.

"We appreciate your help," Kali said.

"It'll take a few days," Gibson said. "I'll have to massage some egos. Sit tight. And don't call me, I'll call you."

"Fair enough, sir," said Thane.

Gibson took out his handkerchief, defogged his glasses again, put them back on, and looked past Thane at the Audi.

"You guys should be renting something cheaper," he said, "like a Ford Fiesta." And he turned without ceremony and stalked away.

Thane and Kali walked back to the car in the rain.

"I'd say that worked pretty well," Kali said.

"Yeah," said Thane, "but I think we can forget about our Christmas bonuses."

ELEVEN

GENESIS

Kali did not see the Audi A6 as he and Thane walked back to the car in a swirl of fog. For just those thirty seconds, he still saw Frank Gibson's mouth in the fleeting moments before, hearing the words . . .

That is a privilege of my position.

And he was seven years old again, back in Lagos on a warm spring day, sitting beside the long built-in swimming pool at the rear of his father and mother's big, beautiful mansion, the one that so many of their friends seemed to wish was theirs.

It was an enormous bright white house of many windows, each with white frames made of carved bamboo wood. The roof stuck out all along the edges, and it too was of the same thick logs of bamboo. In the back where Kali most often played, sometimes with his best friend, Jare, there were four huge Greek columns like the ones he'd seen in those books about Athens. They were holding up a gigantic half circle of marble with a veranda on top, two stories up in the sky. Jare, whose father had died when he was three and who saw Mr. Adeyemi as a foster dad, sometimes remarked with quiet envy that the house was like a king's castle.

Kali's house was so big that it needed double doors in the back to let all the party people inside, and a big garage on one side for the fancy cars and his father's Bentley. There were lots of gardens and palms for him and Jare to chase each other around and hide in, and pretty flowers for his mother to pick for the dining table, although Marabel did most of those chores.

But there was no party today. There were many men inside the house. They'd arrived in their big, dark cars, with drivers who now stood outside in the sun with their caps pushed back on their heads, smoking cigarettes. There was no music leaking from inside, or fancy waiters with trays, or pretty girls in swirling skirts and dresses and those heels that no one could walk in without wobbling. His mom had told him to play outside. His dad had invited the men into his large study on the pool side of the house and shut the big mahogany doors.

Kali hated being banished from the house when his father was doing business. He was a curious boy, and only recently he'd gathered the nerve to sneak back inside—even when it was forbidden—and peek into his father's study from the half wall with the bar that led into the big dining room.

He would be very careful. They wouldn't even see his eyes.

"That is the privilege of my position!" his father shouted.

Kali's father was standing at the head of the long, polished conference table in his study. There were seven other men seated at the table, all very serious looking in their fancy linen suits and silk shirts, but no ties, because it was so hot. His father didn't have one on either; his suit coat was off and his sleeves were rolled up, and Kali clenched his buttocks because he knew his father did that only when he was mad or wanted to fight. He was also smoking a cigar and jabbing it through the air at the men like he wanted the glowing red end to touch them, and hurt them.

"I have been building this consortium for five years, gentlemen, with nothing from you but a few promises and meager investments! First and foremost, the fruits of those labors should be *mine*."

His father was almost shouting. That always frightened Kali, or anyone else who heard it.

"Whatever we're all making, we know it's not innocent, so don't pretend to be so hurt or suspicious because you haven't yet seen your profits. *I* protect you from the authorities. *I* take all the risks. *I* pay the customs agents to look the other way. All of that comes from my pocket, and in the end you're all going to get stinking rich. So, if you don't trust me . . . get the hell out!"

Kali cringed and sank down lower behind the bar. Not even the tip of his nose was showing now. When his father got this way it was dangerous.

"Mr. Adeyemi," one of the other men said. He had his elbows on the table and his hands in a pleading motion, with the palms turned toward the ivory paisley ceiling that Kali's mother had designed. His father didn't like that ceiling so much for his study. He liked darker things. "It is not that we don't trust you, sir. It is only that we would like to know where our money is now, and where it is going."

"Your money is nothing but grease for the wheels, Chibundu," Kali's father snapped at the man. "And don't pretend to be holier than the pope, because every whore and gambler in Lagos knows how it's earned. This consortium has been successful so far due to *my* vision and sweat, and my special connections. You're all going to make returns on investment of more than twenty percent, if you have the balls to shut up and wait for it."

Balls? Kali had never heard his father say something like that before and wondered what it meant.

Then he watched as his father became calmer. He could tell by the way his body went from stiffness to something softer, after a long breath. His father often did that when he yelled at Kali and then felt bad about it. He saw him pull his favorite prayer beads from his pocket and shift them one by one like that Chinese counting thing he forgot the name of. His father talked again to the men but more quietly now. Kali wondered if they'd ever heard his father sing. He sang really well.

"Gentlemen, it is fine that you've come here inquiring about progress. That is a normal state of affairs. But don't ever question my integrity when it comes to doing business with you, or when I allocate monies to make the wheels turn. As I said, that is the privilege of my position. Are we clear?"

The men around his father's big table nodded. They were scary-looking men so it made Kali smile that his father was stronger and made them afraid. The only thing that bothered Kali was that something told him these were all bad men.

His father suddenly seemed to feel something, and he turned his head directly toward where Kali was hiding behind the bar. Kali's little heart thumped so hard he thought it might burst. He pulled his head down, turned, and curled up under the bar like a mouse frightened into a cave by a bobcat.

A few moments later, he opened his small brown fingers where they were clamped over his eyes to see his mom bending her head below the bar and looking at him. She was wearing that pink dress that his father liked so much. It was short and her legs looked like buttery chocolate.

"Kalief, Dad sent me to tell you that if you ever eavesdrop again on his meeting, he is going to use the switch. Now come out of there and eat lunch."

She smiled.

TWELVE

PARWAN PROVINCE, AFGHANISTAN

THERE WAS SNOW ON THE JAGGED PEAKS OFF THE
northern end of Bagram Airfield, but a hot wind was blowing
across the enormous span of empty runway under a brilliant
sun. It was often that way in Afghanistan, the graveyard of empires,
where for thousands of years warriors had died either drenched in
sweat or with ice in their eyes.

Bagram had once been the largest allied military base in the
country, with nothing to compare with it since World War II. Now
it was empty. The gymnasiums and armories were gone. The Pizza
Hut and Green Beans Coffee and the massive dining facilities were
closed. The Hotel California, a clump of wooden "B-huts" for VIP
visitors, no longer had the Eagles wafting from its CD player or
the clacking of journalists' laptops. All along Disney Drive, where
bearded US Army Special Forces, German commandos in leopard
camouflage, and smartly uniformed Danish troops had once hustled to their helicopters to embark on missions, there was nothing
but a few old foreign newspapers spinning pirouettes in the dust.

For more than two decades, Bagram had been the centerpiece
of a fantasy, that Afghanistan could be dragged into modernity by
billions of dollars, goodwill, and guns. Now that dream was dead.

Ziar Baradar stood in the middle of the cracked black tarmac,
just across from where the US Air Force had once launched their
F-16s to rain death on Taliban fighters across the land. He was a
stocky warrior, once tall but now bent with age, with a bushy beard
fringed in tribal henna, a woolen *pakol* cap, and the traditional
blouse and pantaloons called the *salwar kameez*. He had a curved

dagger with an ornate horse head hilt tucked in his leather belt, but no other weapon. He had given up the gun.

Parked about thirty yards behind Ziar sat an armored Land Cruiser with two figures inside—Bilad and Shafik. The men were Ziar's most trusted lieutenants; often quiet, but wise beyond the years of a hundred elders.

Ziar squinted at the distant snowcapped mountains, where the sun was pulling off wisps of steam, and remembered how he, Bilad, and Shafik had once fought those unforgiving peaks as well as the invading infidels who challenged them there. Their unit had been one of the most glorified combatants of the mujahideen, battling the Soviet invaders until the Red Army men had collapsed under their relentless gunfire and fled. During that decade of guerrilla warfare, they'd even been heroes to the Americans and their CIA advisers, though they neither wanted nor needed anything more from them than their Russian linguists and Stinger missiles.

When the Taliban had come to power, they still regarded Ziar as a national treasure and consulted him for his warrior wisdom, religious purity, and love of nation. His name was still the one the people whispered. He was the one they prayed for.

But those days were gone, and along with them, honor.

Osama bin Laden and his al-Qaeda upstarts, along with their chai boys in the younger Taliban factions, had nearly destroyed the country. Ziar had cautioned against overtly attacking the West. He'd pounded on tables at Taliban *shura*—the council meetings of elders. No one had listened. September 11, 2001, had brought a typhoon of infidels to Afghanistan. For twenty more years, he'd been forced to fight again.

But now, despite the Taliban's victory over the Americans and their allies, all of whom had fled in dishonor, Ziar was not a happy man. This new Taliban government longed to be recognized by the West as an emergent power, but they couldn't even keep the electricity on or stop the citizens from rioting for bread. The even more radicalized fanatics of al-Qaeda and ISIS were blowing up mosques, and all of Afghanistan's talented youth who'd had a taste of freedom were fleeing to Western nations.

Ziar still wanted Afghanistan to be strong and independent, and once again to have secure borders. But more than anything now, he wanted peace. Yet he would never say such a thing to his son.

The old mountain fighter turned as Amir Baradar arrived on the tarmac in a large brown Mercury sedan that had once belonged to the US State Department.

Ziar watched as Khalid Mahar, Amir's own lieutenant and best friend, emerged, stomped to attention, and saluted him from afar. Ziar returned the gesture by placing a hand over his heart, then continued looking on as Khalid opened the rear door.

Amir exited and strode toward his father, leaving Khalid at the vehicle. He was a strapping boy in his early thirties, with a trimmed dark beard and green eyes like Ziar's, but he wasn't wearing traditional garb. Amir wore a long brown fur-collared coat to his ankles, black North Face pants, a black T-shirt, black Solomon trail shoes with Russian red soles, and a baseball cap from People's Friendship University of Russia. He carried an M4 rifle, one of those left behind by the Americans, and a smart leather briefcase.

Ziar was proud of his warrior son, yet also wary of his emotions. Amir had fiercely fought the Americans and the British in the Panjshir Valley, though his actions had nothing to do with Islam. He'd rejected his father's traditional beliefs, as well as the entire Quran. He thought that religion was for the weak and stupid. When he'd asked his father to send him off to Moscow for an education, Ziar had relented, but mostly because he didn't want to see his son die in the mountains. Yet five years later, when Amir returned, he'd become completely different. Now he worshipped Lenin and Stalin, instead of Muhammad. He despised global capitalism and wanted to see the decadent West brought to its knees. He had become a "Gen Z" warrior.

Their dreams for their homeland were as different as midnight and dawn. It was the way of the father and son, the veteran elders who'd seen too much war, and the sons who regarded their fathers as tired old fossils and dreamed of a new world order.

"*Saalamaleykum, baba,*" Amir said as he approached and saluted out of respect.

"*W'alekumsaalam, zoweek,*" Ziar said, though he only nodded without a salute. He was done with such things.

They stood side by side and peered to the north over the snow-capped peaks, as if expecting something soon.

"I must tell you, my son," said Ziar. "I am not convinced of your plan."

"I know that, Father." Amir looked down at his rifle. He unwound a green-and-black *shemag* from his neck and used it to clean some dust from the steel barrel. "However, the military council of my faction has approved it."

"I approved it as well, in theory," Ziar said. "But careless men have approved many things in the past, Amir. That is why we have so few cousins."

Amir looked at Bilad and Shafik scornfully, then shifted his gaze back to his father. He respected the old man, but saw him and his older compatriots as obstructions to true power and progress.

"Perhaps I shouldn't have told you about it," Amir said. "Perhaps your strength for the struggle is gone."

Ziar dipped his bushy brows in a glare. "Perhaps I should have sent you off to college in London instead of Moscow. Perhaps I should have schooled your words more often, with my hand or the switch." Ziar showed Amir his large brown hand, its fingers calloused from years of handling weapons and farm tools. It was the hand that had slapped Amir's face more than once.

"I apologize for my impertinence, Father. I am only certain that this is the way for my generation to take its place in the world." Amir looked back at the mountains. "We must rebuild our forces. We must modernize our army and air force. It is just our misfortune that we still need help."

"We shall soon know if this man brings the correct sort of help,"

Ziar said as he also turned back toward the mountains. "We have invited him here together, but I fear that I might regret it."

"We shall see, Father," Amir said.

A small black dot had appeared on the horizon. As it grew in form and shape, the pulse of rotor blades reached Ziar's and Amir's ears.

Amir turned toward the Mercury and nodded, prompting Khalid to peek inside the car and shout an order. Three men emerged, dressed like Amir and also hefting the American guns that were the spoils of war. Khalid walked to the front of the Mercury and pinned a flag to the fender. But it was not the new white banner of the emirate, with a Shahadah in black script: "I bear witness that none deserves worship except God, and I bear witness that Muhammad is God's messenger." Instead, it was a bright yellow flag, with a black hammer, a sickle, and crossed rifles. Khalid and the men then posted alongside the car with one rear door open, as if receiving an honored ambassador.

Inside the Land Cruiser Bilad and Shafik took their weapons off safety and looked on as the helicopter took shape and neared, its rotors scattering dust and paper detritus from the defeated coalition. It was a Russian Kamo 226, piloted by a former Afghan National Army officer who'd been trained by the Americans. The Kamo settled on the tarmac, and the same man whom the mercenaries in Zimbabwe called "Colonel" emerged from the cargo compartment.

He walked toward the men with an expression that was partially arrogant with an accompanying enigmatic smile. His pompous demeanor came from the fact that he had secret sources in both Moscow and Kabul, and was therefore well aware of Amir Baradar's ambitious plans. Not only was the Colonel going to exploit Amir's ambitions, but he also had plans to use Amir's father for his own purposes and profit, all the while making them think he was blessing them with his favors and talents.

Amir saluted the man, who returned the salute and stopped in front of him. They shook hands.

"It's good to at last meet in the flesh, Amir," the man said in English. He had an accent that sounded South African mixed with something else.

"Yes, sir. It is good." Amir smiled, then handed over his leather briefcase. "As we agreed, two million US dollars in cash. I trust that will be more than enough to begin our venture in earnest."

"It will be more than enough, and thank you."

"We are looking forward to the equipment," Amir said, "but it is your professional advice that is priceless."

The man clapped Amir on the shoulder and smiled. Then he turned toward Ziar, walked to him, and offered his hand. Ziar first touched his own chest, then took the hand and squeezed it. The man touched his chest as well and dipped his blond head.

"This is my father, Ziar Baradar," Amir said by way of introduction.

"An honor," the man said. "I am Lucas van Groot."

"It is my honor as well. My son tells me they call you Colonel."

"An old army title." The man smirked. "Such things die hard."

As Amir guided Lucas van Groot toward the big car, Khalid barked an order in Pashto at his men and they snapped to attention.

Ziar followed behind, looking at Van Groot's back, his jungle boots, and the way he walked and carried the briefcase, as if so much money meant nothing. He had the stride of a man whose eyes took in none of the glories of nature, nor would he slow his pace in respect of another, nor would he bend his knees before God. Ziar had learned as a child that you could judge a man by his gait.

He did not like this man.

THIRTEEN

SAUGATUCK, WESTERN COAST OF SARDINIA

THE BLACK BOX HEADQUARTERS SHIP, DESPITE ITS clumsy appearance, was a fast mover. It was already anchored off the western coast of Sardinia, close enough to Europe to launch operations, yet not so close as to draw attention. And like some kind of maritime werewolf, it executed its comings and goings only at night.

An unmarked black Gazelle helicopter had taken a circuitous route, picking up Thane and Kali from Brussels, and then the rest of the team from a small airstrip near Lake Como. It swept in from the north through the star-filled night with its pilots transmitting an encoded permissions request to a pair of gunners manning a minigun on the forward superstructure—so they wouldn't blast it out of the sky. It hovered there long enough for Thane and his crew to jump down, along with Fabio, who was zip-tied and hooded again. Having no leads, they'd decided to hold him until further information came down from Gibson. Then it took off and disappeared, while two armed escorts hustled Fabio somewhere below-decks.

Thane and his crew, all dressed in civilian jeans and sweaters, descended through a roof hatch above Ando's cabin and tramped down the steel stairwell, where his armed guard let them inside. They found Ando behind his desk, studying a thick tome about CIA operations in Southeast Asia. Ando's idea of relaxation was to sometimes review intelligence successes and failures during the Vietnam War, when the agency had first melded spying and special operations into strike teams.

Ando offered no greetings. He placed the book behind him on a shelf, picked up a red file from his desk, crooked a finger, and led the Black Box team through a doorway at the rear of his office. They all climbed down a circular steel stairwell twenty feet deep and emerged into a conference room, where they could work more comfortably than in Ando's office and also make use of visual aids.

The conference space had been constructed inside the ship's former staff officers' dayroom. It had a long, polished table surrounded by office chairs, with a large flat-screen on the wall behind the table's head and a secure encrypted conference call module in the middle of the table. The conference room didn't need to be secured with countermeasures, because the entire ship was a SCIF—a secure compartmented information facility.

Inside the conference room, Ando locked the door while Thane, Kali, Jason, Neveah, and Spencer took seats surrounding the table. Ando took his place at the table's head in a plusher leather version of the remaining seats. He crossed his legs, leaned back, and opened the red file.

"How's everyone doing?" he asked as he flipped some pages.

"We're fine, sir—" Thane began.

"So," Ando continued, "Mr. Gibson has graced us with some intel." He was not uninterested in his agents' welfare, but preoccupied with the issue at hand. "It appears that indeed your theory is correct, Kent. There is an entity out there running some sort of international hostage-taking gambit, while also manipulating the stock markets in concert."

Kali nodded, but he didn't overtly take credit.

"What kind of entity, sir?" Jason asked.

"It's apparently some sort of LLC," Ando said. "A limited liability company, but it's a ghost company handling all the financial transactions, and it dissolves right after all the funds have been moved and all those accounts emptied."

"Were the feds able to nail down the LLC's owners or principals?" Thane asked.

"Well, it's actually not just *one* LLC," Ando explained. "It's a different company for each of the hostage events. And the answer is no, not yet."

"What about the signatories on the company papers?" Kali posed. "The attorneys who filed, for instance."

"All deceased," said Ando. "The SEC determined that all the filings were submitted by people who left this world long ago. Their identities were probably accessed through hacks into Social Security and hospital morgue records. That's why Gibson referred to the entities as ghost companies."

"This sounds like standard operating procedure for a criminal enterprise," Neveah said, while Spencer just listened quietly. High finance wasn't his thing.

"Is this in line with your thinking, Kent?" Ando asked Kali.

"It is, sir," Kali said. "May I have the screen?"

Ando nodded and fired up the flat-screen behind his head.

Kali pulled a keyboard from the conference table's recessed slot and tapped into the Secret Internet Protocol Router Network, or SIPRNet. He had already sent an encrypted file over to the ship, and now a large, multicolored spreadsheet appeared on the screen. Everyone turned to examine it.

"The left column is a list of victims and targets pulled from the last three years," Kali said, "ending at the bottom with Daniella Sietto and Alfred Tizer. The next column is a list of corporations, all publicly traded, that were related somehow to the victims." He looked at his fellow Chameleon. "Jason?"

"The next column," Jason said, "lists fluctuations in those stocks and corresponding dates to the hostage incidents. We've concluded that those trades couldn't possibly have been coincidental. They include stocks, bonds, and Bitcoin transactions."

"And the last column," Kali said, "is our estimate of profits that could have been made from those spiking fluctuations, along with the amounts of ransoms that were paid. We're guessing at more than fifty million dollars, but apparently even with Gibson's help from the SEC and NSA, we can't yet make a guess at the beneficiary."

"I checked their numbers," Neveah jumped in. "The math is right."

"Impressive," Ando murmured as he spun back around.

Thane nodded at his agents with a touch of pride.

"Well, the beneficiary, whoever he may be," Ando said, "is camouflaging all his activities using this scheme. He, or she, is operating through ghost LLCs and cutouts that no one's been able to identify yet. He's extremely careful, uses serpentine investment techniques, and holds no major accounts that can be traced back to his name. His kidnap and hostage operations are resulting in big payoffs, but he's using no overt assets that can be traced . . . He's not like some Russian oligarch showing off his yachts." Ando closed the red file and frowned, clearly exasperated.

"He also uses kinetic and technical assets, sir," Kali said, adding to the conundrum. "He's got contractors like the New Red Brigades, and he had the Comando Vermelho in line for that job until we pulled them offline. We don't know who he used to snatch Alfred Tizer, but my guess is they were also guns for hire . . . He's also got access to some sort of electronic countermeasures. The Swiss couldn't track his jet, and the French cops couldn't get a radar return on the helo that dropped off Daniella in France."

Ando raised an eyebrow. "You're darkening my day, Mr. Kent. Not improving it." He looked at the rest of the team. "Who's got something? We need a course of action. We need a thread to pull."

"Nothing comes to mind just yet," Thane said.

Neveah also shook her head.

"I'm just the driver, sir." Spencer raised his palms.

"Right." Ando knew Spencer was being modest. He was as sharp as any of them—Black Box didn't recruit fools.

"I got nothin'," Jason said.

"We've got Fabio," Kali declared. His teammates turned to look at him. "Maybe our prisoner knows more than he's given us so far. I know he's a low-level guy, but there must be somebody he can actually lead us to. Maybe even if it's just a name . . . something more than 'Orca.' If he knew that much, I'll bet he knows more."

"You're saying he was playing me?" Jason remarked.

"No, I'm saying that this is all we got," Kali said. "We've got to dig deeper."

Ando contemplated as he looked at both Jason and Kali. Then he pressed a key on his command console, and behind him the flat-screen image changed from Kali's spreadsheet to an image of Fabio in his cell. He was manacled to a bunk, hood removed, head down, looking dejected. "We don't seem to have any other options." He looked at Thane, who in turn smiled at Kali.

"You're up," Thane said to Kali. "Don't come back empty handed."

Kali nodded and rose from his chair.

"Good luck, Mr. Kent," Ando said. "We'll be monitoring from here."

FOURTEEN

THE *SAUGATUCK*'S BRIG WAS THE SIZE OF A SMALL-town jail cell.

It was a narrow room with steel bulkheads, two hard bunk beds, and an open toilet and sink. It was a throwback to World War II, when the ship had crossed the Atlantic with cannons on the bow and depth charges racked on the poop deck. Occasionally back then, when under high stress and drinking contraband liquor, the merchant seamen would brawl and get locked in the brig to cool off. But it had also been used for German prisoners who'd been captured from sinking U-boats.

On Ando's orders the brig's bulkheads had been modernized and repainted, with recessed lighting in the ceiling in place of the old bare bulbs. However, he'd purposely left a small cartoon etched on an upright steam pipe by a U-boat prisoner. It was of a submarine captain with a jaunty cap and the words in German *Heinrich war hier*—"Heinrich was here." It had the desired demoralizing effect on Fabio, who'd hardly moved from where he sat on one bunk, head in one hand, wearing a dark blue engine room coverall and flip-flops.

His captors had blindfolded him again and taken him somewhere in a helicopter. From the smell of the sea and the way his prison creaked and moved he knew he was aboard some kind of ship. He doubted that the Giordano Mafiosi had such a thing, but whoever these people were, they'd taken his wallet, cell phone, and cigarettes. He was miserable.

Across the gangway in the guardroom, Kali removed Fabio's captured cell phone from a lead-lined transport box, then a small photo of a pretty Italian woman he'd taken from Fabio's wallet, a blue-and-white pack of Italian MS cigarettes, and a plastic lighter. He wouldn't be going into the cell using any Chameleon disguise. He wanted Fabio to recognize him as the man who'd taken him prisoner. He nodded at a Black Box security man wearing a pistol, and they both walked out to the brig.

The cell door was battleship gray with a small square window. Kali stood to one side while the security man pulled out a key, inserted it, and turned. The door clicked and he pulled it open. Fabio raised his head from his hand—the other one was manacled to the bunk. Kali stepped into the cell, the guard secured the door, and Kali folded his arms and leaned back against it. Fabio's dark eyes went wide.

"*Ricordi di me, Fabio?*" Remember me, Fabio?

"*Sì.*" Fabio stared at the man who'd tackled him on the airport tarmac and smashed his face.

"Good. We're going to do this in English." Kali cocked his chin up at the video camera mounted in the cell's ceiling corner. Fabio looked at it and understood, but he shook his head. His black hair was mussed from combing it with his fingers and he hadn't shaved in three days.

"*Non parlo inglese.*" I don't speak English, Fabio said.

"You speak it very well, Fabio," Kali said. "We have your file from the Carabinieri. Lying isn't going to help you."

"Well, I have nothing to say," Fabio said in English also. He looked up at Kali with a defiant smirk, as if he'd also caught him in a lie. "And you are *not* a Giordano."

"You're right. I work for the US government. The Mafia might kill you, but *we* can keep you forever. You are currently in a prison on a ship with no name."

"*Bastardi,*" Fabio muttered. He was angry.

Kali opened one hand, like a magician producing a playing card, and showed Fabio the photo of the woman.

"Who's this, Fabio?"

"My fiancée."

"She's pretty."

Kali's compliment didn't sound promising to Fabio. "You will not harm her," he said defiantly.

"No, but you'd like to see her again," Kali said, then added in Italian, "*Vero?*" True?

Fabio didn't answer, but his face reddened because this American was using his woman against him.

"Give me something, Fabio," Kali said.

"I know nothing."

"You know about Orca. Who is this Orca?"

Fabio shook his head. "I do not know. It is a name the comrades use. I am only a driver."

"All right. But you must have a contact, Fabio," Kali said. "In case something goes wrong."

"No."

"Tell me about this contact, Fabio."

"There is no such contact."

"Just give me a name, Fabio," Kali pressed, as if it was an easy thing to do. "Come on, I *know* you know someone. Give me something so I can help you."

Fabio laughed as if the idea was absurd. "How can I tell you the name of a person who does not *exist?*" he sputtered, but he looked at the ceiling as if to avoid Kali's eyes.

"What's his name, Fabio?" Kent came off the cell door. His voice stayed controlled, but it wasn't so casual anymore. He pulled Fabio's cell phone from his jeans pocket. "You've got his number in here. Show me."

"*No.*" Fabio stared at the phone, but he laced his thick fingers together as if it were dangerous to touch it.

Kent eased back on the pressure for a moment. He pulled the MS cigarettes from his other pocket and handed the pack to Fabio along with the lighter. The pack trembled in Fabio's fingers as he extracted a cigarette, lit up, and inhaled the smoke as if it were some kind of anesthetic. He slumped and sighed and closed his eyes.

"You do not understand," he said. "If I give you his name, they will hunt me forever." He shook his head harder, as if he'd been asked to kill and eat his favorite pet.

Kali moved over to the other bunk that was facing Fabio, sat down, and leaned on his knees like a concerned parent.

"Listen, Fabio. We're not going to just throw you to the wolves. We're going to protect you. All you have to do is show me the name and number. That's all you have to do."

Fabio pulled on the cigarette with his trembling fingers and the smoke made a blue cloud around his large head.

"I would like a drink please," he said.

"You can have anything you like, Fabio. You can have a bottle of fine wine and some very good food, right here, in just a few minutes . . . but you don't want to be eating and drinking in this cell for years. You know what'll happen. Your fiancée will get tired of waiting around and find another man. You don't want that, do you?"

Fabio looked up at Kali and whispered, "You are bastards."

"And so are you. You took Daniella Sietto, didn't you?"

"But we did this only for *money*."

"The Red Brigades use money to do bad things," Kali said. "Daniella is still missing," he lied. "If she dies, and you haven't helped us, then I can't help *you*."

Fabio spent the next minute thinking, but his options were slim and his future bleak and he knew it. His eyes glazed over and he began to stammer.

"I . . . I will do this, but only on one condition," he said. "Do you hear me?"

"Tell me."

"You must fetch Angela from Milan, and take me and her somewhere far away, where no one can find us."

"Where would you like to go?" Kali had no idea if Ando would agree to such a deal, but he knew that the CIA could arrange it. They'd done it before.

"An island somewhere," Fabio said. He looked up at the brig ceiling while those images formed in his mind. "A warm place, far away, with new names. And money."

"Does Angela like the Caribbean?"

"All Italian girls like the beach," Fabio murmured.

Kali handed Fabio his cell phone. Fabio took it but held the device as if it were a poisonous snake. Then he sighed with a shudder, input his password, scrolled through his contacts, tapped one, and handed the phone back to Kali.

"Who is Maria?" Kali asked.

"It is camouflage. His name is Nabuto."

"Good," Kali said. "Are the rest of your comrades' numbers in here as well?"

"No, they are in my head."

Kali got up, slipped the phone back into his pocket, and the guard unlocked the cell door. Fabio dropped his cigarette onto the steel floor and squashed it with his flip-flop. He stared at Kali with furious resentment.

"What is your name?" he asked as if he were facing his executioner.

"Harold."

"I do not like you, Harold."

"You'll like me better," Kali said, "when you and Angela are drinking margaritas on a beach somewhere."

He went out and the guard closed the door behind him, initiating its electronic lock.

When Kali returned to Ando's conference room, everyone seemed satisfied except for him. He sat down at his place at the table, turning the plastic cigarette lighter in his fingers, but he didn't speak.

"That seemed to go well, Mr. Kent," Ando said.

"You got us a name," Thane agreed. "That's what we wanted."

"It was too easy," Kali said. His training as a Chameleon consisted of much more than just complex disguise. He could read another person's intentions, body language, inflections in tone, the tells that would give him away. Up close with Fabio, he'd observed every facial tic and his darting eyes. "He gave me that name and number too fast. And he was lying. He's not 'just' a driver."

"Well, maybe he was ready to talk," Neveah said. "He wanted a deal, and you gave him one."

"Or maybe that's what he wants us to think," Jason said.

"Let's try to be optimistic," Thane said. "We've got a name and a number. How do we use it?"

No one had anything to offer. Ando rocked back a bit in his chair as he drummed his fingertips on the table, thinking.

"There was a case back in Vietnam days," Ando said. "A Phoenix Program operation, as I recall . . ."

He was referring to a period when the CIA and US Army Special Forces had run combined operations during the Vietnam War. The secret programs were known as Phoenix and Sphinx, and the operators had called themselves roadrunners, performing "wet work" behind the lines against the Viet Cong. Ando's Black Box teams were fully familiar with those operations, having studied the period during training.

"During this one operation in Laos," Ando continued, "they snatched a North Vietnamese Army asset, turned him, and had him offer the Cong a tempting target. They lured an entire VC platoon into an ambush and wiped them all out."

Thane leaned toward Ando. "You're suggesting we try something similar, sir?"

"I'm suggesting we use our imaginations."

"It might work," Jason said, warming to the concept. "We get Fabio to make contact with this Nabuto. He offers him a tempting target, someone whose backers are going to pay off, big-time."

"And how do you expect that to work?" Kali challenged Jason. "They know Fabio's been offline, that he was taken by someone. At this point they won't trust him."

"They might," Jason said, "if we can give him the perfect cover story and back it up with proof positive . . . Look, I'm as skeptical as you are, Kali, but we've got to try *something*. If it doesn't work and they don't bite, no harm, no foul."

Ando looked at his watch, pushed himself away from the table, and got up.

"Work the problem, people," he said. "Give me a brief in one hour."

He went out.

Thane looked over at Neveah, who'd pursed her lips and seemed glum.

"You look skeptical too," he said to her.

"She doesn't look skeptical to me, boss." Jason smirked. "She looks like a hostage."

"Great," Neveah said sarcastically.

But Kali still wasn't happy about any of it.

"It was too easy," he murmured. "Too good to be true . . ."

FIFTEEN

"It is too good to be *true*, George."

Kali's mother was sitting in the front seat of their big Bentley. His father was driving, with his elbow on the windowsill and a cigarette in his fingers. Kali was alone in the back, still not tall enough for his sandals to touch the floor.

"We dress in the finest clothes, George," she was saying. "We dine in the best restaurants, and we have servants and luxuries that most people in Lagos only dream about. And here we are, going off to another party where the politicians will kiss your cheek today, and stab you in the back tomorrow."

Kali looked down at his clothes—dark blue linen shorts and a short-sleeved button shirt with pineapples all over it. He didn't like these clothes and he didn't like adult parties. They were boring. He wanted to be home playing with Jare.

"Yvonne, I don't want to discuss this in front of Kalief." Kali's father sounded stern, but it wasn't the rough voice he used with businessmen.

"But he *must* hear it, George." She turned fully toward George Adeyemi now, laying her wrist across the leather armrest dividing the two front seats, with her gold bracelets jangling. She glanced back at Kali, as if to ensure he was still there, then glared at Kali's father again. "He must learn from our mistakes and watch us correct them. He needs to see which parts of life have value, and which do not. He must learn right from wrong."

Kali's father said nothing. When Kali's mother was speaking it was like a teacher at school. You sat at your desk in silence and listened.

They were driving west on Admiralty Way from Moba, alongside the big, wide river toward the bridge that led over to the Lagos Polo Club. Kali liked this drive because they passed so many fancy buildings, like the Sheraton and Oriental hotels, and the Cactus restaurant. It was the rich part of Lagos with huge villas, lush gardens, towering palms, and fancy cars. Kali's father really liked it too, but sometimes Kali would hear his mother murmuring, "I'd rather be poor."

"You had a dream once, George. You were a wonderful architect with such beautiful plans. You cared so much about people. And then we let the money spoil us both." Kali's mother had taken her hand off the armrest and turned away. She was staring out her open window as the palms flashed by and the air smelled like the salty lagoons. "When we first met, remember? It was all you talked about, that Nigeria had to shed its terrible history of corruption and crime and create new memories and new traditions. Do you remember, George?"

"I remember, darling," Kali's father said, but he was smiling and it seemed like he was patronizing her.

She snapped her head back around.

"Look at me when I talk to you, George. This is a serious matter!"

"I'm driving, Yvonne," he said, but his smile was gone and his voice dropped, as if he was ashamed.

"We are *both* at fault," Kali's mother said. "I also take the blame." She got quieter as she reached out and touched her husband's arm as he drove. "And because of that, I'm ready to give it all up."

"We can do both, Yvonne," Kali's father said. "We can be comfortable and also build something better."

Kali's mother shook her head.

"You cannot be both an angel and a demon, my love," she said. "Nigeria is a sad cesspool of corruption, and it will always be so unless someone as talented and powerful as you makes it change."

"You are asking too much of me, Yvonne."

"I am asking you to do this for your son."

Kali felt something turn in the pit of his stomach. He wasn't sure what they were talking about, but it was very important. Big decisions were being made, and it was all because of him. It made him afraid. It also made him feel loved.

"When we met," Kali's mother pressed on, "you promised me we'd be part of the solution. *Now* look at us. We are going to a fancy affair at a polo club, where only the very richest in Lagos can play, and everyone there is making more money by stealing it from the people. We are now *part* of the problem."

Stealing?

Kali wasn't sure he'd heard that right. His father and mother would never, ever steal. If he even took one more cookie than allowed he could get the switch and be put to bed early.

Kali's father took off his hat and laid it on the seat between him and Kali's mother, as if it could protect him from her judgment. It was a fine straw hat with a purple band.

"I am not prepared to give up our lifestyle, Yvonne," he said. "I will not have us living in the banana fields, and I will not remove Kalief from a fine education. We can do both things."

"If a man makes his money from building casinos, my love," Kali's mother said, "he cannot save himself by building a church. Such a man will end up either in prison, exiled, or dead. Do you want to wind up like your friend Namimbi, speaking your last words to a priest on the beach?"

Where did I see a man speaking to a priest on the beach? Kali thought.

And then he remembered the execution. The idea that his mother was suggesting that might happen to his father sent a terrible shiver up his small spine, even in the heat of a beautiful sunny day on the way to a fancy party. The one thing he'd been looking forward to about that party was the big, beautiful horses when the men played their polo.

Now he no longer cared.

Now he wanted to go home.

SIXTEEN

PRETORIA, SOUTH AFRICA

LUCAS VAN GROOT WAS A GREAT BELIEVER IN THE OLD operational adage "Hide in plain sight."

Naturally, there were times when stealth and camouflage ruled the day, such as long-range reconnaissance or sniper missions, and he and his Selous Scouts were experts at that. But he'd also learned from years of work in the jungle or the veld that sometimes a predator would hold back, hesitate, or simply ignore you because you were right out there in the open.

Once in Rhodesia, when Van Groot was still a captain, he and his commandos had hunted the leaders of Zimbabwe African National Union (ZANU). He'd realized there was no way his men were going to get close to the ZANU chief of operations, Enos Chitepo, so he'd left his men in the bush and had gone into town alone. Dressed in civilian clothes, he'd parked himself on a bench outside Chitepo's home, casually reading the morning newspaper. When Chitepo came out for his morning stroll, Van Groot had dropped his newspaper, shot him in the face, gunned down his security officer, and simply walked away.

Hide in plain sight.

At times it was the most sensible choice. However, while he wasn't going to operate from an underground cavern out in the bush, there was no sense in being a fool about it.

Van Groot's camouflage commercial corporation, Dextor Import-Exports—to which his name was not legally attached and appeared on no corporate papers—occupied a respectable building, but not in downtown Pretoria proper. His affairs had to appear legitimate, yet not to the point of being flashy or renting a suite of luxury offices on Middel Street. His building was a four-story concrete structure he'd selected at an industrial park in Centurion, south of the city outskirts. Dextor Import-Exports appeared to be a mundane business enterprise with worldwide cargo contracts, while Van Groot's operation in profitable acts of violence, stock market manipulation, and international crime ran as an undercurrent below the surface.

Fully aware of the need for security—given the real nature of his business—Van Groot took precautions. He always arrived at his office via an underground garage and never walked in or out of the front door. He rarely invited legitimate business associates to visit the firm, but almost always met them downtown at upscale watering holes. Dextor's roof sprouted all sorts of satellite antenna arrays, which, if necessary, he would have explained away as a monitoring system for worldwide shipping transmissions. And given that most of his employees were former Selous Scouts who'd served with him in hard places, the building was constantly surveilled, from the outside, by armed men in civilian clothes, 24/7.

It was a secret fortress, though on the inside it resembled a small trading firm on Wall Street. One never knew when the South African tax authorities might make a surprise visit.

Van Groot was sitting at a large teakwood desk behind a double-monitor computer array inside his spacious command suite. The walls were decorated with expensive paintings, ancient artifacts stood on marble pedestals, and there were blue leather chairs and a matching couch. Off in one corner stood a marble bust of Alan Stewart Paton, author of *Cry, the Beloved Country*. Van Groot's sense of humor tended toward the ironic. Paton was one of the heroes of South Africa's social justice movement. Van Groot couldn't have cared less.

"Nabuto, let's review this again," Van Groot said. "When did this bloke Fabio make contact?"

"He called me last night."

Nabuto was standing off to one side of the desk holding a tablet.

They were both wearing expensive suits and silk ties. Van Groot insisted that everyone dress appropriately at HQ and that no one use military ranks from the old days. They all called him "VG" in the office.

"And he used the appropriate language?" he asked.

"He mentioned his fiancée, Angela. I checked the code keys for the New Red Brigades. His fiancée's name is actually Federika."

Van Groot nodded as he thought for a bit. He wished he had a cigar or a cigarette, but he never smoked in the office. He had a small vape mod shaped like a large black bullet on his desk, but he rarely touched it. The fog smelled too much like flowers.

"And what's his story about what happened to him and where he's been?"

"He says he was taken by the Giordano Mafiosi as his comrades were getting the girl on the plane."

"Interesting." Van Groot raised an eyebrow. "And then?"

"Claims he escaped, used a ratline to get to Geneva, and has been hiding out there. That's where he spotted this fresh target."

"Has he contacted his Red Brigades comrades?"

"Says he's afraid they might kill him for his cock-up."

"He's right." Van Groot laughed softly. "I'd certainly kill him for it if I were them. And what's his reason now for being so forward thinking and ambitious?"

"Says he knows he screwed up and wants to make it up to us. Claims he's not even expecting a finder's fee . . . unless we'd like to reward him."

"And you checked his cell phone coordinates?"

"Geneva. The cyber boys ran it down."

"All right. Give me the target details."

Nabuto tapped his tablet.

"Maryanne Kreisler. Young woman, around thirty, apparently wealthy, resides in an upscale flat near the lake. She's a vault manager for UBS bank in Geneva. That vault is beneath their headquarters building. It's well known for holding billions in cash, fine art, jewels, and bearer bonds."

"Yes, I know that one." Van Groot nodded and smiled. "Likely still have plenty of Nazi gold down there as well. Those bastards at UBS would sell their souls for a franc or the right piece of ass."

"You're right on the money, VG," Nabuto said with a grin as well. He turned the tablet around so Van Groot could see it. "He sent me a surveillance shot."

Van Groot looked at the photo. It was a grainy, long-range shot of Neveah sitting at an outdoor café. She was wearing a short caramel skirt, high heels, and a tight silk blouse. Her frosted curls swept her shoulders and she was reading what looked liked the *Financial Times* of London.

"They might pay handsomely to retrieve her," he said. "How did he find this girl?"

"He said from his own research, which makes sense. He's part of the recon team that spotted Daniella Sietto and tracked her patterns of life."

"That worked out well for everyone," Van Groot said. "Except for *him*."

He looked at his Audemars Piguet watch. It was a modest Royal Oak Black Dial model and cost only $25,000. "One minute," he said, "while I check something."

Van Groot got up, walked to a door at the rear of his office, and entered a large conference room. It was arrayed with six computer workstations, manned by the same men from the staff tent in Zimbabwe, except that they were all wearing ties with their suit coats draped over their chairs. On the far wall were flat-screens with incoming tickers from the stock markets in New York, London, and Hong Kong. As Van Groot entered, their postures stiffened a bit, but they all kept working the computers and phones, which were all landlines and encrypted. He leaned down to the closest of his brokers, a bespectacled bald man, and spoke softly.

"Martin, tell the lads to start making some acquisitions, but keep them in modest tranches and do them through the more desperate day traders, the hungry ones who'll keep their mouths shut. Get us some Eurail, Air France, Boeing, McDonnell Douglas, and throw in some German pipelines and fuel. Start with five million euros and spread them out so they'll ring no bells. Am I clear?"

"Yes, sir," Martin said as he quickly jotted the details on a notepad. "Is this for a current project?"

"No, it's about something I've got in the works for later."

"Roger, sir." Martin had no idea why Van Groot wanted to make such purchases, but he knew not to ask too much.

"Also, Martin," Van Groot said, "what's the status on our holdings of UBS bank in Geneva? I believe it's UBS Group AG on the NYSE. Should be running around twenty dollars."

"I think we've got about fifty thousand shares," Martin said.

"Excellent. Well, just watch it carefully and let me know if it fluctuates at all. And if it starts to get wobbly, give me a good sell-short position. Understood?"

"Will do, VG." Martin had once been Van Groot's field intelligence officer in the scouts. Van Groot called him a REMF, a pejorative for someone who never saw combat, but he'd sent him to study finance in Paris and he knew his stuff.

"Good man." Van Groot patted him on the shoulder and went back to rejoin Nabuto. He closed the door to the transaction room behind him.

"All right, Pretorius," he said, using Nabuto's real name. "Let's give this one a go."

"Roger, VG. Who would you like to use?"

"Let's try the Germans. How about the Baader-Meinhof offspring?" He was referring to an infamous gang of leftist militants who'd terrorized Europe back in the 1970s. A cell of their descendants were now fanatical anticapitalists, but were also guns for hire, and brutal. "Know how to reach them?"

"I'll call Klaus Debier in Berlin."

"Perfect, and let's have the backup team in here for a briefing." Van Groot walked to a recessed bar behind his desk and started making himself a vodka and tonic. He turned back to Nabuto with the crystal tumbler.

"Tell the Germans their cut will be fifteen percent of a two-million-euro ransom for the girl," he said as he took his first long pull. "But if UBS fails to pay off, they'll still get the standard kill fee." Then he smirked as he added, "And, as a bonus, they can enjoy her company thoroughly, before they get rid of her."

SEVENTEEN

GENEVA, SWITZERLAND

NEVEAH'S FLAT IN GENEVA WAS NOT A SAFE HOUSE. It had been selected by a Black Box Aberration agent in Switzerland called Pierre, and she'd rented it for a full month as Maryanne Kreisler. But it had no concealed weapons, no safe room, and no CIA technicians would be running countersurveillance sweeps on the walls.

She wasn't going to be doing anything there except maintaining contact via an encrypted Black Box app on her cell. She arrived with two Louis Vuitton suitcases full of expensive business clothes, her laptop, and a few books. Just another UBS bank officer making her way in a luxurious world.

The flat was on the second floor overlooking a wide avenue called Rue des Eaux-Vives, which was two blocks south of the lake and ran from the lush green grounds of the Parc La Grange in the east all the way west into the heart of town. Over the past five days she'd maintained her routine.

She rose at seven, showered, slipped into lace lingerie and a silk robe, and sat out on her flower-boxed balcony sipping espresso and reading the *Financial Times*. Then she dressed in a Dior business suit with a plunging neckline, along with Sam Edelman business heels and Gucci sunglasses, and walked all the way down to UBS headquarters at 8 Rue du Rhône.

Black Box reasoned that if Nabuto and his people couldn't spot their target, they were blind.

At UBS, her cover story had been arranged through contacts at the US Federal Reserve. She showed her UBS ID to the lobby staff, then a security guard walked her to a big brass elevator and escorted her four floors underground to the vaults. Once there in the plush reception area for high-wealth clients, she was given a seat beside another woman and two men whose tasks were to escort customers to view their secret holdings. No one asked how this beautiful girl with the olive complexion, stunning green eyes, and long, curling tresses had gotten a job that normally required three years' minimum of dedicated duty. They assumed she was someone's niece from the "God Floor" way up above.

The rest of the Black Box team wasn't so lucky. They were holed up in a safe house down by the water on Quai Gustave-Ador, a dark two-bedroom flat in a building used mostly by immigrants working in the big hotels. Thane shared a bedroom with Spencer. Kali and Jason shared the other. The place was dreary, with warped wooden walls, a salon with a rickety coffee table, a worn brown sofa and armchairs, and a small kitchen whose gas stove barely worked.

They were used to such accommodations, but they'd jokingly cursed Pierre anyway when he led them inside. He laughed and said they were lucky. Pacenza and the Package were staying in a warehouse for antique furniture and artwork five blocks west on the water, and the operators were camped on the cold concrete floor. The operators discreetly trailed Neveah in shifts, back and forth from UBS and whenever she went out for lunch or shopping. No one really thought that Nabuto would have his goons make their move right out in the open, but they couldn't be sure.

Thane and his crew spent the days focused on the mission as the hours ticked by.

Fabio was still in the brig aboard the Black Box ship, but he'd made the call to Nabuto after being thoroughly prepped by Kali about what he should say. Ando's technicians had routed his call through a SATCOM relay hub managed by Pierre, which made it appear that the call was coming from Geneva. But no one would know if the ploy had worked until something happened.

Thane sat hunched in a chair at the coffee table, keeping an eye on his laptop monitor. The surveillance experts aboard ship had hacked into UBS's security cameras, so he had a full view of the bank's lobby and exterior. He listened on comms to the Package transmissions and regularly checked in with Pacenza to see if there was any unusual activity. He would have had the operators field a drone when Neveah was on the move, except that the Swiss police had sharp eyes and forbade such things in their skies.

Jason sat on the couch, keeping his Chameleon skills sharp by reading *The Intent to Live: Achieving Your True Potential as an Actor*, by the Method acting coach Larry Moss. There was a small television on in the salon corner, sound muted, showing images of the latest Russian incursion into eastern Europe. A headline scroll below the images read, "Unnamed source inside White House says, 'POTUS is waiting for the election to pass before deciding how to handle the Ukraine crisis. He doesn't want a decision in either direction to hurt his party's chances of retaining power.'" After reading the scroll Jason murmured, "Election cycles may change, but the games politicians play never will. Damn shame." Kali sat in another chair, studying his German and French and keeping an eye on worldwide stock prices, in particular that of UBS AG. Spencer was perched at the kitchen table in front of another laptop, watching training videos for all sorts of strange vehicles. At all times, they were dressed for the street and ready to move, like patient Rottweilers waiting for someone to slip their leashes . . .

Near the close of banking business on the fifth day, Thane was monitoring the Package, who were about to tail Neveah back to her flat, when Kali suddenly closed the book on his lap. It was Michael Lewis's bestseller about stock trading scams, *The Big Short*.

"I don't think Nabuto's buying this," he said.

"Give it time," Jason said from behind his own book.

"I know, it's only been five days." Kali exhaled a long breath and leaned back in his chair, but it wasn't a gesture of impatience—he was used to long surveillance jobs. It was something else, a sense in his gut. "But it seems like if they thought this target was tempting, we'd have felt something by now . . . light surveillance on Neveah, a probe, maybe an inquiry. Something."

"That's what *you'd* do," Jason said to Kali. "But these guys probably aren't so by the book."

It was a bone of contention that occasionally rose between the two men. Kali did everything according to his training paradigm and regulations, while Jason was more spontaneous, a risk-taker, willing to color outside the lines.

"There's also prep time, travel time, Kali," Thane mumbled as he squinted at a visual on his monitor. "You don't know who they're using for a team, or where they're coming from. Could be a logistics issue."

Spencer didn't chime in. He was focused on a video about Russian helicopter cockpits and controls.

"Anyway, why should they rush?" Jason posed to Kali. "As far as they know, Maryanne might be working for UBS for another ten years . . . Remember when we spent a month hunkered down in Sarajevo?"

"Yes. It wasn't the highlight of my career," Kali said, then added, "But I'll tell you this much. If *I* were them, I wouldn't buy anything Fabio was selling. No matter what he did for them before, or how well we prepped him now."

"You're ruining my day, Mr. Kent," Thane said, "and demoralizing my team." It wasn't really an admonition—Thane encouraged his team members to express opposing opinions. He was pushing back to see if Kali would hold firm.

Kali wagged his head. "He's not going to bite." He opened his book again. "I was right there when Fabio made the call. Something was off."

"I don't agree with that assessment," Jason said. "Nabuto's probably just super cautious, which is why nobody's nailed him yet."

Kali said nothing in retort. He was clearly uneasy.

Thane's cell phone buzzed. He picked it up and read a text as everyone else turned their attention to him and eagerly observed. Thane put the cell back on the table and looked at his watch.

"Pacenza. He says his boys are outside UBS waiting to tail Neveah back to her flat. UBS's workday's over in ten minutes."

"Well, that's another day down," Jason said. "Once she's back in her flat she's off the X."

"Maybe we should send her out to a club tonight," Spencer said from across the room. "Give the opposition more opportunities if they're actually around here somewhere."

"Not a bad idea," Jason agreed.

Thane's cell buzzed again, but this time he straightened as he picked it up and said, "It's Neveah."

No one moved.

"Overwatch," Thane said as he answered, and waited, and listened, while everyone in the room stared and Spencer plucked out his earbuds. A minute later, Thane said, "Roger," then put the cell down and smiled.

"She just got a call from a man named Klaus Debier. Says he's a German art dealer and would like her to please give him an appreciation and estimate, before he commits to the UBS vaults."

Kali dropped his book and leaned forward. The atmosphere in the room immediately turned electric.

"Where and when?" Kent said.

"Tonight," Thane said. "Debier asked her if it wouldn't be too much trouble to do it after hours."

"She confirmed, of course," Kent said.

"She did. And they agreed to meet at our target location, the art warehouse, seven p.m."

"Ya see?" Jason chided Kali.

Kali ignored him and looked at his watch. "We've got two hours to gear up, get the cars, take positions."

"Spencer, get the guns prepped," Thane said. Spencer sprang up and went into the first bedroom, where Pierre had welded a lockbox under one of the bed's steel frames. "And the minidrone with the IR," Thane called, "but don't launch it till after dark."

"Roger," Spencer called back.

Jason had jumped from the couch and was already starting to

prepare his gear and other items for his evening disguise. Kali was doing the same, but as he headed into his bedroom he stopped and turned.

"Wait," he said across the room to Thane. "How do we know this guy's the one? Klaus Debier might be exactly what he says he is, just some rich-guy customer."

"Mr. Kent, your caution is making you cynical, but we'll run a quick background check," Thane said with a smirk. "However, this alleged art dealer calls our very ripe hostage and wants to meet with her somewhere, offsite, after hours, in the dark? If *that's* a coincidence, I'm Maxwell Smart."

No one had a retort for that. They all started moving fast.

EIGHTEEN

THANE HAD INSTRUCTED NEVEAH TO REMAIN AT THE office, as if she were working late. Klaus Debier was clearly somewhere in the area, along with Nabuto's action team, and Thane wasn't taking any chances. If "Maryanne Kreisler" walked home first, as she usually did, they might decide to just take her on the street.

That could result in a gunfight right there in the middle of Rue du Rhône. The Swiss authorities wouldn't take kindly to that.

Thane had dispatched Kali and Jason to fetch Neveah in a black Mercedes E-Class. Jason would be posing as a UBS security man and driver. Kali, having just slipped his transformative beads into his suit pocket, was now in Chameleon disguise as Maryanne Kreisler's Swiss banking associate—his German was good enough to pull it off. Both men were dressed in dark blue suits and pearl ties, but had Glock 19s under their jackets. Spencer and one of Pacenza's men, an operator called Shane, would tail them in an older-model gray Audi, providing running surveillance and backup.

It was already dark and drizzling when Neveah emerged from UBS headquarters and walked down the wide marble stairs to the black Mercedes. Jason opened the rear door for her, she slipped in beside Kali, and they drove off east along Rue du Rhône. As they passed the famous watchmaker Patek Phillippe on the left, Spencer's Audi popped out from a side street and followed a block behind.

Jason glanced in the rearview and spoke to Thane through his bone mic. "Dark Horse One for Overwatch, rolling. Dark Horse Two's tailing."

"Roger," Thane said. He was already down at the art auction warehouse with Pacenza and the Package.

In the back of the car, Neveah asked Kali, "What did you find on Debier?" She was using her smartphone screen to touch up her lipstick.

"*Nicht viel.*" Not much, Kali said in German, then switched to English with German tones. "Age sixty-two; he's an art dealer and real estate investor out of Berlin. Had a few run-ins with the tax authorities, but nothing stuck. Does not do social media."

"So, no images, correct?" Neveah said.

"Correct, except for one photo on his dealership website. I sent everyone a copy."

"He's conveniently modest." Neveah put the lipstick away. "Who's running assault lead on this?"

On combined tactical operations, Black Box would sometimes take point, while other times the Package would have the lead, depending on the potential need for lethal force. Whoever had assault lead would make the call about when to go into action.

"Pacenza," Kali said.

The art auction warehouse was a large lime green building at the corner of Rue du-Roveray and Quai Gustave-Ador, the thoroughfare that ran alongside Lake Geneva's southern tip. Inside was a gray concrete floor the size of a basketball court, with a steel stairway on the far end leading up to a manager's office. Surrounding the floor were stacked wooden shipping crates holding sculptures or antique furniture, and locked cages holding more expensive works of art. Spotlights flooded the space in a dim lemon glow. There were no windows, and only three doors.

The main door facing Rue du-Roveray was an iron affair with two standard key locks, next to another rollup door for truck deliveries, also bolted and locked. At the rear of the warehouse was one more door leading out to a "smoking courtyard" enclosed by apartment buildings. Everything was wired for alarms, and the warehouse floor was covered by IR motion detectors for off-hours, all of which were controlled from the manager's office.

Thane and Pacenza, wearing dark sweaters, jeans, and tac boots, were crouched in the manager's office behind his wide wooden desk. They watched the warehouse floor on their smartphones, via a small video camera they'd stuck on the outside office wall, but they could switch to a feed from a RQ12 Wasp drone that had just been launched by Pacenza's men.

Six of Pacenza's operators were hunkered down behind the crates on both flanks of the main floor. They were dressed like Thane and Pacenza, had compact MP7 submachine guns with Gem-tech suppressors, and were all linked together through earbud comms.

Outside the warehouse, the northeast corner was covered by two operators sitting inside a tinted Sprinter van beside the lake. Not only did they cover their corner from inside the van, but they also controlled the drone that provided bird's-eye surveillance to the team. Across from the main entrance, two more operators were inside a second-floor room of a small hotel—lights off, curtains parted enough to watch the street. And a two-man sniper team had climbed the fire escape on the rear of the hotel and set up on the roof.

At the far corner of that building, down the street from the warehouse's main entrance, was an alleyway where Spencer and Shane could tuck their car but still have a good view of the warehouse.

At the back of the warehouse, across the courtyard, two more operators were tucked beneath an apartment awning. Their task was to stop any "leakers" who might escape out the back.

Except for the snipers, who were each using a suppressed Knights Armament SR-25 rifle, all the operators had silenced Glocks inside their rain slickers.

As Overwatch, Thane had plenty of eyes and ears on the target building. He'd also alerted FedPol, the Swiss Federal Office of Police, through the US consular agency in Geneva, but he hadn't given them the location just yet. He wanted Klaus Debier and Nabuto's gunmen zip-tied on the warehouse floor before he'd summon official aid. Ando would have to handle any diplomatic flak . . .

Jason drove the Mercedes east on Quai Gustave-Ador after cutting over from Rue du Rhône. The expensive yachts lining the lake were rocking in windy swells as the car's wiper blades ticked off the seconds. At 6:45 p.m. he turned right on Rue du-Roveray and parked in front of the warehouse. Spencer, with Shane in the back of his Audi, appeared after half a minute, passed Jason, and then backed into the alleyway on the far southwest corner with the motor running. He had Uber stickers on the front and rear windshields.

"Dark Horse Main for Overwatch," Kali said to Thane from the Mercedes's rear seat. "We're on the X."

"Dark Horse Two for Overwatch," Spencer said from the Audi. "Same status. No sign of the guests."

"Overwatch for Dark Horse, hold," Thane replied, then spoke to Pacenza's teams. "Overwatch for Package, sitrep on street activity. Any surveillance or countersurveillance?"

"Package Alpha for Overwatch," the men by the lake replied. "Negative. Clear from here."

"Package Bravo, clear," said the pair inside the hotel.

"Package Charlie, clear from up here," the sniper team reported.

"Roger," Thane said. "Overwatch for Dark Horse Main, make your move."

Jason turned off the engine, got out with a large black umbrella, and opened the rear door for Kali and Neveah. They walked up the warehouse stairs, Neveah produced two brass keys and worked the locks, and Kali pushed on the door. They went inside and left it two inches ajar.

There was a long wooden table in the middle of the auction floor, for management inspections and paperwork. Jason held back to one side, shaking out the soggy umbrella, while Kali and Neveah walked to the table. They saw no one around, but could feel many pairs of eyes on them. Their ears pricked up as Spencer's voice crackled.

"Dark Horse Two for ALCON," he muttered. "I've got a black Mercedes Sprinter pulling in behind Dark Horse One's ride. Wait one . . . Primary's exiting on the passenger side. Tall, gray hair, black hat, carrying a leather portfolio. Hold . . ." Another few seconds passed. "Okay, here we go. His crew just came out the back. Four men, one woman, Germans."

"Overwatch for Dark Horse Two," Thane said. "Why Germans?"

"They look like Hans Gruber's crew from *Die Hard*," Spencer said.

"Roger," Thane said.

"Package, you're off leash in a mike," Pacenza said in everyone's head as he watched the drone feed on his smartphone. "But hold for my signal."

The warehouse door creaked open. Kali and Neveah turned. Klaus Debier strode in, holding a large black leather artist's portfolio by its handle with his crew following behind. They were dressed in black jeans, boots, and leather jackets. One of the men was blond with a ponytail, the others were darker, one with a beard. The woman had short red hair and looked compact and formidable.

Debier walked up to Neveah and smiled. He had deep lines around his mouth and some sort of scar under his right eye. He left his hat on.

"*Guten Abend, Fräulein Kreisler*," he said with a slight bow.

Jason, standing off to one side with the half-open umbrella blocking his waist, slipped his hand behind it and moved his jacket flap aside, his fingers close to his Glock.

In the manager's office, Thane watched the rendezvous play out on his smartphone. Next to him, Pacenza monitored the drone feed from the sky.

"*Herr Debier.*" Neveah nodded and smiled at the German. "It is a pleasure." She turned and gestured at Kali. "This is my associate, Herr Werner."

Kali nodded at Debier. "*Freut mich, Sie kennenzulernen.*" A pleasure to meet you, he said, but he was peripherally watching the Germans as they moved closer behind Debier.

In the manager's office, Thane suddenly heard the lakeside team hiss in his ear. "Package Alpha for Overwatch, just lost the drone feed." Everyone else on comms heard it too, and Pacenza showed his smartphone screen to Thane. It was blank.

On the warehouse floor, Klaus Debier said to Kali, "*Meine Freude auch.*" My pleasure as well. He switched the large art portfolio to his left and shook Kali's hand.

In the hotel room across the street, the lead operator was trying to warn Thane. "Pack . . . Brav . . . for Overwa . . . Comms . . . going down." His voice trailed off to nothing as everyone's bone mic emitted a terrible squeal. The Package operators quickly turned down their volumes, but Kali, Neveah, and Jason could do nothing but endure the pain.

"My colleague here shared that you might have something interesting for us," Kali said to Debier. The static was screaming inside his head, yet he showed nothing on his face but mild interest, as if he was late for a dinner date.

"Indeed." Debier smiled at Neveah, then looked her over with an inappropriate gaze. "I certainly have something interesting for you."

She smiled in return and revealed nothing in her expression, though her head was splitting with the electronic squeal.

Inside the manager's office, Thane turned to Pacenza. "Someone's *jamming* us," he hissed. "Backup frequency." Pacenza pulled a second smartphone from his pocket and instantly rerouted all the comms.

"Overwatch for ALCON," Thane said over the backup channel. "Comms check."

There was no response. He transmitted again.

"Overwatch for Package, how copy?"

A few tense seconds passed, then . . .

"Package Alpha, good copy," the lakeside team whispered.

"Package Bravo, good copy," the hotel team reported.

"Package Charlie, good copy," the sniper team said.

Spencer failed to report in.

"Overwatch for Dark Horse Two, how copy?" Thane said.

Spencer still didn't answer.

"Overwatch for Package Charlie," Thane said to the snipers. "Give me a sitrep on Dark Horse Two."

"Charlie for Overwatch," the lead sniper said. "I can see the front of the vehicle but not inside. Zero vis, on vic interior."

On the warehouse floor, Klaus Debier was saying to Neveah, "I am sure you will be pleased with my product."

"I am anxious to see it," she said, as she silently thanked heaven that her bone mic had stopped screeching.

But signals were firing in Kali's brain. Something was way off. The drone was down, comms had crashed, now they were up again but Spencer was off comms. It felt like a cold, fast-rushing waterfall, but he had to stay in character. He had to wait until Debier made his move. *Why isn't Spencer responding?*

"Dark Horse One," Thane said to Jason, "excuse yourself and go check on Dark Horse Two."

Jason took a few steps toward Neveah while the Germans eyed him. He stopped, half bowed, took out a pack of cigarettes, showed them to Neveah and said, "If you don't mind, ma'am, for one moment?" Neveah frowned as if she didn't approve of the habit, but nodded.

Jason walked to the front door, went outside, and trotted down the stairs. It was raining hard now but he didn't open his umbrella. He jogged through the downpour to the southeast alleyway and Spencer's Audi. The lights were on and the windshield wipers were swishing, but the driver's door was open. He kept his hand on his Glock as he scanned the area, then tucked his head in the car.

The rear window was punctured with bullet holes and there was blood all over the passenger compartment. Jason's eyes widened even more when he saw Shane slumped on the seat, dead.

Spencer was not in the car.

Jason spoke to Thane through gritted teeth. "Dark Horse One for Overwatch."

"Overwatch," Thane said.

"Shane's KIA, and Spencer's gone."

Inside the warehouse everyone heard Jason's grim report. The Package operators stiffened and looked at each other with furious eyes. In the manager's office, Pacenza's face flushed deep red. He pulled out his Glock and started to rise. Thane reached out and gripped his arm.

"*No*. Don't blow their cover," he barked in a whisper.

"One of my men is *dead*, dammit!"

"Wait!" Thane tried to stop him.

"Get your hands off me or you'll be pulling them out your ass, Thane."

"Colorful! But you're out of line!"

Pacenza stared at him intently. "No, I'm assault lead, which technically means *you're* out of line . . . I'm calling it, now, so stand down."

Thane withdrew his hand and reluctantly nodded. Pacenza kept his eyes focused on Thane as he pressed his transmitter and calmly said, "Madonna, Madonna, Madonna," then rushed out of the office and down the stairs.

Kali knew what was coming. He could feel Pacenza's fury as he came storming down from the manager's office with his Glock in his hand, and the Package were already streaming across the warehouse floor with their MP7s aimed at the Germans. "*Hände hoch! Hände hoch! Auf dem Boden!*" one of them shouted as the shocked Germans thrust their hands at the sky and sank to their knees.

Kali saw only one way to stop Pacenza from killing Debier. He drew his own Glock, jammed the barrel into Debier's chest, and shoved him down hard on his knees. Neveah knew instantly what Kali was doing and why, and she quickly got behind Debier and frisked him head to foot. Pacenza couldn't shoot with two Black Box agents shielding his target. He stopped and snarled, "Get the hell out of my way."

"Not happening, Pac," Kali said to Pacenza as Thane appeared.

The Package were all over the Germans, slamming them down

on their faces, running their hands through their clothes for weapons. Thane nodded at Kali, who was standing over Debier with his Glock, but then an operator walked up to Pacenza, bent his head, and said in a somber tone, "They're all clean, boss. No weapons, no jammers, no comms."

Thane heard that and turned toward Pacenza. The Package commander shook his head, cursed, grabbed his lead operator, and stormed out the front door to confirm for himself that Shane was dead.

Neveah gestured at Debier and said to Thane, "He's clean too. The only things on him are his wallet and business cards." She showed one to Thane.

"Dammit," Thane spat.

Klaus Debier looked up at Neveah and smirked like a man who'd just pulled off a wicked practical joke. "Is this how you treat all of your high-wealth clients at UBS, Fräulein Kreisler?"

Neveah picked up his fallen portfolio and slammed it down onto the table. She opened it and stared at the small painting inside.

"It is a priceless Gustav Klimt," Debier said. "I was expecting a proper appraisal, not this. Are you also going to take our wallets?"

"Who *are* these people?" Kali said to Debier as he tucked his Glock away and waved toward the Germans, who were still face-down on the floor.

"Artists." Debier shrugged. "I was taking them all to dinner at Le Bistrot Dumas." He jutted his chin at the business card in Neveah's hand. "You may check my credentials if you like. I think you'll find them impeccable." He looked over at Thane. "Are you policemen? You do not *look* like policemen."

"Get them up," Thane said with disgust to Pacenza's men.

The Package dragged the Germans to their feet. Neveah did the same with Klaus Debier. Thane pulled Kali off to one side.

"This has turned into a damn circus," he fumed. "But Spencer's missing. That's all I care about right now."

Kali's eyes pierced Thane's but he said nothing. The only thing he heard in his head was the words of his mother: *It's too good to be true.*

"I already know what you're gonna say," Thane said. "So don't say it."

As Kali responded with, "I'm not going to say anything, Thane," wild sirens blared from the street and everyone turned their heads. The front door burst open and five Swiss policemen rushed inside.

Klaus Debier looked at Kali and Thane. His grin was triumphant.

NINETEEN

US CONSULAR AGENCY, GENEVA

WE CAN'T EVEN ESCORT HIM HOME!"

Package commander Dan Pacenza was railing with blind frustration. It was four o'clock in the morning and he'd backed himself up into one corner of the consular agency's basement SCIF, as if he didn't trust himself not to throttle somebody. His master sergeant, a big man whose call sign was Sumo, watched Pacenza carefully just in case the boss lost his cool. That rarely happened, but with Shane dead and a Black Box agent missing, one never knew. Pacenza whipped a hand through the air.

"Not even a dignified return," he fumed. "He's got a wife and a four-year-old girl . . . B squadron's going to have to get him at Dover and handle the funeral. Who's gonna hand that poor girl the flag?"

It was a rhetorical question. Special operations personnel faced these issues on a regular basis. When someone was killed in action, they couldn't just pause operations and take a long break to properly mourn. No one else in the room had a comforting answer, but Thane tried.

"We'll do everything we can for him, Pac."

"Oh, you will, huh?" Pacenza snorted. "You people don't even *exist*."

Thane, Kali, Jason, and Neveah were also there in the SCIF. Ando's disembodied face filled the videoconference monitor at the far end of a long conference table, but the Black Box commander was transmitting from the headquarters ship and didn't have much to offer on this particular emotional matter. The facility buzzed with the electronic countermeasures lining the walls, an annoying hum that only added to the tension.

Jason, clearly on edge as well given Spencer's status as missing in action, paced at the far end of the room diagonally across from Pacenza. Thane sat at the conference table's head, trying to keep everyone even with his measured tones. Neveah was perched on one flank of the long table, working with the ship's Cyber cell via a secure laptop. Kali was leaning back against one long wall, ignoring the high-strung emotions that were fouling the atmosphere as he focused on working the problem that had brought them all to the edge of an international incident.

While Thane tried to calm Pacenza's ire, Kali was mentally reviewing the events of the past few hours. He again saw the fury of a Swiss policeman, like a video playback inside his head . . .

"Que se passe-t-il ici?" What's going on here?

The Swiss police lieutenant had just stormed into the warehouse with four of his men. They were uniformed officers and all had their hands on the butts of their holstered SIG Sauer P228 handguns. The lieutenant stared at the five bewildered Germans who were standing shakily on their feet, and the dapper, smirking Klaus Debier. Six other muscular men were lowering MP7 submachine guns, and he had no idea what to make of Thane, Kali, and Neveah.

Kali had already slipped his Glock back inside his jacket. Thane pulled a leather badge case from a pocket and showed it to the cop as he offered an embarrassed smile.

"Nous sommes des agents Americains du Départment de l'Energie." We are American agents of the Department of Energy, Thane said in fluent French.

"Ah oui?" Oh really? The lieutenant looked at Thane's badge, then glanced up as Neveah produced an identical ID. Then he looked at the Package operators, one of whom also showed him a DoE badge. Still, his expression was skeptical at best.

However, everyone on Thane's team and the Package had DoE

badges and appropriate background stories for cover, though it went much deeper than that. No American agents of any stripe could operate on Swiss soil without preemptive negotiations. Ando, through a CIA liaison officer working with the Department of Energy, had gained official permission from the Swiss Federal Intelligence Service, or FIS, for his "DoE agents" to operate briefly in Geneva. It was an insurance policy, just in case things went south.

"And you have official permission for this?" the lieutenant asked.

"Yes, of course, you may check with FIS," Thane said. "And I'm *terribly* sorry. Apparently we have made an error."

"You certainly *have*," Klaus Debier interjected, but Thane ignored him and went on.

"We mistakenly thought these people were part of a smuggling ring, attempting to sell Russian nuclear materials."

Kali turned away for a moment and spoke quickly to Jason through his bone mic.

"Black Box Main for Two, tell Pac to sterilize it."

"Roger, Main," Jason returned. "He's already on it."

Outside the warehouse, Pacenza had seen the cops arrive. He had his teams moving quickly from their positions, though they had to stall a few times to avoid Swiss pedestrians. The northeast corner team recovered their drone, raced their Sprinter over to Spencer's Audi, and loaded Shane's corpse into the van, while Jason contacted Pierre to arrange to put Shane on ice until they could exfil his body. The hotel team took Spencer's Audi and began driving it north to Lausanne, where another Aberration agent would lock it up in a garage for a full forensics investigation. The sniper team swept the area for evidence and shell casings and withdrew to the Black Box safe house, and just like ghosts, they were all gone without a trace.

Thane had heard Kali's order to Jason in his ear, and knew he had to stall the cops until everything outside the warehouse was clean.

"Nuclear materials?" The Swiss lieutenant's eyes went wide as he looked at Thane.

"Yes, we had what we thought was very solid intelligence," Thane said, and then he embellished. "As I'm sure you are aware, Lieutenant, the Russians have been fielding some highly toxic nuclear materials throughout Europe, including Polonium-210. Mr. Putin has of course denied it, but the evidence of his FSB deploying these materials to kill political opponents cannot be dismissed." Thane gestured at Debier. "Unfortunately for Mr. Debier, one of those Russian FSB agents from their 'wet work' department bares a remarkable similarity."

"Did you inform our governmental intelligence authorities?" the lieutenant asked.

"Of course," Thane said. "The Federal Police were informed."

"This is nonsense!" Klaus Debier spat. "I am an art dealer!"

"That is true," Neveah said as she closed Debier's portfolio with the painting inside and handed it back to him. "We're terribly sorry." Her smile was icy.

Thane knew that Debier couldn't push the issue further. Otherwise, the Swiss cops would be asking him lots of questions.

"Well then," the Swiss lieutenant said. "I suppose these people are free to go." He looked at Thane. "Yes?"

"Of course," Thane said. He took silent solace in the fact that he had Debier's image on a recorded video feed. He didn't know yet when or where it would happen, but Black Box would eliminate this man.

"I will be filing an official complaint," Debier muttered, but he took his portfolio and his bewildered Germans and left.

"I will also have to file a report," the lieutenant said to Thane. "You will have to sign it, Mr.—" He looked at Thane's DoE ID. "Agent Norcross." He handed it back.

"Certainly," Thane said. "Can we all meet at the US consular agency in one hour?" He'd have to arrange that quickly through Ando.

"One hour," the lieutenant said. "You will be there, correct?"

"You have my word, Lieutenant."

One hour later, at the consular agency on Rue François-Versonnex, just five blocks from the warehouse, Thane, Kali, and

Neveah had met with the Swiss cops in a small conference room reserved for the FBI's local legation, where Thane had graciously signed the police report. Thane had also asked the lieutenant why he'd come to the warehouse, and the cop had said he'd received an anonymous tip on his cell phone.

Neveah had then escorted the policemen from the building, and just before they left, she'd smiled and asked the lieutenant for his cell phone number. He didn't know what to make of that, but she was very attractive so he'd given it to her with a hopeful grin . . .

Kali returned to the present with the sound of Pacenza's frustration.

"The whole thing was a freaking setup!" Pacenza was still fuming from his corner in the SCIF.

"That's clear, Mr. Pacenza," Ando said through his video feed.

Kali was tempted to say, *I told you something was off,* but he didn't.

"The issue now," Kali said, "is to find out how they did it, and who did it, and how we're going to recover Spencer."

"I've got something going with Cyber," Neveah said as she worked her laptop. "They pinged the lieutenant's phone from the ship, and slurped all his contacts and his incoming calls from tonight. Given the time frame of events from tonight, they're narrowing a range of numbers, some of which were relayed through dark net hubs."

"Well, tell them to move faster," Jason muttered from his corner.

Then the door to the SCIF banged open; a tall, gray-haired man stormed inside and slammed it shut behind him. He was shaking rain from his golf hat and carrying a dripping umbrella. It was Frank Gibson, the president's national security adviser. Everyone in the room froze as if a vampire had just appeared from a coffin.

"You people are fueling my damn ulcer," Gibson snapped. "I've got the US ambassador to Switzerland on my ass, the DoE director's calling me from Washington, and I've just spent four hours getting here from NATO. So you'd *better* be solving my problem."

"We're working on it, sir," Ando said from the flat-screen.

"You're working on it, huh, Ando?" Gibson said to Ando's stunned expression. "I gave you people every asset I had so you could figure this out, and now you've got a blown operation, a dead operator, and a man missing? You'd better come up with something fast before I have to brief POTUS, or it's not going to be pretty."

"Sir?" Neveah raised a hand from her laptop. "I think we've got something."

Gibson turned on her.

"Talk then, dammit," he growled.

"Cyber cell on the ship just pulled a number, from a range of incoming calls to the lieutenant's phone," Neveah said. "This one was camouflaged and encrypted, and run through three different dark web pools, but Cyber ran an algorithm on it and broke the code. We've got it now."

Everyone in the room watched her. Some of them were praying.

"The tip-off to the Swiss police," Neveah said, "came from the same number that our prisoner called from the ship . . . It was Nabuto."

"Fabio, that *bastard*," Jason nearly shouted as he slammed his fist on the table. "He probably used some sort of a code word to set us up."

Thane turned and stared at Kali, who simply nodded with tight lips, because he'd suspected it all along.

"We need to get back to the ship," Kali said quietly. "I need to interrogate Fabio. But this time . . . differently." Kali looked over at Gibson. "Sir, we're going to need permission for a level five interrogation."

"Kali . . . ," Thane started to say.

"Level five? Are you crazy?" Gibson shouted. "You expect me to go to the president *now*, for approval for level five? He's already dealing with lousy approval ratings from the Ukraine takeover. And you want me to what?! You must have lost your natural mind!" He spun on Thane. "What the hell is it with you people, Thane? Didn't you learn anything from Operation Wisteria?"

No one said a word. That particular operation had gone terribly wrong, and the interrogation techniques used on that op had nearly cost the CIA its full mandate.

"Sir," Kali said to Gibson in a calm, measured tone. "Just as you said, we've got a blown op, one man dead, and another man missing. We need to know whatever our prisoner knows, and fast. And I've got to have your permission to get it."

Gibson thought about that for a moment. He put his golf hat back on his head, his umbrella under his arm, and his hand on the door handle.

"I'll give you level *four*, Kent, and that's it. That's all I can get away with, without having to go to the president. And don't just make it work. You'd better come back with a freaking gold medal."

He stormed out of the SCIF.

TWENTY

SOCOTRA ARCHIPELAGO, ARABIAN SEA

IT WAS A VERY SMALL ISLAND IN THE MIDST OF AN END-less, sparking sea.

It was a place with no name, just three square miles of pink granite, emerald lagoons, and dragon blood trees shaped like giant mushrooms. Its only regular inhabitants appeared to be yellow Egyptian vultures, giant sea crabs, and blue baboon tarantulas. East of Somalia and south of Yemen, the island showed up as merely a dot on the nautical charts of ship captains, and airplane pilots ignored it because there was no place to land.

From the air, or from the lens of a geospatial satellite, there appeared to be nothing there of interest. An occasional boat would dock at its rocky jetty, and there seemed to be palm-thatched roofs across a string of primitive-looking shelters—most likely for sport divers. But in fact there were buildings, all constructed at night in the faces of granite cliffs, and radar arrays hidden in groves of palms. There were Russian-made ZSU antiaircraft guns, concealed by camouflage nets on the cliff tops. There was a sophisticated laboratory, an admin office, six small villas for high-value hostages, and an unmarked helicopter landing pad.

The island was owned by Lucas van Groot. He'd purchased it from the government of Yemen for two million euros, in cash. He called it Geweer, which meant "rifle" in Afrikaans.

A flaming orange sun was just sinking into the sea when the French Gazelle helicopter arrived from the north—the same helo that had delivered Daniella Sietto to a field in France. It settled on the primitive LZ, with coils of dust swirling around the metallic mustache attached to its nose, and the cargo door slid open. Five men emerged, wearing balaclavas and carrying MP5K submachine guns. They reached back into the helo and dragged a prisoner onto the ground.

It was Spencer, blindfolded, with his wrists zip-tied in front. His jacket was gone, his jeans torn at one knee, and his running shoes had no laces. His escorts were Germans, the same Baader-Meinhof offspring that Van Groot had mentioned to Nabuto back in Pretoria. But they hadn't even attempted to kidnap Neveah. Instead, they'd killed Shane and captured Spencer.

Two of the Germans gripped Spencer by the elbows and helped him stumble through the dust as the helicopter pulled pitch and roared away over the sea. The cloud of grit settled, they yanked his blindfold off, and he blinked in the failing light. He desperately needed some water, but he wasn't going to ask for it.

A man was standing twenty feet from him, a large African who looked brutish. Spencer thought this had to be the man Fabio had called Nabuto, but he said nothing. Then another man joined Nabuto, a middle-aged, hard-looking, blond Caucasian wearing a pristine bush jacket. The two men consulted each other in low tones as they looked at Spencer like a laboratory specimen. A satisfied smile touched Van Groot's lips.

"I do love it when a plan comes together," he said. "Klaus played his role to the hilt, the opposition fell for it, and our Germans delivered a fish."

"It could have been two," Nabuto said, "but they had to kill one to get one."

"Fair exchange," said Van Groot.

"Fabio certainly redeemed himself," Nabuto said.

"He did indeed. You've trained them all well, Pretorius."

Nabuto nodded with thanks at the compliment. He jutted his chin at Spencer.

"We can probably get a high price for him," he said.

"Nonsense," Van Groot scoffed. "That's a nineteen eighties Taliban practice, not for us."

Nabuto looked at his boss, confused. Taking hostages and collecting ransoms was how they made their living.

"I don't understand, sir."

"He's some sort of American agent, Pretorius," Van Groot said. "The US government doesn't negotiate with terrorists."

"But . . . isn't that how they recovered that soldier, Bergdahl?"

"That was an anomaly. A public relations ploy." Van Groot slipped his hands into his cargo pockets and cocked his head as he examined Spencer head to foot. "This bloke's a valuable chip, but not in terms of cash. We just have to figure out how to use him, and of course find out who he's working for."

"Interrogation, then," Nabuto said.

"Yes, as usual."

"Who would you like me to assign to it?"

Van Groot regarded Spencer as he considered the question.

"You know what?" he said. "I think I'll do this one myself. Let's find out if I've still got it." He turned and spoke to Spencer's five escorts in German. "*Es ist deinem Drehung. Entlasten Sie die Belgier.*" It's your turn for rotation. Relieve the Belgians.

Van Groot did not only contract international terrorist groups for hostage-takings. He also employed them to secure the island, guard his captives, and provide armed escorts to move them around.

"*Jawohl,*" the German team leader said.

Then Van Groot smiled thinly and spoke to Spencer.

"Welcome to my island, young man. We're going to have a chat."

He turned and walked away with Nabuto, as the Germans dragged Spencer off to somewhere else . . .

The interrogation room was made of stone. It had been cut into a cliffside with jackhammers, like a shelter pit dug by coal miners; then an outside wall with a doorway and one slit window had been fashioned with mud, primitive bricks, and dragon blood wood. It was broiling inside when the sun was high, and freezing by midnight when the rocks surrendered their warmth.

Every hostage delivered to the island called Geweer had taken a turn in the room, but they were never tormented physically. It wasn't necessary. All of them were spoiled, soft, weak-kneed off-spring of high-wealth individuals, and within minutes of being taken inside they freely told their life stories from birth to the present with barely a nudge. Van Groot used their personal revelations to tune his ransom demands and stock market manipulations. All you had to do was reveal to a hostage's father some intimate detail of her childhood, and the man would quickly pay off. Then, while the financial arrangements were made, the hostages "enjoyed" the rest of their stays inside one of the quaint little villas, with all the comforts from linen bedding to fine champagne.

Van Groot was a killer, but he was also a psychological warfare expert.

Inside the interrogation room there was an iron eyelet screwed into the granite ceiling, next to a single lightbulb. A rope led down from the eyelet, through Spencer's elbows—which were cranked behind him with his wrists still zip-tied in front—and back up again. He was sitting on a low, four-legged stool, with his ankles roped to the rear legs and his body tilted slightly forward. The taut rope kept him from falling onto his face, but also from leaning back. It was a stress position. He'd already been there for four hours, waiting in silence, and his shoulders and knees felt like they were going to burst.

Van Groot was now standing inside the room, having just arrived. He was five feet in front of Spencer, smoking a black Balkan Sobranie cigarette and watching his prisoner's facial expressions. The door was closed, a hot breeze flicked through the slit window, and the sweat was dripping off Spencer's nose. Van Groot seemed not to be sweating at all.

"You could save us both time and a lot of discomfort, my chap, if you'd like to tell me who you are."

Spencer said nothing. He just breathed.

"Your credentials said Department of Energy, and the name John Riley. But that isn't your name, is it? And not who you work for."

Spencer just looked at Van Groot's boots. He'd been through multiple iterations of counterinterrogation school, and knew that he had to stall, make this man drag the details out of him, and lie in layers upon layers.

Van Groot opened the cap of a plastic water bottle, took a long, cool swig, then put it back down on a small wooden table.

"I can wait, Mr. Ri-ley." Van Groot elongated the name as if he didn't believe it. "For many more hours, if necessary, while your body dispels every drop of liquid." There was a growing puddle of Spencer's sweat on the dirt floor in front of the stool. "Who do you really work for?"

"I'm just a contract driver," Spencer said in a dry whisper. "For the DoE."

"Interesting." Van Groot took a long drag and looked at Spencer's thighs. They were starting to tremble. "Do you have a family?"

Spencer looked up at Van Groot's eyes. They were ice blue and empty.

"No, my parents died in an auto accident," he lied. His parents were fine and he had two adoring younger sisters.

"Ah, an orphan." Van Groot smiled. "How convenient. No one pays for an orphan."

Spencer made no attempt to reply. He had to choose his responses carefully.

"I was not an orphan," Van Groot said, "until I arranged it." He walked casually over to the slit window and looked outside at the stars as he smoked, his back to Spencer's right flank. "My father was a hard man. I barely knew him. Nothing I did was good enough for him . . . When he thought I was ill behaved, he'd lock me in the basement, much like you are now."

Spencer closed his eyes and just listened. For a moment he thought about his wife back in Virginia, then swept her image from his mind.

"Where did you learn to drive, Mr. Riley?" Van Groot said.

"In the army. They sent me to FLETC." Spencer meant the Federal Law Enforcement Training Course, where government drivers learned their skills. That part was true, and he knew if this man had some way to check, "Riley's" records would confirm it.

Van Groot walked back to his position facing Spencer.

"My name is Van Groot," he said.

Spencer wasn't encouraged by the revelation. When these kinds of people told you their names, they usually expected you to die.

"I was a colonel in the Selous Scouts. Do you know what that is?"

"No," Spencer lied as he dredged up some details from his memory. He had a pounding headache from dehydration and his brain was foggy, but he knew exactly who the Selous Scouts were.

Van Groot bent over, smoking his cigarette casually, until Spencer looked up at him again.

"Whoever you really are," he said, "you know I can make you talk. Everyone talks in the end. Sometimes we have to go through the entire camouflage of lies first, all the things you've been trained to say. But in the end, my chap, it's a terrible waste of time and unnecessary suffering. I've done this before, many times, and I've never failed." He leaned closer to Spencer's face. "It's a point of pride."

Spencer just held Van Groot's gaze. His shoulders were starting to feel as if they'd pop from the sockets, but he knew he could endure a lot more pain—his Black Box training had taught him that. Van Groot was now holding the black cigarette in one finger and thumb, like a syringe.

"From one professional to another," Van Groot said, "I really don't enjoy this part."

He slowly moved the cigarette's glowing tip to Spencer's bare left forearm, just above his zip-tied wrist. But he looked only at Spencer's eyes, and Spencer at his, as the cigarette hissed and sank into flesh.

Spencer went to a place in his mind that he'd always known someday he might have to visit. His lips tightened and his eyelids squinted, but he didn't even gasp.

Van Groot nodded, removed the cigarette from the smoking wound, and placed it back in his lips. Then he reached into his back pocket and pulled out a black leather sap. Its bulbous head was filled with steel ball bearings. He reached out for Spencer's head with his left hand and pulled him forward, so that his knees were on the verge of dislocation. Then he raised the sap high in his right hand and whipped it down onto Spencer's left knee. By the third strike, Spencer was screaming.

Thirty minutes later, Van Groot walked out the door. Nabuto was waiting outside.

"He gave nothing up," Van Groot said. "This young man is a well-trained professional. I haven't seen someone withstand that much pain without breaking since we took that MI6 agent in Morocco. He's working for someone very special . . . very, *very* special." He had lit up another cigarette, but he dropped it and crushed it out with a boot. "I've broken basic agents before. This one's in a different league."

"What would you like to do, sir?" Nabuto asked.

"Let's institute the Reaper protocol," Van Groot said, as he walked off into the night toward his quarters. "Just to be safe."

TWENTY-ONE

BLACK BOX HEADQUARTERS, MEDITERRANEAN SEA

THE DOOR TO THE BRIG FLEW OPEN AND KALI STORMED in like a raging typhoon.

Fabio's manacle had been removed. He was standing beside his bunk, rubbing his wrist with his back to the door, when he spun to the nightmare of Kali's blazing eyes and his balled-up fists. Kali was wearing rawhide tactical gloves with thick leather knuckle protectors. Fabio didn't even have time to gasp because the first punch smashed his nose.

Kent was like a raging bull seeing a bloodred flag. He slugged Fabio hard in the solar plexus, which doubled him over with a grunt, then he yanked him upright and left-hooked his cheek with a blurring fist, slicing it open and drawing more blood. He punched him again, this time straight in the sternum, and Fabio flew back against the wall next to the open toilet and crashed down on his butt as he screamed in Italian, *"Fermati! Fermati!"* Stop! Stop!

But Kali wasn't going to stop until he got what he wanted. With a level five interrogation, you could kneecap a prisoner with a bullet or even bring him to the edge of death, and then resuscitate if it came to that. This was only level four, so he couldn't go that far, but he was taking it to the max.

He bent forward, grabbed a handful of Fabio's hair, and banged his head into the wall. The blood was coursing down Fabio's bruised lips and chin as he tried to cover his face, but Kali punched him again on the other cheek.

"You're on a ship to *nowhere*, Fabio," he roared. Then suddenly,

Kali leaned back an inch and lowered his decibels into a menacing hiss. "Nobody's gonna find you. Nobody's gonna miss you."

Kali was not in Chameleon disguise. He wasn't pretending to be someone else. This was all Kali Kent—every raging muscle.

"I will tell you what you want!" Fabio wailed. "Whatever you want to know!"

Kali still had a fistful of Fabio's hair. He bent low to Fabio's face as he kicked his knees open and pressed on his crotch with a boot.

"How did you set us up, Fabio?"

"There . . . there is a protocol," Fabio moaned. His hands were raised in total surrender and he was shaking all over.

"*What* protocol?"

"If . . . if we are captured, any of us . . . there are certain words we must say, and then they know we are prisoners."

"*What* words?"

"With me it is my fiancée, Angela . . . They have a file on me. They know her real name is Federika."

Kali slapped him, gripped his throat, and started to squeeze.

"If you're lying to me again, Fabio, I'll kill you and feed you to the sharks."

Fabio grabbed Kali's wrist with both hands as his face turned beet red and he tried to breathe. "I am not lying, I swear!"

"Tell me the rest of it," Kali hissed. "Tell me *now*."

"The telephone number I gave you, it is the trigger number. If you call it, that tells them to take countermeasures."

"Is that Nabuto's number?" Kali ground his boot into Fabio's balls. "*Is* it?"

"Yes, but no . . . no!"

"Make up your *mind*, Fabio. Which is it?"

"It is the number to a burner phone, only used for traps . . . and I do not even know Nabuto's real name!"

"Is Nabuto the boss, Fabio? Or is that someone else? Who's the big boss?"

"I do not know his name either! I swear it, on my mother's grave!"

"Is he the one you called Orca? The name you told us before?"

"Yes, yes, Orca! But that is all I know . . ."

"*Liar.*"

Kali banged his head against the wall again. Tears sprang from Fabio's eyes and he clasped his fat fingers together and begged.

"*Mio dio*, I am telling you all that I know!"

"How do they evade radar, Fabio?"

"Radar? You mean with the helicopters? The airplanes?"

"You know *exactly* what I mean."

"They have this thing . . . a device . . . It makes them invisible."

"Is that how they knocked out our drone, Fabio? Is that how they took down our comms?"

"What is comms? Please, I do not know this word . . ."

"Our communications." Kali lifted a fist for a backhand strike. "Don't be cute with me or I swear—"

"I do not know about this! I am nothing! I drive for them and I find hostages for them and that is all!"

"And then what, Fabio? Where do the hostages go? Where do they take them?"

Fabio hesitated now. He sat there on the bloodstained floor, pushing himself back against the wall next to the toilet as if he might somehow be able to disappear. He knew that this was the endgame. If he told this insane American the rest of it, there would be nowhere on earth he could hide.

Kali grabbed the front of his bloody shirt with both fists as if he was going to haul him up off the floor. Fabio whined and resisted and sank down the wall as far as he could, like a sack of cement that couldn't be moved.

"No! I'm telling you true. They take them to an island!"

"An island. What island?"

"It . . . it is in the Arabian Sea, between Somalia and Yemen. They have places there for the hostages until they release them. They have many guns and antiaircraft weapons and other things but I have only been there once. It is very small, like a rock in the ocean, but I do not know exactly where it is. I have only been there one time, one time, and it was at night . . ."

Kali raised his fist again, poised for another awful blow.

"No, *per favore*! I am telling you everything! It is all that I know . . . all of it . . . *please*."

Kali took a long, slow breath, hissing it out through his nose, and released him. He stood up fully, his fists clenched at his sides, and stared down at his bloody work. His voice was calm, measured, and ugly.

"Someone else is going to talk to you now, Fabio. You are going to record every detail of your life, from the time you were born until this very minute. Do you understand?"

"Yes, yes. I will tell it."

"That's right. You will. And if I find out that one word that you just said to me, or to them, is a lie . . . I'll be back, Fabio."

He turned and walked out, leaving Fabio panting and grasping his chest.

Outside the brig, as the guard closed the door, Kali removed his bloody gloves.

"Get a medic," he said to the guard.

"Yes, sir," the guard said and walked off. He'd heard every word of the horrific ruckus inside.

Kali walked down the corridor. A few Black Box support staff crossed his path, moving between the action cells, but they paid him no mind, even though they'd heard the fracas as well. He headed down the gangway to Ando's conference room.

Ando was sitting at the table's head, with Thane, Jason, and Neveah. They'd all seen everything and had heard every scream via Ando's flat-screen and surveillance feed. None of them said a word. Kali took a seat, picked up a plastic bottle of water, unscrewed the cap, and drank half of it down.

"Good thing that wasn't level five," Thane said. "You would have killed him."

TWENTY-TWO

GENESIS

It was only a moment of reflection in Ando's conference room, triggered by Fabio's tale of a secret island. But in that flash of memory, Kali returned to Lagos . . .

And he was seven years old again. It was late in the afternoon. He and Jare were out back on the patio, and Kali was upset because his Game Boy wasn't working. Jare eased it from Kali's hands, slipped a small Swiss Army knife from the pocket of his swim trunks, opened the back of it, adjusted a microchip, and put it all back together.

"Try it now, Kali." Jare grinned.

"It works!" Kali beamed.

Jare beamed too, and he tapped the small tribal markings on his cheek under his right eye, a habitual gesture whenever he was happy. Just then Kali's mother passed by, ruffled Jare's small head, and said, "Maybe you can tutor Kali with his mathematics."

After that the boys had played in the pool. They were Nigerian Fulani warriors attacking pirate ships, and of course they'd sunk them all. Then Jare had walked home and Kali had gone inside to do his homework. It was the mathematics he hated, but his father also insisted it was very important. George Adeyemi always told Kalief that numbers made the world go round.

Now Kali came out of his bedroom and walked down the big, winding stairway to the mansion's main floor. He was barefoot, wearing baggy blue shorts and his favorite basketball singlet, and carrying a plastic model of a schooner. He wanted to show it to his father, but he knew he was working in his office and Kali wasn't supposed to disturb him there. He could hear his mother in the kitchen, talking to their cook, a portly woman named Binobi, which meant "God dwells in my heart." Binobi liked to laugh a lot.

From the big dining room, Kali saw that the door to his father's office was open. He walked to the thick doorframe and peeked around the corner. His father was standing at his big mahogany conference table, looking down at a long and wide sheet of paper that was powder blue and appeared to be a map. His father was wearing an open-necked white shirt, smoking a cigar, and clicking the row of beads that Kali often saw in his hand. He sensed Kali's eyes on him and looked up.

"Did you finish your work, Kalief?"

"Yes, Father."

"What was it?"

"Geometry."

"Good, geometry is very important." George waved a hand, summoning Kali with his long fingers. "Would you like to see something?"

Kali smiled and walked into the office, carrying his ship model carefully in his small hands.

"Ah, you finished your boat!" George smiled, slipped the beads into his pocket, and held out his hands, taking the model and turning it slowly and admiring Kali's work. "It is a beautiful ship," he said as he gingerly placed it on one corner of the big blue map.

"Thank you, Father!" Kali beamed.

Kali looked down at the map. In the middle was a large blue outlined shape, like one of the kidney beans his mother put in their salads. There were other rectangular shapes all over the bean, with arrows and numbers, and outside the bean were curls that looked like ocean waves. At the top of the map were thick red letters that said PEARLAND.

"What is it, Father?" Kali asked.

"It is called a blueprint, my son. It is a plan that architects use when they are designing something that is going to be built."

"Did you make it, Father?"

"Yes, long ago."

Kali's father squinted down at the blueprint. He was smiling slightly, but his eyes also looked sad, which Kali didn't understand.

"Are you going to build it, Father?"

"I would like to, Kalief, yes."

"It looks like an island," Kali said. "Where is it?"

"Not far from the beach in the south, but it is still only land. There is nothing on it yet."

"Is this your dream? Like Mother said?"

George displayed a surprised look, stared at Kali for a beat, then answered.

"Yes," George said. "It has always been my dream. We inherited the land from your grandfather. He purchased it from the government when I was still a child. I want to create something special there, Kalief, buildings and parks and homes for the people of Lagos who have never had something like this." He trailed off a bit and murmured, "But we only own part of it now."

George couldn't explain all those details to Kalief—he would not understand. He had swayed from his dream and sold off portions of Pearland to government speculators, for a good deal of money. But then he'd used that money to buy into the syndicate of illicit import-export shippers and black market traders. If he ever wanted to own all of Pearland again, and turn it back into his longed-for dream, he would have to liquidate his controlling portion of the syndicate and use every penny to buy it back. They might even have to sell the mansion. But Yvonne wouldn't care about that, and he knew it would make her very happy.

"It is very beautiful, Father," Kali said, and George smiled and patted his small head and pulled him closer beside him. "Will there be parks and fun rides for children, and maybe horses?"

George smiled and said, "Perhaps."

They both looked up to the warm, smooth tones of Yvonne Adeyemi's voice. She was standing in the doorway, wearing a flowing printed dress and holding a wooden cooking spoon.

"Yes," she said, and she was smiling broadly. "There will be parks and fun rides and horses."

Kali looked at both his parents. Their expressions for each other were soft and warm, and it looked like they were pulling one another through the air across the room.

"Would you like to see my island, Kalief?" George said.

"Yes, Father! Yes!" Then Kali asked hesitantly, "Can we go get Jare and take him too?"

"Of course, my son. We can take Jare too." George regarded Jare as an adopted son, and sometimes when he drove Jare home, he quietly slipped some cash into his grateful mother's pocket.

"Okay, Dad." Kali grinned.

George looked at Yvonne and she nodded.

"Go ahead, my men. Dinner will be waiting when you get back."

And she turned and walked back to the kitchen . . .

Kali's father had a long, shiny, Chris-Craft Catalina boat. It was nineteen feet in length, with a glossy wooden hull, red leather upholstery, a big white steering wheel, and a Nigerian flag on a mast in the back. It was very fast.

They picked up Jare from his mother's one-room home and drove the Bentley down to the marina, which didn't take very long, and Kali was so happy about the excursion with his father—just he and Jare and Dad, no one else—that his smile almost hurt. The orange sun was already sinking into the crystal blue ocean and the gulls were screeching and diving for fish in the waves, and it was still warm but Kali's father didn't even make the boys wear hats.

They broke out from the marina in the boat, with George standing at the wheel, his cigar unlit now but still plugged in his lips. Kali and Jare wanted to stand up too, but it was bumpy at first and George made them sit.

The ocean breeze full of brine and fish scents was wonderful, and the boat was powerful and its inboard engine roared and they bounced over the crests as Kali and Jare loved it and laughed. And then, after a while, far out on the horizon, Kali saw a looming shape. It was a very long mound of green and brown, emerging out of the ocean like some sea serpent he'd seen in picture books. It shimmered in the evening orange sun, and George pointed forward and said above the waves crashing under the prow, "There it is, Kalief. That is our island." He turned and looked down at the boys, and he smiled and reached out and rubbed a thumb across Jare's tribal tattoo. "It will be yours as well, Jare," he said, and Jare's smile was as wide as Kali's.

Kali and Jare stood up again, and this time George didn't stop them. Kali gripped the top of the curving windscreen and felt a rush of pride as he squinted at his father's distant dream. Then he suddenly realized that they were in the middle of the ocean, very far now from Lagos, and still a long way from Pearland. For a moment he looked down through the crystal waters rushing by, and thought he saw dark shapes there below.

Maybe they're sharks, Kali thought. *Or whales or sea monsters.*

But he wasn't afraid.

He was never afraid when he was with his father . . .

TWENTY-THREE

AT ONE MINUTE PAST MIDNIGHT, KALI AND JASON emerged from a lock-out trunk into the cold, dark waters of the Arabian Sea. On the surface, where a bright, high moon glittered the waves, they held their positions in the indigo liquid as the rest of the assault package emerged from forty feet below.

The lock-out trunk aboard a fast-attack nuclear sub was a large, pressurized chamber that could hold twenty-two divers for special operations deployment. Once inside, packed like sardines, the divers waited as the chamber was flooded and its pressure equalized with the surrounding sea. Then the exfil hatch beside the conning tower was opened, and they slithered out one by one.

Thane had wanted a larger assault package, but Kali had lobbied for a single exfil of all the men. He didn't want to wait for a second LOT iteration. It would take too long, and Spencer was being held hostage on Geweer Island.

"Only one lock-out," he'd said to Thane. "We don't have time."

Pacenza and nine of his operators emerged behind Kali and Jason, assembling in the water like a school of sharks. They would be functioning as the hostage rescue team—primary objective, Spencer, followed by anyone else being held. After them, a second team of US Navy SEALS, led by a master chief, flowed from the hatch and assembled ten feet away. They were there to kill everyone else who might interfere.

All the men were equipped with similar gear. They wore lightweight OCP camouflage utilities without insignia, balaclavas, headset comms, dive masks, IST swim fins, and MK25 Draeger rebreathers that emitted no bubbles. They carried MK18 CQBR assault rifles with suppressors, ammunition carriers, and Glock 19s in thigh rigs. Each team had one M249 SAW gunner and three M72 light antitank weapons.

Kali was operating an underwater navigation board with a depth gauge, dive chronometer, and compass, illuminated by the dim green light of a glow stick. The master chief floating to his right held the same. In the inky gloom of the midnight ocean they could barely discern each other's faces, but the glow was enough to exchange thumbs-ups, and they headed out for the five-hundred-yard swim to the shore.

Kali kicked out a slow, steady pace with his fins, glancing at his compass and correcting his trajectory. Jason and Pacenza swam on his flanks and slightly behind, with the rest of the Package in trail and the SEALs offset to his right. Except for Kali and the master chief, none of them could see their own hands in front of their faces—they kept in formation by gripping buddy lines. Kali pressed onward, hearing only the sounds of his own steady breaths in the Draeger, as he reviewed the target in his mind.

Fabio had given up everything he knew to the second tier of interrogators—of that he was sure—and an overflight of a Keyhole-class reconnaissance satellite had confirmed Fabio's sketchy memories. There were six "villas" for holding hostages, all surrounded by an electrified fence; an interrogation blockhouse cut into a cliffside; a helicopter pad; four primitive huts for rotating security teams; an admin office; and a laboratory of some sort. Russian antiaircraft guns were concealed on two cliff tops under camouflage nets, but Fabio had no idea if there were also MANPADs—man-portable air defense systems. For that reason, Kali had chosen an insertion by sea. If they used helos for the assault, they'd be shot out of the sky before they could land.

He'd briefed the assault package fully aboard the *Mississippi*.

"We've got an E-2C Hawkeye flying comms and a Predator at ten thousand feet," he'd begun, meaning a navy surveillance aircraft and an armed drone. "Now, according to Fabio—the prisoner we interrogated—the protocol on this island is to execute hostages if they're raided. We don't know how many are being held in the villas, but our primary objective is to rescue our agent." He'd then shown the SEALs a photo of Spencer—Pacenza and his men already knew Spencer well. "Primary objective is mine and the Package. Secondary objective, the admin building and lab, is yours," he'd said to the master chief. "After that, whatever we can get from a sensitive site exploration will be good, so try not to blow everything up."

"But that's what we do best," the master chief had said with a wry grin.

"I know," Kali had replied, "but let's keep it to a minimum."

Thane and Neveah were aboard the sub as well and listening to Kali's final brief. Neveah had wanted to participate—she'd passed the Special Forces Combat Diver Qualification with flying colors—but suddenly Jason had lobbied for her to stay behind. Kali thought Jason's paternal behavior toward her was strange, and Neveah had argued, but in the end it was Thane's call and he'd told her to remain on the boat. She wasn't happy about that, but Thane was Overwatch and his was the final word . . .

Up ahead, the water was growing shallower, with the moonlight slanting through breakers and glinting off roiling sand and sharp rocks across the seabed. When the water was neck deep, Kali turned his navigation board over to Jason, removed his dive mask, and wrapped it backward around his wrist—the glass might glint in the night—and let only the top of his head break the surface. As the seawater cleared from his vision, he saw the ominous tableau of Geweer Island.

Directly out front were the six hostage villas—low stucco huts with palm-thatched roofs, each with a single door and one window. They were fifty yards up from the rocky beach, where the waves rolled in with a steady rhythm. Beyond them, he knew, was the helo landing pad, and to the left of that the interrogation room cut into the cliffside. All the villas were dark except one, which had a flickering glow from inside. The villas were surrounded by an electrified, six-foot-high, four-strand fence that stood ten yards out from the buildings.

He spotted only one guard. To the left of the villas at the shoreline was a man's silhouette, about the size of a fingertip, standing atop a jagged slab of granite. He was facing away, looking at the glittering ocean, and he clearly had some sort of subgun.

Kali scanned back around to the right, where a hundred yards from the villas a cluster of low stone buildings hulked beneath mushroom-shaped treetops. These were the admin and laboratory structures, and beyond them was a pair of promontories about twenty feet high, with sharp cliffs facing the sea. The Russian ZSU antiaircraft guns were on those cliffs under camouflage nets—he knew they'd be manned round the clock. From the admin and lab buildings, a pathway led down to the beach to his right, ending in a pontoon wharf floating in the water. But there were no boats docked there for a quick escape—whoever was on the island was expected to fight to the death.

Kali submerged, removed his swim fins, and clipped them to his battle harness, while everyone else on his team did the same. By the light of Pacenza's glow stick, he found the captain, tapped his mask, and Pacenza removed it and they both broke the surface. Kali showed him the sentry. Pacenza nodded, submerged again, found two of his men, and sent them off that way into the gloom.

Kali treaded water and watched the sentry. After a minute, something splashed in the ocean near the sentry, and he turned to the left and looked down. One of Pacenza's operators appeared out of nowhere behind him, looped his throat with a forearm, drove a battle knife into his heart, and laid him down on his back. The only sound was the man's grunt as he died.

Kali reached down to his weight belt and pressed a signal emitter—it chirped underwater like a sonar ping, and immediately the Package and the SEALs began to rise from the water. Then he and the Package headed in for the beach, weapons at the ready, dive masks backward on their wrists. Each man shed his Draeger re-breather at the water's edge, where the last operator would remain behind to guard the gear.

Jason was on Kali's left, Pacenza to his right, and a breacher moved beside Jason. The rest of the Package followed as the cold seawater dripped from their gear, heading smoothly across sand and rock, making no more noise than a flock of walking geese. Kali knew that at this point the SEALs to his right had also broken cover and were moving to their objective, the admin and lab buildings, but they wouldn't assault until he hit the interrogation room on the far side of the villas. One errant gunshot could result in Spencer's execution.

Kali and his point men went prone outside the fence, their uniforms instantly caked with sand. All was quiet except for a few seagulls and the whispers of waves, but then Kali heard German and Belgian French voices in his ear. The E-2C Hawkeye, flying high above in the dark, was intercepting the security teams' comms on the island and feeding them to Kali and his men.

"I'm going for a smoke break," one German reported.

"Someone relieve Pierre," a French voice said with a laugh.

The tones were casual. They had no idea what was about to go down.

The breacher dug in the earth with his knife, pulled up a loop of black cable, and showed it to Kali. Then he came up with a pair of thick rubber gloves and a heavy wire cutter with rubber handles. It seemed like he was taking a moment to pray, then he snipped the cable. It hissed a small shower of sparks, but the fence was now harmless.

The breacher made four quick cuts on the fencing strands, which sprang back and opened a hole. Then the Package split up, with Kali, Jason, Pacenza, the breacher, and two more men moving quickly around to the left outside the fence as they headed for the far side and Spencer's prison. The rest of the Package flowed through the fence, heading for the villas. It would now be a matter of stealth, surprise, and violence of action.

From the E-2C Hawkeye, an observer watching the Predator feed spoke in Kali's headset.

"Hawkeye for Dark Horse Main, I've got thirteen heat signatures to your east on the cliffs, a hundred yards past the admin building and lab. But no movement yet. How copy?"

Kali was moving fast over the ground and he wasn't going to talk now. He clicked his transmit button twice to acknowledge.

"Received that, Dark Horse," the Hawkeye observer said. "Waterboy is in position." He meant the SEALs just south of the admin and lab structures. "Package Two's at the door." That meant the second Package element was ready to assault the villas. "Dark Horse Main, you're almost there."

Kali didn't respond. The cliff face with the interrogation room loomed larger in his vision. He saw a wooden door and a primitive window to its left, but no lights from inside. Slinking low, he and Pacenza reached the granite hut and braced the door on the right, while Jason crouched below the window. The two Package operators went prone, facing outboard and covering.

The breacher slowly approached the door with a crowbar. He would split the lock in one smooth move and they'd all burst inside. But just as he reached the door, something clicked as he stepped on a dirt-covered pressure plate . . .

Bang!

A blinding explosion of white light sent him flying backward as the wooden door splintered and a hundred shards went spinning out into the night. At that moment, a machine gun opened up from somewhere, its bullets raking the building in a vicious spray of tracers. Pacenza spun from the wall and dived on top of his wounded breacher, but the only thing on Kali's mind was Spencer. Even with the shock of the IED and the ambush, he didn't hesitate for a second.

"Hawkeye, jam their comms!" he yelled in his mic so the hostage-takers wouldn't be able to communicate. Then he crashed through the jagged doorway into the room, slicing to the right as Jason burst inside and sliced to the left, guns up.

It was empty.

In the lancing light of their tactical beams, they saw only a meat hook in the ceiling, and an empty chair covered with blood. Kali's instincts told him the blood was Spencer's, and he had a DNA analyzer in his pocket, but the middle of a gunfight wasn't the time to test it.

Bullets pounded the outer wall and whipped through the window, just missing Jason as he dived for the floor. Pacenza and another operator came flying inside, dragging the wounded breacher by his ammo vest as they too crashed to the floor, and a harsh chorus of SEAL guns answered the machine gun from the direction of the admin building and lab.

"Package Two for Dark Horse Main," a voice barked in Kali's ear. "I got a dry hole here at the villas, over."

"Dark Horse for Package Two," Kali barked back above the gunfire. "Same here."

"Waterboy One for Dark Horse Main," the master chief's voice said to Kali over a thunder of gunfire. "We've got a *lot* of opposition out here."

Kali heard the screaming whoosh of a LAW rocket, then a sharp explosion as white light flashed in the room.

"Hawkeye One for Dark Horse Main," came the observer's voice from the aircraft. "You've got a TIC over at the admin and lab structures." He meant troops-in-contact.

"No *shit*," Jason shouted, but he didn't transmit that.

"No visuals on any of your hostages, Main," the observer went on, "but we've got machine guns firing from those AA towers on your position and Waterboy's, over."

"Copy, Hawkeye," Kali said. "How many machine guns?"

"Looks like two, and we're still jammin' their internal transmissions. I know you got your hands full, but you might wanna listen."

"I already am."

There were six Germans and seven Belgian mercenaries on top of the cliffs, and Kali heard a frustrated German team leader shouting into his radio.

"Fritz, this is Dieter. Do you read me? Execute Reaper protocol! I repeat, execute Reaper!"

At the same time, Kali heard Fritz trying to reach his commander.

"Dieter, this is Fritz. Do you read me? Am I cleared to execute the hostages? I'm standing by. What the hell's going on?"

Neither of the men could hear one another due to the Hawk-eye's jam, but Kali knew Fritz was getting ready to kill the hostages somewhere.

Where are you, Fritz? The question screamed in his mind. *Where are you?*

Then he heard Dieter again.

"I can't raise Fritz! Does anyone have eyes on the admin building and can tell me what's going on?"

No one was responding to Dieter.

"If anyone has eyes on the admin building," Dieter transmitted again in frustration, "get over there now and make sure Fritz executes the protocol!"

Dieter didn't realize his mic was still hot, and Kali heard someone shouting right next to him.

"I can't read you either, Dieter, and I'm standing right here!"

"Max, Adler!" Dieter yelled to someone else nearby. "You two come with me. We're going down to the admin building and doing it *ourselves.*"

That's it! Kali realized. *The admin building. Spencer and the rest of the hostages . . . That's where they are.*

Pacenza had heard it all too—his German was good. He scrambled over from the wounded breacher and crouched next to Kali beside the blown-out door. More tracers lanced through the window, ripping chunks from the opposite wall. The Package operator was applying a tourniquet to the writhing breacher. His left leg was gone below the knee and there was a gruesome pool of blood on the floor.

"We gotta get to those hostages, Kali," Pacenza rasped in his ear as more bullets raked the building. "*Now.*"

"I know," Kali said, then he looked across the doorway and shouted to Jason above the gunfire.

"You ready?"

"Like Butch and Sundance," Jason shouted back.

They broke from the building in a hail of gunfire . . .

TWENTY-FOUR

GEWEER ISLAND

TWO HUNDRED YARDS TO THE EAST, PAST THE HELI-
copter landing pad, it was hell in a very small place. The
master chief and his SEALs were pinned down between the
beach and the admin and lab buildings, hunkered behind rocks
and scree as a belt-fed machine gun that sounded like an M60 raked
their positions. It was coming from the antiaircraft cliffs, beyond
the structures to the right, while another machine gun spat tracers
in long orange lances over at Kali's position.

Bullets cracked the air, sparked off rocks, and plowed up gouts of
sand. The SEALs were responding with MK18s, their M249 gunner was firing controlled bursts at the cliff tops, and they'd hit the
closest cliff with a LAW rocket. Its camouflage net was burning,
but the machine gun fire was still relentless and wicked.

One of the SEALs was already KIA and another was wounded.
They couldn't advance, but they would never withdraw. The master
chief and his PO1 were behind a clump of black granite, popping
up, firing, and dropping again. The SEAL team leader had just
heard Assault Lead Kali Kent transmitting as he was pounding
across the ground somewhere on the run.

"It's the *admin* building . . . hostages are in the *admin* building."

And right after that he'd heard the Hawkeye observer from
above.

"Dark Horse, you're not gonna make it. You've got three signatures moving fast toward that building from Tower One."

"Waterboys," the master chief called over the net to his SEALs, "we've got to flank that admin building on the right and stop those Tangos. That's where they've got the hostages."

"We know, Waterboy One. We heard it," one of his men shouted in his headset. "No damn room to maneuver here."

The chief's PO1 was beside him, on his back, reloading his MK18.

"Chief," he yelled above the gunfire, "you know that's exactly what they want us to do, right? Full exposure, right out in the open."

"I got that, Sparky," the chief yelled back. "But we got no choice."

"If they get those ZSU's cranked down at us in defilade," the PO1 said, "we're screwed."

The Hawkeye observer's voice crackled again in the master chief's ear.

"Hawkeye One for Waterboy One. I'm lining up a Predator strike with AGMs on those cliffs." He meant a drone with Hellfire missiles. "But that's not gonna save your hostages, over."

"Roger, Hawkeye," the chief said. His jawline clenched and his eyelids twitched with the gunshots as he considered his options, but he didn't know where Kali Kent was, or even if he was still alive.

Nobody's coming . . . It's up to us . . .

"Waterboys, listen up," he called over the net. "I need an element circling right, behind those structures, otherwise we'll have a bloodbath. Everybody else . . . we're going straight up the middle. Copy?"

"Roger," came multiple replies, and they all got ready to die.

"Hold that, Chief!" The PO1 was peering over the rock and gripping the master chief's arm. He pointed straight out front . . .

Kali, Jason, Pacenza, and one Package operator were pounding across the helo landing pad like marathoners on speed. Closer by, from the villas, the rest of Pacenza's Package were racing to join them. But no one could keep up with Kali. His long strides were slamming the ground as tracer bullets raked the air like lasers, but all he could see was the door of the admin building straight out in front. There were lights glowing inside and the hostages were in there. One of them was Spencer, and he knew he had to beat the Germans racing from the other side, but he also knew the building might be his grave.

He heard the master chief in his comms, yelling at his men to hold fire. He heard the Hawkeye observer warning that he wasn't going to make it. He heard one of the master chief's SEALs saying, "Are you sure Dark Horse isn't a Team guy?"

On the far side of the admin structure, two SEALs had cornered the building under heavy machine gun fire and were engaging Dieter and his two Germans, Max and Adler, with three-round bursts from their MK18s. But the Germans were wearing Russian Ratnik body armor and although one of them jerked hard from a round in the chest, they all raked the SEALs on the run with long bursts from their MP5s. They were only twenty yards from the admin building's rear door.

On Kali's side, an M60 bullet shattered his Glock in its thigh holster, spun him around, and slammed him down on his face, but he was up and running again in half a second. He was ten feet from the admin door when he fired his MK18, blew the lock off, and hit the door with his shoulder, which sprang it open on its splintering hinges. He exploded into blinding light and in a flash of vision saw three hostages strapped to chairs on the left in front of an office-type table, and a man standing over them in leopard camouflage with a heavy HK .45-caliber pistol. The man spun and was turning the gun on Kali when Kali shot him twice in the face and he went tumbling backward over the table.

Dieter, Max, and Adler burst inside through the far door, MP5s up and fingers squeezing triggers. Kali shot Dieter between the eyes as the hostages screamed, and Max was twisting to shoot Kali as Pacenza shoved Kali out of the way from the rear and double-tapped Max in the chest. Jason had already careened into the room and sliced to the left, and he stitched Alder from his groin to his head with six rounds as Adler crashed over another table.

Kali, Pacenza, and Jason kept their rifles trained on that far door, but no one else came in as a firefight blazed next door in the lab building and outside in the night.

"Hammerhead! Hammerhead!" the Hawkeye observer said in everyone's ear, and they all opened their mouths to relieve the overpressure as two seconds later a pair of Hellfire missiles hit the cliff tops. *Boom! Boom!* came in quick succession and there were two thundering balls of fire, obliterating both machine guns. Then the SEALs charged up the promontories, but everyone up there was already dead.

After another minute and a few final gunshots, everything fell to silence.

Kali, Jason, and Pacenza were still breathing hard. Kali looked at the hostages strapped to the chairs with gaffer's tape. None of them was Spencer. One looked like a Brazilian woman. One was only a kid, maybe eleven years old, and Kali's heart filled with pity as he walked to the weeping boy and petted his sweat-soaked head as Jason started slicing his bonds. The third hostage was a girl, maybe eighteen years old. She was sobbing uncontrollably, and she looked familiar. SEALs had begun arriving into the admin office, and one of them whispered, "Holy crap, I think that's Paris Nordstrom. She's been missing for a *year* . . ."

Paris was the heir to a multinational space-exploration company that was traded widely across world markets.

"Waterboy One for Dark Horse Main," the master chief said in Kali's headset. "I'm at the lab. I think you'll want to get over here."

"Roger, Waterboy," Kali said. He was hoarse and badly needed a drink. He took a long pull from his water carrier and went outside.

There were SEALs and Package operators in the night, habitually checking their weapons and magazines because they didn't know what might be coming next. The camouflage nets and the ZSU guns on the tops of the cliffs were burning. A few SEALs were climbing down from the promontories. More men had taken up security positions, weapons outboard, scanning the rest of the island. The master chief was standing outside the door of the lab. Kali approached him with Jason and Pacenza.

"Interesting development, Mr. Kent," the SEAL team leader said. "Show me."

The master chief led him inside. A generator hummed from somewhere and the lights were on. It was a large laboratory, with benches, oscilloscopes, welding torches, computers, and electronic analysis equipment. Two dead men wearing Belgian camo were sprawled in one corner next to their broken rifles. The gunfight had shattered much of the equipment, but the master chief walked to one table and showed Kali a strange-looking device.

It was part of what looked like an antenna array, attached to a microchip that had survived the melee. Kali let his MK18 hang from his neck as he carefully picked it up and turned it over. It looked like part of the strange mustache device he'd seen on the nose of the jet at the Lugano airport.

"Overwatch for Dark Horse Main." It was Thane's crackling voice in his headset, calling from the *Mississippi*.

"Go for Main," Kali said.

"Give me a sitrep on Spencer," Thane said.

Kali looked at Jason and Pacenza, and took a long breath.

"Dry hole, Overwatch," he said to Thane. "Dry hole . . ."

TWENTY-FIVE

KANDAHAR, AFGHANISTAN

THE DASSAULT FALCON 900LX CORPORATE JET LANDED at Kandahar International Airport with a screech of black rubber tires, then reversed its engines and taxied down Runway 23. There was nothing unusual about another civilian jet landing at Kandahar, except this one had a strange sort of silver antenna attached to its nose.

The gleaming white-and-caramel aircraft, the largest model in the Dassault fleet, had a capacity of nineteen passengers and two tons of cargo. But it didn't stop at the old passenger terminal that looked like nine concrete ice cream cones stacked side by side. It kept on going, all the way to the end of the steaming tarmac, and took a right onto a slimmer taxiway. It was heading for the northern DAC, or dangerous air cargo, ramp.

Off to the right of the jet, in front of the old NATO cargo yard, was a strange collection of coalition forces "left behinds," as if the Western allies had finally realized that Afghanistan was unconquerable and were having a weekend fire sale. There were UH-60 Black Hawk helicopters, heavily armored and up-gunned MRAP vehicles, and massive C-130 cargo aircraft, the legendary workhorses of NATO and the West. The Falcon rolled to a stop at the DAC's wide triangular platform, turned 180 degrees, and sat, ready to depart again at a moment's notice.

The passenger door hissed open and its stairway descended. Lucas van Groot paused for a moment, squinted in the afternoon sun, and stepped down. He was followed by Pretorius Nabuto and one bodyguard, a large blond fellow wearing a bush shirt, shorts, and packing a concealed Glock 18. Van Groot and Nabuto were both dressed in jeans, desert boots, open-collar dress shirts, and linen blazers. They were there to do business with Amir Baradar.

Amir was just rolling up from the NATO cargo area in his former US State Department armored Mercury sedan, along with Khalid and three of his men inside and another six troops following behind in an open LMTV 4×4 truck. They parked fifty feet from the Falcon's nose and got out of the Mercury. As usual, Amir was fashionably dressed all in black, despite the heat, but now instead of an assault rifle he carried a custom Kimber .45-caliber handgun on one hip and had a leather business satchel slung from one shoulder.

Amir stopped, tipped up the brim of his People's Friendship University of Russia ball cap, and looked at the nose of the jet.

There was a strange device attached, unlike anything he'd ever seen. It resembled an old-style television antenna, the kind he remembered from black-and-white movies his father had once watched, but it was swept back from the nose on both sides like an eight-foot-long silver mustache. Amir understood from his aeronautics classes in Moscow that something like that would affect the jet's speed and performance, so it had to be very important to Van Groot. He walked toward the South African, followed by Khalid and one bodyguard, both hefting AK-47 rifles. Amir's remaining guards stayed with the car.

Van Groot briefly waved at Amir from twenty feet away and returned his focus to an iPad that Nabuto was handing him.

"Can we get reception now?" Van Groot asked.

Nabuto pulled a small transceiver from his blazer pocket and spoke to the Falcon's chief pilot. "Jeremy, shut down the jammer, please."

The pilot shot Nabuto a thumbs-up from the cockpit.

"The pilots just turned off the device," Nabuto said to Van Groot as he gestured at the mustache antenna. "We'll be getting all the surveillance footage now."

They began watching the playback feed from six security cameras on Geweer Island, which had recorded the entire assault by

Kali, the Package, and the SEALs. Van Groot barely reacted to the gunfire and mayhem, yet was so engrossed in the images that when Amir stepped forward with his men, he brushed him off.

"Mr. Van Groot," Amir said as he pointed at the jet's strange antenna, "I am very curious about that device—"

Van Groot flicked a hand and said, "Not now, Amir," as if he were admonishing a schoolchild.

Amir froze in place, clenched his jaw, and blushed. Being disrespected that way in front of his men was an unforgivable sin. Had Van Groot done such a thing to Amir's father, Ziar, when he was a younger warrior, he would have shot the South African on the spot. Khalid murmured, "*Haywan*," which meant "animal" in Dari. He wanted to kill Van Groot.

"They must have jammed our transmissions," Van Groot said to Nabuto. "That's why our men were hesitant to kill the hostages." He tapped the tablet with a finger. "But I don't like *this* part, Pretorius. They were supposed to blow up the lab if attacked. What's the point of having the Reaper protocol if they're not going to execute it properly?"

"I know, VG, but the two Belgians in the lab probably had their comms jammed too."

"Well, we can't really discipline them now," Van Groot said. "I assume they're all dead. Am I right?"

"As far as we know, yes."

"All right. Make sure we get images of all the assaulters, as best we can," Van Groot ordered. "They appear to be wearing balaclavas, so we won't get facial recognition, but their kit might tell a tale. They were clearly government operators of some sort, probably deployed by submarine. No contractors that I know of possess those means, not even the Wagner Group." He was referencing a Russian private military company—mercenaries with a billion-ruble budget.

"Will do, VG," Nabuto said.

Van Groot handed the iPad back to Nabuto, turned, shot a million-dollar smile at Amir, and walked over to shake his hand.

"Good to see you, mate!"

But Amir left Van Groot's hand empty in midair. He was standing with his feet spread on the tarmac, one hand resting on his Kimber .45, and an expression in his blazing green eyes that hinted at murder.

Khalid wasn't any less upset, as he eagerly awaited Amir's signal to send Van Groot to the afterlife.

"Only my most trusted friend, Khalid, speaks English," Amir said, "which means I can be plain."

Van Groot's smile went away. He slipped his hands into his pockets. Khalid and Amir's bodyguard tightened their trigger fingers on their AK-47s, and the big bodyguard behind Van Groot slowly swept his bush shirt open. Nabuto had a Walther P5 compact tucked in his back but he didn't move his hands.

"You are not in your world here, Mr. Van Groot," Amir said. "You are in *mine*. If you ever dismiss me, or insult me again, in front of my men, or even alone, I will kill you in a very painful way."

Van Groot raised his nose, and nodded slowly. He understood what he'd done.

"I've *insulted* you, haven't I?" he said, yet he didn't apologize. In his world the first man to say he was sorry was usually the first man to die.

"It is worse. You have dishonored me," Amir said.

"I understand. Shall we call it Western ignorance?"

"We shall call it Western *arrogance*, and you will make amends, or this pretty toy of yours"—Amir gestured at the Falcon—"shall not leave the ground."

Van Groot had no choice. Maybe Amir wasn't religious and didn't believe in martyrdom, but all his men surely did. It would take no more than a word from Amir and they'd all be engulfed in gunfire. He decided to debase himself and kill Amir sometime in the future. He pressed his palms together in front of his chest and bowed. Amir raised his chin, satisfied.

Van Groot looked at him again and smirked.

"So, I see you have an interest in my advanced technology," he said, gesturing at the Falcon's nose antenna.

Amir relaxed somewhat, as did Khalid. So did Van Groot's bodyguard, and Nabuto.

"I am actually intrigued by it," Amir said, though still with a hint of bitterness.

"Good." Van Groot walked up and was about to squeeze Amir's shoulder, but he knew the gesture would be too familiar. He smiled instead. "Come, let me tell you all about it." He waved a hand toward the back of the aircraft and began walking in that direction. Amir and Khalid followed beside him, but Amir placed a hand on Khalid's shoulder and stopped him with a reassuring gaze. Khalid nodded, then Amir continued.

"Pretorius," Van Groot said over his shoulder. "Two chairs and a carafe of lemonade. No alcohol."

By the time Van Groot and Amir reached the Falcon's tail, where its high-mounted vertical stabilizer threw an angular patch of shade on the tarmac, the aircraft's crew had already set up two folding director's chairs, a small camp table, a chilled crystal carafe, and two etched glasses. As the two men took their seats, Van Groot's bodyguard stood back in the sun on one side, with Amir's men directly across on the other.

Van Groot took out his pack of Balkan Sobranies and lit one of the black cigarettes. Behind his head on the cargo terminal's blast wall was a sign in Dari, English, and French: NO SMOKING.

"Brainwave," he said, and he stretched out the word for dramatic emphasis. "That's what we call it, Amir. It is state-of-the-art stealth technology. Any aircraft, of any size, that is retrofitted with the avionics, software, and antenna cannot be tracked on radar." Van Groot smiled at the look of amazement in Amir's eyes.

"Where did you purchase such a thing?" Amir asked.

"We did not purchase it. We hired an American scientist from one of their top R&D programs. He was already developing the system. We simply encouraged him."

Amir leaned forward and sipped his lemonade. Van Groot did as well. He didn't like lemonade, but in this part of the world you had to imbibe whatever you offered your guests, or they'd be suspicious.

"In the hands of a foreign military," Amir said, "this could be worth a fortune."

"Yes, of course, but I have no intention of selling it. Brainwave makes my organization's operations invisible. The price would have to be astronomical. Retirement money, as they say . . ."

But Amir's mind was already spinning. The current arrangement he had with Van Groot to upgrade Afghanistan's military vehicles and weapons now seemed almost petty. He sat back again and frowned as he thought about his father's wishes.

"My father wants to rebuild our security and defense structure," he said, "so that Afghanistan will never again be subject to foreign invasions."

"And you don't want that, Amir?"

"Yes, I do as well," Amir said. "But I would like to expand far beyond that."

"Expand how?"

"I believe that Afghanistan can not only fend for itself, but can become a world player. We have already demonstrated our personal courage. No one has been able to defeat us, ever."

Van Groot raised an eyebrow. "That's a very good point, mate." He squinted at Amir and took a drag on his Sobranie. The scent of the smoke slightly camouflaged the rank air, which at the Kandahar airport was a combination of jet fuel, sweat, and the open sewage pools that tainted the whole town.

"You studied in Moscow, didn't you?" Van Groot went on as he leaned over his knees. "Did those Russians rub off a bit on you, perhaps?"

Amir leaned closer too.

"They did, Mr. Van Groot. Although they failed here in Afghanistan, many decades ago, they learned their lesson."

"And what lesson was that?"

"That the West is weak."

"That's a pretty bold statement."

"Think about it. The Russians invaded Georgia, Crimea, and Ukraine with barely a whimper from the West. Yes, NATO made a lot of noise and protested and threw some weaponry and money at it, but as soon as Moscow whispered about tactical nuclear missiles, they went scurrying away like rabbits. They couldn't possibly afford to respond right now. They don't have the political unity or financial means. Their coffers are bare."

Van Groot smiled. "I see you studied your Guderian at Patrice Lumumba."

"Yes, and Suvorov as well. 'Judgment of eye, speed, and attack.'"

"Are you thinking about a joint venture with Moscow, Amir?"

"I am, and so are they. I have already been invited to discuss it."

Amir could tell from Van Groot's reaction that he really had his full attention now. He didn't know much about Van Groot's operations, but from their earlier discussions he knew he was deeply involved in world financial markets.

"Really? And what is the object of the Russian president's next obsession?" Van Groot said. "Do tell."

"One never knows with him." Amir shrugged. "It might be Poland, or Hungary . . . or even all of eastern Europe."

Instantly the potential profits went spinning through Van Groot's head like the old Wall Street ticker tape machines. If he could know in advance about such military moves, and was also fairly certain of the outcome, he could make an absolute fortune in the fuel and stock markets and retire—as could every one of his men. It would be good to quit before they all died, which was inevitable given his high-risk game.

The only problem was that he still thrived on the adrenaline, adventure, and death. Well, he'd have to find some other risky gambit and still have fun until the Grim Reaper appeared.

"So, what do you need from me, Amir?" Van Groot asked.

For the first time that day a shallow smile formed on Amir's lips. "Brainwave," he said.

Van Groot laughed. "We're jumping the gun, Amir. First, let's off-load the items we brought you."

"All right. My father will be pleased with the delivery," Amir said, and he began to hand over his leather satchel, which contained half a million dollars in cash. But Van Groot declined with an out-turned palm.

"Let's make this one a freebie, Amir . . . I think we're going to have much bigger fish to fry."

Amir was somewhat stunned, but he accepted the offer with gratitude. He turned and called out orders to Khalid, while Van Groot did the same with Nabuto.

At the back of the Falcon a cargo door opened beneath the tail. Amir's troops backed up the LMTV, and as he and Van Groot watched, various items were "birthed" from the aircraft's cargo hold and hauled onto the truck bed.

The first was a long wooden weapons crate with EXOCET stamped on the side, which Amir knew to be the name of a French anti-ship missile. It took Khalid and all six of the men from the LMTV truck to maneuver the crate as Van Groot murmured, "They should be very careful with that," and Amir understood and called out cautions. The rest of the items were olive-drab crates with stencils indicating they were avionics and instrument upgrades for aircraft.

With the off-load complete, the LMTV 4×4 truck with Amir's troops drove off down the strip, heading for the Ghandar Mountains.

"I'm afraid I must go," Amir said as he got up, but he didn't shake Van Groot's hand. "Think about a price."

"I will," Van Groot said. "And you take care of that equipment. My chief engineer will contact you shortly with instructions."

"I will take his call."

Amir walked back to his car, got in with Khalid and his guards, and drove off the strip.

Van Groot smoked and watched him go. Nabuto came out of the jet and walked up to his chair.

"Productive, VG?"

"Extremely." Van Groot nodded and smoked. "He's pathetically easy to play. We're either going to make a fortune off of this upstart millennial militant . . . or kill him. I haven't decided yet which one I prefer."

TWENTY-SIX

BLACK BOX HEADQUARTERS, MEDITERRANEAN SEA

ANDO WAS STARING AT THE LARGE DIGITAL TACTICAL map on the wall behind his desk. He was standing with his back to his guests, looking at the current hot spots across Europe, Asia, and Africa. They were outlined in glowing neon borders of yellow, amber, or red, and contained text boxes denoting the real-time issues.

NORTH KOREA LAUNCHES BALLISTIC MISSILE TEST #23: NUCLEAR CAPABLE

ANTI−GAS PRICE AND FOOD RIOTS, BUDAPEST, 120,000 PROTESTERS: 560 ARRESTS

PLA MEDIUM-BOMBER OVERFLIGHT, TAPEI: ROC ARMY SCRAMBLES JETS

RUSSIAN 1ST GUARDS TANK ARMY MASSING, POLISH BORDER

"It's like a game of Risk, except the players are all drunken gamblers," he murmured in disgust, then turned back around again and sat down. He'd been taking a few moments to digest the afteraction reports and intel analyses following the Geweer Island raid.

Kali and Jason had stayed up for the rest of the night after returning to the USS *Mississippi*, typing up their AAR in the submarine officers' dayroom, while Neveah suggested editing changes and Thane plied them all with coffee. It was US Navy coffee—black, thick, and oily. After that, the *Mississippi* had surfaced again off the coast of Saudi Arabia in the northern Red Sea, and an

MH-47 helicopter from US Special Operations Command Africa had picked them up and flown them back to the Black Box ship.

Now they were sitting in Ando's guest chairs. Their faces were drawn, eyes gleaming with fatigue, and that last empty chair that Spencer was supposed to occupy weighed heavily on the atmosphere. Ando fanned through the AAR printout again. It was bound in a tan folder with a red stencil: TOP SECRET: SCI. The "SCI" meant "sensitive compartmented information."

"So, not one prisoner taken alive?" Ando said. "Not even one?"

"It was a gunfight, sir," Kali said. "They weren't going to surrender."

"We think one of them jumped a cliff into the ocean to save himself," Jason added, as if that would be enough to please Ando.

"Did anyone pick him up?"

"Negative, boss," Thane said.

Ando sighed. "We're in the intelligence business, people. You can't get much from dead men."

The Black Box team said nothing. Ando ran his finger down a page.

"You found six surveillance cameras, which we have to assume were operational during your activities onshore. Therefore, if they had a remote feed, we can assume Orca has clear images of all of you . . ."

"Sir, we were all wearing balaclavas," Kali said. "He's got nothing."

"Yes, of course," Ando said, as if he'd momentarily forgotten that his people were the best in the business. He looked at Neveah. "Were you able to finally get us something regarding that island?"

"The island was leased from the Yemenis some years back," she said. "Using a cutout, naturally."

"Naturally." Ando dropped the file in disgust. "Have the analysts in Tank Two see if that cutout matches any of the ghost firms Orca's used to make stock buys and sells. They can cross-reference with Kali's and Jason's previous spreadsheet."

"Yes, sir." Neveah jotted his instruction in her small notebook. She always had one with her.

"And where are the surviving hostages currently?" Ando asked.

"Should be arriving at our station in Malta just about now," Thane said. "They'll need some treatment and recovery time, then we can start gently asking questions."

"We'll want the transcripts of those interviews, Thane," Ando said.

"You bet."

"What about our wounded and KIAs?" Ando asked.

"Pacenza's breacher is at the hospital in Ramstein," Thane said. "He and his men are all going there first, and then back to Bragg. Master Chief had one KIA and three wounded. They're all en route to Norfolk. Got to take care of the families."

"So do we," Ando said, and everyone knew what he meant.

Spencer had a wife, Janie, and two little girls. At the moment he'd been missing in action for over a week. It wouldn't be long before Janie would know that something was up, if she hadn't already sensed it by now. Spencer was the kind of devoted husband and father who always stayed in touch, no matter what.

After the hostage rescue on Geweer Island, Kali and Jason had gone with Pacenza back over to the interrogation room to help stabilize the officer's gravely wounded breacher and prep him for exfil by helo. Soon a MH-60R Seahawk helicopter had set down on the primitive landing pad to whisk the breacher out to the US Navy's Sixth Fleet, and they'd turned their attentions back to Spencer's unknown fate. Kali had sampled some of the blood from the floor in front of the chair using his DNA-analysis probe, but he didn't transmit the biometrics out to Black Box in the Med. He wanted to make absolutely sure and preferred to deliver it by hand.

Something flashed on one of Ando's computer monitors, briefly turning his face silver blue, and he leaned closer, squinted, and sat back again with another sigh.

"It's the lab, Kali. Your hunch was unfortunately spot on. Blood belongs to Spencer."

Neveah wanted to curse out loud, but she didn't.

"Any idea about where they might have taken him?" Ando posed. "*If* he's still alive."

"One of Orca's previous locations," Jason said. "A fallback position."

"You mean like Africa, where they found the Tizer boy?" Thane asked.

"Or Italy, near Lake Como," Neveah said.

"He's operated in South America before as well," Thane said.

"None of the above," Kali said. "He won't take him anywhere he's been before. He interrogated Spencer, and whether or not Spencer talked, Orca knows he's some kind of American special agent. He's going to plan this one very carefully. He's not bringing him anywhere easy, especially after what he knows we just did to his island fortress."

Ando nodded.

"I'm afraid I agree with Mr. Kent, though it pains me to admit it's that bleak."

A phone chirped on Ando's desk. He picked it up, said, "Go ahead," and listened for a while as his team members watched his expression, which revealed nothing but one raised eyebrow. Then he hung up.

"All right, Tank Two has finished their analysis of that strange piece of antenna array you found, Mr. Kent. Without being overly dramatic, they say it's like nothing they've seen before. It has a partial plasma microchip, which, as you may know, involves wave technology that is still theoretical."

"Any guess as to the source?" Kali asked.

"DARPA," Ando said.

The Defense Advanced Research Projects Agency. It was the most sophisticated, carefully guarded, top-secret development laboratory for defense projects in the United States, and probably anywhere else in the world. DARPA developed computers, weapons, and subminiature infiltration systems that could be imagined only by fans of *Star Wars*. If a drone the size of a dragonfly flew into the bedroom of an ISIS leader and killed him with a poison stinger, it was likely a DARPA product.

"DARPA wouldn't sell advanced technology like that to a guy like Orca," Thane said.

"No, but a guy like Orca might steal it," Kali said.

"Correct, Mr. Kent," Ando said. "Pack your bags, get to Boston, and find out."

"Roger, sir."

Ando turned to Jason and Neveah.

"You two, go pay a visit to Spencer's wife. Don't tell her any fairy tales, but try to make it hopeful."

"Yes, sir," Neveah and Jason said together.

"Where would you like me to go, boss?" Thane asked.

"Right here," Ando said. "Go below, get some sleep, come back here in four hours. Maybe two old brains can come up with one brilliant idea."

TWENTY-SEVEN

KALI DROVE TO THE MASSACHUSETTS INSTITUTE OF Technology's Lincoln Laboratory from Waxy O'Connor's Irish pub.

He'd stopped at the saloon not because he was hungry or wanted a drink, but to review his research and cover story, and to prepare. He'd sat in a gloomy corner booth, reading technical materials on his smartphone while he shifted his father's beads in his hand, and by the time he slipped them back into his pocket he had fully transformed. He finished his coffee, left some cash on the table, and went outside into a brilliant midday sun. He got into a royal blue nondescript Ford Edge and headed down Hartwell Avenue for Wood Street.

It was only a few blocks, but on the way he passed the gas station of one of the Big Five oil companies. There were protestors blocking the pumps. They had handmade signs: NUKE MOSCOW FOR STEALING UKRAINE! STOP BUYING AN INVADER'S OIL! OPEN THE RINGSTONE PIPELINE! RESTORE UKRAINE OR RUSSIA WON'T STOP! He shook his head and drove on.

MIT's Lincoln Lab was a work of art. At least that's what the front entrance looked like. It was a multistory, all-glass tower, which curiously suggested complete transparency even though everything that happened inside was classified. The Lincoln Lab was entirely funded by the Department of Defense, and subtly advertised its expertise in such things as space control; tactical systems; advanced technology; artificial intelligence; air, missile, and maritime defense; and military air traffic control. For this reason, the lab wasn't located at the sprawling MIT campus in Cambridge proper. It was tucked away in one corner of Hanscom Air Force Base in Lexington, where security forces armed with assault rifles could respond to breaches in a flash.

The Lincoln Lab was an amalgam of brilliant young minds from a top-tier Ivy League school, the needs of the DoD, and a $1 billion annual budget, much of which came from the Defense Advanced Research Projects Agency. DARPA decided which technologies were the most important to national security, and called all the shots.

Kali parked the Ford in one of the lab's vast lots and ambled over to the circular drive at the front entrance, glancing up at the crystal blue tower and its surrounding roofs, all of which had huge antenna arrays or radar domes, like white mushrooms sprouting in a concrete garden. He was wearing a dark blue suit, a pale pink shirt, and a pin-striped tie, and carrying a federal law enforcement SIG Sauer P226 in a concealed belt holster. His glasses seemed a bit sporty for a federal agent—retro Ray-Ban Clubmasters. He walked in the front entrance under its elliptical white portico and presented his FBI credentials to one of the friendly-looking desk guards.

"Special Agent Anthony Hartwell, at your *service*, chief," he drawled to the guard in a North Carolina twang and shot him a blinding grin. "I believe I have an appointment with Dr. Marguerite Taylor."

"I'm right here, Jim," a voice said as the scientist came walking across the polished floor from a doorway. She was around forty, with striking red hair and large brown eyes, and she wore an open white lab coat over a sharp-looking green blazer and skirt, as if she'd just come back from lunch at Oak Long Bar + Kitchen in Boston. A pair of fashionable bifocals hung from her neck on a bead chain.

"He's all yours, ma'am." The security guard handed Kali's FBI badge wallet back to him.

Dr. Taylor looked Kali over and seemed about to riff on the guard's remark, but thought better of it.

"Come along with me, Agent Hartwell." She turned and headed

down a long corridor lined with corporate artwork, most of which seemed to exalt the wonders of deep space. Kali caught up with her.

"Thank you for giving me some time, ma'am," he said as they walked. He handed her an FBI business card, then nudged his glasses onto the bridge of his nose with a fingertip and smiled.

"Well, when the FBI calls, we can't really pretend we're too busy." She put the card into her lab coat pocket.

"You mean I shouldn't be flattered?" Kali lifted his eyebrows as if he'd been hurt, and she laughed.

"You southern men are all charm. Where are you from?"

"Field office in Asheville, North Carolina, ma'am."

"It's pretty down there."

"As a picture, ma'am." He smiled at her again, and she knew he was complimenting her and slightly blushed.

Kali had asked the intel team on the ship to do some research on the lab and the personnel who'd most likely be able to help him. After that, he'd selected Dr. Taylor, chief of advanced wave technology—if anyone would know the intricacies of radar, it would be her. Then Thane had arranged for his FBI cover, which always required negotiations between Langley and the J. Edgar Hoover building (favor for favor). After that, he'd contacted the lab, already posing as a genteel FBI agent from the South, Anthony Hartwell, and secured the appointment.

At the end of the long hallway, Dr. Taylor opened a door and let him go first. He stepped into a laboratory about fifty feet long, where all the furniture, including the computer desk modules, the electronic microscope benches, and the chairs, seemed to be primarily white. However, right away he understood that this wasn't a matter of decor selection, but a practical choice. The lab tables and computer desks held all sorts of microchip and related components, many of them subminiature. No matter how steady your hands were, occasionally these tiny things could get dropped. It would be much easier to find them against a blinding white background.

A young blond man wearing a lab coat was sitting at the far end of one bench. He looked over at Dr. Taylor, she cocked her head toward the door, and he got up and left. She offered Kali a seat in one of the plush white chairs. He quickly sank into it and crossed his long legs, a posture that would make her feel like she wasn't being interrogated, and again he adjusted his glasses, which would make him seem even less threatening. Meanwhile, she chose to stand and leaned on the edge of a lab table. She smiled and looked down at him.

"So, to what do I owe the pleasure, Agent Hartwell?"

"I was wondering if you could identify something for me, Doctor."

"A corpse perhaps?" She raised an eyebrow. "That could make this exciting."

"Nothin' like that." He laughed softly. "It's actually a piece of evidence we collected, but we're not quite sure what it is."

Kali reached into his pocket and came up with a slim plastic case with a transparent top that he'd gotten from electronic warfare crew on the Black Box ship. Inside was the partial circuit board that had been attached to the broken antenna array on Geweer Island. He had that piece of antenna in his car outside, but visually it would suggest the purpose of the technology, and he wanted Dr. Taylor's unbiased assessment. He handed her the case.

She opened it, pulled out the small board, and turned it over in her manicured fingers. She held it up to the light and turned it again. Then she twisted around, slipped it into the clips of an electron microscope, pushed off the table edge, bent over, and plugged her eye into the eyepiece.

"Well, that's something," she murmured. She pulled her eye back, hit a switch on the microscope, and a large image of the board appeared on a monitor behind the scope.

Kali saw only the black board, like a thin wafer with one corner torn off, with a pattern of tiny blue lines and gleaming gold dots. There were none of the standard microchip elements or printed circuit clichés.

"What is it, ma'am?" he asked.

"Honestly, I'm not sure," she said. "But if I had to venture a guess,

I'd say it's plasma or counterwave technology, but from two years down the road."

"What do you mean, 'down the road'?"

"I mean it hasn't been fully developed just yet, though we had one department working on it."

"Had?"

Dr. Taylor turned off the microscope, replaced the board in its case, and handed it back to Kali.

"Yes, had," she said. "Past tense. That department was headed by one man who's no longer with us."

Kali just waited. He knew when not to push. *Just let it unfold.*

"Do you know what RCS is, Agent Hartwell?" She folded her arms.

"I believe that means radar cross-section," Kali drawled as he massaged his chin pensively with a thumb and finger, as if stroking a goatee. "It's also called a radar signature, of any object you're trying to track. The bigger the object, the bigger the RCS."

"Very good," Taylor said, clearly impressed. "Now, since we're having a radar lesson, I'm assuming you know how radar works."

"Well, yes ma'am," Kali said and adjusted his glasses again. "Basically, you bounce a signal off a moving object, the signal returns to the source, and you get an image of the object you targeted."

"Correct. And how does stealth technology impede or defeat radar?"

"I believe you alter the surface of the target object, so that instead of the radar waves being bounced right back to the source, they get scattered in all directions, so you can't get a picture."

"Precisely. Now, have you ever heard of plasma stealth?"

"No, ma'am. That sounds like science fiction." He smiled.

"That's because it hasn't been invented yet in a practical way. In theory, we could cover an object—let's say a reconnaissance aircraft—in a plasma cloak, rendering it unreadable to radar. However, the plasma generators are much too unwieldy, heavy, and expensive at the moment. Needs a few more years for that."

"So, no Klingon cloaking device just yet."

"No, but we do have the makings of something else. Something much more practical that's on the books, but not quite cooked up yet. It's called active cancellation."

"I'm all ears," Kali said. He leaned in over his knees toward Taylor, as if hers was the only voice in the world.

"Active cancellation is based on a wave and quantum physics theory. We would develop a device which, when mounted on an aircraft, for example, would generate a wave exactly proportional to the radar wave being beamed at the target. In effect, the two would cancel each other out, making the target invisible."

"And why don't we have that yet?"

"Because all radar waves, types, volumes, and ranges are different. Our active cancellation device would basically have to have a very powerful brain on board, a brain that could instantly analyze the encroaching radar signal *before* it arrives, then instantly produce its clone and cancel it out. We're not there yet, though we did have someone here working on it, as I mentioned before."

"Who was that, ma'am?"

"A lovely man, basically an Einstein throwback. Dr. Emmanuel Leiter." Taylor's shoulders slumped a bit and she sighed. "He was fairly obsessed with the idea and was working on it for years in one of the subbasement labs. I think management considered him a bit *off*. Then he seemed to grow despondent. Perhaps he had some terminal illness. At any rate, he took his own life just last year. It was very sad."

Kali's pulse rose a notch, but he showed nothing on his face as he nodded with that revelation. A brilliant scientist, on the verge of inventing a radar-defeating technology that could change the face of modern warfare, suddenly gets depressed and kills himself?

"What happened to all his materials?" Kali asked. "His notes and so forth."

"Never located. He left nothing in his safe here, and our own security people gently questioned his widow, Nora, in Marblehead.

She knew nothing about it. Didn't even appear to be aware of his work on this, though at one time she was a radar researcher herself."

"She was?"

"Yes, big fan of Hedy Lamarr, that actress from the nineteen forties. Did you know she developed radio wave guidance technology for the Department of the Army?"

But Kali was already focused on something else.

"If this technology were able to be fielded, Dr. Taylor, how effective would it be?"

"Oh, you could hide a C-130 transport airplane right under somebody's nose. Of course you'd still have the issue of engine noise, but at night, even at a low altitude of a thousand feet, no radar operator could see it."

"And, ma'am, in theory . . . if that sort of thing was deployed . . ." He rubbed his chin once more as he considered his question. "What would it do to communications? Let's say in the immediate vicinity?"

"It would probably jam everything in line of sight."

Kali nodded and showed her the board again in the case. "So, if you didn't develop this here . . ."

"We didn't. I'd know—"

"Who might be able to do it?"

"With Emmanuel Leiter's help? In theory? A number of countries. France, the UK, Israel, even South Africa. The Chinese could also back-engineer and duplicate it."

"Is Dr. Leiter's widow still alive?"

"As far as I know. Sweet woman. I really should call her . . ."

But something had crawled into Kali's head. Leiter had invented Brainwave, but before he could get the project rolling at the Lincoln Lab, someone had found out and either threatened, blackmailed, or bribed him. Now he was gone, and perhaps the only person who knew exactly what had happened, yet hadn't told a soul about it, was Nora Leiter.

If she wasn't already dead.

He got up, shook Dr. Taylor's hand, and said, "The FBI can't thank you enough, ma'am. Not *nearly* enough," and headed right for the door in loping strides.

"Wait, Agent Hartwell!" she rose and called to his back. "I was going to invite you to dinner. There's so much more to discuss . . ."

But Kali was already gone.

TWENTY-EIGHT

SILVER SPRING, MARYLAND

JASON AND NEVEAH PULLED TO THE CURB IN FRONT of Spencer's pale blue, split-level house, and stopped the discussion they were having as they stared at the Wind agent's home. There was a red Jeep Cherokee in the driveway, but they knew Spencer kept his cherished emerald green 1983 Mustang under wraps in the garage. A curving flagstone pathway bordered with flowers led up to a covered porch and the white front door, which loomed in their minds like the entrance to a funeral parlor.

They stalled for a minute, gazing at each other, then finally nodded and got out. It was warm and sunny. They were wearing T-shirts and jeans, like any other casual neighborhood visitors. Neveah cautioned Jason as they started up the path.

"Let's try to be gentle about this," she said.

"Of course," Jason said. "As much as we can be with the way things are."

They walked to the front door, and Janie pulled it open before they got there. She was petite yet athletic like a college gymnast, wearing purple sweats, with short blond hair cut in messy bangs over her forehead and bright blue eyes. She usually had a dazzling smile, but it wasn't quite there today. Jason and Neveah had called her from Dulles airport to arrange the visit, so she already knew something was up. Behind her off to the right in the living room, Spencer's twin girls, age five, were playing on the floor with a big Lego set. They had fire red hair, like Spencer.

"Come on in," Janie said. She briefly hugged them both as they walked into the living room across a parquet floor. "Coffee?" she asked.

"No thanks, Janie," Neveah said. "I think we're already overcaffeinated."

"Kylie, Miranda," Janie said down at the twins. "You remember Jason and Neveah from Daddy's baseball team?"

One of the girls looked up and said, "The one called feebee?"

Janie smiled. "Not feebee, honey. FBI. Now say hello."

The twins looked up, smiled, said "Hello," and went back to their Legos. Jason and Neveah sat down next to each other on the couch, while Janie took a seat across from them in a chair.

"Place looks great, Janie," Jason said as he looked around.

"Thanks," Janie said. "It always looks better when the man of the house isn't around here making a mess." She tried to smile.

Neveah swallowed. "It's good to see you, Janie."

"Same here," Janie said.

"We just thought we'd check in." Jason's remark sounded so hollow to him that he almost blushed.

"Well, you were always such good friends," Janie said kindly, but her use of the past tense chilled them both.

Jason glanced down at the twins. Janie understood and said, "Girls, you can grab Mommy's iPad and go upstairs and watch *PAW Patrol*."

"Yay!" both girls squealed.

"Make sure you play nice. I don't want to hear any fighting over who gets to pick first. You know Mommy's rules."

The girls got up and happily bounded up the stairway to their bedroom above. They giggled about something and a door closed.

"Okay," Janie said to Jason and Neveah as her blue eyes gleamed. "You can cut the crap now."

She waited as they shifted on the sofa, then Neveah spoke.

"Spencer's gone missing," she said.

Janie took a deep breath and looked at the ceiling. "I thought it was something like that." She looked at them again and asked, "Missing? Or taken out?"

"Missing," Jason said.

"What's the time frame?" Janie asked.

"About a week," Neveah said.

Janie nodded, got up, and went off into her piano room. When she came back, she was holding a glass with some sort of green smoothie in it and she was wiping the corner of one eye with a knuckle. She sat down again, sipped her drink, and said, "I'd offer you some, but I don't want to repeat what happened when I made you this stuff in Croatia."

They smiled and watched as she sipped some more. Her fingers trembled a bit.

"Ando's running a full protocol, I assume," Janie said.

"Yes," Jason said. "He's got multiple action teams engaged."

"Was it a decept snatch?" Janie asked. "That's the only way somebody could get one of you guys."

"Yes, it was," Neveah said. "But we're working it."

"If I was still in Black Box, I'd work it myself," Janie said.

She was not your average government or military spouse. She'd actually been a full-fledged member of Black Box herself, a Ghost agent, for nearly six years before she'd quit. That's where she'd met Spencer and they had fallen head over heels for each other. But Black Box regulations strictly stated that intimate relationships between agents were forbidden. The only way to maintain such a relationship and carry it onward was for one of the agents to withdraw from Black Box.

Spencer had actually volunteered to quit first, but Janie had said no. They wanted to have a family and she wasn't going to leave him home alone to raise their kids. When he'd said that at her retirement party, everyone had laughed.

Janie looked at her glass and swirled the smoothie, as if somehow the liquid might provide an answer or comfort of some sort.

"So, what are his odds?" she whispered.

"We don't know yet, Janie," Neveah said. "But we're doing everything possible."

"I know you are," Janie said. She looked up again and her blue eyes were brimming. "I appreciate you coming here in person."

"Ando didn't want us to do this with a call."

"That's Ando," she said. "Thank him for me. I know this is hard for you both."

The fact that she was trying to comfort them made their hearts hurt.

Janie finished her drink and got up. They did too. She hugged both of them again, but longer, as if Spencer were a part of each of them, which he was.

"Okay," she said. "I know the rules, and I don't want to put you guys in a position to get you in trouble. But if there's anything you can share, it'll be appreciated." Janie no longer had a security clearance.

"Yes, you know the rules," Jason said. "I can't say yes, but I won't say no."

"Thanks. I think I'll go be with the girls." She smiled wanly. "Do you mind letting yourselves out?"

"Sure thing," Neveah said.

Janie walked to the stairs and turned for a moment. "Please find him, if you can."

She headed upstairs to see her girls. Jason and Neveah looked at each other. They didn't know if she was going to tell the twins something to ease them into the possibility that their dad might not be coming home again, or if she wasn't going to say anything at all. They got up and left, closing the front door quietly behind them. They walked to the car, got in, and Jason started the engine. A letter carrier waved at them with a smile as he stuffed something into Spencer's mailbox.

Jason was about to drive away when Neveah touched his arm to stop him. He looked at her. She offered her hand, and he took it in his and squeezed it. They sat that way for a moment.

"This is when being involved with someone in our business can get ugly and sad," Neveah said.

"I know, NV," Jason said. "I know."

They looked at the house one more time, Jason put the car in gear, and they left.

TWENTY-NINE

MARBLEHEAD, MASSACHUSETTS

KALI HAD THE GAS PEDAL JAMMED ALL THE WAY TO the floor. He was racing north on I-95, weaving among trucks and cars, but the Ford Edge wouldn't do more than a hundred miles per hour—he wished he'd rented a Dodge Charger. He wasn't concerned about the state police pulling him over, because he'd slapped a magnetic police light and siren onto the roof and had federal license plates on the car.

Typically this would be a job for the Patriot program, which was a Black Box unit of Wind agents, Ghosts, and Chameleons who operated only within the United States, but Kali had no time to alert them. He had to get to Nora Leiter before someone else got to her first. He had no doubt they'd kill her.

Kali hadn't asked Dr. Taylor for the widow's address or phone number. As soon as he'd loped from the Lincoln Lab, jumped into his car, and spun it toward the highway, he'd pulled out his cell and tapped a camouflaged icon. That opened a SATCOM link to the Black Box ship and a voice from the Intel Tank had said, "Transmit."

"Dark Horse Main here. I need a location fix and a contact number in Marblehead, Massachusetts."

"Roger, Dark Horse. Go."

"Last name, Leiter . . . Lima Echo India Tango Echo Romeo. First name, Nora . . . November Oscar Romeo Alpha. Age range . . . five-zero to six-zero, plus. Watch for duplicates. Over."

"Good copy, Dark Horse. Wait one."

A truck hauling wobbly propane canisters suddenly jerked from the right lane in front of Kali's speeding car. He didn't touch the brake pedal but stomped harder on the accelerator instead. He zipped around the truck on the left, nearly ripping his side-view mirror off on the concrete highway divider, and kept on going, faster.

"Dark Horse," the Intel Tank operator said, "your target's at two-two Davis Road, all the way at the end, northeast tip of the peninsula. No duplicates." The operator meant there were no other individuals with that name or description. "Transmitting a nav patch and a cell number. Want me to route a call? Over."

"Affirmative. Out," Kali said.

The icon on his cell flipped over to an encrypted navigation system similar to Waze. Immediately a series of telephone numbers appeared and Kali heard ringing on the other end. After a few rings . . .

"Hello, this is Dr. Nora Leiter—"

"Dr. Leiter," Kali started to say, but she kept on talking.

"I'm sorry I can't get to the phone right now—"

"*Dammit.*" He banged the steering wheel, then the navigation voice broke in.

"Your ETA is twenty-three minutes. Heavy traffic. Exit right in three miles to Routes 128 and 114."

It felt like the longest twenty minutes of his life. The offshoots from I-95 were slimmer and packed with good-weather traffic, people taking off early from work to cruise to lunches in picturesque Salem or visit their boats all along Marblehead's piers. The seaside town was one of the prettiest in New England, but Kali didn't see any of it. He weaved among motorcycles, convertibles, pickups hauling sailboats on trailers, and finally turned sharply north off of 114 and pushed it hard through the small streets and colorful colonial maritime houses. He tried calling Nora Leiter again.

"Hello, this is Dr. Nora Leiter. I'm sorry—"

He hung up, pushed his suit blazer open, and pulled out his P226, keeping it low in his lap as he press-checked the action, confirmed a seated round, and put it back into the holster. He slowed as he reached Grace Oliver Beach, pulled the beacon back in from the roof, then turned north again on Crowninshield Road and onto the last little finger of the peninsula. That road then turned into a slim lane called Davis.

The quaint New England homes were spaced out there, in a remote, peaceful spot away from the tourists. "ETA, one minute," his nav system said. He slowed as he spotted a mailbox that had only 22 stamped on its side, at the end of a long, curving driveway leading off into the trees. Beyond that he could see the bright blue ocean and seagulls winging over a beach.

He didn't enter the driveway. He parked on the shoulder of Davis, got out, walked to a pair of stone pillars, and pushed one eye around the corner. Up along the driveway he could see a dark van, no markings. If it was a service truck it would have a stencil of some sort. He circled back and made his way behind a thick row of pines lining the driveway.

The house was canary yellow, with white window frames, open shutters, and a wraparound front porch. It was surrounded by a white picket fence. Some sort of instrumental jazz wafted from inside, maybe Herbie Hancock, but that gave him no comfort. Either Nora Leiter was enjoying a languid afternoon, or someone wanted to camouflage her screams.

He moved carefully behind the row of pines, head on a swivel, checking his surroundings in case someone had posted security. No dog barked, but the birds in the trees weren't chirping either. Birds always knew when there was bad mojo in the air. He stopped outside the house's right flank and peered through the trees. No movement. But he wasn't going to try the front door.

He vaulted the white picket fence without a sound and made it over to a side window. It was neck high, but there was an air-conditioning unit on the ground just below, and the window's shutters were open. He slithered up onto the box, letting only his eyes rise over the sill. He saw a long, shadowed front hallway leading straight away, with a living room off to the right—no movement in there either. The window was screened, with tall double panes inside that hung on hinges. He pulled a spring-loaded tactical knife from his pocket, flicked it open, carefully sliced a long slit through the screen, popped the window latch, and wriggled inside. He dropped like a cat onto the polished oak floor.

"But I didn't *say* anything to anyone!"

It was a female voice, pleading from somewhere deeper inside the house, on the same floor but the far side.

"Oh, we think you *did*, Mrs. Leiter." A man's voice, heavy and dark.

"I didn't! He warned me to keep quiet about everything and I did. I kept my end of the bargain. I never told a *soul* . . ."

Kali heard the smack of a palm against flesh and a woman's scream. He moved quickly along the hallway's right wall, the knife in his right fist—a razor-sharp four-inch Benchmade. He glanced into the living room before crossing its threshold—there was a sofa, stuffed chairs, lamps, books, a rolling bar, but no people. The jazz was coming from a CD player.

"You're lying, *bitch*." That voice was foreign. "We *know* you talked to somebody."

"*No!*" she wailed. She was crying now.

"Were there any government agents here before us?" It was that menacing, deep, dark voice again. "Asking you questions?"

There was an open doorway on the right, up ahead, across from the house's front entrance. The voices were growing louder as Kali slinked along. He was almost there . . .

"Better tell us right now, Mrs. Leiter," the foreign voice snarled again. "Or I might have to cut off your *ear*."

She screamed and sobbed pathetically. "Please, *no!*"

For a moment Kali heard nothing, as inside the room the man with the dark voice was peering out a window at pedestrians passing by the end of the driveway. Then Kali heard him say, "Marcel, she's making too much damn noise. Go outside and make sure nobody heard her."

"All right," the foreign voice said.

Then a man popped out of the doorway five feet in front of Kali. He was tall with buzz-cut blond hair, gripping a suppressed pistol, and he instantly sensed Kali's presence and spun. But Kali was already on him. His left hand shot out, clamping the pistol's slide, and he snapped the gun backward and broke the man's trigger finger as he drove the knife full force up through his throat and into his mouth. A gruesome sound squealed from the man's gullet as his eyes rolled back. He crumpled to his knees and collapsed as Kali took the pistol away, then racked the slide.

Nora screamed like she hadn't before.

An arm flew around the door sill, gripping another silenced handgun. Three rapid shots coughed in Kali's direction as he slammed himself face-first onto the floor and fired two shots one handed through the sill, sending splinters flying. The shooter dropped the handgun, tumbled sideways out into the hallway, holding his blood-gushing neck with both hands, and crashed down into the front door foyer.

Kali knew that whoever was still in that room was ready for him now. He leaped up and spun back toward the living room, racing to flank them from behind. He heard the cough of another suppressor shot and a thump as a chair flipped over, and as he came around the corner a huge man pounded into him in a flying tackle. They both crashed over the back of a sofa, Kali's skull banged into a side table, and his captured pistol went skidding across the floor.

His assailant was a bull, with wide shoulders in a leather blazer and hands like meat slabs. He rolled off the floor next to Kali with his silenced handgun still in one huge paw. He grunted something in a Slavic language and jerked the gun up and fired. The bullet cracked past Kali's left ear as he grabbed a bronze standing lamp and swung it like a Louisville Slugger, smashing the pistol from the man's fist. But that didn't stop him. He bent low and charged.

Kali sidestepped fast to the left, grabbed the top of the man's suit jacket in back, kicked his right leg from under him, and flung him face-first into the rolling bar. Glass decanters exploded and alcoholic beverages sprayed everywhere, but the man shook it off and turned, streaks of blood coursing down from his skull. Kali shin-kicked him hard in the groin, nearly lifting him off the floor, but the beast wasn't done. He swiped the blood from his eyes and came on again. Kali reached down for the lamp, ripped the electric cord from its base, gripped it two fisted, whipped it around the man's bull neck, and spun him fully around. Then he crashed to the floor on his ass, pulling the man's full weight down between his legs, locked his ankles in front, crossed his fists behind the huge head, and twisted the cord as hard as he could.

The man tried to scream. His huge arms flailed backward over both sides of his head as he tried to gouge out Kali's eyes. Kali tucked his face down beside the man's bulging neck and used every muscle in his arms, until the man flailed his feet in the air a few times and, at last, shuddered, collapsed, and stopped moving.

Kali crawled out from under the corpse. He staggered across the floor, picked up the bull's silenced handgun, walked back over to him, and looked down. The big man's eyes were wide open, all the blood vessels burst. Kali walked back out into the hallway.

Keeping the pistol trained on the splintered doorway, he looked down at the foreigner, who was clearly dead, then he moved to the second man lying in the foyer and prepared to finish him off. A large pool of blood was spreading from under his head, but his neck wound had stopped pumping. He was gone.

Kali still couldn't be sure there were only three of them. He gripped the pistol two handed again, fully extended, and cornered in through the bullet-splintered doorway.

It was a beautiful sunroom, bright, airy, and drenched in light from the ocean. There were flowers everywhere, and a small gardening table with stuffed printed chairs. Nora Leiter was sitting on the floor on the left, her legs sprawled open and slumped back against a flowered window divan. She was in her fifties, had gray-blond hair, and was wearing gardening coveralls and a pretty pink blouse. There was a bullet hole in her sternum and her small hands trembled in her lap. She was breathing in long, shallow drafts and she looked up at Kali as if he were some kind of apparition.

He tucked the pistol into his waistband and lowered himself to the floor beside her. He slipped his left arm around her shoulders and with his other palm gently applied some pressure to her froth-ing chest wound. But she was fading fast and he knew there was nothing he could do for her.

"It's all right, Mrs. Leiter," he said. "You're safe now."

"Are they gone?" she wheezed. There was blood on her lower lip and Kali knew it was coming from her lungs.

"Yes. Do you know who they were?"

"Van Groot's men," she managed.

"Who, Mrs. Leiter?"

"Lucas van Groot . . . I'm sure." She coughed and laid her head back in the crook of Kali's arm. She looked up at him. Her green eyes were glassy. "He's the man who tormented Emmanuel . . . made him work for him . . . made him give him all of his research about Brainwave."

"Brainwave, Mrs. Leiter?"

"Emmanuel was so smart," she whispered, and a weak smile crossed her bloody lips. "He was so kind, so wonderful . . . but he wasn't an evil man, like Van Groot. He couldn't resist . . ."

Her hands dropped limply to her sides and stopped trembling, and then she died.

THIRTY

GENESIS

"They are trying to kill me, Yvonne!"

George Adeyemi stormed outside to the pool through the tall french doors at the rear of the family mansion. He was holding a sheet of crumpled white paper in one fist and a bone-handle knife in the other.

"Yesterday they nodded and smiled, like *snakes*," he railed. "They all said they understood my wishes and that all would be well. But today those bastards want their pound of flesh!"

"My love," Yvonne said as she sat up from her lounge chair and twisted around toward George, "please calm yourself and tell me."

She'd been lying by the pool, wearing a floppy straw hat and a flowered wraparound, and sipping sparkling water with a sprig of thyme while she read one of her favorite books. Kali was in the shallow end of the pool with Jare. They were playing one of their favorite imagination games, inspired by those American black-and-white detective programs they sometimes watched together on TV. They often argued over who was going to be good and who was going to be bad.

"I'll be the good cop now," Kali was insisting. "It's your turn to be Mafia!"

"Okay, okay," Jare said, "but then *I* get to be good!"

"*None* of those people are good," George growled as he heard the boys' exchange, then tossed the crumpled paper in Yvonne's lap. She took off her big sunglasses, unwrinkled the paper, and squinted down. The short message was in all capitals and had been done with a typewriter. There was a gash between the two sentences.

THE ISLAND WILL NEVER BE YOURS
YOU ARE EITHER WITH US, OR AGAINST US

Yvonne looked up at George. The overt threat alarmed her, but she didn't want him to see, therefore she knew it was best not to say anything yet.

"With a *knife*, Yvonne," he hissed down at her as he showed her the gleaming blade. "With a knife, in our front door!"

Kali was standing stock still at the far end of the pool now, waist deep in the water that had felt so warm before, but now felt cold. His hands were clutched in small fists by his sides. Jare seemed not to notice anything unusual and was playing with a submarine toy because Kali had dropped out of their roleplaying game.

"You see what happens when I try to do the right thing, Yvonne?" George slammed the knife down onto the small side table next to his wife, making her tall drink tremble. He took off his purple-banded hat and swiped sweat from his brow with a forearm. He was wearing a short-sleeved silk shirt and gray trousers. "You see what happens to a man who tries to leave the consortium?"

It was a question, so Yvonne saw her opportunity to answer, in a tone that was as calming as she could manage.

"We knew it would be difficult, George—"

"Difficult? It's impossible, Yvonne!" He began shouting his grievances in rapid succession. "I offered them my shares! I offered them my controlling percentages so I could finance the island and all the developments! I even offered to borrow a portion of their future profits at an interest rate a full point *higher* than the banks! And do you know what they said?"

"You already told me they said yes—"

He cut her off. "Let me finish, Yvonne! They said they would be *disappointed* if I left, but pretended to compliment me and all my efforts! They said Pearland was a fine idea and they'd be happy to participate! And you know what? They are *liars*!"

At the other end of the pool, Kali's breaths were quickening and his eyes were wide. Jare had finally stopped swimming around—he realized now that something bad was happening and he stared at his friend.

"They have always been that, George." Yvonne got up from her lounge chair. She touched his arm where the muscles were rippling because both his fists were clenched. "Let me go get you a drink and we'll talk—"

"I don't want a drink!" He yanked his arm away. "And I don't want to talk anymore. This is never going to work. Not if you still want me *alive.*"

Kali was staring at his parents the way he did whenever they fought. But somehow he knew they weren't fighting each other. They were struggling with something else, something bad, and his eyes filled up because he felt so helpless. He wanted to do something for them.

"They are simply trying to scare you, George," Yvonne said in her soothing, maternal tone. "They want to frighten all of us. It's very threatening to them that one of their own might turn away from their evil ways, George."

Evil ways?

Kali did not understand. He knew that his father's friends were strong men and sometimes they scared him with the way they talked, but his father would not be with evil people. If they were evil they could hurt him. That image was awful to Kali.

"Well, it is working, Yvonne," George said. He picked up her drink from the table and drank half of it down. He was breathing hard with the emotion. "I have worked with the consortium for so long that I forgot what these men are made of. Chibundu called me yesterday after our meeting and said it would not go so smoothly. He said that they talked about going to the governor. I didn't believe him. I thought they'd sent him to bluff me so they could get a better deal."

Yvonne reached up and touched his cheek.

"Do not let them do this to you, George," she said. "Do not let them steal your dream."

"What am I supposed to do then?" He swatted her hand away. He could not be comforted.

"You must be strong, and you only have two choices," she said. "You can either capitulate, or go straight and show them all."

But her words only seemed to infuriate him further. He picked up the knife, jammed it into his pants pocket, spun around, and started walking back to the house. But immediately he turned and snapped again.

"You don't understand, Yvonne. Your principals are nothing to men like these. It is like trying to leave the Black Axe." That was a reference to a vicious Nigerian gang, notorious for drug running, human trafficking, and murder—they were akin to the Italian Mafia who ran the streets of New York in the 1970s and '80s. He steamed for a long moment, picked up his hat, and jammed it back onto his head. "I am going to see Chibundu, right *now*."

Kali could stand it no longer. He rushed to the stairs at the corner of the pool, crawled out dripping, and ran down the cement to his father. He grabbed him around one leg of his trousers and hugged tightly.

"No, Dad, don't go!" Kali pleaded. "I don't want you to wind up like that man on the beach, like Mom said before!"

George looked down at his son and peeled him away from his leg. His trousers were stained now with pool water but he didn't seem to care.

"What do *you* know, Kalief?" he said. "You're a boy. These are man things."

And he stormed off back through the rear of the house, back toward where his Bentley was parked out front.

Yvonne pulled Kali down to the lounge chair. She sat beside him, hugged him close against her chest, and petted his soaking wet hair. Jare appeared from the other end of the pool and put his hand on Kali's shoulder.

"It will be all right, Kalief," Jare said. "Your father is strong."

But Kali didn't believe him. Bad things happened to strong men too.

THIRTY-ONE

AFLIGHT OF SIX SUPER TUCANO STRIKE FIGHTERS roared in from the north over the snowcapped mountains. They were in perfect V formation, like a flock of metallic geese, and they swept over the runway, then broke from each other and arced for the sun, spewing colorful smoke from their tails.

After that came three lumbering C-130 military cargo aircraft. Their cargo ramps were open and they spewed bundles of equipment and ammunition crates, which floated down to the field under blossoming silk parachutes. Ten Black Hawk helicopters followed the C-130s, with five smaller Little Bird helos buzzing proudly in trail. And then came seven Russian Mi-17 heavy-lift helos, as if the world's greatest superpowers had decided to join just this once in a brotherly aerial celebration.

It was an impressive display, because all of these aircraft had been left behind by Western coalition forces, and only a year before had been deemed unflyable.

As the last aircraft passed overhead, the audience erupted in wild applause and many rifles were fired happily straight up in the air—apparently the celebrants thought this new Afghan air force was immune to bullets.

There were more than two hundred folding chairs set out on the long runway's apron, in the front of the old Soviet control tower that the Americans had once proudly acquired, and had then left empty to the rats and wild dogs. The chairs were occupied by high-ranking Taliban warriors, officials from the new Afghan Islamic

Republic, heroes of the wars of liberation against the allied co-alition, and many members of the international press.

Not one of the guests was a woman. Afghanistan was no longer pretending to be enlightened on that score or liberated in terms of its female population.

Lucas van Groot had a front-row seat for the military parade, along with Ziar Baradar, Bilad, and Shafik on one side and Amir Baradar on the other. To the right of Amir sat a nondescript beefy man wearing a woolen blazer—despite the heat—and his trans-lator. The beefy man's credentials said he was a minor vice-consul from the new Russian embassy in Kabul, and Amir had led his fa-ther to believe that he was merely an old chum from his days in Moscow. But he was actually Vitaly Chok, a four-star general in the Russian army.

A thunder of engines grew from the north end of the field, and then captured and refurbished coalition vehicles began to roll down the strip in perfect formation. There were Humvees, heavy-armored MRAPs, and M113 armored personnel carriers, clanking along on treads. All of them flew the whipping white flags of the new republic, and all had proud Afghan warriors standing straight up from their hatches, saluting smartly as the audience clapped and roared.

Ziar Baradar sat in his chair, nodding in approval as every new element of the parade passed by. He was wearing the traditional *salwar* and a *pakol* cap, but now he also turned a walking stick in his brown farmer's fingers. His hips were telling him that his days in the mountains would soon be over, but he felt proud that he would be leaving this legacy of strength when he passed into the next world. He, along with Bilad and Shafik, was still wary of this foreigner, Lucas van Groot, but they had to admit that the man had done wonders.

"It pleases me, Mr. Lucas," he said above the roar of engines—in formalities Afghans often used the first name instead of the last. "Afghanistan will once again be strong. Our borders will be re-spected."

"It pleases me as well, Chief Ziar," Van Groot said, using the African title that he knew Ziar found flattering. "I have to say, my contractors and engineers worked very hard."

"Indeed they are expert professionals," Ziar agreed as he continued to admire the passing, gleaming, freshly washed vehicles. "Where do you find them?"

"They are the backbone of wars." Van Groot smiled. "The pilots and tank commanders are important, but it's the mechanics who make them fly and roll."

Amir Baradar was listening to the exchange between his father and Van Groot. He was dressed in his typical countercultural fashion—a pale linen shirt with neatly rolled cuffs, jeans, and Red Wing boots. He leaned toward Van Groot.

"The question is," Amir said, "just how *far* will they fly?"

"With the add-ons my people are installing," Van Groot answered, "triple their usual range."

"And what add-ons are those?"

"Robertson fuel tanks, mate," Van Groot said. "They're American-manufactured supplemental fuel bladders, with bulletproof casings. You simply bolt them into a fuselage, connect them to the internal tanks, and top them up. The Yanks left more than a thousand behind."

"Are they very expensive?" Amir asked.

"Yes, but worth every penny." Van Groot turned and looked at Amir, while Ziar continued to admire his unfurling dream of national power. "By the way, Amir, I'm curious . . . How are you financing all this?"

"Poppies," Amir said.

The Americans and the coalition had thrown huge efforts behind suppressing Afghanistan's traditional trade in cocaine harvests and heroin processing on its northern border with Iran. But with the foreigners gone, that business was once again booming.

"The hunger for heroin is very strong in America," Amir added.

Van Groot laughed softly. "I'll have to look into that. One of these days, smack is going to be publicly traded."

Amir smiled and nodded. He knew all the American slang words for drugs, and the Russian ones as well.

The Russian general, Vitaly Chok, leaned to his left toward Amir. His interpreter was perched in the next row of chairs behind him and had been whispering a translation of the exchanges between Van Groot and the Baradars in the general's ear.

"Forgive me for eavesdropping," Chok said to Amir in Russian. "But I understand your client claims he can triple the ranges of the aircraft."

Amir, fluent in Russian, didn't need to wait for the interpreter's translation.

"Yes," Amir said. "And perhaps more."

Vitaly Chok shrugged. "We also have such equipment," he scoffed. "This is nothing special."

Van Groot heard the next bit of translation from the interpreter, and before Amir could answer the Russian, he leaned across Amir and locked the general's eyes.

"Can you also make them invisible?" he asked.

"No, of course not," the general said, just after his interpreter's translation.

"Well, *I* can," Van Groot said, and he sat back and lit up one of his black Balkan Sobranie cigarettes.

The Russian stared at the strange South African, then Amir caught his surprised gaze and nodded in confirmation.

"I will believe this when I see it," Chok said.

"Then you will believe it soon," said Amir.

Amir turned and glanced surreptitiously at Bilad, Shafik, and his father, but Ziar Baradar had paid no attention to the significant exchange among Amir, Van Groot, and the Russian, as he was too enthralled with the celebration and in jubilant discussion with Bilad and Shafik.

The parade of vehicles had finished their display and were arranging themselves on the far end of the strip. Now formations of Afghan warriors were marching from the north end, led by a sole figure a few feet ahead—Amir's most trusted lieutenant and friend,

Khalid. Some were dressed in flowing white warrior robes and carried scimitars, but an entire battalion was outfitted in left-behind American camouflage uniforms, with Velcro patches of the new regime's national army and American rifles, machine guns, body armor, helmets, and night-vision goggles. It would have been hard to distinguish them from US Army Special Forces freshly arrived from Fort Bragg. The audience applauded even more wildly, and another thunder of approving AK-47s fired off into the air.

In the midst of the raucous reception, someone tapped Van Groot on the shoulder from behind. It was Nabuto, dressed in casual business wear like Van Groot, except that he was packing a Glock under his summer linen blazer. Van Groot leaned his head back as Nabuto bent to his ear.

"We just got news from Boston, VG."

"Good news, I assume."

"It cuts both ways," Nabuto said. "The woman's dead, but so is our element."

Van Groot turned and looked at him. "All three?"

"Affirmative. Somebody took them out, but we don't know the order of the incident."

"Meaning?"

"We don't know if she might have talked to the person or persons who eliminated our team, before she died."

Van Groot smoked for a moment, just thinking.

"Media reports?" he finally asked.

"*Boston Globe*'s reporting it as a robbery gone wrong. They're saying that three foreign assailants, who are yet to be identified due to the absence of fingerprints, apparently used their weapons on each other."

"Nonsense," Van Groot said.

"Of course."

Van Groot waved Nabuto off. Quickly, he turned to Ziar, Bilad, and Shafik, shook their hands, then faced Amir and did the same. He rose from his chair.

"I am afraid I have to take my leave, gentlemen," he said. "I have an emergency that requires me to take some time off."

Both Ziar and Amir rose in respect as Van Groot made to depart, but Bilad and Shafik stayed seated, glanced at each other, then eyed Van Groot suspiciously.

"We'll be able to continue our current arrangement, though?" Amir said. He looked worried.

"Naturally," Van Groot replied. "I would never leave such good clients in the lurch."

He walked away, joined up with Nabuto, and left the airfield.

Two hours later, Nabuto arrived at a small village called Silwar, in the mountains sixteen kilometers west of Bagram. Almost all the mud and stone buildings had been wrecked and abandoned, because Silwar had once been a Taliban stronghold and had been repeatedly gunned and rocketed by American A-10 Warthog fighter planes. But one house on the highest hill was standing, virtually intact. Its rough brick walls were washed in pale blue, its front door was the traditional Islamic green, and its roof was thatched and perfect.

Nabuto pulled up along the rocky, twisting access road in a tan Humvee, parked, and got out. The house was guarded on all four corners by some of Van Groot's most trusted men—former Selous Scouts wearing camouflage tunics, cargo trousers, and boots, hefting M4 rifles and ammunition carriers, and all wearing green-and-black *shemags* wrapped around their bearded faces. One tipped a finger at his brow in salute, and Nabuto nodded and went up the stone stairs and inside.

The house looked empty and clean, but many Afghan homes held little in the way of furniture, and instead had colorful carpets and comfortable pillows arranged along all the walls. Another guard was posted in the salon, and Nabuto passed him and walked to the rear of the house.

The back room was also large and essentially empty, except for some unusual furnishings and equipment. The large missile crate that had been delivered by Van Groot to Kandahar sat open against one wall. There was no Exocet missile anywhere in sight—instead, the crate was lined with soundproof quilted material, a small pillow, a large oxygen tank, and a regulator lying on its side.

On the far wall at the back a huge flat-screen was mounted, powered by a humming gasoline generator that was blimped to keep it quiet. The flat-screen displayed a curious bucolic landscape of rolling, lush green mountains, a clear silver river running from left to right, and flocks of birds winging in a blue sky with cottony clouds. Nothing else moved in the scene—there were no vehicles, people, sheep, or horses—but it looked like a peaceful valley at the foot of the Alps somewhere in Europe.

Spencer was sitting in front of the flat-screen in a wooden armchair, facing a small video camera on a tripod ten feet in front of him. He was dressed in fresh jeans and a plaid woolen shirt, and though his red hair had been washed and combed, his face still displayed dark bruises. He was also barefoot. His wrists were roped to the chair arms, his ankles to the wooden legs, and his chest was roped to the chair back.

"Good afternoon, Mr. Riley," Nabuto said.

"Kiss my ass," Spencer said.

Nabuto smiled. "I'm afraid that's not possible in your current position."

He walked over to Spencer, looked down, and grasped the fingers of Spencer's left hand. Spencer tensed, expecting Nabuto to snap one of them and break it, but the big African simply examined his ring finger, peering at it carefully. He ran his fingertips over the flesh between Spencer's two knuckles.

"You are wise not to wear your wedding ring," Nabuto said. "It's the sign of a professional. I do the same."

He examined the finger further, feeling for that slight indentation and the faded evidence of where the sun never bled through the metal band. He released the finger, looked into Spencer's eyes, and smiled.

"Maybe your government doesn't care about you, Mr. Riley," he said. "But your wife will . . . if you're lucky."

THIRTY-TWO

THE CIA BLACK SITE WAS AT THE END OF A SIX-MILE road that wound away from the small town of Allendale.

The paved two-way lane was lined on both sides by thick green forests, but since it led to nowhere on any map, there was little traffic. At the end was a turnoff, a small sign that said GOVERNMENT INSTALLATION: NO TRESPASSERS, then another half-mile road that arrived at a perimeter fence and an iron gate. A guard booth beside the gate held three CIA security men wearing body armor and carrying M4 rifles. Beyond them was a structure that looked like the top half of a flying saucer, but it was covered in topsoil and thick, weedy grass, with a single steel entrance door that led underground.

From the air, it would look like these men were guarding a golf course green.

Inside the black site was a facility similar to the Black Box headquarters ship—much smaller, but with matching support systems. There were active intelligence, research, analysis, and armory shops; two barracks rooms for agents, security, and support staff; a small kitchen; and a dayroom. A long corridor ran from the entrance to the back of the site, at the end of which were two holding cells on each side for "national security guests," and finally an observation and admin room. An air-conditioning system drew fresh air from the forest outside, and the entire facility smelled like a mixture of sweat and pine.

Ando was sitting at the black site commander's steel desk in front of two large flat-screens, drinking from a coffee mug with a

CIA seal. Thane, Kali, Neveah, and Jason were arranged in front of him, in custom chairs with fold-down worktables that resembled airline seats. Two CIA security personnel, a man and a woman, sat at a pair of desks in a far corner, watching four smaller monitors providing interior views of the site's four cells.

"Lucas . . . van . . . Groot."

Ando stretched out the name as if he were speaking of Dracula. He was scrolling through fresh intelligence on the computer in front of him, and seemed anything but pleased to be there. Ando didn't like leaving the Black Box ship, but once in a while even he had to come in from the cold and meet with his CIA superiors. He had an office at Langley, but he preferred the black site over the hustle and bustle of headquarters.

"So far, nothing on him," he said. "No criminal history, no arrests in South Africa or anywhere else, no known criminal associates. He actually donates substantial sums to select charity organizations. On the surface he's clean as a missionary."

Thane and his crew all had their laptops open, looking at screens that mirrored Ando's intel file.

"Not a single link to questionable stock trades through Dextor Import-Exports either," Jason said. "As a matter of fact, no trades at all except for a few environmental start-ups."

"Not even a traffic ticket," Neveah said. "He's like Mother Teresa."

"I'll bet if we had the South African cops raid his place in Pretoria," Thane, seeing through the facade, said sarcastically, "they'd find nothing but bibles and Beanie Babies."

"Believe me," Kali said as he squinted at his screen, "he's a killer."

Neveah looked over at Kali, but he didn't notice, because he was reading the intel file intensely. They'd all read his detailed after-action review following his killing of Van Groot's three men, and their murder of Nora Leiter, but as always after such incidents, his demeanor was placid as a wading pool.

"Scroll down," Ando said. "Some background intel's flowing in from the ship."

Everyone scrolled down their laptop screen, while Ando read the report aloud.

"Forty-eight years old, an only child. Former Selous Scout, rank of full colonel. Father was a hardnose cop, confirmed apartheid supporter. Mother was—" Ando paused. "This is interesting. She was a former prostitute."

"Maybe she was one of dad's arrests," Jason suggested with a smirk. "Trophy wife, in the literal sense."

Neveah didn't react or look at him. They'd become experts at utilizing their Black Box skills to ignore one another personally while at work.

"Apparently from this," Thane said, "the father treated Van Groot like dirt. Look at this school psych report."

All of them perused the next paragraph.

"Abused kid," Kali said. "Regular beatings, locked in the basement. Even hospitalized twice. Mother apparently had no influence."

"That could explain a lot," Neveah remarked. Her minor in college had been psychotherapy. "Sins of the father, and so forth . . ."

"Yes," Kali said, "but look at his military record. Operations all over Africa, multiple combat and valor medals, and no disciplinary actions."

"The African killing fields," Thane said. "Makes for a fine finishing school if you're getting into the business of hostage-taking and murder."

"There's not a single shred of evidence of any of that," Ando said in disgust as he slapped his hands on the desk. "Comes out of the service, opens an import-export firm, gets rich, and lives the life of Riley." It was an older-generation expression that meant living in the lap of luxury, but they all fell silent for a moment—everyone knew that Riley was Spencer's cover name. Ando ignored his unintentional gaffe and went on.

"By the way, Mr. Kent," he said, breaking the momentary somber mood. "What is the status on that item of DARPA Lincoln Lab microtechnology?"

"It was actually two items, sir," Kali said. "The chip and a partial antenna. I had them couriered this morning to Science and Technology." Kali meant the CIA's "Q Branch" down at Langley. Black Box agents rarely visited headquarters. For deliveries of hard-copy files, gear, or materials, they used specialized couriers.

"Very good," Ando said. "Did you follow up to get an initial assessment?"

"I got shrugs over the phone, sir. Chief engineer said something like, 'How am I supposed to reverse-engineer and develop a counter-countermeasure for a countermeasure that doesn't exist yet?'"

"Cynical," Thane commented, "but the man has a point."

A secure telephone buzzed on Ando's desk. He picked up, answered with his name, and listened for a moment.

"You've got to be kidding me," he finally said. "Are you sure about that?"

Everyone just watched him.

"When?" Ando said into the phone, then, "All right, feed it to me." He put the phone down and looked at his team. "You're not going to believe this. Open Source Media on the ship just picked up an interview with the BBC in Barbados. It was Van Groot, talking about some water-resource charity effort!"

"No *way*," Jason said.

"Well, it's coming over now," Ando said as he spun around to look at one of the big flat-screens on the wall.

The screen came to life, with an image of a television studio set. There was a large, curving glass desk with a digital map of all the world's continents behind it, with the African continent as the centerpiece and various hot spots outlined in red. Lucas van Groot was sitting on the right, wearing a perfect linen summer suit, a cream silk shirt, and blue tie. Facing him was a tall blond female reporter in a purple pantsuit, who seemed to be gushing with admiration.

"*Please* do tell us more, Mr. Van Groot . . ."

"I firmly believe that those of us who've been so fortunate to be successful must give back wherever and whenever we can," Van Groot was saying with a modest smile. "That is how I was raised."

"Good *Lord*," Neveah whispered.

"And how exactly are you doing that with Dextor Import-Exports, Mr. Van Groot?" the reporter asked in her unctuous tone.

"Well, with the issue of famine encroaching once again throughout Africa," Van Groot said, "we are committing three million euros to improving water resources and access, in particular for remote peoples and tribes."

"Three million euros!" the reporter nearly squealed. "That's quite a generous opening gambit!"

"Oh, I think it's the least we can do," Van Groot said with a self-deprecating shrug. "After all, I am South African born and bred. Charity begins at home, doesn't it?"

"It does *indeed*, sir," the talking head said as she turned to the camera and smiled with a bright white row of veneers. "We should *all* take an example from this man, Mr. Lucas van Groot, who is clearly a rare fellow amongst the world's one-percenters."

She turned and shook Van Groot's hand, and he almost managed a modest blush.

"Thank you, sir, for speaking with us, and for all you're doing," she said.

"It was my pleasure," Van Groot said, and the interview faded away to a commercial.

Ando clicked off the screen and spun back around, facing his team, who, except for Kali, all looked somewhat shocked.

"What the hell does he think he's doing?" Jason said. "Talk about balls."

"The unexpected," Neveah said. "It's a perfect move."

"Think about it for a minute," Thane said. "The man knows somebody's after him, somebody with assets and power. He just lost his island base of operations and knows it was some kind of government job. So, what's the best next move? Hide in plain sight. Make yourself out to be an international environmental crusader and benefactor. Make anyone who comes after you now look like a villain, while you look like a martyr."

"That is precisely his plan, Thane," Ando said. "Perfectly analyzed."

"Yes, just like a Chameleon," Kali stated, as the rest of the group looked at him. He meant that Van Groot was copying their most effective operational technique—transformative camouflage. "But there's something else," Kali added.

"Elaborate, Mr. Kent," said Ando.

"It's a challenge to us. It's a counterintelligence move," Kali said. "Van Groot's assuming his cover is now blown as a result of what happened in Marblehead. He can't be certain that his name was revealed, but he's smart to make that assumption. So, while he knows that whoever is hunting him has no proof of anything criminal he's done, he's drawing us into the light."

"He wants to find out who's tracking him," Neveah said.

"Exactly," Kali said.

Thane looked over at Kali. "I say let's counter his countermove. I say he wants to see who we are, so let's show him."

All of the Black Box team turned to Ando for his reaction. Ando nodded.

"Off to Barbados," he said. "If he's still there . . ."

THIRTY-THREE

BARBADOS, CARIBBEAN SEA

THERE WERE MANY BEAUTIFUL LUXURY HOTELS ON the island of Barbados, but the Fairmont Royal Pavilion was no less than spectacular.

Sprawled across half a mile of beachfront property on the western coast, its long, twin, two-story structures provided each five-star suite with breathtaking views of the dazzling azure ocean and pristine sands. Towering palm trees shaded the hotel's pools, handsome servants carried tropical drinks on silver trays, and rainbow-colored parrots squawked in the trees. The Fairmont was favored by the international singing sensation Rihanna, a Bajan native, giving the property its highest endorsement.

Lucas van Groot arrived from a meeting in the capital, Bridgetown, as the sun was setting. His appearance on the Barbados Public Broadcast Service had drawn attention from government officials, and he'd been asked to consult on an ongoing effort to improve the island's freshwater resources. He'd happily complied—further enhancement of his charitable reputation could only fortify his cover.

He was driving a rented silver blue Lamborghini Huracán convertible, which he couldn't push anywhere near its top speed on the narrow left-hand-drive roads. But the speed didn't matter—only the impression. He was coming over to the Fairmont for a dinner date with the fawning TV journalist, Samantha Winston. He'd clearly made an impression on the reporter, and she'd contacted him with the demure invitation. The car would enthrall her even more after dinner, when he planned to take her for a nighttime drive.

Van Groot's growling Lamborghini was led by a black Mercedes

SUV in front, and one in back, each holding two of his security men—for a man of his stature such precautions would be expected. The small convoy drove across the Fairmont's access bridge and onto a circular drive to its impressive lobby entrance of flamingo-colored archways. A parking valet appeared right away and hustled toward Van Groot's sports car. She was slim, Bajan, and beautiful, wearing a tight, pink, short-skirted suit. She hurriedly opened Van Groot's door.

"Good evening, good sir," she said in a lilting Bajan accent as he exited the car. She handed him a parking card. "Dining with us this evening?"

"I am indeed," Van Groot said. He was wearing a cream linen suit with a blue silk shirt open to his tanned throat. He handed her the car fob as he wolfishly looked her over. "Perhaps later you'd fancy a ride . . ."

Before he could finish his sentence, the valet jumped in the driver's seat and drove away.

Van Groot watched her go, thinking the girl would be a seductive challenge if things didn't work out with Samantha Winston. Then he strode off toward the airy lobby, while two of his security men discreetly followed. The other two parked their own cars.

"The Palm Terrace, please," Van Groot said to an impeccably dressed doorman who graciously opened the glass front door.

"Right along here, sir," the Bajan said, and he escorted Van Groot to the left and into a spacious, sprawling restaurant. Its walls were all graceful pink arches, its high ceilings made of woven rattan, and large twirling, hanging fans provided a mild breeze.

There were no windows—everything was open to the nearby sea and starry sky. All the tables were finely dressed in white linen with plush, thick blue armchairs, and shelves of liquor decanters were backlit in royal blue behind the long bar. A maître d' approached Van Groot with a tablet.

"Dinner this evening, sir?"

"Yes, I believe the reservation is under Samantha Winston."

"Right along here, sir."

The maître d' led Van Groot to an oceanfront table. He chose a seat with his back to the sea, giving him a view of the entire establishment. One of his security men walked to the bar and pulled out a stool in the middle. The other stayed in the lobby watching the arrivals. Guests were flowing inside for dinner, and the room was full of soft banter, clinking silverware, and toasting wineglasses.

"May we get you a drink now, sir?" the maître d' asked.

"No thanks, mate. I'll wait for my partner."

The maître d' bowed and left.

Ten minutes passed. Van Groot took a few sips from the sparkling water in his glass and looked at his watch. He was always punctual and had to suppress his growing annoyance. He looked at the Palm's entrance to his left and saw no one arriving who resembled Samantha Winston. He took out his cell phone and looked at it—nothing . . .

Kali emerged from the men's room behind the left-hand side of the Palm Terrace bar. He was holding his cell phone to his head, walking slowly, and using the cell to cover his muted conversation with the team.

Thane had contacted an Aberration agent named Andre, on permanent station in Barbados. He'd instructed Andre to pose as a Bajan agent of the Financial Intelligence Unit, a branch of the Anti–Money Laundering Authority. Andre had then found Samantha Winston at the broadcasting studios and asked her to arrange the dinner invitation with Lucas van Groot—with gratitude from the Bajan government. Kali would take her place.

Thane was now sitting in a rental car just outside the Fairmont property. Jason was perched at the right-hand corner of the bar, wearing a pair of fashionable Prada glasses and also using his cell phone as cover. Van Groot's security man was seated at the center, his back turned to the bar as he watched his principal and sipped sparkling water. Neveah was there somewhere as well, but only as a whispered voice in Kali's earpiece.

There were no other Black Box agents on station for the mission, and none of Pacenza's Package. The team was engaged in a heated discussion they'd been having over the past two days, about how much Kali should reveal to Van Groot. Neveah was voicing her objections.

"I hate to sound like a broken record, but this is going to screw Spencer," Neveah said in Kali's ear. "I looked at all the data and analytics like you told me to, Thane. The minute we reveal you're with a government agency, it'll put Spencer's life in further danger."

"NV may be right on this, Kali," Jason murmured into his cell. "We know what could happen. Once Van Groot knows, there's no turning back."

"Spencer's already under intense pressure somewhere," Kali countered. "If he isn't already dead . . ."

"This is all we *have*, people," Thane said, making the final decision. "I don't want to hear any more of it. We have to do this."

They'd all agreed that the dinner's objective was to put Van Groot on notice, apply pressure, get him off balance. But more than that, they wanted to be able to track him. Andre had confirmed that Van Groot's private jet at Grantley Adams International Airport did not have a Brainwave antenna attached—the man wasn't stupid. Instead, Science and Technology at Langley had provided the team with a prototype device. It was a small, transparent patch of microencapsulated cells, stuck to the inside of Kali's right palm. Squeezing Van Groot's palm in a handshake would burst the tiny capsules and embed Van Groot's skin with nanoparticles that emitted microwave signals. Even if Van Groot washed his hands, he'd be trackable by a CIA satellite for at least one week.

Kali would just have to strike a careful balance between deadly and friendly . . .

Van Groot was just about to give up and leave when his eye caught a man approaching his table from the right. The tall Black man was dressed in a blue linen suit as fine as Van Groot's. He stopped directly opposite Van Groot and looked down at him.

"It looks like your date stood you up, Mr. Van Groot," said Kali. "Mind if I join you?"

Over at the bar, Van Groot's bodyguard started to rise from his stool. Jason's hand moved toward the Glock under his jacket . . .

Van Groot squinted up at Kali, but he didn't say anything. He just opened a palm toward the opposite chair. Kali nodded, pulled it out, and sat down.

Van Groot's bodyguard settled back onto his stool, and so did Jason. The maître d' appeared at the table again, looking embarrassed and frustrated.

"I am sorry, sir," he said to Van Groot as he looked again at his tablet. "I believe you were waiting for a Ms. Samantha—"

"No, it's quite all right, my friend," Van Groot said.

"It's actually Sam, not Samantha," Kali said to the maître d'. "Must have been a booking error."

"Yes, of course," the maître d' said, relieved. "Drinks then, gentlemen?"

"I'll have a gin and tonic," Van Groot said. "Tanqueray, with a twist."

"Sounds like a taste of summer," Kali said. "I'll have the same."

The maître d' left a pair of menus on the table, along with a wine list, and walked away.

Neither man spoke for a minute. They looked at each other like mountain cats of different species, suddenly locked in the same cage.

"So, to what do I owe this pleasure, mate?" Van Groot finally said.

"I thought it was time to get acquainted," Kali said. He considered offering Van Groot a handshake, but it would be too obvious and too early.

"Are we old school chums?" Van Groot tilted his head. "No, you're too young, and your face isn't familiar."

"We're in the same business," Kali said. "At opposite ends of the spectrum."

"I see." Van Groot nodded slowly.

The maître d' returned with the drinks, accompanied by a waiter. "Have you gentlemen decided what you'll be having?" he asked.

"Not yet, mate," Van Groot said without taking his eyes off Kali. "We're just catching up."

The two servers withdrew. Van Groot reached across the table, took Kali's gin and tonic, pushed his drink across the table to Kali, and smiled.

"Cheers," he said, taking a long sip. Kali did the same.

At the bar, Jason casually turned his head so he could see Kali's right hand. The Prada glasses had digital lenses sensitive to microwave transmissions. He could see the nanoparticles in Kali's palm patch, turning from green to yellow.

"We've got about another two minutes," he murmured.

"So, you're a government stiff of some sort." Van Groot smirked at Kali. "US, I assume."

"Not stiff. Extremely flexible."

"Well, let's see, mate . . ." Van Groot perused the rattan ceiling. "Can't be DEA, because those blokes can't work overseas unless it's a drug-related matter. NSA stays in their nerd hooches. FBI's domestic, unless I happen to be wanted on an international basis, which I'm not." He looked back at Kali and smiled. "That leaves only Langley, the purveyors of illegal coups the world over."

"We do other things on occasion," Kali said, confirming Van Groot's CIA guess without actually saying it.

"Ahh, the men who killed JFK." Van Groot sneered.

"You read to me as too smart for conspiracy theories, Lucas."

Van Groot took another swig of his drink.

"I see we're on a first-name basis," he said. "What's yours, or the cover name you're using today?"

"Abasi."

"African. It's a respectable name."

"I'm a respectable man," Kali said.

Van Groot leaned closer, his green eyes gleaming. "You're also out of your league, Abasi. You've got nothing on me. Both you and I know that's the reason you're here."

Kali leaned forward as well. "And why are you here, Lucas? Out in the open?"

"I just wanted to see who was interested in me."

"I'm interested," Kali said. "And I've got more than enough on you, more than you can imagine."

Van Groot laughed and sat back again, appearing fully relaxed.

"Ah, the lies of the spies," he said. "So bloody obvious. The only one here who's holding anything of value is *me*, Abasi."

He stared fully at Kali. They both knew what he meant—Spencer. But Kali showed nothing in his expression.

"That item of value should be carefully guarded," Kali said. "Its loss could result in kinetic action."

"Ah, so you're threatening me?"

"Let's call it a guarantee."

Thane whispered quickly in Kali's ear. "Move this along, wrap it up. Get the *handshake now*."

Van Groot nodded, then swirled his glass slowly. The ice clinked.

"I should tell you that I was raised in a threatening environment. Such things don't faze me."

"Not even the sins of the father?" Kali asked.

Van Groot raised a thick blond eyebrow. "You've done your homework. I suspect that your father might have been similar. That's what often drives us."

"My father had numerous faults," Kali said. "But child abuse wasn't one of them."

Van Groot's expression darkened, but he stayed cool. "Is he proud of your current employment?" he asked.

"If I could tell him what I do, I'm sure he would be."

"A man happy that his son deceives people for a living," Van Groot scoffed. "I think we're both the products of fatherly sins."

"I'd like to think redemption," Kali said. "But you're something different, Lucas."

Van Groot fixed Kali again with his sniper's glare. He'd clearly had enough already.

"Well, this has been interesting," he said. "But if I see you again, Abasi, it won't be so pleasant."

"That implication works both ways," Kali said.

The waiter appeared by the table again. "May I take your orders now, gentlemen?"

"I'm afraid this just isn't my menu," Van Groot said. He fished in his pocket, peeled off some bills, and handed them to the waiter. "Perhaps my friend here still has an appetite."

The waiter murmured "Thank you" as he stood there fidgeting. Van Groot pushed away from the table and got up. Kali rose too, smiled slightly, and extended his hand.

"Good talk, Lucas," he said sarcastically. "Let's do it again sometime soon."

Van Groot looked at Kali's hand.

Jason, still surreptitiously watching, saw the nanoparticles turn from yellow to red. "Shake the damn *hand*," he whispered through gritted teeth. "Come on, shake the damn *hand*."

Van Groot said to Kali, "Don't call me, *mate*. I'll call you."

He left Kali's empty hand in the air, then turned and exited the restaurant. His security man left the bar and followed.

"Shit," Jason whispered.

Kali sat back down and ordered a glazed shrimp salad, then the waiter trotted away.

"Dark Horse One, here," Kali murmured. "He wouldn't shake my hand."

"*Dammit*," Thane said in his ear . . .

Outside the lobby, Van Groot's two men called for their security cars through their earpieces. The beautiful valet appeared again. When she turned toward Van Groot, it was actually Neveah. She smiled at Van Groot and recovered his parking card. He looked her over.

"I don't suppose you're getting off duty soon?" he said charmingly. "I've decided to have dinner elsewhere."

"Oh, I would *love* to, mister." She beamed. "But you know, a girl has to earn her keep. I'll be back with your steed in a minute."

She sauntered off into the parking area, and soon returned with Van Groot's Lamborghini. He looked at her long, fine legs as she exited the car, then handed her a substantial tip.

"Thank you so much!" Neveah said, as she touched her chest. She then reached out for his hand. He took her hand in his and squeezed, then lifted it to his lips and kissed the back of it.

"Some other time then, beauty." Van Groot slipped into the Lamborghini. Neveah shut the door and waved as he roared away through the palm trees, braced front and back by the black Mercedes SUVs.

Her smile faded as she slipped the bills into her suit jacket pocket, then spoke into her earpiece.

"NV for Black Box One," Neveah said. "He didn't shake your hand, Kali . . . but he shook *mine*."

She looked at her hand, where a secondary microencapsulation patch was attached.

Just then Jason emerged from the restaurant. Their eyes locked onto each other, and as Neveah closed the palm of her hand, she stared at him and said, "I still think this was a bad idea . . . It's going to hurt Spencer."

THIRTY-FOUR

THE EASTERN ATLANTIC

AT TWENTY-EIGHT THOUSAND FEET ABOVE THE ocean, the cargo compartment of the C-17 Globemaster transport jet was bone-chillingly cold.

It was an enormous steel cavern, eighty-eight feet long, about the size of three subway cars end to end, but much wider. The four-engine monster could hold 102 jump-ready paratroopers, or an M1 Abrams tank, or two folded-up Black Hawk helicopters, or three Stryker armored vehicles, or a mixture of combat troops and eighty-five tons of palletized loads. The C-17 was a miracle of modern American aeronautical technology, but its heating system sucked.

Thane, the Black Box team, Pacenza, and sixteen men of the Package were arranged along the aircraft's fold-down web seats, backs against the curving fuselage. They were all wearing heavy arctic sweaters, tactical gloves, desert *shemags* wrapped around their throats, and woolen hats. They had headsets on with short boom mics, plugged into the aircraft's comm system, but none of them were feeling chatty.

The air force jet had staged at Hurlburt Field in Florida with the Package already on board, waiting for a signal to launch from Thane and his crew in Barbados. Two long, torturous days had passed while Lucas van Groot lounged by the pool at the Hilton resort on the island. Each hour that ticked by meant that the nanoparticles in his pores were draining down through their single week of effective transmissions, but there was nothing anyone could do about it.

And Van Groot, being no fool, assumed he was being observed by "Abasi" and his US government comrades.

But at last, he'd summoned his private pilots and told them to prepare his Falcon. Andre, the Aberration agent, was lying in the tall grass outside the international airport's perimeter for two days and nights with a pair of night-vision binoculars. He thanked heaven when at last he witnessed the Falcon being rolled out from a hangar, and contacted Thane, who gave the order to Pacenza to launch from Florida. That evening, as Van Groot took off in his jet with his security team, the C-17 had landed, picked up Thane, Kali, Jason, and Neveah, and the chase across the ocean had begun.

"I think this whole thing's a cluster," Pacenza said to Thane through his mic. He was leaning back against the bulkhead next to Thane, eyes closed, arms folded. To Pacenza's right was his master sergeant, Sumo, in a similar pose. All of the Package's personal gear and weapons were in a palletized load in front of their boots. The container had cargo parachutes packed on its roof, but it also had skids so it could be unloaded on land.

"Haven't you ever chased a target before, without knowing where he's going?" Thane asked. He had a thick Alienware laptop open on his legs, on which he was tracking the Falcon's course and receiving updates from Ando.

"Only about fifty times," Pacenza said. "And half of those were clusters too."

Pacenza still hadn't fully recovered from losing Shane in Geneva, or having his breacher seriously wounded on Geweer Island. The combat losses in his life had accumulated to the point where he'd begun to wonder if retiring to his farm in West Virginia might be the wisest option. But he still had scores to settle.

"I want this guy's head, Thane," Pacenza said, meaning Lucas van Groot.

"We all do," Thane said. "But we need hard evidence. So far, all we've got is the accusation of a dying woman."

Kali was sitting to Thane's left, also with a laptop open. It was well past midnight, but sleep didn't interest him. There were all sorts of operational options to consider, and he was devising action items, each with alternatives and backups. It was like writing a computer program, using "ifs" and "thens." *If this happens, then we do this . . .*

Running toward the tail from Pacenza's right, his Package men were all slumped in their seats and sleeping—they'd learned long ago to grab Zs whenever the opportunity arose. Past their boots in the cargo hold's center was another palletized load holding all their HALO parachute gear, in case that was how they were going to insert and either rescue Spencer—if he could be located and was still breathing—or take out Van Groot and his minions. All options were on the table, the only problem being that no one had any idea what Van Groot was going to do next, or where he might go.

Past the palletized loads, farther toward the cargo ramp, three Ranger Special Operations Vehicles, or RSOVs, were tied down with vibrating web straps. They were manufactured by Range Rover and looked like the old desert combat vehicles of World War II, with mounts for heavy machine guns, grenade launchers, and steel jerricans full of water or extra fuel.

Jason and Neveah sat across the fuselage on the other side, but not next to each other. They always tried to arrange their seating so that they couldn't look at one another. The wrong glance, witnessed by the wrong person, could give them away.

Jason was working on a laptop linked by secure SATCOM to the Intel Tank on the Black Box ship. He was urging the analysts to scour all sources for anything related to a man named Nabuto—the only name they'd gotten out of Fabio. But there were thirty-seven such identifiers tagged for combat-hardened individuals all across Africa, and Jason rightly suspected that it wasn't his actual name. Neveah was studying a book on special operations raids and hostage rescues, penned by Admiral William McRaven. Her focus was rescuing Spencer, and she was researching all the techniques that might prove useful in his case. As a Ghost, she was calculating the options of somehow getting in close and performing crucial reconnaissance.

"What's the status, Overwatch?" Ando's voice said in Thane's and Kali's headsets. Kali answered for Thane.

"Overwatch is working, sir," Kali said as he looked over at Thane's laptop. "Target's going to go feet dry over Europe in thirty mikes."

"Did he file a flight plan out of Barbados?" Ando asked.

"He did, according to Andre," Kali said. The Aberration agent had gone into Flight Operations at the Barbados airport after Van Groot left and had sneaked a look at the manifests. "He filed for Marseille, but that doesn't mean he'll stick to it. He might have his pilots change route and report the diversion later."

"That's what I'd do," Thane murmured. He was half listening and half working.

"Sir," Kali said to Ando. "I know this is delicate, but we need Mr. Gibson to pressure his federal financial investigators. If Van Groot's past activities are an indicator, he's going to make another move. We need to know about any recent heavy stock activities, worldwide."

"All right, Mr. Kent," Ando said with an audible sigh. "I'll stick my head in that noose one more time."

"Thank you," Kali said. "And one more thing."

"Go ahead, Kent."

"What's the status on the countermeasures for Brainwave?"

"I was just about to get to that," Ando said. "Science and Tech says it's the most technologically advanced thing they've seen in years. Could take them months to unravel it."

"Would be good if they'd move faster," Jason chimed in from across the way.

Ando ignored his comment and continued.

"They also discovered a significant connection, using intel supplied by our shop, between this fellow Nabuto and a computer engineer in Nigeria. Taking Brainwave operational would require some genius talent."

"Please tell me they were able to get us a real name, sir," Kali said. "Not some encrypted cover like Orca or Nabuto."

"Affirmative. They pulled his real name after running some decryption algorithms." Ando held up a photo of a middle-aged Nigerian man with two unique tribal markings under his right eye. "The man's name is Adejare Zabu."

Kali said nothing, as suddenly his voice was paralyzed. Hearing that name and seeing the unique tribal markings from a past once lived froze him in his seat like an ice sculpture. *Adejare Zabu.* The name of his best childhood friend, Jare! He hadn't seen Jare in decades, yet already at eight years old the boy had been a computer and mechanical prodigy. *No*, he thought desperately, *this can't be . . .* As Ando looked on, awaiting some sort of reaction, Kali found his voice again.

"Copy that, sir," Kali said. "Adejare Zabu."

"Correct. Images will be coming your way shortly," Ando said, then addressed Thane. "Thane, your team might want to pay this fellow Zabu a visit."

"Thinking the same thing, boss," Thane said.

"Okay people," Ando said. "Stay on Van Groot's tail, and don't lose him."

"Will do, sir," Kali answered robotically.

"Keep me informed." Ando clicked off.

Thane looked over at Kali, then glanced down at Kali's list of options and countermoves.

"What's your best guess?" he asked.

Kali quickly recovered from the shock of Ando's news.

"If Van Groot really does have Spencer he's not going to wherever he's holding him," he said. "He's not that stupid."

"Agreed."

"And we'll only have tracking capability on those nanoparticles for another five days," Kali said. "If he lands somewhere and decides to go to a party or hang out in some fancy hotel, he'll just be running out the clock and we might lose him before he takes off for his final destination."

"Well, if he lands, then we'll have to land too, but not on the same strip," Thane said. "We can't just fly around and air-refuel until he makes the next move."

"Right," Kali said. "I told the pilot in command to plan on Sigonella." It was an American naval airstrip in Sicily, with rapid access to both Europe and North Africa.

"Best move, I suppose," Thane said.

Kali nodded and leaned his head back on the bulkhead. Between the two palletized loads, he could see Neveah ensconced in her reading. For a moment she looked up and spotted his eyes across the fuselage, but then went back to her book. She hadn't approved of any of these tactics, for Spencer's sake, but Kali had unemotionally run the options over and over again in his mind. It was either do their best to rescue Spencer, or leave him to die at the hands of Van Groot, or worse. They had destroyed Van Groot's island headquarters, but maybe he had another secret location somewhere. The idea of Spencer spending years in some hole until he withered away and died was no option either. Death would be preferable.

"Sometimes there are no good options," Kali said to himself, and at last he tried to sleep. But his childhood with Jare kept flooding his mind, and sleep was elusive . . .

THIRTY-FIVE

GENESIS

The boys were hiding out in the cabana way past the farthest end of the pool. It was made of thick bamboo poles and a thatched roof, with a teakwood door. It sat in the lush grass in the shade of tall palms and was used only for storage. There were rows of lounge chairs and cushions inside, plastic floats for the pool and chemicals for its buzzing filter. Sunlight stabbed through the cracks in the bamboo.

Jare sensed Kali was avoiding his mother, so that she wouldn't be able to find him and make him do chores. But in truth, Kali had received his report card that morning at school. All his grades were perfect, except mathematics, for which he'd received a 79. It was an unacceptable grade and Kali knew it. Nigerian culture strongly emphasized education and no good parent would stand for such laziness.

Kali knew he was in trouble. So instead, he was focused on *Tetris*, the game he and Jare were playing on the Game Boy that Jare kept alive for Kali with his magical fingers and tools.

"I am going to beat your score!" Kali said breathlessly as he sat on the cabana's tiled floor, legs crossed, bent over, fingers flying as he played.

"*No one* ever beats my score," Jare hissed at Kali as he squatted behind him and peered over his shoulder. "No one at school, no one at boys' club, not even the chess nerds!"

"Shh! I am going to do it! Watch me!"

"Never!" Jare wailed with a grin, as he really wanted Kali to be able to do it.

"Here it comes . . . ," Kali whispered intently. "Just one more . . ."

The colored squares were appearing so fast now on the small Game

Boy screen that Kali was sweating. Added to that the heat of the baking cabana, and his printed short-sleeved shirt and shorts were soggy. His report card was stuffed in his shorts' side pocket and that was probably soaking wet now too.

The Game Boy dinged; Kali jumped up from the floor and leaped into the air like Muhammad Ali after a title fight in New York City.

"I did it!" he yelled as he spun and jumped and waved the Game Boy over his head. "Five thousand points! I am the king!"

"You did!" Jare joined in, jumping up and down too. "I can't believe it!"

The door to the cabana flew open. Both boys stopped jumping and stared. Yvonne Adeyemi was standing there with her fists on her hips, looking furious.

"Kalief," she said. "What are you doing?"

Kali swallowed. The boys were eight years old now, and taller, but Yvonne still towered over them.

"We were just, um, playing a game, Mom," Kali stammered.

"I just spoke to your teacher." She stuck out a hand, palm up. "Where is it?"

Kali bent his head and fished in his side pocket. There was no hiding anything from his mother. He handed her the soggy report card.

She looked at it and her eyes grew dark and furious. "Come with me," she said. "And you too, Jare."

The boys followed her out to the pool patio. The sun was starting to set and the air was cooler. Jare was supposed to stay for dinner, but Kali sensed that wouldn't be happening now. She spun on both boys.

"Do you think your education is a game, Kalief?" she demanded.

"No, Mom."

"Do you know what happens to boys who fail their subjects?"

"I . . . I didn't fail, Mom. I know it's not a good grade, but look at the other ones . . ."

"And *you*, Jare." She turned to him and he took a step backward. "Don't you care about your best friend's future?"

"I, well, of course, Mrs. Adeyemi."

She jabbed a finger at Jare's frightened face. "You will tutor him,

Jare. You will make sure this never happens again, if you want to keep coming over here to play. Do you understand?"

"Yes, ma'am," Jare whispered.

None of them really noticed that George had arrived in his Bentley and had driven it around to the back toward his garage. But he'd coasted to a stop and heard the exchange through his open window. He was exiting the shiny car and said with a smirk, "She really meant to say 'please,' Jare."

Kali was relieved for once to have his father intervene. When it came to schoolwork, his mom was scarier.

"Don't make a joke of this, George," Yvonne snapped as she handed her husband the report card.

He looked at it, nodded, and said, "I'll take care of this, Yvonne."

She huffed and stormed off toward the house. Kali noticed she was carrying her big wooden soup ladle and was glad she hadn't smacked him with it.

George smiled down at the boys. He ruffled both their heads. He seemed very happy to Kali today.

"You men better step up your game, and I don't mean *Tetris.*"

Kali smiled with relief at his father. "I will, Dad. Promise."

"I'll help him, Mr. Adeyemi," Jare said.

"I know you will, Jare," George said. "You're a good friend."

Jare grinned. He always felt such pride whenever Mr. Adeyemi praised him.

"Now, Jare," George said. "I think you'd better run along home. Dinner might not be so pleasant tonight."

Kali cringed, but he knew his father was right. Mom would have a lot more to say and Jare wouldn't enjoy it.

"Okay, Mr. Adeyemi." Jare started to walk away.

"Just one moment." George fished in his suit pants pocket. "I borrowed some money from your mom the other day for cigarettes. Please give this to her and thank her."

He handed Jare a hundred-dollar bill. Jare stared at it. He knew Mr. Adeyemi was lying, but it was sort of a game they played. They were both the secret guardians of his mother's pride.

"Thanks, Mr. Adeyemi. I'll tell her." Jare started walking away, then turned once more and grinned at Kali. "See ya later, champ."

"See ya." Kali waved.

Jare walked off down the side driveway, and George turned back to Kali. He saw that his son was still gleaming with sweat, which he knew was more from his mother than the waning heat of the day. He took out a handkerchief, bent down, and gently wiped Kali's face with it.

"Thanks, Dad," Kali said. "Sometimes she *scares* me."

"Well, you'd better improve that grade. But today I want you to be happy, because today is a day to celebrate."

Kali presented a curious smile. "Celebrate?"

"Yes, my son. Our island is almost finished, Kalief." The words coming out of George's mouth gave him great pleasure. Only months before he'd nearly given up on his dreams of Pearland, but he had decided to ignore the threats, defy the consortium, and push through. "I just came from there. The parks are going to open, with all the things you and Jare love to play on. The big buildings and shops are almost complete and people are reserving apartments and storefronts. They're going to be very fancy, but there are also going to be places for the less fortunate folks of Lagos. There is going to be a ribbon-cutting ceremony soon. You're going to love it."

"I can't wait, Dad!" Kali jumped and hugged his father's waist.

George took off his nice straw hat, the one with the purple band. He wiped his brow with the same handkerchief and Kali saw that his father's eyes were gleaming. His dad never wept over anything, but maybe Pearland was making him that happy. George slipped his big hand around Kali's small shoulders and began walking him toward the back of the house.

"I did it with you, Kalief. I did it with your mother. I was able to do it because of how much I love you both, and how much you love me too."

They walked off into the house, for a dinner that Kali knew wasn't going to be much fun.

But he didn't care. He was happy.

THIRTY-SIX

SILWAR, AFGHANISTAN

THERE WAS THUNDER IN THE HILLS AND VALLEYS, BUT it didn't wake Spencer. It was nighttime and dark in the back room of the village's highest hillside house, except for the occasional flash of lightning. Spencer was still strapped to his chair, wrists and ankles rubbed raw and his knee still terribly swollen. Exhausted, his chin resting on his chest, he slept in jerky fits of bad dreams.

A light flicked on, bathing Spencer's prison in glaring yellow. Nabuto walked in from another room. He had a pistol locked in his thigh holster and a cell phone in one hand. He looked at a secure text from Van Groot and smirked.

Wake him up, the text instructed. But be extra nice.

Nabuto knew what that meant. He walked up to Spencer, cocked his right hand back, and slapped his face so hard that had Spencer been awake the blow might have knocked him out. Spencer gasped from the slap, then moaned as the pain shot through his cheek. His eyes fluttered open and he raised his head, grimacing with his cracked, dried lips.

Is he awake now? Van Groot texted again.

Very much so, Nabuto texted back.

Good. Deafen him while I debrief you.

Nabuto walked over to a metal cabinet, extracted a pair of noise-canceling headphones, went back to Spencer, and jammed them onto his head. Just for good measure, he tapped a button above one earpiece and the headphones roared AC/DC's "Hells Bells" in Spencer's ears. He rolled his eyes, then shut them hard.

All clear, Nabuto texted Van Groot. A moment later, his secure Signal channel buzzed.

"Go ahead, VG," Nabuto said into his cell.

"I had an interesting meeting with one of Mr. Riley's colleagues," Van Groot said, referring to Spencer, who was still maintaining his DoE cover. "They're CIA."

"Why the hell would they show that card, VG?" Nabuto asked.

"They think they can scare me, mate," Van Groot scoffed.

"Then they don't know their customer, do they? Did you get it all on tape?"

"Of course," Van Groot said. "The button works well. Do you have yours ready?"

Nabuto looked down at a button on his safari shirt. It concealed a pinhole digital camera with a Bluetooth feed to his cell. "Affirmative," he said.

"I'm sure they've been tracking my movements," Van Groot went on. "Following our protocol like good little sheepdogs." After each one of Van Groot's hostage and stock market operations, his protocol was to operate out in the open as if he were innocently doing regular business. *Hide in plain sight.* "I've got them chasing me all over Europe."

"Perfect," Nabuto said. "What's the next move?"

"Riley's of no use to us now as a hostage," Van Groot said. "We know who he works for and he's not likely to give anything else up. But we can't get rid of him just yet. His death would be too coincidental right after my Barbados adventure. Let's toy with him for a while. I've got a better idea of how to use him. Where is Amir?"

"Outside, waiting with the Russian."

"Good. Let them wait till we're ready. Let's have a chat with Mr. Riley."

"Roger."

Nabuto yanked the headphones off Spencer's head and dropped them onto a small side table. Then, as Spencer stiffened, Nabuto picked his chair up off the floor, with him in it, and cranked it around to face the large flat-screen on the rear wall. The screen flickered and came to life, and there was Van Groot's full facial image against a white digital background.

"Good evening, Mr. Riley," Van Groot said.

Spencer stared at the screen. His heart rate quickened for a moment, but then he realized Van Groot was somewhere else and couldn't torture him remotely. However, that wouldn't prevent the big African standing next to him from beating him senseless. He just looked at Van Groot and said nothing.

"I've discovered some interesting information," Van Groot said. "I know who you work for, Mr. Riley . . . or whatever your real name is."

Spencer's facial expression registered no change.

"You're an intelligence agent of the CIA." Van Groot smiled and examined Spencer's body language and facial expression, looking for any reactions or tells, but Spencer didn't react. "What *is* your real name?" Van Groot asked.

Van Groot's mention of the agency hitched Spencer's chest, but he assumed the man was just fishing and said nothing. Van Groot nodded at Nabuto, who suddenly cracked his palm across Spencer's face again, whiplashing his head to one side. Spencer grunted, but then just looked up at Nabuto and whispered, "Water."

Nabuto looked at Van Groot, who nodded. Nabuto pulled a plastic water bottle from his side cargo pocket, gripped Spencer's red hair, and spilled a stream into his parched mouth. Spencer swallowed as much as he could while the rest dribbled down his lips and soaked his torn shirt.

"John Riley," Spencer croaked.

Van Groot leaned closer to the camera. His face looked huge.

"Your people don't care about you, *John*," Van Groot said. "Whatever the branch—Clandestine Services, Special Activities Division—they simply don't give a damn, mate. They outed you. They wouldn't waste a single dime to save your bloody hide." He paused to let that much sink in. "You'd be much better off working for *me*."

Spencer didn't believe a word of it. His Black Box training had prepared him thoroughly for all attempts to deceive him or turn him against the agency. He looked at Van Groot and forced a trembling smile. Van Groot sat back and folded his arms.

"Oh, so you think I'm lying," he said. "All right, let's burst your bubble, shall we?"

Van Groot reached out for a device of some sort. The screen suddenly went blank for a moment, and when it flickered back on, there was Kali Kent's face. He appeared to be sitting at a table in some sort of fancy restaurant and looking at someone just above the camera lens. Spencer's guts tightened when he saw Kali, but he just watched in torturous silence.

The first voice was Van Groot's, off-screen.

"NSA stays in their nerd hooches. FBI's domestic, unless I happen to be wanted on an international basis, which I'm not." There was a long pause, and then, "That leaves only Langley, the purveyors of illegal coups the world over."

"We do other things on occasion," Kali said.

The blood started pounding in Spencer's ears. Kali had just admitted to being a CIA agent. *Why on earth?*

"Ahh, the men who killed JFK," Van Groot said off-screen.

"You read to me as too smart for conspiracy theories, Lucas," Kali said with a thin smile. Then the screen went blank again, and Van Groot's face reappeared. His triumphant expression was ugly.

"Believe me *now*, John?" Van Groot said. "You see? Your colleague and I are even on a first-name basis."

"I've never seen that man before in my life," Spencer managed to say, though his heart was pounding in his chest and the sense of betrayal was nearly overpowering. Still, he trusted his Black Box comrades with his life. There had to be a reason for Kali's behavior, some kind of strategy or tactic . . . "No idea who he is," he said. "I told you. I work for the Department of Energy."

Van Groot slowly wagged his head in amazement.

"You really are loyal, John," he said. "You really are special. After your own people turn on you, you're still not breaking. I wish I had more men like you on my side . . . but something tells me you're not open to other employment."

Van Groot looked at Nabuto.

"Let's invite the customers in for an inspection, Nabuto." Even though Spencer was helpless, Van Groot wasn't going to use Nabuto's real name. "Turn the bloke back around, but let's not have him be too chatty."

Nabuto picked up Spencer in his chair again and faced him the other way, with his back to the flat-screen. Then Nabuto took off a sweat-soaked *shemag* that was wrapped around his neck, and stuffed the end of it into Spencer's mouth. Spencer labored to breathe through his nose.

Nabuto went to the door, called out to someone, then stepped back into the room. A moment later, Amir Baradar appeared, along with Vitaly Chok, the Russian general. The two men stood stock still as they stared down at Spencer, with Van Groot's smiling face hovering behind on the screen. Nabuto stepped to one side, turned so his chest was facing only Amir and the Russian, and clicked a recording app on his cell phone.

"Who is he?" Vitaly Chok asked as he stared at Spencer.

"An American CIA agent," Van Groot said.

Amir stared at Spencer, whose eyes were flicking from one man to another. Amir hated the CIA.

"My God," the Russian exclaimed. "You've got an American spy?"

"That's correct, General," Van Groot said. "I don't waste my time on small fish."

Chok looked Spencer over as calculations of his incredible value flashed through his mind. Since the war in Ukraine, the Americans had captured five Russian oligarchs who were close associates of the Russian president. He turned to Amir.

"Do you know what we could do with such a prize?" Chok said to Amir in Russian.

"An exchange, perhaps," Amir said. "He is priceless."

"Moscow could get two for one for a man like this. Maybe three!"

"Perhaps you should propose something, General," Amir said.

Vitaly Chok turned back to Van Groot.

"I will give you ten million dollars for him," he said in English. "No questions asked, no negotiations."

Van Groot raised an eyebrow but said nothing. It was exactly what he wanted. He'd sell off Spencer to Moscow and profit highly from the sale. But first, he'd make certain that sometime soon after the exchange, Spencer would die in Russian hands. That would take a bit of finesse, but he knew he could do it. In the end, his own hands would be clean of Spencer's fate and all the blame would fall on Mother Russia.

"Well, give me some time to think about it," Van Groot said to Chok. "I'll get back to you."

Amir glared at Van Groot. They were about to close a deal to sell Brainwave modules and all sorts of modified combat aircraft to the Russians, and he didn't want Van Groot to endanger that arrangement. Van Groot shot him a nearly indiscernible wink and Amir relaxed somewhat.

"All right," Amir said. "General Chok will hear from you soon about this?"

"Very soon, gentlemen," Van Groot said. "Very soon."

"I'll drive you both back to Kabul in a few minutes," Nabuto said. "Make yourselves comfortable in my vehicle."

Amir and Chok nodded at Van Groot, then walked back through the door and out of the house. Spencer was breathing hard, his face flushed from the filthy *shemag* stuffed into his mouth, but Nabuto ignored him.

"Did you capture all that on video?" Van Groot asked.

Nabuto smiled and tapped the camera button on his chest.

"Indeed I did, VG," he said. "Indeed I did."

THIRTY-SEVEN

KALI STARED AT HIS IMAGE IN THE MEN'S LATRINE mirror. He knew he didn't have much time. The planning session outside in the red-roofed aircraft hangar was nearing its final phase and he had to make a decision.

Van Groot had already landed in Rome in the Falcon. A Black Box Aberration agent on permanent station in Italy was keeping track of him with assistance from satellite surveillance, but two more Ghosts from another team had been sent in by Ando as backup, just to make sure. The nanoparticles embedded in Van Groot's skin were still active, but the clock was ticking. The South African was playing hide-and-seek, and everyone knew it.

The C-17 had set down in Sigonella, where everyone, including the air force crew, had been sequestered in a hangar reserved for special operators. Since Sigonella was a navy base, those personnel were usually SEALs or other naval spec ops forces from NATO. However, Ando was authorized to use any real estate he needed.

Kali examined his own eyes in the mirror. He'd never used his Chameleon techniques before against his own people, but this would have to be an exception. The risks were enormous. He'd gone through multiple, endless, down-drilling security and background checks to get into the program. He'd revealed many things about his childhood in Nigeria, except for childhood friends like Jare, which weren't relevant. However, if it were to come out that he did have a link to Jare, it could mean the end of his career.

He had always done everything by the book, followed every Black Box regulation, no matter the consequences. And he'd always insisted that his teammates also adhere to those rules. If an agent couldn't be trusted to keep his personal and professional life completely separate, he could be a mortal danger to Black Box. Now Kali was about to break his own ironclad oath, but he felt that he had no choice. Nothing else was going to work.

He slipped his prayer bracelet from his trouser pocket and began turning the beads in his fingers. He wasn't going to become someone entirely different. He was simply going to immerse himself in the belief that there was only one way to do this. He was going to lie to his comrades.

He began whispering the lines of an essay by the famous African American poet and novelist James Baldwin.

"All of us know, whether or not we are able to admit it, that mirrors can only lie, that death by drowning is all that awaits one there. It is for this reason that love is so desperately sought and so cunningly avoided. Love takes off the masks that we fear we cannot live without and know we cannot live within."

He placed the beads back into his pocket and walked out into the hangar.

It was a cavern the size of a basketball court, with a concrete floor, corrugated walls, pneumatic hangar doors, and an arching steel girder ceiling. Off in one corner was a V-22 Osprey, looking like some sort of prehistoric flying beast with its engine nacelles and black rotors tilted upward and its cargo ramp down. In the hangar's center was an array of folding tables, with one long row laid out with ten HALO parachute rigs, oxygen-supplied jump helmets, night-vision goggles, and weapons carriers. Two of Pacenza's men, who served double duty as the Package's riggers, were going over every strap, buckle, and grommet to make sure the ram-air parachutes would properly deploy.

On a large square array of two tables pushed together in the center, three surveillance-reconnaissance and SIGINT specialists from Langley were pulling overhead ISR satellite feeds of an area northwest of Lagos, Nigeria, called Kétou, in the middle of the jungle forest of De Dogo. Part of their equipment package was a superwide printer, so they were using the retro method of printing out overhead surveillance photos and maps of the target area, which they'd taped down to the table. Thane, Pacenza, Jason, Neveah, and the men of the Package surrounded the central plotting table. Thane had somehow acquired a long, collapsible antenna, which he was using as a pointer as he tapped various waypoints on the map. Ando was observing the proceedings via a laptop screen set up by the SIGINT people.

"All right, so here's what we've got so far," Thane said. "Adejare Zabu's residence, a ten-room mansion out in the jungle, twelve klicks north of where the A3 and A4 highways intersect about sixty klicks northwest of Lagos." He looked over at the SIGINT people. "Give us the challenges, please."

"Sir, you've got a double security fence laid out fifty meters from the target building on all sides," said a young woman as she clicked and zoomed in on images on her laptop screen. "It has one gate on the east side with an access road through the jungle from the A1. Can't tell from ISR whether or not it's sensored or electrified."

"Just the fact that he's got it makes him suspect in my mind," Pacenza muttered as he watched and listened.

Kali had taken up a position behind Pacenza, peering past his shoulder, but said nothing.

"Okay, give me the rest," Thane said to the surveillance analyst.

"From heat signatures over the past four hours, looks like one main resident is moving throughout the mansion. There's also constant movement around the perimeter, seven personnel who appear to be security, plus two dogs."

"Dogs," Sumo, Pacenza's master sergeant, growled to himself, but everyone heard it. "I hate that."

"Bring your bite suit and a raw steak," Jason quipped to Sumo, whose thick lips twisted into a smirk.

"What else you got, ISR?" Thane said to the female analyst.

"Well, sir, our best possible spot for a drop zone is that open patch in the jungle, three klicks west of the mansion. It's not large and the surrounding trees are minimum fifty feet tall, but it's big enough for the whole team if they jump at intervals in trail."

"What about the exfil?" Jason asked her.

"It's also large enough for the Osprey, but just barely," she said.

"All right." Thane turned to Jason. "You're assault lead on this, so let's hear your plan."

Kali stiffened as Jason took Thane's antenna pointer from his hand. The Package operators stepped aside to make room for him.

"Okay," Jason said as he began tapping the map. "Myself, Pacenza, Sumo, and seven more will HALO from twenty thousand feet at oh-one-hundred tonight, actually tomorrow morning. That hour should give us an awareness reduction on the part of the target, Adejare Zabu, and his security team. We'll hit the DZ, stow the chutes, then hump it three klicks through the jungle to the mansion. Good so far?"

"Roger," Pacenza said. "Go on."

"We'll tranq the dogs, then breach the fence," Jason said.

"What are your ROEs, Jason?" Thane asked, meaning "rules of engagement."

"If we can, we'll take the guards without killing them—zip ties and gags. We don't need to leave corpses all over Nigeria. But if there's no choice, suppressors."

"Roger." Pacenza looked at his men. They nodded.

"After that, I'll go up the middle with Pacenza and Sumo while the rest of you pull security. I'll make positive ID on Zabu with an image relay and fingerprint relay back to here, and once confirmed, we'll call in the V-22, haul his butt back through the jungle, and exfil from the same DZ."

"All right," Ando broke in via his video monitor. "Sounds like a solid foundation, Jason. Now work all the contingencies and we'll review it again."

"Roger, sir," Jason said.

"It's not going to work," Kali said from the back of the group.

Everyone turned slowly to look at him. He pushed his way past

Pacenza and up to the table, directly across from where Jason was standing with the antenna pointer.

"Explain yourself, Kali." Thane cocked his head at him.

"This man's Nigerian," Kali said. "He's highly educated, most likely raised by an honorable family, but he's gone bad somewhere along the way."

"Okay, Kali, we know all of that so far," Neveah said. "So?"

"He's made himself a fortune doing something he knows is highly illicit," Kali said. "He's dishonored his name and his family's name. He might even realize that what he's done with Brainwave has resulted in deaths or even murders. But he's never been confronted with that before."

"What's your point, Kali?" Jason was getting a bit edgy. He wanted to move on, work the contingency details, discuss the backup plans, and get ready to launch.

"My point, Jason"—Kali turned on him—"is that, no offense, but an assault package of big scary white guys breaching his house at two in the morning is going to shock him to the point of no return."

"Go on, Kent," Ando said from his screen, and Kali turned to his image.

"Sir, he's armed, for certain. But he won't try to fight it out. He'll most likely kill himself right then and there. I know this culture. I grew up in this culture. I should take this one as assault lead, because if he sees another Nigerian, someone who speaks his language and culture, I'll be able to talk him down. Jason won't."

"Oh for damn's sake," Jason spat and slapped the antenna down on the table, making the maps rattle.

"I'm sorry, brother, but you know I'm right," Kali said to Jason. "I'm the best hope for taking this guy alive. I grew up in Nigeria, you didn't. I know how this man's going to react, you don't. If he terminates himself, we've got nothing."

Neveah was staring at Kali. There was something about his demeanor, something about his insistence on this, that seemed off. Perhaps it was his emotional connection to Nigeria, to Lagos, and to his long-lost childhood, but she couldn't be sure. She glanced over at Thane, who turned from Kali and looked at Ando's wavering image from the Black Box ship.

"Mr. Kent's logic is sound, Thane," Ando said. "Change assault leads."

Thane nodded at Jason, who shook his head, but he maintained his professional cool. He picked up the antenna pointer and extended it across the plotting table, where Kali gripped the other end. But Jason didn't let go right away. He locked eyes with Kali, whose expression gave him nothing, and then he released the pointer and turned over command.

"All right," Kali said as he tapped the map. "Let's rework a few things here . . ."

THIRTY-EIGHT

KÉTOU, NIGERIA

FROM TWENTY THOUSAND FEET ABOVE THE NIGERIAN jungle, the drop zone looked like a bright red ruby sitting in the middle of a thick black salad.

There was no pathfinder on the ground to mark the DZ for the parachutists, so instead a Predator was deployed at an offset altitude of ten thousand feet, firing an invisible laser beam down into the target's coordinates. Kali, Pacenza, Sumo, and the other seven men were all wearing night-vision devices sensitive to the full IR spectrum. All they had to do was exit from the Osprey's ramp, keep an eye on the ruby, free-fall for ninety seconds, deploy their RA-1 Advanced Ram-Air Parachute Systems at two thousand feet, glide into the hundred-foot-diameter patch of clearing in the jungle, flare for a landing, and get out of the way for the next man to slide into home.

Too easy.

But it was freezing cold at twenty thousand feet, despite the temperature hovering at 100 degrees Fahrenheit on the ground. They were wearing old-style French camouflage jungle fatigues (except for Kali, who was dressed as a Nigerian colonel), which would make them difficult to identify if they were spotted by any locals, and the uniforms whipped and flapped in the roaring wind stream like racing banners on the back of a Formula One car. The NVGs attached to the tops of their MICH helmets banged around like steel golf balls in a clothes dryer, their oxygen masks sounded like fire extinguishers in their ears, and every hard corner of their weapons and tactical gear punished their ribs like a pissed-off prizefighter.

HALO, or high-altitude, low-opening parachute-insertion tech-nique, was one of those things that seemed really cool the first time you tried it. After that, it was simply torture, and there wasn't a single commando, no matter how tough, who couldn't wait till the whole thing was over.

Kali was first off the Osprey's ramp when a crew chief slapped his shoulder, and he dived into nothing but inky blackness with a few errant stars winking above. Pacenza, Sumo, and the rest fol-lowed at set short intervals, maintaining enough separation so that they could track behind Kali—who had a small IR beacon on the back of his helmet—but not overshoot one another or get lost. Kali immediately went into delta freefall position, with his long arms thrust back alongside his hips, the palms of his gloves facing up, his legs bent slightly upward, and his head angled down at the DZ far below. The more you shaped yourself like a bullet, the faster you'd zip through the sky, which meant you'd be on the ground that much faster as well.

He'd done this so many times before, in training and in real-world deployments, that he didn't have to check his wrist altimeter but once, when he sensed he was approaching two thousand feet. To make sure he didn't roll over on his back, he cranked his right arm up over his helmet and brought his left wrist up to his goggles. Sure enough, the muted neon numbers were spinning down like a one-armed bandit in Vegas, and when he saw 2,000 disappear, he braked by spread-eagling his limbs, reached back for his pilot chute pocket, yanked the ball, and got rewarded with a *whoosh* of canopy nylon, two riser buckles smacking the sides of his head, and a harness yank in his groin that drove his manhood back up into his pelvis.

Perfect.

He popped the oxygen mask off his face, reached up for the steer-ing toggles, and looked down past his boots. The wind was at his back and it was pushing him quickly toward the DZ. He was still too high and was going to overshoot, but that couldn't be helped and he'd simply correct it. His boot tips flashed past the glowing ruby in his night vision at five hundred feet, then he yanked hard on the right-hand toggle, executed a slick hook turn that whipped his boots around in an arc, and came straight into the middle of the DZ at ten feet and flared for a classic stand-up landing in the lush, wet elephant grass.

He could have won some sort of competitive award with that landing, but there was no one around to see it.

Pacenza came in next, but he slightly misjudged his altitude and skidded in on his ass through the elephant grass like a kid on a toboggan. Sumo, on the other hand, landed like a ballet dancer, pulled his chute right down into a messy ball, and strode off the X to make way for the next man. The other seven landed more or less with grace, then Kali made a soft sound like a jungle sugarbird and they all gathered around him in the dark near the edge of the tall trees.

"Chutes in one pile under that tree," Kali whispered as he prepped his MK18 suppressed rifle and checked his load-bearing gear, ammunition, and suppressed Glock 17.

"You want to leave security with them?" Pacenza asked, meaning someone to stay behind and make sure the chutes weren't found or destroyed by some jungle beast.

"Negative," Kali said. "We're not parachuting back *out* of here, so we can take the risk."

"Roger," Pacenza said.

Kali took a knee in the utter darkness. The rest of the Package gathered around as he showed them an overhead surveillance graphic glowing from a tablet module on his left forearm.

"Okay, here's the route." He pointed off due east through the jungle. "There's a straight path from here, three klicks through the bush and right up to the front gate. They probably use a Land Rover on it and come out here to pick up supply drops. See it?"

Everyone nodded.

"All right. Stay off it," Kali said. "Might be sensored somehow or have minisurveillance cams in the trees along the route." He looked at Pacenza. "Pac, I'll take you, Sumo, four more, and we'll right-flank that path. The rest of you, mirror us on the left flank," Kali said, referring to the other half of the Package. "Stay away from the front gate, breach the fence on the flanks, then Pac, me, and Sumo will head up the middle. Copy?"

"Roger," everyone whispered.

"Who's got the tranquilizers?" Kali asked.

Sumo showed him one gas-powered pistol, while another operator displayed his as well.

"Okay, if you can put the dogs down easy, use them. Otherwise, kill them, suppressed," Kali said.

The men raised thumbs-ups in the dark.

"Okay, let's go."

Kali moved straight down the middle of the clearing toward the slashed-down mouth in the trees where the vehicle path to the mansion was flat and clear. Then he raised his right hand and turned off to the right, and Pacenza, Sumo, and four more operators followed along in spaced intervals. Right away, the jungle was thick, clawing, steamy, and hot. Although the air above the high palms was post-midnight cool, nothing penetrated through the canopy, and it was like a sauna on the ground. The men's footsteps made soft squishing sounds on a bedding of leafy mush, and macaws and wild monkeys barked in the distance like the background track of a cheap horror film. Long vines seemed to reach out from the trees, snatching at their uniforms and weapons, but they hadn't brought along any sort of machete to cut through the jungle, because the slashing would make too much noise.

The path to the mansion was three kilometers long and they flanked it off to the right by ten meters. By the time Kali's team was halfway there, they were pouring sweat and sucking long drafts off their water carriers. Then Kali heard something on the path itself up ahead and off to the left. He raised a fist, took a knee, and heard the men in trail behind him do the same. There were human footsteps on the pathway, moving in their direction. But there were also the sounds of animal pads and claws scraping the jungle floor.

Dogs. He hadn't expected the guards to come out this far from the mansion and patrol with their canines. But then he thought that might make it easier to take them out without Jare hearing anything from inside his house.

He turned and signaled for everyone to remain in position, then crooked a finger at Sumo, who moved up beside him. Kali pointed to Sumo's tranquilizer gun. Sumo nodded and they moved stealthily through the thick trees bordering the path on the left. They could take down the dog and his handler from right there beside the path.

Then Kali saw a pair of eyes glowing in his NVGs, just a few feet away. They were strange eyes, very large, and had weird vertical pupils that didn't seem canine. The animal growled, then a human voice grunted something, a leash disengaged, and a beast went hurtling through the bush, left the ground in a leap, and sank its teeth into Sumo's left forearm just as he yanked it up to protect his face and throat.

It wasn't a dog.

The guards were using damn hyenas!

Sumo crashed onto his back. The beast was the size of a Rottweiler, patched in yellow and black prints over its spiky fur, with a black pig's nose, bladed ears, and dripping fangs. It ripped and tore at Sumo's arm but Kali was on it in a flash as he whipped a razor-sharp boot knife from a scabbard and put the beast in a headlock from behind. But the hyena wouldn't release Sumo, and the three of them rolled and crashed over the jungle floor as Kali tried to get his blade around to the hyena's throat without slashing Sumo's jugular. He finally managed to grip the beast's jaw in his left hand and squeezed with all his might, and as the hyena screeched and released, he arced the blade around and cut its throat from ear to ear.

Kali and Sumo lay on their backs hyperventilating, with the bloody hyena twitching between them as it wheezed its last breaths. Then its handler, a large Nigerian in jungle fatigues carrying an MP5, came stomping at them out of the bush, furious that they'd slaughtered his "pet." Sumo drew his suppressed Glock and shot him twice point-blank in the chest. The man crashed down on his back and lay still.

Sumo looked over at Kali. "Hyenas," he said as he looked down at his bloody forearm. "Hate 'em even worse than dogs."

"You've fought a hyena before?" Kali said.

"No, but I watch the nature channel."

Kali helped him up off the ground.

"ISR must not have been able to pick them up under the triple canopy," Kali said.

"Yeah, and they've got good noses and sniffed us out."

They checked the guard to make sure he was dead, signaled to Pacenza and the rest, and moved on.

Kali had to assume that the dead guard with the hyena was wearing comms and had reported in before he was killed. He called over his headset, "Dark Horse Main to ALCON, move," and then he, Pacenza, Sumo, and the rest of his team cut over to the main path and started pounding toward the mansion. It didn't matter anymore if the pathway was under surveillance. The element of surprise was gone.

Another wild hyena came racing at them straight down the pathway from the direction of the mansion's main gate. Pacenza gunned it down with a suppressed Glock bullet to the brain. Kali, sensing that right behind the beast was its furious handler and maybe more security, waved his team to split to both sides of the path, just as an MP5 opened up and a line of red tracers spat straight out and mowed down plants and palm bark. Pacenza jinked off to the right, burst from the bush, and gunned down two Nigerians with double taps from his MK18, just as Kali took Sumo and the rest of his team up the middle.

"Watch for Claymores," Kali whispered in his headset, meaning the wicked antipersonnel mines that could be set up in ambush for just such an occasion.

On the far side of the path, the second Package team also encountered a pair of wild hyenas and their handlers, but they'd al-

ready been briefed and warned by Sumo, and those animals were
dead before they leaped into the air. Their handlers ran back toward
the mansion's front gate, where they had a German MP40 light
machine gun mounted on a tripod behind an inch-thick bulletproof
shield salvaged from a British armored car. They got off a single
burst from the high-rate-of-fire weapon, but were gunned down in a
volley by Pacenza's men assaulting from the left flank.

One guard, who'd seen the fate of his comrades but apparently
thought that honor was better than surrender, charged out of the
trees as Kali and his team were just hitting the right-flank perimeter fence. At that moment, all the floodlights in the compound
flashed on and the Nigerian guard's wild eyes looked completely
insane as he drew a wicked curved kukri knife with one hand and
came on firing a .45-caliber handgun with the other.

Kali shot the pistol right out of his hand, but the man seemed
drugged, or insane, and leaped at Kali as he slashed with the kukri
and tried to cut Kali's ear off. Kali trapped his knife arm with a
left-hand slash and wrist grip, jammed his shoulder under the man's
armpit, hurled him over his shoulder, and slammed him down on
his back. For a split second he thought about taking the man prisoner, but that thought died as Pacenza shot him in the head.

At that point, with all the sodium lights blazing and gunfire
banging through the jungle, stealth had been lost, and Kali's only
thought was to get inside the mansion and stop Jare from either
fleeing into the bush, or, worse, destroying everything that Black
Box would need for information and intelligence about Brainwave.

"Package, forget the wire," Kali barked in his comms as he got up
from the man Pacenza had just killed. "Blow the gate."

"Roger," someone said in his ear and a breacher blew past him,
racing for the steel rolling gate fifty meters from the mansion's front
door. It had a titanium padlock where the two sides met in the
middle, and the breacher slapped half a brick of sweating C-4 on
the lock, jammed a remote detonator into the clay, yelled "Cover!"
and sprinted away as everyone went prone and ducked his head. A
blinding flash and an echoing boom sent the gate flying open on its

hinges. Kali got up, jerked his head at Pacenza and Sumo, and they charged straight up the middle toward the front door.

It was then that Kali realized something that curdled his guts. He was sprinting toward the mansion's entrance, and he suddenly saw that the building was nearly an exact copy of his father's house in Lagos, the house where he'd grown up as a child. *Everything* was the same—the white-framed windows made of bamboo, the columns and portico, and the beautiful, ornate front door. It was a clone. It was an architectural ghost of his and Jare's childhood. It almost made him weak in the knees.

Pacenza got there first. He tried the door handle—locked. Sumo arrived, unslung a cut-down twelve-gauge Remington shotgun from his back, and blew the lock off. Kali kicked the door open and then charged inside, guns up.

It was dark. But from outside, the sodium lights were bleeding in like the moon, and the rooms were eerily silent and large and overpowering in Kali's mind. His heart was racing as he absorbed the tragedy of the moment. Here he was, back in a house that was a replica of his own childhood, with all those losses and the things he thought he'd never see again, except in his mind.

There was his mom's white piano. There were pictures sitting on the top of its cover. He walked over to the row of framed old black-and-white photographs, and sure enough, there was one of his parents, with him and Jare standing between them, smiling and eating ice cream cones, down by the beach in Lagos. The beach where good things happened, and also very bad things. He picked up the photo and slipped it into his cargo pocket. He started walking through the dining room toward the back, where in his old, beloved home, his father's study had been. He passed a muted television set that had images of Russian customs officers checking passports at the Poland–Old Ukraine border. A banner at the bottom of the screen read, FIRST RUSSIANS TO USE NEW RUSSIA–OLD UKRAINE BORDER ENTRY.

Pacenza and Sumo were close on his heels, turning with their MK18s leveled and ready, scanning the winding stairway that rose up to the second floor, and the archway opening to the big kitchen in back. When Kali arrived at the door to "his father's" office, he motioned for both men to stay back. He braced the left-hand frame of the doorway, took a breath, and peered around the frame inside . . . but right that second a burst of automatic gunshots shattered the doorframe just above Kali's head!

He jerked his head back and crouched low as another burst flashed the office bright yellow, and for a moment Kali saw the clone of his father's study, with all its bookshelves and books, the long white curtains billowing in the open windows, and even the paisley ceiling decor that his father hadn't liked very much. But the big conference table was thrown over on its side like a barricade, and from behind that a man in silhouette was firing an AK-47 and yelling.

"You come to my house?!" *Bang, bang, bang,* each word punctuated by gunfire. "You dishonor my home with your filth and your guns?!"

Bullets ricocheted off the plaster walls and punched ragged holes just above Kali's head. Pacenza gripped his shoulder hard as if he were ready to charge inside and slice the pie, but Kali pushed him back and waved off Sumo with a fiery look.

"I will kill you! All of you!" the man's hoarse voice screamed again from inside, and he fired five more shots and then Kali heard a bolt lock back. The man cursed as he fumbled for a fresh magazine to reload.

At that moment, Kali edged his right eye around the corner of the splintered doorframe and took aim with his MK18. The gunsight's reticle framed the sweat-slickened face of the man barricaded behind the table, but Kali's finger stopped squeezing his trigger.

The face in his gunsight was Jare's, with the same childhood tribal tattoo beneath his right eye.

THIRTY-NINE

STILL YELLING AND FURIOUS WITH THE ASSAULT ON his house, Jare struggled to reload his AK-47 so he could kill the men who'd dared to defile his home. But Kali's finger touched the button on his rifle's laser-targeting beam, and suddenly a burning red dot appeared on Jare's chest just below his throat.

Jare looked down and froze. The bright scarlet pinpoint gleaming in the sweaty curls of his chest meant that one false move and a bullet would rip through his heart. He stood there behind the table barricade, just breathing, and Kali did the same, where he was locked in position behind the shattered doorframe.

"Take him out," Pacenza whispered in Kali's ear.

"No. He's useless to us dead." Kali cocked his head toward the curving stairway, the one that had once led upstairs to his precious bedroom—or at least this duplicate version of the same. "Pac, take Sumo and check the second floor. Might be a laboratory up there."

"And leave you here solo?" Sumo said from across the open office doorway, where he was pulling a flash-bang from his combat vest and getting ready to use it.

"Yes," Kali said. "I'll handle him."

Pacenza looked at Kali. He didn't quite understand what was going on in Kali's mind, but Kali was assault lead and always cool under fire.

"Roger," Pacenza said. "Call us on comms if you need backup."

Pacenza and Sumo moved toward the stairwell and disappeared up into the gloom. Kali hadn't taken his eyes off Jare's face through his gunsight and he saw that his nostrils were flaring, his eyes wide and gleaming, and his hands were twitching because part of him wanted desperately to finish prepping his AK and open fire.

Without moving his right hand from his rifle, Kali first turned off his comms with his left hand, then reached into his cargo pocket and stroked his fingers over the images of his family and Jare that he knew were right there. It was as if he was absorbing something through his skin, something that would change his spectral as well as mental colors. When he finally spoke to Jare, it was not in his own voice. It was in the voice of his father, George Adeyemi, from long ago.

"You are a very good friend, Jare," Kali said in George's deep Nigerian accent, the one that had once expressed wisdom, anger, and love all in the same breath.

Across the darkened office on the other side of the overturned table, Jare blinked. His hands were trembling where he held the AK-47, still poised to reload and continue the gunfight. But suddenly, the sound of a deep voice from the past, a voice that had comforted him so many times and filled his void of a fatherless childhood, made his brow crease.

"But there is a price for doing bad things," the voice of George Adeyemi said from the bullet-pocked doorway again. "A heavy price, my son . . ."

Jare swallowed hard. This could not be. He was hearing George's voice coming out of the darkness, and it seemed to be coming from this soldier or commando or whatever he was who was about to kill him with gunfire. Was it possible that he was already dead? Had the man already shot him in the brain and now he was swirling through a vortex of purgatory on his way to heaven or hell, and George Adeyemi's voice was nothing but a rushing stream of expiring memories from his past? George couldn't possibly be here in this room on this night! George was long gone. George was dead!

"I always treated you like a son, Jare," the voice said from behind the glowing gunsight across the room. "Now you will treat me with respect. Put down the gun."

It was as if Jare were hypnotized. Over the decades of a very hard life, during which he'd had to become ten times as tough and resilient as the gentle, intellectual boy he'd been as a child, he'd learned to push down his emotions and terrible loneliness. He'd learned to erase the past. But now the sound of George's voice was completely overpowering. He swallowed, and obeyed, and his trembling hands lowered the Russian assault rifle to the floor. When he stood back up again, he was looking intently at the man in the doorway with the glowing green night-vision tubes in place of eyes, and he watched as the man lifted them up away from his face, and also lowered his gun.

Jare stared at him.

Kali stared at Jare.

"Who are you?" Jare said.

"You know who I am, Jare."

"No. This is some sort of a trick."

Neither had seen the other for many years, but they'd been brothers in everything but blood and had been torn from one another under terrible circumstances, something that neither would ever forget. Jare still had the tribal scars beneath his right eye. Kali still had those eyes that could never be disguised by age. And still, Jare thought he was hallucinating, because none of this made sense.

"It is not a trick," Kali said. "It is a twist of fate. I am Kalief."

"Kalief is gone. Kalief ran away from Nigeria years ago."

"Kalief is here, right now, in front of you, Jare."

"No. A moment ago, George was here too. I am dreaming. I am dead already."

Kali took a step into the room. Jare's body jerked and he stepped back. Kali raised a hand out, palm up, in supplication.

"That was me, Jare. We both remember my father's voice. *Our* father's voice. I used it to remind you."

"He was never my father. I had no father."

"He was the best father either of us ever had, Jare."

Jare suddenly swept a hand through the air as if none of this could be happening and he could swat it away like a swarm of mosquitoes.

"He abandoned us!" Jare yelled. "He left you, he left me, then you and your mother ran away like dogs and left me and my mother with nothing!"

"We had nothing, Jare. Don't you remember? Everything was taken from us."

"You abandoned me too! And so did your mother! Is that what a mother does to her son even if the father has gone?"

Kali took off his helmet and let his rifle hang on its sling from his neck. He wanted Jare to see him fully, and he stepped in closer. He could see tears now streaming from Jare's eyes.

"Who are you now, Kali?" Jare asked in a trembling voice. "What have you become?"

"I am an American, a sort of government security officer."

"But you are dressed like a Nigerian colonel."

"This is a disguise, Jare. See me for who I really am."

"Did you come here to kill me? Is that your idea of a childhood reunion?"

"No, Jare. I came here to save you."

"From myself?" Jare almost laughed bitterly. "I am beyond saving. I have done things that cannot be redeemed."

"That is not true. Remember what our father always said about redemption?"

"That didn't help him get off scot-free, did it?"

Kali took a breath. At last and at least, Jare was no longer rejecting the idea that George had been a father to both of them.

"You can help us now, Jare. Whatever you did with that technology is going to be used for something very bad, but you can help us stop it."

"You have no idea how bad it will be," Jare murmured.

"You will tell me," Kali said. "And I will help you so that you can live a full life again, without paying a terrible price. There may be some punishments for what you've done with this man Nabuto, and others above him, but I can prevent it from being too cruel."

"You have that power now, Kalief?"

"I do. But you must also promise me something."

"What is it?"

"Our relationship. It can't be discovered by the people I work for. We have very strict regulations. You must *promise* to keep that just between us, and we will make it seem like we are simply two Nigerians who understand one another. Favor for favor, a blood brother pact."

"Why should I do that?"

"Because your other option is a prison island somewhere."

"You expect me to trust you?"

"Here I am." Kali's voice dropped and his tone changed to a heavy accusation. "I'm the one who should be questioning trust after what you did to me and my father."

It was as though Jare were punched in the gut by those words. "All right . . . All right," he muttered, and he let out a long breath and looked around the office. "I will do this . . . What will happen to my house? Did you notice the house?"

"I did, Jare. Nothing will happen to it. Maybe someday you and I will come back here and sip lemonade by the pool, like we used to do with my mother."

"That would be good."

"Come to me now," Kali said as he crooked a finger. "I'll have to bind your wrists behind you, but that will only be for a show, for the men I'm working with. And when we leave here together, I will be this Nigerian officer you see now, disguised in my voice and form. You will not know me, and I will not know you. When we speak to one another, it will be like our old game, 'good cop and Mafia.' Do you remember?"

"Yes, I remember."

"Good. Now come."

Jare came out from behind the table. He was wearing a short-sleeved bush shirt and shorts, and the image reminded Kali of their childhood and so many times when they played together in the park or out by the pool. He swallowed as Jare turned his back to him and laced his fingers together. Kali took out a zip tie and bound his wrists, but not tightly. He led him back through the house. Pacenza and Sumo were already at the front door, waiting.

"Nothing up top," Pacenza said to Kali.

"No laboratory," Sumo added.

"It is of no matter," Kali said. His voice was now heavy with a Nigerian accent, but Pacenza and Sumo had seen him work that kind of magic before. "I will uncover his secrets in due time."

"My lab isn't out here," Jare whispered as Kali led him past them and outside.

Kali walked, gripping Jare's elbow as he would do with any other zip-tied prisoner. He slung his rifle over his right shoulder, more like a Nigerian special forces commando than an American, and led him toward the blown-out gate at the front of the house. Pacenza's men were arranged on both sides of the perimeter fence, pulling security and watching the jungle. Already the sounds of the Osprey's rotors were growing louder in the predawn sky as it headed in to pick up the Package from the DZ three kilometers back in the jungle.

Jare stopped for a moment as he spotted the corpses of some of his security men lying twisted and dead in the glistening grass. One of the hyenas was lying there dead too. He turned and looked one more time at the house he'd built from his memories.

"Nothing will happen to it?" he said to Kali without using his name. Jare was still very sharp and understood the discretion of Kali's demand.

"Nothing at all," Kali said. "The Americans asked me to aid them, and in turn I am the man who decides how to treat any Nigerian prisoners and their properties. Nothing here will be touched by anyone."

Jare looked at him. "Good, because there are no materials here," he said. "The materials are all in my head."

Kali nodded and started walking Jare down the jungle pathway toward the drop zone. The Package men followed, turning this way and that and watching the trees, in case a guard or hyena was still out there somewhere.

Kali and Jare ignored them and walked, side by side. They were not holding hands, but it was as if once again, like so many years ago, they were walking down to the beach in Lagos. But this time there would be no execution.

FORTY

GENESIS

There were three Lagos police cars out in front of the Adeyemi house.

It was early evening and Yvonne had just finished preparing a fine meal with Marabel in the kitchen, but that wouldn't be happening now. The cherry lights on the roofs of the cars were spinning and flashing through the mansion's windows, and Kali's mom was now trapped in the kitchen and yelling at a female police officer, who wouldn't let her leave.

Kali and Jare had run down the stairs from Kali's bedroom when they heard the sirens outside, thinking there might be some sort of exciting event out in the neighborhood—maybe a chase after a thief. But then they'd realized the police were coming into the house itself, and they'd slithered under the big bar just outside George's office, while uniformed and plainclothes men stomped through the mansion and went into all the rooms.

Kali was very frightened. Jare held on to him and tried to keep him calm, though Jare was frightened too.

The boys peeked out from behind George's bar with only their eyes above the polished mahogany slab and their small fingers gripping it till their fingernails turned pale. George was inside his office, facing two men whom Kali had seen before. They were men of his dad's consortium. One of them was Chibundu, whose big, sweaty face Kali knew well, and the other was Reki, who he remembered was usually so quiet when George's council was arguing.

Now they were facing Kali's father across his big conference table. They were wearing suits, and on the outside pockets hung shiny detective badges. Kali had never known that Chibundu and Reki were actually policemen. The thought crossed his mind that all this time they'd been hiding that fact from his father, but then he realized, for some instinctive reason, that his father had known they were policemen all along.

They were bad policemen.

"What the hell is this, Chibundu?" George was shouting and waving his arms.

"You know what this is, George," Chibundu said. He had his palms out and turned at the ceiling, as if he were apologizing. But Reki, the quiet one, wasn't apologizing at all. He had a revolver in one hand as if George might be dangerous or would suddenly try to escape.

"Yes, I know what this is!" George shouted at Chibundu. "It's a betrayal of everything we did together! Of everything the consortium accomplished before you fools decided there was only one way, the most corrupt and criminal way possible!"

"You were naive, George." Reki finally spoke, yet his tone was disrespectful.

"Shut up, Reki," George hissed. "And put that stupid gun away."

Chibundu nodded at Reki. "Put it away."

Reki's face flushed as he tucked the revolver back in his waistband.

"You two, *playing* policemen. It's laughable," George said.

"We tried to warn you, George," Chibundu said. "We could not *possibly* have made it more plain."

Kali was listening very carefully, though below the bar his legs were trembling. He'd never seen anyone threaten his dad, especially with something like a gun. He had no idea what his father might do. Jare reached out and gripped Kali's forearm as they watched from the shadow of the bar.

"Oh, so that stupid note was from you, Chibundu?" George scoffed.

"You'd better be careful, George," Chibundu warned.

"Me be careful? Coming from someone who sends notes like a jealous little schoolgirl?"

Kali's ears burned when he heard that. He remembered the threatening note that had been stabbed to the front door of the house. His father's friends would do something like that? It didn't make sense. Why didn't they just tell him they were unhappy?

"Yes, it was from me," Chibundu said calmly, knowing that he had the upper hand. "I could think of no other way to get you to back off of your crazy ideas. The consortium loved working with you, George, but you went too far . . ." He looked away in anger and frustration. "You have no idea what they wanted to do to you! Very bad things, believe me!"

"Too far?!" George yelled and the sound of his booming voice vibrated the crystals of the beautiful chandelier hanging from Yvonne's paisley ceiling. "Too far? I followed my vision for a better Lagos, Chibundu. I built something that none of you could ever imagine. I financed it myself, out of my own pocket, by giving the consortium back every damn penny of my investments and doing all that backbreaking work myself over the years! Too far? You all could have joined me and benefited yourselves, but you are nothing but jealous fools and you know it!" George's voice dropped to a threatening tone. "All of you are criminals, all of you are corrupt, and all of you will pay the price for that."

"Only you will be paying the price, George," Reki finally said in his deceptively quiet tone. His hand was still resting on the butt of his pistol.

"Oh, I see." George turned to him and almost smiled. "The snake finally hisses when you step on its tail."

Reki's eyes widened with the insult. A young police sergeant came walking past the bar where the boys were hiding and stuck his head into George's office. He was carrying a cardboard evidence box overflowing with papers. He spoke to Chibundu. "We've got a lot of materials, sir," the young sergeant said. "There was stuff hidden under the kitchen cabinets, including cash."

It was then that Kali realized he could hear his mother crying.

"There is nothing illegal about keeping travel documents and extra cash in one's house, you government lackeys," George said.

Chibundu ignored the insult and said to the sergeant, "After we leave, gather up everything in the office here, including all the blueprints."

"Yes, sir," the cop said and went out.

"Oh, so you're going to pretend now that none of Pearland was my idea?" George almost laughed at the thought. "Chibundu, you barely have the talent to draw a proper dollhouse using crayons."

Chibundu just shook his head, almost mournfully.

"I tried to warn you, George," he said. "Now turn around and let's not make this harder than it is."

George hesitated and challenged the men with his eyes for a long moment. But then he turned around and laced his fingers behind his back. Reki approached him carefully with the handcuffs. He was afraid of George and he clipped them closed quickly and stepped back. George turned around again.

"I will want my attorney the moment we arrive at headquarters," George said. "He'd better be there."

"I'll call him myself," Chibundu said as he took George's elbow and began leading him out of the office.

It was then that George spotted the two pairs of large, frightened eyes poking just above his bar. He knew they belonged to Kalief and Jare, but he wasn't going to reveal the boys to the cops. He trusted none of his former associates now. He had no idea what they might do to pressure him.

However, as he passed by, he turned his head just enough so that Kalief would understand that his father knew he was there, and would listen carefully.

"A man must sometimes do what a man must do, no matter the consequences, my friends. I decided to change my life, to turn it around, to transform my not-so-admirable deeds of the past into charity and good works for the future."

Chibundu and Reki were looking at George curiously as they walked him past the bar, through the big dining room, and toward the front of the house, where the police beacons were still striping everything in a sort of hellish crimson hue. But George kept on talking, and only Kali and Jare knew that his words were meant for them.

"If a man does the right thing—If a man does the things that he knows he should do, no matter the consequences, then a man can die in peace. There is no greater gift than that."

As Kali heard those words, his eyes watered, and those words would forever be engraved on his mind.

Then Kali and Jare heard the front door close and George was no longer talking, but they could still hear Yvonne softly weeping in the kitchen. The boys slipped from the bar and sank to the floor amid the washed glasses on the shelves and the cans and small bottles of spices and garnishes that Kali's parents liked to use to spruce up their drinks for their honored guests.

But Kali sensed that there would be no more parties in the house. A tear rolled down his cheek, and then one rolled down Jare's cheek too.

FORTY-ONE

AIRSPACE ABOVE THE PAKISTAN–AFGHANISTAN BORDER

LUCAS VAN GROOT LED THE BLACK BOX TEAM ON A wild countersurveillance chase across three continents, and relished it thoroughly.

Just as the special operations V-22 Osprey was landing back at Sigonella—after extracting Kali, Jare, and Pacenza's men from the Nigerian jungle—Van Groot took off in his Falcon from Rome. The nanoparticle tracking team at the National Reconnaissance Office shot a flash message to Ando, and that left Kali and the rest with barely enough time to off-load from the Osprey and hustle all their gear back onto the C-17. The chase was on.

First, Van Groot's Falcon turned due east toward Asia, as if he were planning a visit to Moscow. Then suddenly, the aircraft heeled over and headed south for Cairo, Egypt. When it set down in Cairo, it stayed on the runway for only an hour, just enough time to refuel and change crews. The Black Box team aboard the C-17 landed in nearby Alexandria at a military airfield, but by then Van Groot was off *again*, this time heading toward South Africa.

For the third time in twenty-three hours, the C-17 was back up in the air. The pilots had to summon a KC-130 tanker from Africa Command (AFRICOM) for midair refueling—they didn't have time to land in South Africa before Van Groot was moving once more. He took off from Pretoria, sped north above the Arabian Sea, and landed in Islamabad, Pakistan.

At that point, the nanoparticle technology planted in Van Groot's palm was the only thing saving Black Box from losing his zigzagging trail. They were embedded in his skin. He couldn't hide that.

But the bots were finally fading on the very last day of Van Groot's trip, and surveillance experts at the NRO were relaying the bad news to Ando. To make matters worse, Van Groot got out of his jet in Islamabad to have lunch at an airport café with some unknown person, during which time the trackers were pulling their hair out because the particles were turning from yellow to red. Then, just as he reboarded the Falcon, the nanoparticles finally blanked out.

Now there was no way to track him except by closely tailing his jet. But as Black Box soon discovered, his lunch appointment in Islamabad was a head fake—he was stalling while his engineers rolled the Falcon into a hangar and mounted the airplane's Brainwave antenna to the nose. Then he took off again, headed straight for the Afghan border, activated the Brainwave, and the jet disappeared . . .

"Dammit!"

Aboard the C-17 chase plane, the pilot in command cursed and threw up his hands. Van Groot was entering Afghan airspace, which was now forbidden to US aircraft, and he was probably going to land somewhere. The C-17 had to turn back and fly a wide oval track on the Pakistani side of the border, while Ando, Thane, and other people above their pay grades argued about what to do next.

Meanwhile, Kali had just started his interrogation of Jare . . .

The two childhood friends were alone, inside a modular secure communications compartment that looked like a beige ceramic box. It had a single door with a one-way mirrored window. The "Cube," as it was called, was strapped to the C-17's cargo floor up forward near the cockpit and was essentially a miniature SCIF.

Inside the Cube there was a drop-down table with two high-end laptops, secure SATCOM phones, a flat-screen for video communications, two office chairs, and one over-and-under bunk bed, because sometimes the intelligence analysts inside weren't allowed to leave. That's why the Cube also had an open toilet and a sink, like a prison cell. It was also sometimes used as an interrogation cell, with a full suite of surveillance cameras inside.

Kali and Jare sat across from each other in the office chairs. No one had witnessed their private reunion or secret agreement back at

Jare's mansion, so as far as the Black Box personnel were concerned, this was an ongoing deep interrogation by Kali of a villainous computer engineer. Even during the trip back to Sigonella, Kali hadn't broken from his Chameleon state, in which he was utterly convincing as a Nigerian colonel who'd never seen Jare before. And Jare, understanding that he had to stick to his deal with Kali about not revealing their past, was still going along.

But both men knew they were walking a tightrope without a safety net. Their conversation inside the Cube was being monitored by Thane, Jason, Neveah, Ando, and the Package, so they'd have to use hints and double meanings, while Jare "reluctantly" revealed the crucial intelligence that Black Box needed.

Kali was still wearing his Nigerian jungle camouflage, while Jare was dressed in the bush shirt and shorts he'd been wearing when his mansion was raided. He also had on a pair of boat shoes, making the contrast between his and Kali's attire strikingly weird.

Kali stared at Jare and gave him a stern nod. *I'll be the good cop. You be the Mafia.*

It was the roleplaying game they'd often played outside the back of Kali's house in Lagos. Jare understood exactly what Kali was going to do. But this was real life, not just a game, and he was anxious about it.

"All right, Zabu," Kali said, still deep in his Nigerian accent and purposely using Jare's last name. "Tell me everything about Brainwave."

Jare sneered as he sat back and folded his arms. "You expect me to tell you anything after you dragged me out of my own home? I want an attorney."

Kali nodded as if he understood. Then he got up, cranked his right hand back, and slapped Jare across his face, hard. "*There's* your attorney," he said as the slap echoed in the Cube.

"Holy *crap*," Thane exclaimed from his seat in the C-17, where he was sitting next to Pacenza and watching the proceedings on his laptop.

"He's starting a little rough," Pacenza agreed.

"You pig!" Jare sputtered at Kali as he touched his stinging cheek. "You are a traitor to all that is honorable in the Nigerian armed forces! You think violence is going to make me tell you things?"

Kali started to get up from his chair again and Jare realized he was going to play his role to the hilt. Kali was cocking his arm back to deliver another blow, yet instead of flinching, Jare spoke with arrogance.

"It was developed by an American DARPA scientist," he said calmly with his chin raised. "Dr. Emmanuel Leiter. But that is *all* I am going to say. Anything else is going to cost you." A grin slid across his face. "And I *still* demand an attorney."

Kali of course already knew that much from the deceased Mrs. Leiter, and Black Box knew it too. But he wanted it to appear to Thane, Ando, Jason, and Neveah that he was setting a baseline for truth, like a polygraph examiner. However, speaking to Jare this way, after so many years and the painful things that had happened between them, would still make it hard for him to use his most brutal techniques. It wasn't lost on Kali that that's why Black Box had such strict regulations about personal relationships. He knew nothing about Jason's and Neveah's secret tryst, but if he had he would have exploded with indignation.

"And this Dr. Leiter," Kali said. "What happened to him?"

"Am I not speaking English?" Jare snapped in the same Nigerian accent that he still had from their boyhood in Lagos. "Do you want me to say it in Yoruba? *Gba mi niagbejoro, Colonel!*" Which means, "Take me seriously, Colonel." Then Jare demanded a lawyer again and called Kali "Colonel" just to remind him that they were acting their roles.

Kali pretended to steam at Jare's attempts to needle him. He balled his fists and his next question came through clenched teeth.

"Did Leiter pass the technology on to you, Zabu?"

"No. I read it on the back of a cereal box," Jare said with dripping sarcasm. "I think it was Corn Flakes."

Kali leaped up from his chair, caught Jare by the throat, dragged him up on his feet, and banged his head into the top half of the bunk bed. He held him there with one hand as Jare's eyes bulged.

"Overwatch, Black Box Primary here." It was Ando speaking to Thane from his land-based headquarters in Virginia, where he was watching the proceedings. "What the hell is going on in there? It looks like Kent's going to kill this guy before we get a damn thing out of him!"

"Sir, he knows what he's doing," Thane said, though he wasn't sure.

"*I* should have been assault lead for this," Jason mumbled from across the huge cargo cabin. "He's too emotional about it."

"It looks like a Nigerian-versus-Nigerian ego issue," Neveah agreed. "Jason might be right—"

"Stand down and freakin' listen," Thane ordered them all, then quickly addressed Ando. "Not *you*, sir."

Back inside the Cube, Kali was choking Jare, who was barely managing to stay in character. He blinked rapidly at Kali, a signal that he was going to pass out. Kali threw him down onto the ceramic floor. Jare got to his knees, turned his head, and spit on the floor in defiance. Kali marched toward him and yelled down, "Tell me about Leiter, now!"

"You will get *nothing* more from me. Do you hear me? Nothing!" Jare shouted up at Kali. "You come to my house, dishonor me, kill my personal bodyguards, destroy my property. Why should I tell you anything else?"

"Because if you don't," Kali said, "I might have to get serious with you."

He pulled a black Benchmade folding knife from his uniform pocket and flicked it open. It had a long, gleaming, serrated blade.

"That's enough!" Thane barked from his seat, jumped up, and started stumbling over the legs of Pacenza's operators. He rushed to the Cube, but Kali took one long stride toward the door and locked it. "Stop!" Thane pounded his fist on the door and stared through the one-way window. "Colonel, I want you out here right now!"

"Your boy in there might be finally losing it," Pacenza called over to Thane.

Inside the Cube, Kali was ignoring Thane's rants from outside. He loomed above Jare with the knife and brought the gleaming blade very close to the cheek under his eye where he had no tattoo.

"I see the witch doctor failed to complete his job," Kali said, because he knew the story of Jare screaming so loudly that the witch doctor had stopped the ritual. "But *I* will."

Just then the C-17 hit a pocket of turbulence and Kali jolted forward. The tip of his blade flicked a slice in Jare's cheek and a trickle of blood ran down.

"Dammit, Colonel!" Thane yelled again through the door as he held on to the frame and tried not to tumble to the floor.

"Overwatch! Black Box Main!" Ando snapped in Thane's and Kali's earpieces. "Stand down from this *now.*"

But Kali ignored the order and with his other hand raised five fingers in the air behind his back. Thane stared at the signal, dropped his head, and mumbled, "Shit. He's going to level five."

"That is *not* authorized," Ando said in their ears.

"Colonel!" Thane yelled as he pounded again on the door. "Stand down!"

Kali ignored Thane's fist slamming the door and the urgent voices in his ear. He leaned even closer to Jare as the blood ran down Jare's cheek and stained his collar.

"You can take a lot of punishment, Zabu," he said with false admiration. "You can even take a good beating. The question is . . . can your mother take a beating too?"

Jare froze, just staring at Kali. He had no idea that during the Osprey flight back to Sigonella, Kali had pulled everything from the Intel Tank that he could on Jare Zabu—his past and present, his foibles and weaknesses. He would use them now without mercy, for the sake of further deceiving his Black Box team.

"She has cancer, I know, the poor thing," Kali said. "You send her for treatments to London, just like all the other corrupt Nigerian officials do." He cocked his head. "You'd be surprised at how much information Nigerian special forces can obtain."

"This has *nothing* to do with my mother," Jare said. He was suddenly breathing hard. "Leave her out of this."

"I can leave her out of it, or I can simply cancel all of her future trips to London. We both know that the survival rate in Nigerian hospitals for patients with her type of cancer is less than one percent . . . But that decision is up to you."

Jare's eyes brimmed over with tears. One ran down his cheek, mixing with the blood from Kali's cut. Kali was talking about the only precious family member left in Jare's life, his mother, whom George Adeyemi had once nurtured and kept alive. Ando, Jason, and Neveah were watching Jare's face on their monitors, while Thane still stared through the one-way window in the Cube's door. Kali's tactics were effective, but terribly cruel.

"He's good," Neveah commented softly. "But I wouldn't want to be on his bad side."

"Bastard," Jare hissed up at Kali, but he wasn't playacting now. "I will talk, but only if you guarantee to leave her alone."

Kali pocketed the knife, pulled Jare up from the floor, and dumped him back in his chair.

"And I want it in writing," Jare said. "An official document."

"Tell him you agree," Ando said in Kali's ear.

"You will have it," Kali said to Jare, and he sat down again too.

Jare took a long breath. "Leiter passed the technology to my contact in the organization, a man named Nabuto," he said.

"Nabuto." Kali repeated the name as if he didn't already know that Nabuto was Van Groot's infamous cutout—always the fall guy, the name that everyone knew, from Fabio to Mrs. Leiter. "Have you ever met this Nabuto?"

"I have met him twice," Jare confessed. "He is South African, a native, not a Boer. Very smart, very cruel."

"What did he have you do?" Kali demanded.

"He had me back-engineer the device. Then I manufactured operational versions."

"How much did they pay you for that work?"

"*Millions.*" Jare snorted as if Kali were asking a ridiculous question. "You saw my house, didn't you?" He sneered. "Didn't you like my house, *Colonel?*"

That remark stung Kali like an electroshock. Jare's house was *his* house, a carbon copy of all that was left of their childhoods. Jare clearly wanted it to hurt Kali as much as Kali had already hurt him.

"Yes, I saw your house," Kali said to Jare. Then he raised his chin. "It would be a shame if your mother could not return to it. Keep talking. Who is this man called Orca?"

"He is the top of the pyramid." Jare seemed exhausted now. "I've only heard he's a South African . . . white. But I have never met him."

"That's a lie," Kali said.

"*No.* I actually do not know anyone who has met him. I worked with some of Nabuto's technicians to make Brainwave modules, even at a special island laboratory, but I *never* saw this man, Orca."

"I want his name!" Kali reached out for Jare's shirt again, like he was going to rise from his seat and inflict more pain.

"His name won't *help* you," Jare snapped. "Because only *I* know how to track this man."

After a moment, Ando spoke in Kali's ear. "Mr. Kent, listen up. Pursue that angle *now.* Find out what your source has on the technology and his ability to track it, and do it without harming him further. That's an order."

Kali released Jare's shirt, though Jare was watching him as if no longer sure that Kali was sane.

"All right, Zabu," Kali said. "You mentioned there is a way to track a Brainwave device aside from radar technology. What is that way? Is there something about it that nobody knows?"

Jare's lips curled into a smile. He seemed amused by some sort of irony.

"When I was a child," he said, "there was a wise man in the neighborhood. He would often tell us boys, 'Always have something on your opposition, as well as your partners. Trust is beautiful, but insurance is better.'"

Kali's jaw clenched. That expression was his father's.

"What is your insurance policy then, Zabu?"

"I added a component to Leiter's technology," Jare said with pride. "Every Brainwave module attached to an aircraft, no matter the size, emits an ultrahigh radio signal that's off the standard spectrum. It is like one of those transmissions that come from faraway planets, and is only detectable by SETI."

He meant an acclaimed US nonprofit in the California desert called the Search for Extraterrestrial Intelligence, which used massive dish antennas to pick up potential signals from other life-forms in distant galaxies.

"Are you saying that we'd need to work with SETI in order to track all the Brainwave modules that Orca might deploy?"

"No, you need only work with me," Jare said. "And my smartphone. May I have it, Colonel?"

Kali spoke out loud to Thane in his thick Nigerian accent. "Mr. Zane," he said, using one of Thane's cover names, "the American soldiers have Mr. Zabu's cell. Can you deliver it please?"

A minute later, Thane again pounded the door, but this time Kali unlocked it and retrieved the cell from Thane's hand. Thane was about to admonish him for going too far, but Kali just slammed the door.

He handed the smartphone to Jare, which appeared to be a standard iPhone model.

"I wrote the entire tracking program in here," Jare said.

Kali gestured at the phone. "Could you use that device to tell me where the modules you developed currently are?"

Jare looked down, tapped an icon, and glided his fingers over an app. As he did so, the eyebrow above his cheek with the tribal tattoo arched, as if he was surprised. Then he looked up at Kali and spoke again.

"He is being very careless," he said.

"Who is?"

"Orca, or whatever his real name is. He is already in Afghanistan. However, it appears that all of the Brainwave antennas and modules I built are also in Afghanistan. *All* of them."

"How do you know that?"

"They show up on my tracking program, like radio stations on one of those worldwide listening apps. They are all there, Colonel, all inside Afghanistan's borders. As a matter of fact, they all appear to be in the same place."

"Where would that be?"

"At Bagram Airfield."

"Do you know why they would all be there?"

"I assume because Orca is going to use them as Nabuto told me he would."

"And how is that?"

"He intends to sell them to a very high bidder, who will then use them to attack a sovereign nation. There will be no way for that nation to defend itself against combat aircraft if its ground and air defenses can't see them. He would have to do nothing else. He would make billions on the sale."

Kali was thinking, *And billions more on the stock transactions that will tumble like an avalanche after such an attack.*

"Why would he tell you such a thing?" Kali asked.

"Because he had to, in order for me to develop the technology for its intended mission. I would have to know what kinds of air defenses would be used against Brainwave in order to tune it properly. Do you understand?"

"Yes, I understand," Kali said.

"Then you must be very good at mathematics, *Colonel,*" Jare said to Kali with a stone-cold stare. They both knew what he was referring to. They could both hear Yvonne admonishing them about Kali's grades.

Kali leaned forward over his knees. He looked at Jare fully, examining his eyes for any lie or body-language tell that might happen with his next question.

"Zabu, is there a way to stop these machines you developed?"

Jare sat back away from Kali, his arms folded in arrogance, because he knew that he now held all the cards.

"Yes, there is a way. They are controlled from a central module."

"Where is that module? Do you know?"

"I have no idea. But there is only one man who can turn it off, and make every Brainwave fail in midair."

"And who is that man, Zabu?"

But Kali already knew the answer, because of the way Jare leaned back and smirked, and so did everyone else who was watching the feed.

"You'd better start treating that man well now," Ando said in Kali's earpiece. "You might have to take him with you."

Kali dipped his chin in the affirmative, a signal to Ando that he knew the boss could see.

Then he nodded at Jare, who understood they'd succeeded with their game.

And Jare nodded too . . .

FORTY-TWO

BAGRAM AIRFIELD, AFGHANISTAN

LUCAS VAN GROOT'S FALCON WAS HIDDEN DEEP IN-side one of the old F-18 hangars that had once belonged to the US Air Force. Its Brainwave antenna, like a bristling steel mustache, was mounted on its nose, but it couldn't be seen now by American Keyhole satellites. Through a formal agreement with the New Afghan Emirates government, no American Predators or other high-flying drones were allowed anymore in Afghan airspace. The eyes of the Western powers that had once ruled the skies were now blind.

The rest of Afghanistan's newly upgraded squadrons were also arranged inside the long rows of abandoned hangars and fitted with Brainwave devices. There were thirty-two strike fighters armed with missiles and bombs, eighteen Black Hawk helicopters, and twelve Russian heavy-lift helos, all retrofitted with long-range fuel tanks. Only the largest cargo aircraft—the left-behind C-130s and KC-130J tanker-refuelers—were outside on the tarmac, but those were covered with camouflage netting. To the eyes of any surveillance satellites, the Bagram airstrip looked like a paltry aircraft boneyard.

It was nighttime. On the eastern side of the airstrip, where the Green Beans Coffee trailer had once served thousands of homesick American troops, the fires of a *shura* council's traditional gathering made the coals glow red under strips of lamb. The Western picnic tables and benches had been removed, and in their place was a circle of colorful braided pillows and Afghan rugs.

The pillows were occupied by many men, some in traditional

Afghan garb, some in Western clothing, with armed bodyguards standing back in the flickering darkness. Lucas van Groot was there, along with Nabuto, the Russian general Vitaly Chok, his translator, and a Russian air force commander dressed in plain clothes. Across from them sat Amir Baradar, his lieutenant, Khalid, four of Amir's new military junta officers, and three Afghan chief pilots who had supervised the technical upgrades. Those upgrades had been accomplished by Van Groot's South African contractors, but those men were not invited to a meeting of such high caliber.

This was the final phase of what Amir was now calling "Operation Hurricane." It had become clear to Van Groot that Amir was the one who was running the show. His ambition to reconstitute Afghanistan into a major world power was his primary motive; he was using the Russians' ambition to carve out another chunk of eastern Europe as the catalyst for his own grand coup. However, Van Groot had delivered the method and means—Brainwave, the aircraft upgrades, and the long-range capabilities.

In forty-eight hours, the squadrons were going to launch from Bagram and lead a Russian spearhead to attack Poland and Hungary, just as they'd done in Ukraine. Using Brainwave to remain invisible, the fighters, helicopters, and cargo aircraft filled with Russian paratroopers—picked up en route—would lead a blitzkrieg into those former Soviet satellite nations that could not be stopped. Thereafter, the rest of the West and the United States would be their final target. Amir, though an Afghan himself, would become a hero to the Russians along the lines of Georgy Zhukov, the greatest tactician of World War II, and also obtain the revenge that he'd sought since America invaded his beloved Afghanistan. Then, his follow-on ambitions to not only rule Afghanistan, but also hold sway over Pakistan, Turkmenistan, and even Iran, would have full Russian support.

Van Groot loved the idea. He had no ambitions to rule the Western world or become a modern Charlemagne like Amir. NATO would finally collapse. The United States wouldn't dare respond except with idle threats and pathetic sanctions. Worldwide stock markets would tumble, oil prices would soar. And since Van Groot had pushed his financial wizards to buy up huge tranches of stocks and options, only to sell short, his enormous payday, coupled with the sale of his Brainwave technology, would be the last he would ever need.

"Gentlemen, it is a momentous evening."

Amir had just pushed his plate of rice and kebab away from his pillow. The men had been eating their meal and conversing to one another in low tones, but now that was done. Amir snapped his fingers twice, and immediately his adjutants moved around the circle, offering baklava for dessert and pouring tea. Amir sat cross-legged in the traditional fashion, but he was wearing a black T-shirt, a buttery leather jacket, jeans, and his favorite crimson kicks. The only sign that he wasn't a millennial European playboy was the small Russian Makarov pistol tucked into his waistband. He was speaking in English, while Khalid muttered the meaning to their indigenous guests.

"First, we must thank Colonel Van Groot for his technical assistance. Without his expertise, Operation Hurricane would not be taking place."

He nodded at Van Groot, who dipped his chin in thanks, while the men in the circle also nodded at the South African in appreciation. Amir had paid Van Groot a total of eleven million US dollars for the Brainwave modules, aircraft upgrades, and long-range fuel tanks, but to Van Groot it was only a token sum. He'd be making his real money on the chaos that would shortly ensue.

"Then, of course," said Amir, "we owe great gratitude to General Vitaly Chok, who will spearhead the conquests of what will soon be thought of as New Noble Russia."

Vitaly Chok listened to his translator, then smiled and touched his forehead and chest in thanks to Amir.

"I'd also like to thank my most trusted friend, Khalid." As he heard his name, Khalid turned to Amir, surprised, while he humbly continued to translate. "Despite being absent from our homeland for years, you have remained a good friend to me, and a great help to my father, Ziar. Without your loyalty, dedication, and support, none of this would be possible . . . And so, I thank you." Khalid put his hand over his heart, then saluted Amir, who reciprocated the gesture.

"And finally," Amir said as he looked at the Afghan chief pilots, "we owe our gratitude to our Afghan pilots and crews, who will soon be the heroes of Hurricane, and the spearheads of a new world order."

The pilots heard Khalid's translation, then smiled while dipping their heads in thanks.

"They will *not* be heroes," Ziar Baradar, Amir's father, said bitterly in Dari. He had suddenly appeared out of the darkness, accompanied by his lieutenants, Bilad and Shafik, who'd gone off to warn the elder of what was transpiring at the *shura*. "They will be thought of as villains by the entire world!"

Amir's expression of confidence and control froze on his face. He didn't look at his father, but he saw how Khalid swallowed, reluctant to pass Ziar's message on.

"Father," Amir said as he turned toward Ziar, who was still dressed traditionally in his *salwar* and *pakol* cap. "This is not the time for the old ways. This is the time for my generation, not yours."

"You and your generation have forgotten the holy word, Amir," Ziar said. "The way of our ancestors is peace, not ambition. The way of our fathers is faith, not power and riches." Then he turned to Khalid with a pointed finger. "And you! I expected more from you, Khalid! I expected you to be a leader of warriors, not the follower of a fool . . . even if that fool is my own son!" Khalid looked down in subtle shame.

Amir's face reddened, but he waved off his father with a dismissive hand and rose to his feet. He called out to two of his adjutants, giving them orders. They hurried away, then came back with small ornate glass cups and bottles of something that was not tea. As they distributed the cups to the guests and filled them, General Chok saw the fury crawling over Ziar Baradar's face.

The liquid was arrak. Alcohol was forbidden by the devout, and

Amir was rubbing his blatant Westernization in his father's already festering wounds. Chok leaned over to Van Groot and spoke in English.

"What is this boy doing, Colonel?"

"He is building his empire, General," Van Groot said.

"It appears to me that he is causing a deep fissure in the ranks of his people, perhaps endangering our entire venture."

"It is a family matter," Van Groot said. "Let's see if the boy tends to it."

Nabuto, on Van Groot's other side, leaned toward his boss. "VG, we could wind up having a bloody gunfight here."

"Don't worry, Pretorius." Van Groot patted Nabuto's knee, though he was watching Ziar as the old man conversed heatedly with Bilad and Shafik, who appeared to be urging him to leave. "And by the way, what's the status with Mr. Riley?" he asked, meaning Spencer.

Nabuto didn't answer, because Vitaly Chok was too close. Instead, he quickly typed a message into his cell phone and showed the text to Van Groot.

We'll inject Riley this morning. Chok already transferred the ten million to us. By the time they get Riley to Moscow, he'll be a corpse.

Van Groot nodded and nudged the cell phone back into Nabuto's lap.

"And so, gentlemen." Amir raised his glass of arrak to the circle of guests. "A toast, in the manner of all civilized nations!"

They all raised their glasses as well, although some of the Afghan pilots seemed hesitant. They had never in their lives before sipped any sort of forbidden drink but knew that now they were expected to change.

"To the new Afghanistan!" Amir continued. "To the New Noble Russia! To a new world order where the dying West will show us the respect we deserve! Never again will they think that Afghanistan is their colonial playground, that they are our masters, and we are their slaves! To honor and victory!" As Khalid translated it became clear to Amir that despite the volume of his translation, his heart—having been challenged by Ziar—was in a tenuous place. This enraged Amir further, and he harnessed his anger to repeat his thunderous finale.

"To honor and victory!" all the guests called out, in Pashto, Dari, English, and Russian, as everyone but Khalid downed his arrak, while the imbibing Afghans sputtered and coughed.

"I will celebrate nothing!" Ziar lunged forward, snatched the heretical cup from his son's hand, and threw it to the ground, where it smashed into pieces on a warming rock. "We agreed that our mission would be to make Afghanistan and her borders secure forever, and instead you have sold our souls to the devil! This is not honor! It is blasphemy!" He spun on Amir in fury. "You are no longer my son. You are nothing but a Western lapdog."

Ziar swept his checkered *shemag* around his neck and stormed off, back into the night, calling out prayers of entreaties and forgiveness to God. Bilad and Shafik, having just witnessed Ziar's unforgivable insult to Amir, fled in a different direction and disappeared.

All the men, in particular the Afghan warriors who knew the great Ziar Baradar's reputation, looked embarrassed and glum with the display. Amir raised a hand to quiet their whispering discomfort and said, "Gentlemen, gentlemen. Do not be disturbed." He smiled, though his lips were tight. "I will resolve this one outstanding issue."

Khalid looked on with concern as Amir put down his glass and walked off into the darkness, following his father, leaving the fires and the glow of the *shura* behind. He found Ziar standing on the old Bagram perimeter road, where the high concrete T-walls the Americans had erected to protect themselves from Taliban snipers and rockets still stood. But the old high wire concertina fencing was gone now, and the lanterns of the villages in the valley twinkled like fireflies. Ziar was standing there staring at his beloved country. His shoulders trembled because he was still livid and breathing hard.

"You must stop your rebellious talk, Father," Amir said from a few feet away.

Ziar spun on him, walked up to Amir, and slapped his face.

"You are not my child! You are a nightmare to me and your blessed mother, may she rest in eternal peace!"

Amir slowly turned his face back toward his father. The rage of an unjustly punished small child was in his eyes.

"I . . . must . . . *warn* you, Father." His fists were balled at his sides.

"Warn me? How dare you speak to me this way, and in front of infidels no less! I will not let you do this. I will not let you execute your foolhardy plan and destroy all that we have fought for all these terrible years! We threw them out, we vanquished them all, we have a chance to be men of honor, and free, and at peace. You will destroy us all!"

"I will not tell you again, Father," Amir said. "I will not let you keep us all in the Stone Age. Do not test me. I am who you made me to be now."

"You are a slave to them, Amir," Ziar hissed. "You will do this over my dead body!"

And Ziar raised his calloused palm to slap his son once again, but Amir pulled a Karambit arc-shaped knife from his waistband and swiped the blade across his neck. Blood rushed down Ziar's shirt. He grabbed his wound with both hands, his eyes blinked hard, and he tried to say something, but instead toppled back in the dust, dead.

Across the road and hidden by a dilapidated building were Bilad and Shafik. They looked on in horror but maintained their silence out of fear that they would be next.

"So be it," Amir whispered.

He stood there, shaking with rage. The tears sprang to his eyes, but he swatted them away with the back of his knife hand and murmured a prayer that he hadn't evoked since he'd given up the faith. He folded the knife, tucked it into the back of his jeans, then turned to walk back to the *shura*, but stopped in his tracks.

Lucas van Groot was standing there on a small rise, looking down at him. The South African sighed, almost as if he were sympathetic. He snapped his fingers twice and Nabuto and another one of Van

Groot's men emerged. Nabuto and the man walked past Amir and unfolded a body bag by Ziar's corpse.

"Where did he go, mate?" Van Groot asked.

Amir gave him a confused look. "What?"

"Unless you want to start a civil war, you're gonna have to come up with a good cover story for this."

Amir turned from Van Groot and watched as Nabuto and the man put Ziar in the body bag and zipped it up.

After waiting a few seconds for an answer from Amir, Van Groot spoke. "Let me help you out . . . Your father stormed off, you caught up with him, and he said he was going to his third wife's village in the Kunduz mountains to clear his head. Didn't specify for how long but asked that you be gone by the time he's back. That sound about right?"

"Yes," Amir muttered. "That's what happened."

"Good. They'll make sure not a bone or ash is left. It will be as though he disappeared from the face of the earth and only us four will know the secret to the magic trick," Van Groot said before nodding at Nabuto and the man. They picked up the heavy body bag and walked off into the dark of the night, leaving Van Groot and Amir alone.

As Bilad and Shafik continued to look on from their hiding place, Van Groot walked down to Amir, slipped an arm around his shoulder, and began walking him back to the meeting.

"Never mind, Amir," he said. "Sometimes there's only one way to move forward, mate . . . It was business, not personal."

FORTY-THREE

THE WHITE HOUSE, WASHINGTON, DC

IT IS CALLED THE TUNNEL OF SPIES, BUT VERY FEW PEOple know it exists. Two blocks away from the presidential residence at 1600 Pennsylvania Avenue, there is a small, nondescript alleyway on H Street nestled between Bay Atlantic University and a parking garage. At the mouth of the alleyway a thick steel vehicle barrier rises up from the cement, with a red-and-white drop pole just above that, both controlled by Secret Service agents in a recessed bulletproof guard post behind.

If you can get past the agents—and you'd better have a good reason to do so—you then walk two blocks between the high, redbrick alley walls to the rear of the Treasury Department annex, where a double-thick pair of heavily barred doors made of brass looks like the entrance to a gigantic lion's cage.

If someone will open those doors for you, you then pass through a long, musky tunnel that leads to the White House basement. The whole thing was constructed during World War II as an escape route for Franklin D. Roosevelt, in the event that the Nazis bombed the White House into rubble. The fear wasn't far fetched, as during that time the Germans were bombing London and the Horse Guards were often sending Winston Churchill down to "the tube" to keep him alive.

Now the tunnel is rarely used, except for discreet visitors, presidential paramours, and intelligence agents who can't be seen wandering through the West Wing like tourists.

Ando, the director of Black Box, fit the bill.

Ando waited outside the tall brass doors while the uniformed

Secret Service agents inside the tunnel looked him over on a security monitor. Then both sets of doors swung open and they motioned him inside, where a pair of plainclothes agents inspected his
CIA identification card. They'd already been notified by the presidential chief of staff and national security adviser, Frank Gibson,
that Ando was going to arrive, but they were still professionally
cautious.

"Are you carrying, sir?" one of them asked, meaning a personal
weapon.

"Only my cell phone and a wallet," Ando said.

"Do you mind if we check?" the other agent asked.

"Feel free. My tailor does it all the time."

Ando was wearing a dark blue suit and a tie. If you were meeting
with the president, you didn't show up in jeans and a windbreaker.
He opened the suit jacket and the agents looked him over, but they
didn't use their hands. Their expert eyes would spot any object that
"printed" in his dress shirt, waist, or trousers. They nodded and he
rebuttoned his jacket.

"Mr. Gibson's right down there," one of the agents said as he gestured down the length of the dimly lit tunnel.

Ando walked. Gibson was standing there in the shadows, looking like a gray ghost. He was wearing a double-breasted herringbone
suit, like a throwback to Eliot Ness, and Ando guessed he was also
wearing suspenders. Gibson reached out and shook Ando's hand.

"I'd say that it's good to see you, Ando," Gibson said, "but my
blessed mother taught me not to lie."

"Same here, sir," Ando replied. "It's not exactly a happy occasion."

"Let's go." Gibson walked toward the White House basement,
which was another two blocks through the secret passageway, with
Ando walking beside him. "I received your classified briefing an
hour ago. You're sure about this?"

"As sure as we can be at the moment," Ando said. "Van Groot
is already inside Afghanistan, currently at Bagram Airfield, along
with some of his cohorts. The source we captured in Lagos has pin-
pointed more than fifty aircraft of various types at the airfield, which

we assume to be combat aircraft, all fitted with radar-defeating Brainwave devices. That same source claims that the devices were tuned to defeat air defenses in Hungary and Poland."

"Fuck my life," Gibson grunted, surprising Ando with the raw profanity, but the emotion was sincere. "Any further bad news?"

"Well, we firmly believe that our agent, the one that was cap-tured in Geneva, is also being held somewhere in that AO," Ando said as they walked, using military jargon for "area of operations." There was no one else inside the tunnel, which made it seem like a one-way passage to hell. "We drew that conclusion based on Van Groot's double-talk during his meeting with Kent in Barbados, as well as the fact that Van Groot's now in Afghanistan. He knows US forces can no longer operate there, so it's the perfect spot to hold our man hostage."

"That's another layer of feces on an already shitty cake," Gibson growled.

Ando agreed with that dark assessment, but he didn't want to dwell on Spencer's fate. "Did you have time to brief the president?" he asked.

"I made an effusive attempt," Gibson said, "but his sole focus right now is the upcoming election. Afghanistan is the last thing he wants to hear about. That's why you're here. He tends to listen to the spooks. He's a spy novel fan."

"All right, sir. I'll do my best."

At the end of the tunnel two more plainclothes agents stood guard at a heavy steel door. They opened it using a digital keypad, then turned an industrial key inside the door's pneumatic lock. Ando and Gibson stepped out from the tunnel into the White House basement, where they turned left, trotted up a short set of stairs, and entered the Situation Room in the sublevel under the West Wing. The centerpiece of the Situation Room was a very large conference space with a long, polished table, plush chairs for VIPs, backup seats for staff, flat-screens, secure communications telephones, and encryption modules. It was the place where the president planned wars and handled international crises with his cabinet and Pentagon staff, but today there was no one there. Instead, the president was tucked away in a private side office with yellow-framed secure telephones and another flat-screen, behind a large desk that faced a few more guest chairs. A stern Secret Service agent was posted outside the door.

"All right," Gibson murmured to Ando as he knocked. "Let's see if we can twist his arm."

"Come on in, boys," the president called out, and they went in.

President Jack Turner was sitting behind his desk, squinting at a computer screen and scrolling through numbers with a mouse. His suit jacket was off, his blue silk tie pulled open. He was a tall man with swept-back gray hair, a college quarterback's handsome face, and a smooth Oklahoma accent. He didn't look up at Gibson, whom he spent most of his professional days and nights with, but he glanced at Ando, grinned his best electioneering smile, and stretched out a hand.

"Travis Ando, Mr. President," Ando said. "CIA."

"You don't strike me as a Travis," the president said.

"Come again, Mr. President?"

"I'm just kidding." He chuckled at his own joke. "Lighten up, CIA."

"Yes, Mr. President," Ando replied with a false smirk and nod.

"Which division y'all from?"

"Mr. Ando's with Black Box, sir," Gibson said.

"Superspies! All right, have a seat."

"That's all right. We'll stand, sir," Gibson said. "We don't have much time."

"Frank, you're always so darn dramatic." The president pointed at his monitor. "Have you seen these poll numbers today? It's like I'm Charles Manson now or somethin'."

"I'm afraid they're going to get worse, sir, if we don't attend to this problem."

Turner sighed, sat back, folded his fingers behind his head, and looked at Ando with a good-ol'-boy expression.

"All right, let's hear your pitch, Mr. Ando."

"Mr. President, as I believe Mr. Gibson has already informed you," Ando said, "we've got a critical situation in Afghanistan."

"That situation isn't critical anymore," Turner said. "We're out."

Ando ignored the interruption and went on.

"Sir, our target, this South African colonel, Van Groot, has been taking wealthy civilian hostages, collecting ransoms, and manipulating worldwide stock markets. Now he has provided heavily armed, reconstituted air squadrons inside Afghanistan with devices that defeat air defenses and radar. We believe, through fresh, actionable intelligence, that the Afghan faction commanding those aircraft is going to cooperate with the Russians for a redux of their Ukraine invasion, but this time taking out Poland and Hungary, with the intention of moving on to decimate NATO. What we're asking for is clearance for a small contingent of special operations troops, along with our teams, to go in and stop them before they can launch."

The president blinked at Ando, then smiled as if Ando were putting him on.

"Is that all, Mr. Ando?" He laughed. "The big bad Russkies are gonna take over the world? Like Dr. Evil?"

"It's not a joke, Mr. President," Gibson said. He'd thrust his bony hands into his suit pockets, as if he didn't trust them. "This is serious business."

"Well, gentlemen, unless you've got proof positive . . . and I assume that much of this is speculation, sort of like all those WMDs in Iraq . . . I don't know if I can commit to that. If you're wrong, and we send troops back into that hellhole, and some of them come home in flag-draped coffins . . . Hell, we've got an election coming up."

"Mr. Ando isn't wrong, sir," Gibson said. "His people are top notch. He's got a source from inside Van Groot's organization, the very man who developed the radar-evading devices. You know I'm a skeptic, sir, but their information is close to ninety percent, if not higher."

The president unspooled his fingers from behind his head and raised his hands and face to the ceiling.

"Oh, Lordy, where have I heard this before?" He looked at Gibson. "Frank, you and your conspiracy theories! Everybody said Ukraine was going to be my Waterloo, it was gonna be a nuclear nightmare, and now the whole thing's calmed right down." He shook his head. "Nope, not gonna do it. Sorry, gents."

Before Turner could get "gents" out, Frank pulled a hand from his pocket and slapped the president's desk in fury. "What's wrong with you people?!"

Turner slightly flinched, not expecting his most loyal staffer to erupt. Ando too looked on with a mixture of surprise and concern.

Then Gibson, realizing how out of bounds he was, tried to collect himself. His eyes shifted past Turner to a row of framed pictures on the wall behind the POTUS's chair—presidents and politicians grinning and shaking hands—and he could no longer control his fury.

"That's the problem with *all* you politicians, Mr. President!" He jabbed a finger at Turner, who leaned away in his chair. "Republicans *and* Democrats! You care more about elections than you do actual people! And fail to realize that it's about lives! Human lives! Men, women, children, your allies, your foes, and everyone in between!"

Gibson took a brief pause and both Turner and Ando knew darn well not to take his break as a sign to interject.

"A lot of people can die, and here you are playing this ridiculous political game just for votes—so you can what? Ensure that your political party maintains power? Keep the other side out, huh? Well, let me tell you something, this isn't the United States of Republicans or the United States of Democrats, it's the United States of America! And unless we can put aside our unilateral goals and work together to make decisions for the greater good of humanity, then the trauma's just going to keep getting worse!"

Gibson was shouting now. Ando actually took a step back, and the president recoiled from Gibson's flying spittle.

"We've completely lost our credibility as the leader of the free world because of what we allowed!" Gibson pointed to a digital map that showed Russia highlighted red, and next to Russia stood what was once Ukraine, which was also highlighted red and with the text "New Russia."

"That happened because of a lack of balls, and the voters think those balls are *yours*. So if your numbers are tanking now, wait till the Russians and their Afghan partners blitz their way through Poland and Hungary and take out NATO! Your election's going to be in the shitter! And if you're *not lucky*, what's going to happen over there will quickly be coming to a theater near *you*! But I guess you'll be fine in this underground bunker. Isn't that right, Mr. President?"

The Secret Service agent opened the door, poked his head inside, looked around, and said to the president, "Sir, everything all right in here?"

"Yes, Sean, yes . . . It's all right." The president waved him off. "Family matter."

The agent nodded and withdrew, but Gibson wasn't finished. He shot a thumb in Ando's direction.

"This man and his agents risk their lives for us all on a daily basis. You think I'd bring him in here for this if it wasn't real? Is that something I'd normally do?"

Ando was actually shocked. Gibson always gave Black Box such a hard time, and now he was defending what was usually a thorn in his side.

"All right, Frank." The president put out his big hands and waved them up and down, like he was trying to calm a hysterical child. "Cool yourself down before that old heart of yours busts." He contemplated his chief of staff's outburst for a moment, drumming his fingers on his desk. Then he looked over at Ando, but now his expression was grim. "You think this is all that serious, Mr. Ando?"

"As a heart attack, like you just mentioned, Mr. President."

The president rubbed his big chin. Gibson was standing upright again, but he was still trembling with emotion. Ando waited for whatever was coming next.

"Well, hot damn," the president said. "What other options do we have?"

"None that we can think of, sir," Ando said. "And we've explored them all. Either you approve this action and take the risk that we might be wrong, or you deny us permission, it turns out we're right, and, as Mr. Gibson said, your upcoming election efforts won't matter."

"Damn," the president muttered. "That's a devil's alternative."

"That is correct, sir," Gibson said. He'd calmed somewhat and backed off from the president's desk. "That's why you get the big bucks."

"Hell, I should have stayed a governor. Biggest issue was lousy roads and school lunches." The president looked at Ando again. He knew that whatever choice he made now would follow him till his end of days. "How much time do we have, Mr. Ando?"

"Twenty-four hours, sir. Tops."

"All right, gentlemen. Have an action plan on my desk in two hours. Then I'll make a final decision."

Ando looked at Gibson. The chief of staff nodded. It was the best they could do.

"Now get out of here, people," Turner said. "I've got a fundraiser tonight, and so far, my speechwriters are making me look like Jimmy Carter."

"We'll be back in two hours," Gibson replied.

"Can't wait," the president quipped sarcastically, and pointed at the door.

Gibson and Ando nodded in thanks and walked to the door as the Secret Service agent opened it. They were almost out of the office when Turner spoke once more.

"And Mr. Ando," he said. Ando respectfully turned around. "If you're wrong about this . . . you're fired."

"Understood, Mr. President," Ando said, and then he and Gibson quietly closed the door and headed back out toward the tunnel of spies.

FORTY-FOUR

FIVE MINUTES TO ROMEO," THE C-17 PILOT IN COM-
mand said into his headset. He was working the joystick, throttles, and flaps, trying to keep the big beast under control. The
headwinds were slapping the cockpit at forty knots and it felt like
wrangling an eighteen-wheeler in a hurricane.

"I can't believe we're actually doing this," his copilot grunted as
the aircraft pitched and rolled in the midnight darkness.

"Well, Gator," the PIC said, using his partner's call sign, "the
green light came directly from sixteen hundred."

"That proves it, Razor," the copilot said in return. "POTUS has
finally *manned up.*"

"Romeo" was the code word for the border between Pakistan
and Afghanistan. They were at twenty-six thousand feet above the
Khyber Pass, a plot of space in the sky where only fools dared
to fly. The pass had been a notorious graveyard for ambitious con-
querors across the centuries, where the bones of British, Russians,
Indians, and even the warriors of Genghis Khan still lay bleaching
in the Afghan sun. But the Khyber Pass was braced by mountain
ranges and enormous peaks that swirled up furious lightning and
thunderstorms—maelstroms of Mother Nature that tore aircraft
out of the sky like shotguns ripping apart quails. That made it the
most unlikely place for an American military aircraft to trespass
into Afghan airspace, but it was also a bitch to navigate.

Added to the challenges of wind and weather was the lack of
tactical intelligence on the ground. Since the fall of Kabul, there
were no longer any American or coalition recon troops or UAVs to

report on the New Afghan Emirates' military activity. All that was left was a handful of Black Box Aberration agents who maintained CIA ratlines, just in case other clandestine agents or Tier One operators had to move in and out. They also provided "atmospherics"—information on the current environment—but without the cover of coalition forces, and due to so many Afghan interpreters being killed by the Taliban, they were spread too thin to be as effective as in the days of old.

"Five minutes to Romeo!" Pacenza, in the rear of the cargo hold with the Package and all of the Black Box team, repeated the pilot's call and shot five fingers up at the C-17's ceiling. All of them were running a final gear check of their ram-air parachutes, helmets, oxygen rigs, weapons, and ammunition. They were beyond the three special operations vehicles still strapped down to the floor, which they weren't going to use tonight, but the vehicles were bouncing around as if they might break their bonds, roll to the rear, and crush everyone in their path.

"I am *not* staying behind, Jason!" Neveah said as she continued to gear up with her parachute and weapons. "*You* stay, if you're so convinced we have to leave someone on board."

"But you're the best C3 operator we have," Jason countered, though it was obvious to Neveah that once again he was trying to protect her from what could certainly be a suicide mission.

They were having a heated discussion about the deployment. Protocol required that a subject matter expert should remain behind on the aircraft—in most cases that would be Thane, as Overwatch. However, in this case, once the Package was deployed, someone would also have to liaise and manage operations on board, because the C-17 would then be serving as a C3 (command, control, and communications) aerial platform for the follow-on mission over eastern Europe. Ando had ordered Thane to deploy with his team—the mission was so critical he wanted his Overwatch on the ground. Now they had to decide who would remain behind. Jason was lobbying hard for that person to be Neveah.

"I've got five combat tours in the AO with MARSOC," he argued further, meaning the Marine Forces Special Operations Command. "I know the territory, and obviously Thane and Kali and his Uber passenger have to be down there too."

Kali was wearing a Butler TT-600 rig, a large tandem parachute capable of handling six hundred pounds. Jare was wearing only a harness that would be snap-linked to Kali's chest. He was also wearing an oxygen rig and a helmet with a headset, but the terror of the entire ordeal had him mumbling in his Lagos accent, "I do not want to do this! *Why* do we have to do this!?"

Kali ignored him.

"That's bullshit, Jason," Neveah said—such expletives were rare for her.

"Stand down, people, and let me *think*," Thane ordered as he worked over his gear.

Just ten minutes prior, President Turner had finally green-lit the mission, but he'd made it clear to Ando once more that if the operation failed, or if any of the Package or Black Box personnel were captured, Ando would be seeking other employment—and so would Thane's entire Black Box team. Ando had *not* relayed that to Thane; he'd have enough to worry about as Overwatch on the ground. But Thane was smart enough to know that if this mission was a failure, it would leave a lasting blemish on Black Box's track record.

Just after the president's reluctant blessing, Frank Gibson had then told President Turner he'd have to place American F-16 and F-15 fighter squadrons in Germany on full alert, as well as inform the governments of Poland and Hungary, so their fighter squadrons could also fuel and arm up. Turner had wanted to murder his chief of staff, but he knew he was right, so he'd done it.

"Ms. NV is right, Zane," Kali finally said, still in his Nigerian "Colonel" accent, as he pulled Jare's back into his chest and locked him to his tandem harness. "We might need her on the X."

"I am *not* jumping out of an airplane!" Jare continued to wail. "It is not natural. I will not do this!"

"*Gbenu so un!*" Shut your mouth, Kali hissed.

Thane considered the makeup of his operational team for another moment, then said, "All right. We *all* go. Air force has a good-enough C3 and nav guy in the cockpit. He'll manage it."

Neveah looked over at Jason with both triumph and fury in her eyes. He turned his face away and kept on gearing up.

This time, the assault package was going to HAHO into their drop zone. The insertion technique—high altitude, high opening—meant exiting the aircraft, deploying parachutes right away, then gliding through the night over many kilometers and landing with a whisper, undetected by radar. The target was a small town deep inside Afghanistan called Chelgazi, on an open plain thirty kilometers west of the Khyber Pass. Two Black Box Aberration agents, who'd been in deep cover in Kabul and Jalalabad for a decade, would rendezvous in Chelgazi with the assault package and provide them with five nondescript vehicles, as well as any actionable intelligence they had. But first the C-17 had to penetrate five kilometers into Afghan airspace, deploy the Package, and turn back around.

Tonight, all thirty operators of Pacenza's full Package would be going in. They were lined up in two sticks on opposite sides of the fuselage, facing the huge rear cargo ramp, which was still closed. They were wearing various Afghan-style jackets, with *shemags* wound tightly around their necks, and baggy pantaloons temporarily bloused with thick rubber bands over their boots. They were gripping the aircraft's fuselage spars to keep from being tossed to the floor in the turbulence.

"One minute to Romeo," the pilot in command called over comms.

"One minute!" Pacenza repeated, holding up one finger now.

All at once, the entire raid contingent fell silent. Like Jason, every one of the men had operated in and out of Afghanistan at one point or another, some on multiple tours. They'd all left that hellhole, under what they considered dishonorable circumstances, but now they were going back in. Crossing that border again, but this time in the other direction, was a meet-your-maker moment for each of them.

"Romeo, Romeo, Romeo," the pilot said. Now it would be a fast five more kilometers through turbulence and unknown threats, and then they'd fling themselves into space. They all started moving closer to the ramp. As Pacenza's boots neared the ramp's massive hinges in the steel floor—

"Missile, inbound!" the pilot snapped over comms. "Brace, brace, brace!"

"Shit!" barked one of the two crew chiefs manning the ramp. They were both wearing oxygen masks but their eyes were huge as they grabbed fuselage spars.

There were antiaircraft batteries in the Khyber now, but the pilots didn't know that until the missile came screaming at them. All of the Package and the Black Box team grabbed on to whatever they could and braced, but the C-17 banked hard to the right in a crazy evasive maneuver. Thane, Jason, Neveah, and Kali with Jare smashed into the starboard fuselage. On the port side, Sumo's grip was ripped from a spar and he plunged to the tilting floor. Two more operators tumbled onto their backs atop their parachute cases, flailing their arms and cursing. Another operator smashed down onto his face, fracturing his right wrist. It was absolute chaos.

In the cockpit, the glass instruments were flashing wild numbers and a stall warning screamed as the two pilots, angled hard to the right against their harnesses, took the steel monster into a dive that was way outside its manual's warnings.

"Here it comes," the PIC said as a glowing object raced up from between two craggy peaks far below in the night. The pilots punched their countermeasures buttons, launching chaff—clouds of aluminum strips to confuse radar-tracking missiles—and a pod of magnesium flares to foil heat-seeking warheads, which lit up the night outside like giant flashbulbs.

"Where the heck did that come from, Razor?" the copilot said as he helped his chief grip the vibrating joysticks and rudder pedals.

"It's a freakin' Russian S-300. We're not the only ones who left those bastards some toys!"

The missile roared past the aircraft's port side, with a tail like dragon fire spewing from its engine. Then it found the burst of white-hot flares and exploded, smacking the fuselage with its aftershock like a chorus of steel ball bearings.

"Let's get this bitch back on course, Gator," the PIC said as sweat dribbled down from his helmet.

"Roger, Razor," the copilot said, and they both manhandled the aircraft, turned left again, and climbed.

In the aircraft's rear, Thane and his crew, and Pacenza and his Package, were just regaining their footing and trying to breathe through their hissing oxygen masks. Some of Pacenza's men were injured, but they just gritted their teeth and prepared to jump.

"One minute out," came the pilot's warning.

"One minute out!" Pacenza again jabbed a finger up at the ceiling, then he turned and looked at both sticks and held up a questioning thumb. They all returned the gesture, except for Jare, who was shaking like a leaf in a hurricane.

"Ramp," the pilot called.

"Ramp!" the first crew chief repeated, then he pressed a module button attached to a long steel cable. A heavy pneumatic whine vibrated through the cargo hold, and the long, wide ramp at the back started to come down, revealing a black sky with roiling purple clouds below and a night full of blazing stars above. Then the ramp jammed, halfway down.

"Mother of God." The crew chief hammered the button again, but the ramp wouldn't move. A piece of shrapnel from the exploding missile had pierced a pneumatic feed line. The ramp was stuck at a 30-degree upward angle. He looked at Pacenza with utter despair in his eyes.

"Forget it," Pacenza boomed in his mic. "We'll climb it." He turned to both sticks and made a fist in the air. "Come on!" he yelled.

Pacenza and his operators started climbing up on the ramp, some of them so weighed down with weapons and explosives that they had to do it on all fours. A jump claxon sounded in the cargo hold and at the rear of the fuselage, and then a large beacon that had been glowing red for an hour suddenly went out as another beacon burned bright green.

"Second missile, inbound!" the PIC called out again, and the airplane cranked hard once again to the left.

"Get out the damn plane!" the crew chief yelled. He and his partner were tethered to the fuselage by long web straps, but they were pushing the tumbling operators up the ramp. Another rack of decoy flares burst from the C-17's belly, and the second missile's warhead hit the flares and exploded, its blast wave banging the fuselage like Thor's hammer.

"Go, go, *go!*" Pacenza barked as he reached the top of the up-angled ramp, got to his feet in a crouch, and jumped. His men followed him, crawling, falling, some tumbling back down and climbing again as the plane twisted and turned, until at last they hurled themselves into the night.

Thane, Jason, and Neveah crawled up the ramp like crabs, then dived into the sky from the up-tipped ramp. But Kali was burdened with Jare attached in front of him like a wailing toddler—pushing him, kneeing him in the ass as his childhood friend resisted and screamed, "I am not going! I am *not!*"

Outside in the freezing night sky, all of Pacenza's men had already deployed their ram-air parachutes, forming a long, drifting, descending line in the dark. All of them had also now pulled their night-vision goggles down over their eyes, and each had an infrared LED beacon on the back of his helmet. But they also had IR signal emitters on their wrist-mounted altimeters, and each of them clicked it once to let the man behind him know they were good to go.

Jason, floating beneath his large square canopy and working the toggles, clicked his "Okay" signal, then twisted his head around to look back up at Neveah, who was fifty meters behind him and thirty meters higher. But when Neveah clicked her signal back at him, she did it four times, as if to say, *I'm effing* fine. *Stop treating me like a baby.*

Back aboard the C-17, the pilot in command yelled it this time— "Third missile, inbound!"—and his evasive maneuver was a hard diving bank to the right. Kali and Jare were almost at the lip of the ramp when the aircraft skewed hard and downward. Kali threw out his hands over Jare's shoulders and gripped the steel ledge to keep them from being hurled back into the crevice between the ramp and the fuselage, where their ribs would be crushed like toothpicks in the maw of a shark. Then, like a mountain climber who had only one hope of surviving, he dragged himself and Jare up over the top and rolled them both over into the sky.

But they were instantly falling on their backs, totally unstable, and starting to spin clockwise. Jare was flailing his arms, making it impossible for Kali to flip over and get in a proper freefall position. They were screaming toward the ground at 180 feet per second, and Kali knew if they didn't open soon, they would wind up landing so far from the target that Thane would have to tag them as missing in action. The wind was furious, slamming their faces and bodies. Kali reached forward, gripped Jare's flailing arms, pulled them back hard, kicked one long leg far out in the sky, and rocked his body hard to the right. They flipped over, he released his grip on Jare's arms, and then threw his own arms and legs out like a starfish. As soon as he felt they were stable, he reached back and snatched his pilot chute from the pocket.

There was a rush of whipping nylon, a thundering flutter, and then it was deathly quiet. They were hanging under their parachute. Kali looked up, checked that it wasn't shredded, then reached up for the steering toggles and dragged a long, cold breath through his oxygen mask. Jare was hanging in front of him, head down, arms dangling, like a limp puppet.

"I will curse you *forever* for this, *Colonel*," Jare rasped in Kali's headset.

Kali pulled down his night-vision goggles and looked forward into the darkness, spotting the distant line of IR beacons on the back of the assault package's helmets. They were half a mile away, but if the winds were kind he thought he could catch them.

Then suddenly, a roaring explosion split the night. He and Jare twisted their heads around and looked up. A missile had just torn through the left wing of the C-17. Its fuel burst in a flower of orange flame, as half the wing tore off and went spinning away into the roiling clouds.

They watched as the aircraft slowly turned to the right and down, corkscrewed helplessly into a mountain, and exploded.

Kali maneuvered the parachute to regain their course. There were no sounds now but the wind and the rippling of nylon. Jare turned his head to look at Kali. His eyes behind his jump goggles were brimming, as he realized that Kali had just saved his life by forcing him to jump.

Kali looked down at Jare.

"Be at peace," he said. "We're alive . . ."

FORTY-FIVE

GENESIS

Kali was almost nine years old, walking down to the beach again in Lagos. His hand was grasped in his mother's, though she gripped his so hard it almost hurt. It was a brutally hot day in the summer without a wisp of breeze. The towering palm fronds were still as pitchforks and Kali's bare toes stung from the scorching sand. He had always been happy whenever his parents surprised him with a family outing, but today there would be no such thing.

Kali and Yvonne were being escorted by Chibundu and Reki, one on either side. Both corrupt policemen were wearing ties, but no jackets, with their detective badges gleaming on their belts, next to their pistols. They had come to the house and called Yvonne outside. She'd cursed at them and said she would go but she would not bring Kali. With a squad of armed cops at Chibundu's and Reki's rear they'd made it clear that she had no choice.

Jare and his widowed mother, Uloma, were also walking down to the beach. But they were staying thirty feet back from Kali and Yvonne. Kali turned his head to look at his best friend and was quickly met with the sense that Jare would come no closer. It was as if Kali and his mother had the dengue fever.

Kali fixed his gaze back in his direction of travel, trembling as he trudged through the sand. His vision was blurry and his heart was racing. There were so many people at the shore, tall men in colorful shirts, ladies all wearing headscarves as if they were going to church. They all had such stern expressions, and today even the sea seemed angry. The waves were roiling at the lip of the beach, kicking up broken seashells and stones. No one was swimming.

Once again there were many policemen in their blue uniform shirts and peaked caps, along with soldiers in their thick green uniforms and orange berets. Some of the policemen held snorting horses and many of them had fierce-looking guns.

Chibundu had a big hand on Kali's small shoulder. Reki held Yvonne by the arm. They stopped walking. Kali looked toward the water and felt weak in the knees.

Kali's father was standing on a wooden platform in front of a great pyramid of blue and white oil drums, wearing dark blue prisoner's pants and a pale blue shirt. He was tied to the drums with white rope. The Lagos State Government Free Cinema Unit truck was parked down there again, and next to it in the sand was a wooden coffin. The sight of it made Kali want to vomit. He slipped his trembling free hand into his shorts pocket and gripped the bracelet of prayer beads his father had given him.

Some sort of government official mounted the platform next to George. He was fat, dressed in a dark suit, with a collarless top like a Nehru jacket. He had small black eyes, held a silver microphone, and began reading out charges from a piece of paper.

"George Adeyemi, you are sentenced this day to execution," he said with no hint of pity or emotion.

Kali swallowed. Tears sprang from his eyes and rolled down his cheeks. Yvonne gripped his hand harder.

"You have been found guilty of embezzlement, fraud, extortion, and theft of public property. From this day forward, the island called Pearland and all its properties shall be retained by the Lagos government. Thereafter, Abeo Chibundu will be in charge of Pearland, and all the rights and holdings of the Adeyemi family shall be taken away . . . Theft has a price, and you must pay it, Mr. Adeyemi."

"It is a lie!" Yvonne suddenly screamed as she jolted forward. "These are false charges! George did everything the right way. That was all *our* money!"

Reki crushed Yvonne's arm in his grip, pulled her back into place, and bent close to hiss in her ear. "Shut *up*, Yvonne, if you know what is good for you."

She wrenched her arm from his grasp, but she covered her mouth with her hand and sobbed quietly. She was thinking now only of Kalief.

The government official smiled. He looked out at the crowd and spoke again into the microphone.

"Is there anyone here who would like to testify as to this man's character?" he asked as he perused many pairs of frightened eyes. "We just need *one* witness, and we shall consider a stay of execution, a postponement." The government official smiled more broadly. He knew no such thing would be forthcoming. "*Anyone?*"

Kali twisted his head around in desperation. He looked directly at Jare, standing there at the front of the crowd with his pauper mother, whom Kali's father had always supported. She was wearing a colorful kerchief while also holding Jare's hand.

Say something, Jare! Kali pleaded with only his eyes because he didn't dare speak. *Say something, Mrs. Zabu, please!*

But Jare intentionally avoided Kali's gaze. Instead, he stared straight ahead, as if his best friend weren't even there. Yvonne turned her head, also hoping for some kind of salvation, but Mrs. Zabu caught Yvonne's eyes for only a moment, and then looked down at the sand.

"I shall ask one more time," the official said from the podium. "Is there anyone? Anyone at all?"

Then Kali saw Mrs. Zabu looking directly up at the official, and he turned to see the official staring at her with a deadly squint in his eyes. It was clear that the surviving members of the Zabu family, and all the rest of the crowd, had been warned.

Kali snapped his head back around, looking at Jare with an anguished plea in his brimming eyes. But Jare turned his face away, once again avoiding Kali's burning stare, and so did his mother.

Kali turned his back on them, furious with the betrayal. But he looped his thin arm around his mother's waist and held her. In his tortured heart, he knew that soon he would have to be the man of the house.

The corpulent government official looked satisfied. He held the microphone up to George's lips and said something to him. George raised his chin and grew taller in his posture, and he looked directly at Kali and Yvonne.

"I am an innocent man," he said. "In my heart of hearts, I know that I did the right thing. May God forgive my enemies. My God, watch over my loved ones."

A priest in black robes began climbing the platform's stairway. George waved him away with a look. The priest retreated.

There was a large circle of sand between Kali's bare toes and his father, and all at once it was empty. Then a soldier was barking something, and three other soldiers marched into the circle with rifles. They stopped and stomped in the sand, like the British soldiers of old, then turned toward George and raised their rifles.

Yvonne keened a terrible sound and covered Kali's eyes with her hands. But Chibundu leaned down and pulled them away.

"He must watch, Yvonne," he said. "The boy must understand what happens when men like us are crossed, so that he may never make the same mistake."

The commander of the firing squad barked, "Ready!"

Kali gasped as the men took their rifles off safety.

"Aim!"

Yvonne crushed Kali's hand harder.

"Fire!"

Bang!

Kali slammed his eyes shut. Reki gripped the back of his neck and tried to force him to watch, but he wouldn't.

Bang! Bang! Bang!

There was a long moment of silence, with no sound other than the curling waves on the shore. Kali forced himself to open his eyes. His father was staring at him, taking his last earthly breath, as blood flowed from his gunshot wounds. Then his head fell to his chest.

Kali buried his face in his mother's belly and hugged her as she wept . . .

FORTY-SIX

CHELGAZI, AFGHANISTAN

KALI AND JARE PLOWED INTO THE EARTH JUST EAST of the Rodat–Deh Bala road.

The parachute landing was routine for Kali, but another horror for Jare, who squeezed his eyes shut as they swept through the night and the ground came rushing at them. Then all at once their four bootheels were skidding through dust. Kali sat down hard on his butt to stop their skid, the parachute collapsed, and Jare slumped back against Kali's chest and muttered "Thank God" in Yoruba.

But they were a mile short of the drop zone, which was due east past the small village of Chelgazi, in an open bowl of desert at the foot of a range of craggy hills. Kali wasted no seconds. He unhooked his harness from Jare's and jumped up, leaving Jare still breathless in the dirt, then quickly dragged the parachute in by the risers. He didn't have time to bury the huge nylon "kite," so he shed his harness, stuffed the chute back into its deployment bag, slung the whole rig over his shoulder, and draped his MK18 rifle strap around his neck. Then he dragged Jare up off the ground and said, "*Come on.*"

They ran due east. The clouds had cleared from the purple-black sky and the starlight showed shadows of rocks and outcroppings, enough so that Kali could lope at top speed. But Jare was shorter, and scared out of his mind, so he instantly fell behind.

"Why are we running, Kali?" Jare rasped from his burning lungs.

"Do *not* use that name," Kali warned in his Nigerian accent, not swaying from his Chameleon disguise. He turned and glared at Jare's wide eyes. "I am the Colonel. Do not forget that for a moment."

Right after the president had approved the mission, Thane had pulled Kali aside aboard the C-17 and reminded him not to break character. He'd said it was crucial that Jare keep believing that the "Colonel" would harm his mother if he failed to complete the mission. Kali, of course, had agreed, though he knew that *both* he and Jare were deceiving Thane about the nature of their relationship.

"All right, *Colonel*," Jare said. "But why must we run like this?"

"Because we are short of the drop zone," Kali said. "If we do not arrive in time, they will leave us."

"Leave us? Alone? Here?"

"*Run*," Kali urged.

Something was gleaming from a dip in the ground up ahead. It ran from north to south like a winding silver ribbon. Then Kali realized the ribbon was a river, between him and Jare and the hulking huts of Chelgazi beyond. There was no way around it.

"I . . . I cannot swim!" Jare exclaimed as he tried to stop before the rushing waters.

"Liar," Kali said. They'd swum together in Kali's pool a hundred times as young boys.

He spun around, gripped the sleeve of Jare's Afghan *salwar*, spun back, and pounded into the river, dragging Jare with him. The tumbling water was freezing cold but it appeared to be only waist deep, and the river was just twenty meters wide. When they climbed out the other side, they were soaked from their stomachs to their sloshing boots.

"I will *never* forgive you for this," Jare gasped.

"I have heard that before," Kali said as he started running again.

They skirted the village of Chelgazi, giving the cluster of dark huts a wide berth, then pressed on across a plain of hard-packed earth and thorny scrubs as hungry vultures wheeled in the black sky above. Then Kali spotted a thick grove of poplar and hazelnut trees in the distance, at the foot of a low ridgeline. He ran faster, with Jare panting behind, and through his night-vision goggles he saw an infrared beacon winking. He punched the signal button on his altimeter so Pacenza and his men would hold their fire.

He slowed, jogged up to the rally point, and stopped. Behind him, Jare stopped too, then bent over, coughed, gripped his knees, and drooled in the dust. Pacenza and his men appeared to all be there, digging shallow graves in the dirt for their bunched-up parachutes, although four of them were sitting on the ground being tended to by a medic. Five civilian vehicles that looked like a mix of Isuzu vans and Toyota pickups were tucked back into the trees, and Kali saw two figures in full Afghan garb, their grins glinting white in the starlight as they shook both of Thane's hands and whispered in Dari, the Afghan dialect of Persian.

"You look very good for an old man!" one of them, a woman, was saying.

"We never thought we would see you again!" said the other one, a man.

Kali understood that these were the two Aberration agents. Thane had spent many years as an Aberration agent himself, so he clearly knew them from past adventures.

"I always show up when you least expect it," Thane said in English, and the two agents laughed.

"I see you took an Overwatch billet," the man said.

"Not *took*," Thane said. "More like forced."

Pacenza was standing close by, along with Sumo, Jason, and Neveah. Kali heard the medic saying to one of the operators on the ground, "That wrist is busted. It's no good."

"It's as good as your mom was last night," the operator scoffed. "That's why we train to shoot with both damn hands."

Now Thane was looking down at the Aberration agents. His expression had turned serious.

"Tell me you've got something good," he said to them in English.

"We think so, Thane," the male agent said. "But we cannot be sure." He had bronze skin, his head was swathed in a rough burnoose, and he had a heavy Pashtun accent. He and his partner were

Americans, yet they'd been in deep cover within Black Box's Aberration program for so long that they seemed like native Afghans.

"We will show you," the woman said. She was dressed in a full burka that covered her from head to toe. She pulled an acetate map from a cardboard tube, squatted, and spread it out on the ground. These agents were still old school.

Ando had sent an encrypted message to the Aberration agents—whose cover names were Ali and Sadaf—as soon as President Turner had hinted that he might consider the mission. Ando had informed them that one of his Black Box agents was possibly being held somewhere in the Afghan AO, and they should quickly scour all their sources for actionable intelligence. As the male agent, Ali, placed rocks on the corners of the map, Sadaf pulled a small red penlight from her burka and flicked it on. Everyone squatted to look as she touched a spot with her sun-brown finger.

"This is our best guess," she said. "A place called Silwar. It is a small mountain village six kilometers west of Bagram."

"Why there?" Kali asked.

The two agents looked at him. He was dressed like all the rest, in Afghan mufti, but he looked African and had a thick Nigerian accent. However, they'd been working with Black Box for more than a decade and nothing surprised them.

"We have a very wide network after all this time," Ali said to Kali. "Even though the Taliban have found many and killed them, some are still very brave. One of them lives in a village near Silwar. He did reconnaissance while herding his goats and told us if he were hiding a hostage, Silwar would be the place."

"There is one building," Sadaf said now to Thane, "with strange activity. It is heavily guarded by foreign fighters—white men who look like Europeans, and one Black man who appears to be African."

Kali looked over at Jason and Neveah, who both gave him confirming nods. They were thinking the same thing . . . *Nabuto!*

"Other men come and go too," Sadaf continued. "An Afghan dressed like a Westerner, and perhaps one Russian."

Thane turned to Kali. Behind Kali, Jare was sitting in the dirt, brooding.

"What do you think, Colonel?" Thane said.

"As you Americans say," Kali said, "I would put money on it."

"Six klicks from Bagram," Pacenza said, shaking his head. "That's a logistical problem."

"Right," Thane said as he looked at Pacenza. "That means we'll have to split our forces, and we're already understrength with the wounded."

"Wounded?" Pacenza scoffed. "We've only got a couple of broken bones, a concussion, and a back injury . . . My guys'll fight even if they've lost a frickin' arm. It's what we do."

"All right," Kali said to both of them, "but we must still confirm that your agent is at that location."

"Yes, gentlemen," Ali broke in. "We would need a Ghost for that."

Thane looked at Ali and smiled. "We happen to have one," he said, and he looked over at Neveah.

She was working her long hair into a braid after removing her jump helmet. She nodded at Thane, then looked over at Jason and skewered him with a triumphant stare.

"*Khoob!*" Good! Ali said in Dari.

Thane stood up from the map. Everyone rose along with him. As assault lead for the mission, he was the one to make the call.

"Okay, people," he said. "We're going to split our forces. But both hits have to happen simultaneously. If we hit Bagram before Silwar, they'll execute Spencer on the spot . . . if he's actually there."

"I will lead you to Bagram," Ali said. Then he looked at Neveah and Jason. "Sadaf will lead your team to Silwar."

Pacenza turned to his master sergeant. "Sumo, go split up the squadron. Give the jacked-up guys the M249s and LAWs so they can work covering fire from the vehicles. I'll take Bagram, you take Silwar."

"Roger, boss," Sumo said and took off.

"Colonel," Thane said to Kali, "we need to know the status of those aircraft and Brainwave modules at Bagram."

Kali nodded, walked over to Jare, and pulled him up from the dirt.

"It is time for you to work, Zabu," he said, and he walked him over to the circle.

"Mr. Zabu," Thane said to Jare. "We need to know the current location and status of the aircraft and your Brainwave modules."

Jare sighed, then pointed at his trouser pocket. Inside was his cell phone with its encrypted tracker, but Kali had told a medic on board the C-17 to sew it closed so it couldn't be lost. Kali took out his knife—the same one he'd bled Jare with during their interrogation. Jare flinched, but Kali only sliced his pocket open, pulled out the cell, and handed it to him. Jare turned it on and scrolled through his tracker, as the rest of the element held their breath.

"All of the aircraft are still at the airfield," he said. "But they will not be there for very much longer."

"How do you know that?" Thane asked.

"In order to function, Brainwave modules must first be charged up with an auxiliary power unit," Jare said, "the kind of APUs we find on military aircraft. Once they are fully charged, they must be used or they will bleed off energy." He tapped the app with a finger. "My tracker shows the charging percentages of each module."

"Tell us the readings, Zabu," Kali said impatiently.

"They are at ninety percent," Jare said as he squinted at his tracker. "They will be ready to fly very soon."

Thane turned to Ali. "How far to Bagram, Ali?"

"It is one hundred kilometers," Ali said as he pointed northwest into the night. "Through Jalalabad and Surobi."

"And six more from there to Silwar," Sadaf added.

Thane looked at Kali, then at Pacenza.

"Hustle up, Pac," he said. "We're moving out. *Now.*"

Six minutes later, the five vehicles packed full of operators and weapons were speeding northwest along the Rodat–Deh Bala road. It was a narrow, unlit lane, barely wide enough for the vans and pickups, and the dust roiled up from the tires and splattered the windshields. From afar, the convoy looked like a ragtag group of locals en route to their morning deliveries, which was exactly what the Black Box team was going for, a total blending into the environment.

Ali and Sadaf had covered the headlights with circles of red cellophane, which doused the road ahead in bloody hues, but would keep anyone at a Taliban checkpoint from seeing them coming. Sadaf was in the lead in an Isuzu van, but Sumo was driving because women were no longer allowed such freedoms in the New Afghan Emirate of Afghanistan. Neveah, Jason, and five operators were tucked in the back, and behind them was one Toyota pickup, completing their element for the recon and assault on Silwar.

After that came another Isuzu van, with Ali at the wheel, Thane beside him, and Kali and Jare huddled in the rear with four more operators. They were followed by Pacenza in another packed van and the tail vehicle, the last Toyota pickup.

"Think we're going to make it, Colonel?" Thane called back to Kali as he squinted through the windshield and the primitive road tortured their spines.

"Only God knows, Zane," Kali said. "Or Allah, or Yahweh."

Thane took no comfort in that. He turned his head slightly and spoke to Jare. "What's the status, Mr. Zabu?"

Jare hadn't torn his gaze from his tracker the whole way, seeking comfort in his technology.

"The modules are approaching ninety-eight percent," he said.

"I would suggest that you drive faster, Ali," Kali said from the rear.

But Ali had no control over that. Only Sumo and Sadaf at the point could see what lay before them, and suddenly the road simply ended at Chaghari and turned into nothing but dirt. Sadaf urged Sumo to keep on driving, and the convoy jerked and banged hard over ruts and clawing dunes, until at last they bounced back up onto the Rodat road and sped north.

"Got any spare tires in these junks?" Sumo asked Sadaf as he floored it.

"Only one for each vehicle," she answered. "Pray."

The convoy turned a hard left onto the Jalalabad–Torkham high-way, and then they were flying west. None of the injured men in the back of the last pickup muttered a complaint as they pulled their jump goggles over their eyes and ate the whirlwind of dust. Instead, they tried to keep their M249 light machine guns and LAW rock-ets from being swallowed in the dirt. When the lights of Jalalabad appeared up ahead, Sadaf made Sumo turn left on the bypass road that skirted the city.

"Dammit," Thane cursed. "This is gonna add more time."

"Your agent knows what she is doing," Kali said. "We could be stopped in Jalalabad by ambitious policemen."

They careered down the highway, hugging towering mountains that loomed like sleeping giants in the dark, then jinked left at Su-robi and were suddenly breaking out into Kabul Province. Just east of Kabul, Sadaf took them north again on a narrow farm road. Kali opened his side window and leaned out. In the distance he could see the floodlights of Bagram Airfield, like the illumination over an enormous football field.

Sadaf spoke to Thane through his headset comms. "Thane, we are leaving you now," she said. "We will see you soon again, *Insh'allah.*"

"Good luck," Thane said as he watched the two lead vehicles turn sharply left, heading for Silwar.

At two kilometers from Bagram, Thane ordered his three vehi-cles to stop. They slowed and pulled off the farmer's lane. Thane got out, along with Kali. Pacenza jogged up and joined them. He looked at his watch, then up at the sky, which was turning from black ink to navy blue.

"It'll be light soon," Pacenza said.

"Right," Thane said. "While we've still got some cover, let's douse the lights and get the vehicles as close as we can."

"We should recon on foot from there," Kali said. "Hunker down and wait for your Ghost's signal."

They remounted the vehicles, doused the lights, and rolled slowly closer to the airfield's perimeter. Kali, using his night-vision goggles, leaned out his window, scanning the airfield, and was glad to see that its thick concertina fences were gone. He reached forward, gripped Thane's shoulder, and said, "Here."

"One hundred percent now," Jare said.

"Damn," Thane said. "This is going to be close."

Kali said nothing. Now it was all up to Neveah, and how quickly she could somehow infiltrate Silwar and tell them whether or not Spencer was there.

They pulled the vehicles behind a small grove of trees. Pacenza ordered his men to form a security perimeter, but be ready to jump back into the vehicles and move. His operators followed his orders without a whisper.

Kali opened the van's rear door, got out, and pulled Jare with him.

"Where are we going?" Jare whispered.

"For a walk," Kali said.

Thane and Pacenza joined them, checking their MK18s and ammunition. They were wearing old Russian load-bearing vests over their Afghan garb, making them look like mujahideen.

The four men moved slowly over the dry grass of the wide-open field just south of the air base. Then, as they got closer, Thane motioned for all of them to drop and crawl through the bush. It was thorny, and it clawed at their clothes and scratched their arms and faces. Jare, despite the heat of the night, was shivering and whining. Kali dragged him along and warned him to keep quiet.

They lay in the brush, just two hundred meters from the airfield's perimeter road, for half an hour. None of them spoke. Kali shared water from his carrier with Jare, who was pouring sweat and shaking. Thane just listened to his comms, but nothing came through his ears but soft static. Pacenza's expression was stony.

Then there was a growing roar from the airfield, a sound like prehistoric beasts clearing their throats. It grew in volume, then started to scream like a hundred locomotive engines. The sky was turning to silver as the first aircraft, a fighter, rose from the strip and roared off over the mountains, heading due north toward Europe. And then there were more takeoffs—waves of fighters, helicopters, refuelers, and assault aircraft.

Kali pulled out his binoculars and saw that each of the aircraft had a Brainwave mustache antenna attached. He handed the binoculars to Thane, and said, "We are too late." Thane looked through them, and saw it was true. Within ten minutes, the last aircraft had left, and the strip fell to silence as the stench of scorched jet fuel reached out and stung the men's nostrils.

"I told you," Jare whispered.

Kali turned and glared at him. "Just tell us where the control module is," he said.

Jare looked at his tracker, then pointed a trembling finger across the wide airstrip at a conical tower that looked pink in the breaking dawn.

"It is way over there, on the other side," he said. "In that old Russian control tower."

Thane shifted the binoculars from the sky to the tower, then spoke into his comms. "Dark Horse Actual, this is Overwatch."

"Send it, Overwatch," Ando replied.

"We have eyes on Brainwave's HQ. Break. The Falcons have left their nest and are heading northwest toward their target. How copy?"

"Good copy, Overwatch. Initiating the command for NATO to launch Eagle Claw," Ando said over comms, referring to the code name for the air-to-air assault, which would take place once Brainwave was turned off and all Amir's planes were visible on NATO radar. "Confirming, general heading for coalition pilots. Break. Southeast, approximate bearing 116, toward Afghanistan?"

"That is correct, Dark Horse Actual."

"Received. Eagles are departing Aegis Ashore NATO base in Romania in five mikes, so get Brainwave off ASAP."

"We're on it," Thane said before ending the transmission.

"When can we hit it?" Pacenza whispered to Thane.

"That's up to Neveah," Thane said. "All we can do now is wait . . ."

FORTY-SEVEN

SILWAR, AFGHANISTAN

THERE WAS A SMALL STONE HOUSE IN A SHALLOW valley just south of Silwar. The house belonged to Jasim, the goatherd who'd provided intelligence to the Aberration agents Sadaf and Ali. Next to the house was a thick grove of walnut trees, where the first assault element had hidden their two vehicles just as dawn was striping the hills and the valley in tangerine hues.

Sumo had already dispatched ten operators to stealthily make their way into cover positions surrounding the target building at the top of Silwar—they knew not to get too close. Soon he would follow, along with Jason, but first—and quickly—they all had to figure out how to get Neveah into that building. From their position in the valley, they'd just witnessed the waves of aircraft roaring off the strip at Bagram six klicks to the west. The clock inside Jason's head was ticking like a time bomb, and Kali wasn't helping the issue.

"Colonel here for Dark Horse Two," Kali's voice whispered in Jason's headset in his Nigerian accent. "Can you please give me an update?"

"We're working on it," Jason said. "Stand by."

Rescuing Spencer was crucial for Black Box, but it wasn't the primary objective. If it didn't happen soon, Thane would order the assault on Bagram, and Kali and Jare would have to get to the Brainwave controls. They were all on the precipice of a potential World War III.

Jason and Sumo were standing inside Jasim's small house, along with the goatherd, his daughter Fatima, Neveah, and Sadaf. Jasim, though forty years old, had a big, bushy beard dyed henna red and looked like a sixty-year-old version of Moses, complete with a shepherd's staff. No one could guess Fatima's age, because a blue-black burka covered her form and features. Jasim was talking about her to Sadaf in Pashto.

"Fatima brings food every morning to two houses in Silwar, as well as to those men in the large house on top," he said.

"What do you bring them?" Sadaf asked Fatima.

Jasim's daughter pointed to a straw basket with a handle. It was filled with hard-boiled eggs, flatbreads, and fruit.

"I bring it to the white men up there," she said. "But they do not ever let me inside."

Sadaf translated that for the team.

"Good," Neveah said to Sadaf in English. "Then that's what we've got. I'll take Fatima's place."

"Do you think that's going to work?" Jason asked Neveah, although he'd seen her pull off miraculous Ghost missions many times before.

"If it doesn't," she said, "you'll know what to do."

He did indeed. When it came down to business, they put all their personal stuff aside. He and Sumo would initiate a full-on hostage rescue raid on the house, whether or not Neveah was still alive.

"All right, gentlemen," Neveah said to Jason, Sumo, and Jasim. "Please wait outside."

Jason and Sumo complied, taking Jasim along with them.

"Sadaf," Neveah said to the Aberration agent. "Tell Fatima that she and I are going to switch clothes."

As Sadaf explained to Fatima what was going to happen, Neveah was already stripping out of the rough Afghan shirt and pants she'd worn on the jump. Fatima took a step back, shocked by the sight of Neveah's underwear, even though her bra and briefs were modest.

"*Beleh koah!*" Sadaf said to Fatima, the Pashto expression for "Hurry up!"

Two minutes later, Neveah, followed by Sadaf, stepped out of the house, with Neveah wearing Fatima's full burka and carrying her food basket. Her suppressed FN 509 compact pistol was tucked in the belt from her pants, which she was now wearing under her robes, along with a titanium lockpick set and a slim commando blade strapped to her thigh. In one ear she was wearing a bone mic, but no one could see that either. Jasim stared at her, not quite sure if this was his daughter or not. But Jason already knew and had full confidence in Neveah's talents.

"Ask Jasim how Fatima gets to the village," Neveah said to Sadaf, who translated for the goatherd. Jasim pointed his staff at a small, battered motorized vehicle. It had tricycle wheels and just enough room in the front for a driver and one other person.

"Tell him to please take me," Neveah said to Sadaf. "Now."

Sadaf translated again for Jasim, and he nodded and motioned for Neveah to follow. He got in the rickshaw-type vehicle and started it up. Neveah, with the food basket, squeezed in beside him. She turned to Jason before they left.

"The call sign is Sparrow," she said. "I'll give the signal if I'm under duress, or I'm ready for you guys to come in."

That call sign would also be the signal for Kali to initiate on his end.

"All right. Go do what you do," Jason said as he looked at her warmly. She turned away, and as Jasim's rickshaw rumbled off, Jason and Sumo headed north on foot, low and fast along the valley floor. At the end of that hustle they would slither up the hills and join the rest of the Package in the brush outside the target. Sadaf would remain behind with Fatima.

It took Jasim a good five minutes to reach the skirts of Silwar in his motor-tricycle, during which he and Neveah exchanged no words, since they had no common language. At the first small hut—one of the few still standing in the bomb-shattered village—he flicked his calloused fingers at the front door. Neveah dismounted with her basket, walked toward the hut, and a hefty woman came out. She muttered something in Pashto as she plucked two eggs and two pomegranates, dropped a coin into the basket, and went back inside. Neveah exhaled a breath, got back in beside Jasim, and they trundled on.

The next delivery was similar, though a man came out. He spoke to Neveah and even called her by Fatima's name, but as he made his selection she only nodded, and he paid her, then left. At that point the sun was rising, and she was starting to sweat.

There were no more deliveries after that, except for the only one that was crucial. Jasim stopped the motor-tricycle at the foot of a winding dirt drive, above which the target building loomed. It was three stories high, with rough brick walls washed in pale blue, a traditional green door, and a wide thatched roof. Neveah could see three corners, outside of which stood burly white men wearing *shemags* and carrying automatic weapons. She couldn't see the back of the building but assumed that was guarded too. She took her basket and started to trudge up the drive, the hem of her burka wafting up powdery dust. A plan had already formed in her mind.

She headed straight for the front door. A sentry at the closest corner marched over, mounted the stone stairway, and stopped her with an outstretched palm.

"You're late," he said in a heavy South African accent. "'Bout time."

She nodded submissively as he looked through the remaining food in her basket. Then he grabbed the straw handle from her hand and said, "We'll take the whole thing." He dropped some coins onto the ground and turned away to go into the house. Keeping in character, she snatched the coins from the dust and spoke to his back in a heavy Pashtun accent: "T . . . toi-let."

He turned and sneered at her.

"Need the loo? Well, you won't be using ours." He jutted his chin toward the northwest corner. "Go around and piss in the bush."

Neveah shifted from foot to foot. She was wearing Fatima's worn leather sandals.

"Toy-elett!" she said more intensely.

The sentry called over to another man at that corner. "Pike, take this girl around to the bush and let her squat."

The second sentry walked over and went to grab Neveah's arm, but she pulled it away and shrank back.

"Don't touch her, Pike," the first sentry said. "Her brother'll have your balls."

Pike laughed, crooked a finger at Neveah, and she followed him around the corner. There was a hedgerow of low, leafy bushes a few feet back from the house's high walls. He stopped and pointed. Neveah walked into the bushes and turned to face him. But he eyed her in a way to say, *I'm not leaving.*

Her green eyes narrowed at him through the slit in her burka. She mimed lifting her robes up, but only an inch, then wagged an angry finger at him.

"Don't give me this modesty crap," he said. "Do your *business.*"

But Neveah wouldn't move. "Toy-elet!" she snapped.

"Oh, bloody hell," Pike said. Just then the first sentry appeared around the corner. "She won't pee in front of me, Reese," Pike fumed.

"Of course not." Reese snorted. "If she does, her village will have her stoned. Give her a break."

The two men walked away, back around the corner. Neveah counted their footsteps in her head . . . four, five, six, seven, eight . . . then they stopped. She figured she had about twenty seconds.

The house had no windows on its side wall, only rough stones, but plenty of hand- and footholds. Neveah burst from the bushes and sprinted to the wall, her sandals barely touching the ground as she counted off the seconds in her head. Then she was on it like a cat, climbing steadily upward without a sound, like a giant spider clothed in a cape. A hundred meters to the north, Sumo and Jason had just hunkered down in a grove of thick olive trees. Sumo had pulled out a pair of binoculars and was watching Neveah as she slithered up fast.

"Look at her go," he whispered in admiration.

Jason didn't need the binoculars. He'd seen her do this before, but his breath was hitched in his lungs.

Neveah reached the thatched roof, got two handfuls of thick, dry straw, and hauled herself up over the top. Just as her sandals cleared the ledge, Pike and Reese came back around the corner and stared at the hedgerow where she should have just finished peeing.

"Where'd she go?" Pike said.

"Hell if I know." Reese looked up at the house, but there was nothing to see there. Just then the sound of Jasim's engine coughed from the bottom of the winding dirt drive as he rumbled off. "Guess she took off down the hill," Reese said as they shrugged and went back to their posts.

Neveah lay flat on the primitive thatched roof—which was thirty feet long and almost as wide—scanning for some kind of hatchway into the house, but there was nothing. She slithered slowly to the rear ledge and exposed just her left eye. Below her she saw another sentry, his back turned toward her, smoking a morning cigarette and facing the surrounding groves of trees.

Less than a meter down from the ledge on the house's stone wall, there was a single window, but it was closed with a green metal shutter and locked with a rusty iron padlock. She slipped her hand under her burka, removed her lockpick set, and very slowly stretched her body over the ledge.

In the grove of olive trees, Sumo and Jason both had binoculars now. Sumo whispered as he watched Neveah, "She's out of her freaking mind," and then he put the binoculars down and raised his rifle, training the red-dot sight on the rear sentry's chest.

Another Package operator, a sniper fifty meters to their right in the bush, spoke to Sumo over his headset.

"Pack Two, Gravemaker here. Standing by for your green light."

"Hold fire, Gravemaker," Jason whispered. "Let her work."

And Neveah worked, hanging halfway over the ledge, her slim fingers moving like those of a brain surgeon with a pick and a slim steel needle inside the lock. After a moment the shaft popped, and she removed the padlock from the hasp, reached up, and buried it in the hay of the roof.

The next issue was the green metal shutter, mounted on a pair of rusty hinges on its left side. She held her breath, pulled on the shutter's handle to release pressure on the hinges, and slowly swung it out from the house until it was fully open. Then she silently rolled onto her back, stretched the top of her body nearly in half, and gripped the top sill of the window upside down.

"No effin' way," Sumo whispered on comms.

"Just watch," Jason whispered back while he clenched his guts.

Neveah executed a perfect backward somersault, and her entire body speared into the window without making a sound and disappeared. A moment later, her hand reached out and quietly closed the shutter.

"Frickin' ninja," an operator whispered on comms from somewhere.

Jason gave an affirming nod.

She was inside the house in the dark. As her eyes adjusted to the light, she saw that she was in some sort of third-story storage room, like a hayloft. There was a single window in front streaming morning daylight, and a slim, rickety wooden stairway that led downstairs. She listened for a long moment but heard nothing inside the house. Then all at once multiple engines were roaring up the dirt drive, with the sounds of tires spitting stones. She braced herself against the front wall and peeked outside.

An entire convoy had just arrived, five military-style vehicles with a desert Range Rover in the lead. More than twenty gunmen who looked like the ones guarding the house—along with heavily armed Afghans—spilled from the trucks and took up security positions. From the Range Rover, a muscular Black man who looked like an African emerged, followed by an older thick man in a herringbone jacket, who appeared to be Slavic. She was instantly certain the African man was Nabuto.

"Reese! Pike!" Nabuto called to the sentries. "Any suspicious activity about?"

"No, sir," Reese called as he walked partway down from the house.

"Well, some sort of military aircraft went down near the eastern border last night," Nabuto said. "Our Afghans think it might be part of an American rescue move."

"No Yanks floatin' around here, sir," Pike said from his post.

"Nabuto," the Slavic man said in a thick Russian accent. "Let us retrieve my merchandise and get out of this place."

"Right, General," Nabuto said. "Wait here. I'll be right out."

Vitaly Chok frowned, but assented. He had no idea that Nabuto was going to inject Spencer with a deadly toxin that would take full effect only in Moscow, laying his death at the feet of the Russians.

Nabuto snapped out some orders for the men to cover the access points down the drive as well as the house's exterior. Then he took Pike, Reese, and two more men, and started for the entrance, telling them to take up defensive positions inside.

From a hiding spot deep in a hedgerow and facing the house, one of Pacenza's snipers keyed his mic.

"Dark Horse Two," he whispered to Jason, who was still in position around the back, "you've got twenty-plus pax outside here, and five making entry."

"Roger," Jason said. "Pick your targets and hold." He didn't have to signal Neveah, because he knew she'd heard that.

On the second floor, Neveah flattened herself against the wall, her heart racing. She knew from the exchange outside that Nabuto and the Russian were talking about Spencer, and she also knew she only had seconds to rescue him. Jason's voice was hissing in her ear as she moved silently to the wooden staircase and started slinking down.

"NV, I'm not sure if you're seeing this out here, but you're running tight on time," he said. "Don't be cheap on giving me that signal."

She ignored him, pulled out her suppressed FN pistol, and press-checked the action as she started for the steps. The stairway from the loft stopped halfway down at a landing on the second floor, with an open door to a room on the left, and more stairs leading down to the right. Her sandaled feet barely touched each step as she floated down like a wraith, then smeared herself to the right-hand wall as she heard footsteps. A gunman appeared on the landing. She shot him twice in the heart, point-blank, and caught his rifle as he slumped back against the landing wall. Then she lowered his twitching corpse into the room on the left, laid him down on the floor, backed out, and silently closed the door—as quietly as a ghost.

She slinked back into her cover position by the stairs and eased her eyes around the corner. No one else was moving up, so she floated downward, her eyes darting left and right through the burka. At the bottom, a small hallway led to the left and the front door. She peeked around to the right.

She was looking into a large room at the very back of the house. There was a flat-screen on the far wall, and in front of that, strapped to a wooden chair . . . Spencer!

Nabuto was standing there, opening a small medical case. He had a syringe in his hand with a thick steel needle and was just finishing extracting some kind of liquid from a glass vial. Spencer looked up at Nabuto. His eyes were glazed, and his face was swollen with bruises. Nabuto sneered down at him.

"Don't worry, Mr. Riley," he said. "This won't hurt much at *all.*"

"Screw you," Spencer slurred.

Nabuto laughed as he raised the needle to jab Spencer's bare arm.

Neveah had her pistol gripped in both hands, aiming directly at Nabuto's face as she squeezed the trigger . . .

A figure flashed out from the right and kicked her pistol hand. It was Reese, and for a split second, as Neveah's gun went spinning across the floor into the room, he stared at her in disbelief. She lashed out with her bladed right hand, crushing his Adam's apple, and he went flying onto his back. She jerked her burka up, snatched her commando blade from her thigh rig, and whipped it across the room, where it plunged into Nabuto's right shoulder. The impact jerked the syringe up and away from Spencer.

Neveah had no time to go for her handgun. She charged across the room, head down, rammed her skull into his chest, and sent him slamming backward into the flat-screen, smashing the glass into exploding shards. He bounced off it and came at her with fury in his eyes, the long syringe gripped in his right fist, as he sliced it down at her throat. She jerked to the right as he missed his mark, and she spun and kicked him in the groin. He grunted but it didn't take him down.

Outside in the back, Jason was hearing the scuffle.

"I hear what's going on in there, NV," he said. "We're standing by for the signal."

She didn't answer, because Nabuto came back at her, raising the needle again, while Spencer jerked and bucked in the chair, trying to break his bonds. Neveah's right hand yanked the bloody blade from Nabuto's shoulder. Nabuto drove the needle down to stab her, this time in her eye, but she blocked his blow with her left arm, drove her commando blade hilt-deep inside his armpit, spun, and flipped him over her shoulder.

He crashed down onto his back. She straddled him, ripped the syringe from his hand, and plunged it into his heart. Then, just to be sure, she yanked her bloody blade from his armpit and drove it down into his throat.

Neveah snapped her head up as she heard someone enter the house's front entrance, pounding toward her down the hall. She dived for her handgun on the floor and jerked it up just as Pike appeared. His eyes caught Nabuto's corpse—and the delivery woman in the burka now wielding a weapon—but before he could fire his assault rifle, she shot him between the eyes. He jerked back and fell as his trigger finger twitched and his rifle sprayed the ceiling in a wild burst.

Outside, there was no mistaking the sound of gunfire. Jason barked in her ear.

"Give me the damn signal, NV! Give it to me now!"

But she wasn't going to give it until she had Spencer free. She spun around and jerked her blade from Nabuto's throat, and as she went to go for Spencer, she saw Reese starting to recover and get up from the floor. She shot him in the face and kept going.

She reached Spencer and he stared at her as she sliced through the web straps holding him down.

"It's Neveah, Spencer," she said. She pulled up her face covering and reiterated, "It's me."

His eyes bugged and he muttered, "Thank God." She hauled him up on his feet. He was exhausted, malnourished, beaten, and dehydrated, but the rush of being rescued sent adrenaline coursing through his body. Neveah darted over to Reese's corpse, yanked a Glock 19 from his thigh holster, came back, and shoved it into Spencer's trembling right hand. She knew he was ready to fight when he press-checked the action.

"You good to go?" she asked him.

"I'm good," he said.

"NV, for Black Box Two," Neveah said to Jason over comms, then finally gave him the signal. "*Sparrow.*"

A wicked hail of gunfire erupted outside. In an instant, bullets were flying in both directions, inbound and outbound, cracking off the house's stone walls. Neveah and Spencer started moving toward the hallway and the house's front entrance. Then a man came tumbling inside and hustled toward Neveah and Spencer. It was the Russian and he was holding a Makarov pistol. He saw Nabuto, dead on his back, cursed something in Russian, and opened fire.

Neveah dived to the left, Spencer to the right, both taking cover behind the hallway arch. Vitaly Chok's bullets were taking off chunks of plaster as he screamed. Spencer looked down and found a triangle of shattered glass from the exploded flat-screen TV. He picked it up with his left hand, slipped it out from the arch just enough so he could see the Russian's furious image, then thrust the Glock barrel out with his right hand and shot him twice in the chest.

Outside the house, Jason, Sumo, and the Package were engaged in an assault on the building from all sides, but the Package snipers had already killed most of the South Africans and Afghans with well-placed single shots to their heads. Jason raced through the brush at the back of the house, leaped over the sentry that Sumo had just shot from close range, and sprinted around to the front.

Neveah and Spencer stepped around Vitaly Chok's corpse and made their way toward the front door, both gripping their handguns at the ready. There was still some gunfire outside—the Package was finishing off "leakers." It sounded like it was almost over, but Neveah couldn't be sure, and she tucked herself and Spencer behind the jamb of the open front door and yelled, "Clear, inside!"

The gunfire outside stopped, its echoes resounding through the valley.

"Clear, outside!" Jason yelled back.

Neveah nodded at Spencer. The two of them stepped out of the house. There were corpses everywhere and the stench of burnt powder filled the air, but none of the bodies belonged to any of the Package. She pulled off the entire burka as if it were a customized tear-away jumpsuit, then looked at Jason, who was standing there breathing like a marathoner.

"NV for the Colonel," she said over comms to Kali as she looked over at a bloody and beaten Spencer. "Sparrow. I say again, Sparrow. We're consolidating on you."

FORTY-EIGHT

BAGRAM AIRFIELD, AFGHANISTAN

KALI WAS ALREADY RUNNING.

The minute he heard Neveah's first "Sparrow" signal, he knew she had Spencer in her hands. Then sporadic gunfire had come over comms, followed by a wicked firefight. By the time Neveah gave him the final confirmation, he'd already jumped up from the thorns, grabbed Jare by the back of his shirt, and started charging for the airfield's perimeter road. Thane was assault lead and Kali knew he should wait for his order, but there wasn't time for command formalities.

Thane and Pacenza sprinted behind Kali and Jare. On the run, Pacenza called to his Package in the three vehicles still camouflaged in the trees.

"Execute Tobruk. I repeat, execute Tobruk."

"Roger, Pac," came three replies.

It was a preplanned tactical strategy, like a football play. During World War II in North Africa, the British SAS had executed deadly effective airfield raids against the Germans defending Tobruk—so Pacenza's operators knew what to do. The two Isuzu vans and the pickup truck broke from the trees, bounced across the dry fields, went careering up onto the perimeter road, and split up—left, right, and center—with the operators' guns already jutting from the back truck windows.

"Colonel!" Thane shouted at Kali's back as they sprinted. "Hold and cover right there."

Kali turned and saw Thane pointing to a retaining wall next to the old Green Beans Coffee shop. He dragged Jare behind the wall, shoved him down, and crouched, both of them pouring sweat in the heat as the morning broke bright and hard. Thane and Pacenza joined them, all of them panting.

"You can't take Jare right up the middle right now, Colonel," Thane said to Kali. "It's too dangerous. We'll hold till the Package clears the field."

"All right," Kali said, even though he desperately wanted to charge the tower and destroy those Brainwave controllers. By now all the planes had been in the air for nearly two hours and the lead fighters would be crossing the Caspian Sea. At that moment he heard Ando's voice in his ear, transmitting from the Black Box station in Virginia. "Dark Horse, we've got a Keyhole satellite over your position. It's intercepting all comms over the AO. I'll relay pertinent opposition intel, as needed."

The first Isuzu van came roaring up from behind. Thane waved it down, ran to the van as it stopped in a cloud of dust, and yanked open the side door. He immediately locked eyes with Ali and gestured for him to dismount.

"Ali, you can't be part of this," Thane said to the Aberration agent. "After the smoke clears you still have to operate here. If I get you killed, Ando will have my *nuts*."

Ali smiled, nodded in assent, and took cover behind the old coffee hut as the van drove on, straight for the airstrip.

Kali, Thane, and Pacenza pulled out their binoculars and braced their arms on the retaining wall, while Jare peeked over the top. Kali saw an array of left-behind coalition vehicles arranged in front of the old Russian tower. There were five soft-skinned Humvees, which wouldn't be much of a problem. But there were also four MRAPs, the mine-resistant, sixteen-ton monsters, with turret-mounted .50 calibers and M240B machine guns.

"Here they come," Pacenza said as they all watched the center Isuzu racing straight up the middle across the airfield. "Good luck, boys," he added as the second Isuzu appeared from the left and the pickup truck roared onto the field from the right. Then, every Package operator opened up from the vehicles. The Isuzu on the left raked the Humvees with MK18 fire, punching through the flanks and windows at close range. A few Package operators who were injured on the jump stood up in the pickup on the right and raked the MRAPs' turrets with two fully auto M249s. The center Isuzu careered straight at the vehicle array as its roof popped open and an operator jumped up with a LAW. At a range of less than thirty meters, he fired the rocket, taking out an MRAP turret and bursting it open like a tuna fish can. The detonation combined with the fuel inside created a mushroom cloud of black smoke and a boom that echoed across the airfield.

In the center of the field, the three racing Package vehicles just missed each other by a yard—like the Blue Angels jet fighters at an air show. Their tires screeched as they all sped away toward the airfield's perimeter, then turned back around and floored it for more killing.

Kali peered at the vehicles as they set themselves up for another run. Their volume of fire would be the best cover he could hope for. He dropped his binoculars and looked at Thane.

"There is no time like the present, Zane," he said.

"Agreed," Thane said. "Let's get some."

The four men got up and ran, with Kali gripping Jare's arm as his childhood friend yelled, "Should we not wait until it is over?!"

In the Russian control tower, Lucas van Groot spun away from a bank of six Brainwave control modules bolted to a semicircular steel console, and ran to the slanted Plexiglas windows. Two of his technicians were seated at the console, where the air traffic controllers had once perched, and they turned in their chairs with quizzical expressions. They didn't understand what was happening, but Van Groot did. He leaned on the steel window ledge and looked down as the first MRAP exploded, and he saw the wild ballet of the Package vehicles as they raced across the field in figure eights, slaughtering Amir Baradar's machines and men.

"So," he said with a strange, almost demented smile. "The cavalry has arrived."

Then he ducked below the sill as a burst of automatic fire punched through the windows and shattered them into spinning shards of razor-sharp plastic, while his technicians dived to the floor and curled up like panicked hedgehogs. From a stairwell at the back of the cramped tower, Amir suddenly appeared. He was holding an AK-47 assault rifle and started walking toward Van Groot, when another spray of automatic fire whipped into the tower through the shattered windows, exploding a rack of fluorescent lights overhead. But Amir strode defiantly over to Van Groot and took a knee amid the gunfire.

"I will handle this, Colonel," he said. "They taught us a lot more than just economics in Moscow."

"All right, Amir," Van Groot said as the gunfire raged outside. "Let's see what you've got." He jabbed a finger in the Afghan's chest. "You *can't* let the bastards get up here."

Amir rushed off down the stairwell, calling for some of his men to join him below. Van Groot pulled out a cell phone, swiped open an encrypted texting app, selected "000" as the recipient, then quickly typed Initiate Zero protocol. He pocketed the phone and began crawling low across the carpet of window shards toward a wooden box. When Van Groot finally arrived at the box, he flipped it open, revealing a Russian RPK light machine gun. He grabbed it, then slammed a hundred rounds into its breech.

"You two!" he yelled above the gunfire to the two technicians curled up on the floor. "Get back to your stations. If those Brainwave modules fail, I'll bloody kill you myself."

The technicians were nearly in tears, but they crawled back into their seats.

Outside, across the wide tarmac, Kali, Jare, Thane, and Pacenza slammed their boots on the steaming blacktop as they charged across the runway. Pacenza called over comms to his drivers and the three Package vehicles raced out in front of them and formed a flying wedge. The volume of gunfire from the Delta men was murderous, providing a shield of bullets for the sprinting team. Another LAW rocket screeched from the back of the pickup and exploded through the windshield of another MRAP, sending its turret gun-

ner flying. From the roof of the right-hand Isuzu, an operator fired
an M203 grenade, flipping a Humvee over on its side.

Kali dragged Jare in a pounding jog behind the pickup's tailgate,
while Thane and Pacenza ran behind the bumper of the left-hand
Isuzu. Jare was panting with the terror of death, and sweat was
pouring from his scalp.

"Do not worry," Kali said to Jare in the thick Nigerian accent.
"We are almost there, and opposition is light."

But just then the tables turned. From the top of the control tower,
a machine gun opened up in defilade across the field, its bullets
chunking up showers of blacktop and raking the vehicles. One of
the already injured operators in the back of the pickup jerked back
and fell in the steel bed. The windshield of the right-hand Isuzu van
shattered as RPK rounds killed the driver and destroyed the engine.
It skidded to a stop and the rest of the operators inside burst out,
firing up at the tower as they hit the ground.

"You call that *light*, Colonel?" Jare wailed as Kali slammed him
down on his face and covered him with his body.

In the control tower, two of Van Groot's Selous Scouts had
rushed up the stairway to join him. They were bracing him on both
sides, firing down with their assault rifles as he burned up the entire
belt of Russian bullets.

"That should give them something to think about, Rod," Van
Groot said to the man on his right, just as a bullet from a Package
sniper lying prone on the tarmac took off the top of Rod's skull.
Van Groot turned to look at his second man, Brick, but Brick was
clutching his throat where a second sniper round had just severed
his jugular, and he collapsed to the floor like a rag doll, spraying
Van Groot with a stream of blood. Van Groot sat down fast on the
floor, crabbed backward with the machine gun to the wooden crate,
and loaded another belt.

Outside at the foot of the control tower, Amir Baradar had calmly
mustered twelve of his Taliban fighters. Much of his training at the
former Patrice Lumumba School in Moscow had consisted of Russian small-unit tactics, and he was putting those tactics into play.

In front of the tower was a row of concrete vehicle barriers that the Americans had used for airfield control. All of his men had been in combat before, and he had them spread out across the concrete array, carefully shooting at whoever these assaulting commandos were. Amir was striding behind his men with his short Krinkov submachine gun, directing them calmly like an American officer at the invasion of Normandy.

"Kill them all," he called to his men in Dari. "Every one of them."

One of his men took a burst of M240B rounds from a Package operator that blew off his head, but Amir just stepped over his twitching corpse and kept walking. The firefight had ground to a stalemate now, and that's what he wanted. No one was going to get up to that tower until the planes reached Hungary and Poland.

Back behind the pickup truck, Kali was still smearing Jare down on his face.

"Please get off me," Jare whined. "I can't *breathe*."

"You can breathe later on," Kali said in his ear as hot empty shell casings rained down on them from the back of the truck. He looked to the left, where Thane and Pacenza were hunkered down behind the Isuzu. It was peppered with bullet holes and the men inside had hustled out and taken cover behind a burning MRAP as they fired back at Amir's men. Thane called out to Kali, but not over comms.

"We've got to get up to that tower, Colonel," Thane yelled.

"Maybe we can flank it from the left," Kali called back. "If we've got enough covering fire."

"We can blow the whole thing with a couple of LAWs," Pacenza called out.

"No!" Jare shouted from under Kali's weight. "If you destroy the control modules, I will not be able to turn Brainwave off!" Then he pounded his fist on the pavement as he realized he should've kept his mouth shut and let them save him the trouble.

Just then, Ando's voice echoed inside all their earpieces.

"Dark Horse, this is Dark Horse Actual. Keyhole has intercepted a message from Van Groot. It doesn't have much bearing on your current circumstance, but it does change things. Break." Ando took a brief pause before he continued. "Your orders are no longer kill or capture. We want Van Groot alive. This is a capture only. Copy?"

Thane looked at Kali. Kali eyed the carnage all around him as a way to indirectly say, *Impossible*, then looked back at Thane and doubled down by shaking his head.

"Who did Van Groot message?" Thane asked Ando over comms.

"It's above your pay grade. I repeat, capture only. Copy?"

"I don't want to hear that above-my-pay-grade shit! We're dealing with a damn circus down here! We've already lost men, all of Bagram is on our ass, and now you want us to do something for Van Groot that we may not even be able to do for ourselves!" Thane took a brief breather as a volley of bullets snapped around them, then continued. "If you're asking us to turn water into wine, I need to at least know why."

After a long beat a smooth and somewhat soothing southern-sounding voice spoke over comms. "Dark Horse, this is the commander in chief. Do you read me?"

Kali's eyebrows raised as high as they had when he saw the fleet of aircraft with Brainwaves attached departing from Bagram.

"Read you loud and clear, Mr. President," Thane said calmly and with a surprised look that matched Kali's.

"Good. I can see what you boys got going on down there and you're doing a hell of a job," POTUS said with no hint of jive. The Keyhole satellite was also relaying images to the White House Situation Room. "What Dark Horse Actual requested is actually from me, no pun intended. We can't go into the details now, but I can assure you, capturing Van Groot alive is a matter of the utmost national security. Now, given your current situation on the ground, I'll soften my ask. If you can find a way to shut down Brainwave and get your team out, while at the same time capturing Mr. Van Groot *alive*, I'd appreciate it. If you can't, you can't, no harm, no foul. Fair enough?"

Thane looked at Kali. After a three-second stare-off, Kali gave Thane a subtle nod as if to say, *I think we can figure it out.*

Thane focused back on his comms. "Understood, Mr. President. We'll try our best."

"Thank ya. That's all I'm asking for," POTUS said in his southern twang. "Now, we won't armchair quarterback you anymore. Get back to the circus."

Kali called out to Thane. "So much for the LAW option, Zane."

"All right," Thane called back. "Left flanking movement it is. We'll try to keep you both alive."

"Ditto, Zane, ditto. Leading us out," Kali said, before positioning Jare behind him and taking off as Pacenza, Thane, and a few operators laid down cover fire.

After a thirty-yard sprint Kali stopped by a cinder block barrier, shoved Jare to the ground, and started laying down cover fire so Thane and the Package could move up. Just then Van Groot started firing again from the tower. Kali quickly shifted his sight from the hostiles on the ground up to Van Groot's position. As he turned the nob on his scope Van Groot came into focus.

Kali had a clear shot and thought, *What makes this man so important that the president of the United States wants him alive?*

AMIR BARADAR TURNED HIS MEN ON KALI'S POSI-
tion and ordered them to finish him off. All eleven barrels
of their AK-47s raked the cinder block barrier, sending
chunks spinning off as Kali threw himself onto Jare again while his
childhood friend screamed. Amir added a burst from his Krinkov
to the mad-minute volley, then pulled a satphone from his pocket
and made a call.

"Khalid, this is Amir," he yelled above the gunfire in Pashto. "Do
you read me?"

"Yes, Amir. I can hear you," Khalid replied. Prior to arriving at
Bagram, Amir had positioned Khalid with two full companies of
men, which included some Selous Scouts, near the local Taliban
HQ and had ordered Khalid to execute any Taliban elder who exited the premises before the operation was completed. He wanted
to ensure that no one sympathetic to his father would interfere with
the Brainwave operation. "What is it?"

"We are under attack by elite Western forces," Amir said. "I need
you and all your men to the airfield *now*."

"On our way," Khalid confirmed before hot-micing a rally cry to
his men. They were camped halfway between Kabul and Bagram—
it wasn't far.

"Very good. Out," Amir said, and he turned back into the fight.

Kali was crushing Jare as cinder block splinters rained down on
them from above. Then he heard Ando's voice calling Thane.

"Overwatch, be advised," Ando said. "Intercept just picked up
a call from the airfield. Someone just summoned reinforcements.
They're en route. Over."

"Roger," Thane replied. He, Pacenza, and five more operators were close behind Kali, but not close enough. They were taking cover at the back of a burning vehicle and firing at Amir's men, trying to keep them off Kali. But Van Groot was trying to kill them all with his RPK from the tower.

"Colonel, don't move," Thane said to Kali over comms.

"I couldn't even if I wanted to," Kali called back as bullets cracked through the air above his head.

"Stand by, people," another voice said in their ears. It sounded strangely like Spencer, but no one thought that could be, because Spencer had just been freed after weeks of torture in captivity. Yet they all turned their heads to the left, where an MRAP was roaring across the airfield, straight for Amir's position.

Spencer, Neveah, Jason, Sumo, and all the operators from the rescue operation at Silwar had just broken through Bagram's west gate, using Nabuto's Range Rover and the surviving command cars from his convoy. Just inside the gate, they'd come upon four parked MRAPs, and Spencer had pointed at one and said, "That one's mine."

Jason tried to stop him, but Spencer was having none of it. Despite a half-swollen face and bruises all over his body, he straightened his back, pulled Jason's headset off, jammed it onto his own head, and grabbed a brick of C-4 and a detonator from a breacher. He dismounted from the Range Rover, picked up a large rock from the ground, and took off, while Jason, Neveah, and the rest of their men rushed from their soft-skinned vehicles and jumped into the remaining MRAPs.

Spencer gunned his MRAP, and through its inch-thick windshield he now saw Kali prone on the tarmac behind a pile of shattered cinder blocks, covering someone else's squirming body on the ground. To Kali's right, he saw Thane, Pacenza, and a cluster of operators behind a burning Humvee, taking heavy fire and shooting back. To the left, in front of the control tower, he saw an Afghan commander directing about a dozen troops to kill his teammates—it was Amir.

He crouched as low as he could, floored the gas pedal, and drove the iron beast straight at Amir's concrete barrier positions. He smeared the brick of C-4 down onto the truck's center console, pulled the four-second-delay detonator from his pocket, plunged it down into the explosive clay, and slipped one finger into the ring pin. He saw Amir and his men turning on him, and then their bullets were banging and ricocheting all over the truck. He saw the bursting cough of an RPG tube and the rocket racing toward him through the air, and he jinked the wheel hard to the left as it whipped past the vehicle's right flank and exploded somewhere behind him. Then he swung the wheel back, regained his trajectory, and slammed the gas pedal harder.

At twenty meters from Amir and his men, Spencer bent over the wheel, locked the accelerator pedal with the rock, and yanked the ring pin from the detonator. Then he spun from the driver's seat, scrambled to the MRAP's rear, cranked the rear hatch open, and jumped out. He hit the tarmac hard and rolled three times in a blurring somersault, with all his bruises being hammered and skinned again, but he wound up flat on his stomach and looked up.

The Afghan commander and his men were scattering in all directions like a school of panicked fish. The MRAP crashed into the concrete barriers, reared up in front like a spooked stallion, and the C-4 detonated inside, blowing out both front doors and exploding the windshield into spinning shrapnel, instantly killing three men. A second later, its fuel tanks exploded in a black mushroom cloud that boomed up into the air.

Up in the tower, Van Groot felt the building tremble with the explosion and looked down, seeing the fire, smoke, and carnage below. He loaded the machine gun with yet another ammunition belt.

"I am not stopping this time, Zane!" Kali yelled as he dragged Jare up off the tarmac and charged. He shot one of Amir's surviving men at close range on the run, then another who came at him around the burning MRAP. Thane, Pacenza, and their men joined the charge, firing as they sprinted and killing Amir's shell-shocked men as Van Groot tried to pick the Americans off with his RPK from the tower.

Kali raced past the burning MRAP, pulling Jare along with his free hand. To his left, he saw Spencer rising from the blacktop with a Glock in his fist. Straight ahead, he saw an Afghan commander, dressed like a Eurotrash kid, taking cover inside the entrance to the control tower and turning a Krinkov subgun on Spencer. Kali switched his MK18 to full auto and flayed Amir with a burst of spinning bullets from his groin to his face. Kali had no idea who he was, but he was certainly dead now, along with all his men.

Thane, Pacenza, and their element blew past the burning MRAP to the foot of the tower, just as Jason, Neveah, Sumo, Sadaf, and the rest of the Silwar Package roared up in three more hijacked MRAPs from the left.

The firing from Van Groot's machine gun stopped. The entire Black Box team and the Package were now too close to the tower for him to be able to shoot down at them without being taken out. Thane called out for everyone to quickly form a defensive perimeter with the MRAPs around the front of the tower, then looked at Kali, pointed at the tower stairwell, said, "Colonel, on me!" and started to move.

Just then, an incredible volume of gunfire exploded on them from the western gate, where Khalid and his companies had broken through. Bullets sparked off the MRAPs and pocked ragged holes in the base of the tower. One of them tore through Thane's right thigh, spinning him around like a top, and he went down hard.

The Package swung their MRAP turrets around to the west and opened up on Khalid's quick-reaction force with the American .50 calibers and M240Bs that had been left behind. But so many Taliban fighters and Van Groot's men were pouring through the west gate that even as some were hit, more came on. It was as though all of Afghanistan were descending on the airfield.

Pacenza dragged Thane over to the tower and leaned him back against the pink stone facade. "Medic up," Pacenza called. One of his operators hustled over and bent to Thane as he ripped open his med kit and extracted a tourniquet.

As Amir and Van Groot's QRF bullets cracked overhead, Thane

said to the medic, "Never mind that now," as he turned to Kali. He was crouching next to Thane with Jare ducking behind his back. "Get up there, Colonel, and grab Van Groot," Thane said.

Jason and Neveah ran over to Thane. Spencer arrived on the run. He was gripping his Glock, and still barefoot.

"We'll go with him, Thane," Jason said.

"No," Kali said. "What has happened to you, Zane, may be a blessing in disguise. We must try to take Van Groot alive. The more targets he has, the more likely we'll have to put him down."

"The Colonel's right," Thane said to Jason, Neveah, and Spencer. "He and Jare *only*. Alone. You three will be more useful holding the line."

Neveah and Jason nodded in unison. Spencer picked up an enemy AK-47 and then all three of them jumped back into the fight.

Thane reached up, grabbed Kali's ammo carrier, and pulled him close.

"Just get it done, Colonel," he said before turning his gaze to Jare. "The whole world's in Nigeria's hands now . . ."

Kali nodded, checked to make sure he had a full magazine in his MK18, set Jare behind his back, and headed into the tower up the steel stairwell. Kali hugged the left-hand side, assault rifle up, one eye focused on his holographic sight and the other eye scanning ahead and above. He saw one steel landing where the stairwell zigged the other way and from the height of the tower guessed there were three levels. The darkened stairwell boomed and shuddered with the volume of gunfire outside.

On the first landing, nothing happened, and they turned and started up toward the second. Just as they reached the lip of that platform, Van Groot's machine gun roared from above, shooting a long spray of bullets downward that sparked off the steel and chipped cement off the walls. Kali ducked, smearing Jare behind him against the wall. As soon as Van Groot's first volley stopped, Kali leaped forward and up, cranking off rounds that ricocheted off the stairwell's stone ceiling and drove Van Groot back inside the top doorway.

Up in the tower, Van Groot looked down at his last belt of ammo—he only had twenty more rounds. The two technicians behind him at the console were still working—because it was that or die—and they were pouring sweat as they flinched with the gunfire and worked the controls to keep all the Brainwave modules alive. Van Groot took a Belgian minigrenade from his pocket, pulled the pin, and tossed it through the stairwell doorway.

Kali saw the grenade come bouncing down the stairwell. He caught it in midair, whipped it back up the stairs, and crushed Jare down as the grenade detonated above, sending shrapnel whipping through the tower. He felt a steel splinter puncture his right calf and ignored it. Then he pulled a flash-bang grenade from his load-bearing vest and got ready to charge.

Outside in front of the tower, the Black Box team and the Package were engaged in the fight of their lives. AK-47 rounds were cracking the air like spinning demons; an RPG had blown through the engine block of one of the MRAPs, setting the vehicle on fire; but the Package gunners were still hammering away with their machine guns and using up lots of ammo.

Thane, with a tourniquet squeezing his thigh wound, was back in the fight, firing his MK18 from one of three MRAPs arranged in a defensive V. He called over to Pacenza and Sumo, who were directing fire from behind the remains of Spencer's destroyed MRAP.

"Pac, I just called Ando for some fire support," Thane said. "He's got two armed Avenger Predators tasking from the Pakistani border at Torkham. I told him to have them steer clear of the Khyber so they don't get shot down."

"What have they got?" Pac asked.

"Hellfires," Thane said, meaning the powerful air-to-ground missiles.

"They better get here fast," Sumo broke in. "Otherwise, we're gonna have an Alamo situation here." Sumo unslung his ruck and pulled out a handheld SOFLAM, a targeting device to direct the incoming missiles. "I'm gonna go lase some targets," he said as he took off, weaving between the cordon of MRAPs and ducking low through the gunfire.

Up in the tower, Van Groot leaned out into the stairwell doorway and squeezed off his last twenty rounds of machine gun ammo. But just as the belt ran dry, a cylindrical object came flying up over his head, bounced on the floor behind him, exploded with a flash as bright as the sun, and sent him careening sideways against the tower wall. His technicians screamed for mercy, fell off their chairs, and balled up in a corner as white smoke billowed and filled the room.

Van Groot hit the floor, crawled behind the wide console, and pulled a Browning Hi-Power pistol from his hip holster. Kali's rifle barrel appeared around the corner of the stairwell doorway.

"Mr. Van Groot," he called out. "There is no way for you to leave here alive, unless you surrender."

After a moment, Van Groot answered back.

"There is no way for you to leave here alive either, mate. Unless you think you can fight off hundreds of Taliban fighters."

"Let us discuss it in peace," Kali said. "I am lowering my rifle."

Kali dropped his MK18 down along his chest on the strap and came out from the doorway. He saw the smoke and wreckage inside the small room, and the two technicians now balled up on the floor under the shattered windows, but no Van Groot. He reached back and pulled Jare past his left thigh and into the room. He pointed over at the consoles and motioned for Jare to stay low. Jare started sneaking through the smoke and debris, crawling like a lizard, and muttering prayers to every deity he could think of.

Slowly, Van Groot rose from his cover behind the bank of electronics and stood up, facing Kali, his hands raised in the surrender position. He looked through the drifting smoke at Kali, and then he smiled.

"I thought I might see you again somewhere, mate," he said.

"Yes, just as I told you," Kali said, though he was maintaining his Nigerian accent, which Van Groot picked up on right away.

"So, who are you today, Mr. Abasi?" Van Groot sneered as he gestured at Kali's Nigerian camo. "In Barbados you were all-American. And now?"

Kali ignored the inquiry. "Come along with me now in peace," he said, "and we will have plenty of time to continue our dinner discussion."

"Sounds like a reasonable idea," Van Groot said, "but I think we should have this discussion right here, right now . . . like men."

He still hadn't spotted Jare, who was inching along through the smoke on the far side of the tower. His eyes were focused only on Kali, and he reached back slowly, plucked his Hi-Power from the back of his waistband, and laid it carefully on the edge of the console.

"I've killed many men of war with these hands," Van Groot said as he looked down and slowly slipped off his combat gloves. "Polish GROM, MI6, SAS, Mossad, even Wagner Group alum. But never one quite like you. If you would indulge me, mate, you may end up being my most prized trophy." Van Groot dropped the gloves on the deck, then looked up at Kali. "What say you?"

Kali recognized the challenge but stared at Van Groot for a few seconds as if he was considering the question in order to buy Jare a bit more time. Finally, he unslung his MK18, laid it to his right on the floor, then pulled out his Glock from his thigh holster and set it down there too. A hand-to-hand fight without guns would be the best way to take Van Groot alive.

But Van Groot had other ideas. "Good choice, my boy," he said as he came out from behind the console with his fists postured at his sides, and the dance of violence began.

He faked a left jab at Kali's head. Kali blocked the fake with his right and tried to palm-strike Van Groot's chin, but Van Groot ducked, grabbed the top of Kali's ammo vest, and yanked it hard while he drove his forehead into Kali's nose. The blow blazed stars in Kali's eyes, but he gripped Van Groot's bush jacket with both fists, spun to the left, and hurled him over his hip. Van Groot crashed down on his back.

Jare had finally reached the consoles. He was trying to ignore the thunder of gunfire outside and the grunts of the melee behind him as he crawled up into a chair and started turning dials on the Brainwave controllers.

Van Groot sprang to his feet. Shards of Plexiglas from the shattered windows had pierced his back, and his bush jacket was stained with blood. Kali tried to kick him full in the groin, but Van Groot blocked the blow with a downward forearm strike, then struck Kali straight in the throat with a tiger fist. Kali flew back against a steel rack of power modules, his bootheels skidded on the floor, and he went down hard on his ass.

Jare pulled a keyboard out from under the controllers. His fingers hovered over the board while he fervently tried to remember the code. Then suddenly, the letters and symbols came flooding back into his brain. Jare pulled up his sleeves with a smile and started typing as fast as a stenographer.

At that moment, Van Groot spotted Jare. Immediately he realized what was going to happen and his face flushed red with fury. "Bastards!" he roared. As he started for Jare, Kali cranked himself off the floor and charged him.

Kali grabbed Van Groot's shoulder and spun him around. He punched him hard in the face, swept his leg with a reverse kick, and smashed him down on his back again. Kali slammed his knees down onto Van Groot's chest and grabbed his throat to choke him out, but adrenaline and fury were surging in Van Groot's veins, and he twisted hard to the left, spinning Kali over onto his spine, and used both legs to try to arm-bar him and break his elbow.

Jare was inside the Brainwave system now. He was reducing all the transmissions, one by one, to every long-range aircraft that was using Brainwave as a cloak. Once that sequence was done, he'd be able to completely cut the power.

Van Groot saw what was happening. He gave up on arm-barring Kali, heel-kicked him in the stomach, and scrambled upright. Kali grabbed Van Groot's leg and Van Groot fell to the right on the floor, but he yanked his boot from Kali's grasp and charged to the right of the console for his gun.

Jare reached up on the controllers for a pair of levers that looked like aircraft throttles. He held his breath as he pulled them downward, and then all of the module's lights blinked and went out.

"It is done!" Jare yelled as he thrust both hands in the air.

But by that time, Van Groot had snatched up his Hi-Power. As Kali charged toward Van Groot it was as though time slowed: Van Groot turned, squinted his nondominant eye, lined up his sight square on Jare, and fired. The bullet sailed across the room and found its mark just under Jare's right arm. Jare screamed as the bullet punched through his ribs.

Kali roared as he lowered his head like a ram and connected with Van Groot's chest, taking him to the ground. It was the moment when Black Box's tight regulation about having no personal relationships made all the sense in the world, but his emotions trumped his logic. He grabbed Van Groot's gun hand before he could shoot Jare again and twisted it around toward the South African's chest. Van Groot tried to break Kali's jaw with his free hand, but Kali didn't even feel the blow. He headbutted Van Groot with such force that his eyes temporarily rolled back and blood gushed from his nose. Kali felt Van Groot's hand loosen on the gun and knew that one more headbutt would knock him unconscious, and subsequently end the brawl in a way that would sustain Van Groot's life. But as he contemplated his next move, his childhood friend's screams were too much to bear. Kali stiffened his face, jammed the Hi-Power under Van Groot's chin and jerked the trigger.

The bullet exploded through the top of Van Groot's skull. He fell back against the tower wall, smearing the pink stones with blood and brain matter as he slid to the floor, with his lifeless eyes rolled back in his head. Kali leaned back and whispered angrily to Van Groot's corpse, "I guess you're my trophy now, *my boy.*"

He got up and ran to Jare, who was lying on his back, blinking up at the ceiling. The blood was pouring from his chest wound. Kali helped him sit up as he groaned, then slipped his forearms under Jare's armpits and held him there.

"Water," Jare whispered.

Kali knew it wasn't a good idea with that kind of wound, but he let Jare take a long pull from his water carrier. Kali jutted his chin at the console.

"You *did* it," he said in Jare's ear.

"I . . . I know . . ." Jare gasped, but he also smiled. "It was just like *Tetris*."

Then he toppled forward and passed out . . .

Kali spoke into his comms. "Dark Horse Actual, this is Dark Horse Main, Brainwave HQ has been shut off. You should be able to see enemy aircraft. How copy?"

"Good copy," Ando said over Kali's comms. "All enemy aircraft popped up two minutes ago. NATO planes will intercept in T-minus thirty minutes. Great work. Break. What's Van Groot's status?"

Kali looked over at Van Groot's dead body, then turned to Jare to pick him up. "Stand by, Dark Horse Actual," Kali said, intentionally not answering Ando's question. He slung Jare's arm over his shoulder and started moving toward the exit. He was hoping Jare was going to make it . . .

FIFTY

A strong ocean breeze was blowing through the Adeyemis' house.

But even though all the windows were open, the breeze moved none of Yvonne's beautiful curtains, because they were gone. The stately mansion was empty, with all its fine furniture taken away, and only Yvonne's mournful footsteps echoed inside the hollow rooms.

Outside the front entrance, where so many well-dressed guests had once happily trotted in and out, Kali sat waiting. He stared at a cluster of bloated suitcases at the bottom of the stairs, holding everything they had left in the world. He was wearing a pair of long pants now and a short-sleeved dress shirt, and his father's bracelet of beads was inside his pocket. Kali held his beloved Game Boy in one hand, with the other hand inside the pocket.

He turned the beads through his fingers, wishing he could be someone else as he waited for Jare to arrive, so they could say their last goodbyes. They hadn't spoken since his father's execution, and the pain of betrayal was still a deep wound in Kali's heart. But Jare would always be his best friend, and even though Kali was very young, he sensed there would never be such a friendship again. A week earlier, Kali had swallowed his pride and sent a short note to Jare's house, asking him to come by. He'd heard nothing in return, but he still had hope.

Yvonne came out of the house. She was wearing George's favorite dress. It was long and billowy, covered with jungle flowers. Her glossy hair was piled up inside a wide-brimmed white straw hat. George's signature hat, the one with the velvet band, was carefully tucked into one of the suitcases. Yvonne looked up at a sign on the polished mahogany doors of her house that read PROPERTY OF THE LAGOS STATE GOVERN-MENT, then closed the doors with a soft, eternal click. She placed her purse next to Kali, sat down next to him, and caressed his hunched shoulders.

"I don't think he is coming, Kalief," she said.

Kali didn't look up at her. He was staring off in the distance. He couldn't see George's dream from there, but he could picture Pearland as he'd once seen it from his father's boat, like a fairy-tale castle rising from the ocean.

"Maybe he will, Mom," he whispered. His voice sounded weak and liquid. "Can we wait a little bit longer?"

"You know I would wait as long as you wish, my son," she said as she rubbed his small head. "But I'm afraid the airplane will not."

A car appeared from the road on the left and parked in front of the house. It was long and black, with two men in the front. They were not wearing uniforms, but Kali knew they were policemen.

The authorities had informed Yvonne that they would be delivering her and Kali to the airport and making sure that they got on the plane. The driver stayed where he was, while the other man got out, opened the trunk, and came over to get the suitcases. But there was no defer-ence in his eyes, and he didn't look at Yvonne or Kali. He closed the trunk and opened the rear door. Yvonne took Kali's hand. They got up, walked to the car, and slipped inside. Kali couldn't bring himself to look once more at their house as the car drove away, so instead he looked down.

"Have you found a place for us to stay in the Apple?" Kali asked as he slumped in the big back seat and gazed at the passing palms.

For the first time since George's death, Yvonne let out a light chuckle. "You mean New York City."

"I heard you call it 'the Big Apple' when you were on the phone last night," Kali muttered.

"It's a nickname, my attentive and astute son," Yvonne said as she pulled Kali close to her. "Aunty Adelola is going to let us room with her until we get back up on our feet. We'll be staying in a part of 'the Apple' called the Bronx."

On many occasions Kali had watched as Jare's mom pleaded with George for money, "until Jare and I get back up on our feet." So, after hearing Yvonne parrot those same words, Kali heard nothing else. That familiar phrase just lingered in his head for what seemed like an eternity.

"Did you hear me, Ka . . .?"

Before Yvonne could get Kali's name out of her mouth, he muttered, "Are we poor now, Mom?"

"No, we will never be poor, my son." She kissed him on the top of his head. "We have each other."

After a moment, Yvonne leaned forward and spoke to the driver and his colleague.

"If we have the time, would you mind going by way of Front Street?" she asked.

Front Street was where Jare lived. Kali sat up straighter in his seat as his heart thumped. His mother was so kind.

The two men looked at each other. The driver checked his watch and shrugged. The big man on the right nodded.

After some turns and curves, they cruised down Front Street, past rows of dilapidated homes that hulked in stark contrast to the wealthy enclave where the Adeyemis had lived. Kali crawled over his mother's lap, because he was sitting on her left and they were passing the houses on the right. Yvonne rolled down the window and he gripped the sill.

There was Jare's house, looming toward them. It was white, just a single story, with a sagging roof and window boxes with blooms going brittle in the Nigerian sun. There was one large picture window in front.

"Slow just a bit here, please," Yvonne said to the driver. He complied, though rolling his eyes at his partner.

Kali stared at the house, searching for his friend. No one was outside, and Jare's battered bicycle, that he'd rode over to Kali's house a thousand times, lay crooked against the front stoop. Then he spotted Jare.

He was inside the house, right there at the picture window, with his small palms pressed to the glass. Kali smiled and waved with both hands, though his vision was blurry now. Jare weakly raised a hand to wave back, and Kali could see that his friend was also crying. Then Jare's mother appeared from somewhere inside, said something harsh to Jare, and dragged him away from the window, as if he were toying with demons.

Kali sank back into the car and laid his head on his mother's shoulder.

She hugged him close as they drove away, to another life somewhere . . .

FIFTY-ONE

OUTSIDE IN FRONT OF THE TOWER, THANE STUCK his head out from his cover position and looked up. Something was streaking through the sky like a blurring black spear. It lanced overhead toward Khalid's quick-reaction force, and exploded among his fighters, sending bodies flying and turning vehicles over on their sides.

"That'll hold them off for a while," Pacenza called over to Thane.

"Don't get too optimistic," Sumo said in their ears. He had crawled up into one of the MRAP turrets and was using his SOFLAM to lase targets. "Those Predators only got three more."

Spencer was flat on his stomach beside one of the MRAPs, scanning the field with a pair of high-powered binoculars he'd gotten from Pacenza. As a Wind agent, he was always focused on mobility, and since their situation looked critical, he was searching for some means of extraction. Suddenly he froze, turned the focus dial, stared for a second, then spun around on his belly and crawled over to Thane under fire.

"There's a C-123 Provider down there inside one of the hangars!" he yelled above the gunfire to Thane. He meant a twin-engine, medium-range cargo aircraft. "No idea what condition it's in, but it won't hurt for me to go check. Right now we've got no other way outta here."

"All right," Thane said. "Take one MRAP and some guys and go look it over."

"Roger," Spencer said before running off.

Thane called over to Pacenza on comms. "Pac, Spencer's gonna go check out an aircraft on the east side of the field. Lay down some covering fire."

"On it," Pacenza said.

Another Hellfire missile came streaking in from the east. They all watched as its warhead exploded between Thane's Package and the assaulting Taliban and Selous Scouts, blowing chunks of tarmac and a plume of black smoke skyward. There were numerous corpses strewn across the runway now, but Khalid's people were not coming on like mindless suicide bombers. They were highly trained professional soldiers, using cover and concealment, making their bullets count. They waited until the smoke from the missile cleared, then opened up again. Another of Pacenza's operators went down and a medic ran to him and dragged him behind an MRAP.

Just then, Kali appeared at the bottom of the tower stairwell with Jare over his shoulder in a fireman's carry, his head down and lolling. Thane looked over from his cover position at the unconscious engineer.

"Did he do it?" Thane asked Kali.

"He did," Kali said.

"And Van Groot?"

"I tried," Kali said. "But he gave me no choice. I have already informed higher. They received it well."

"All right," Thane said. "At least you tried . . . as the president asked."

"What is your plan for getting us out of here?" Kali asked. He was keeping Jare under cover inside the tower's entrance.

"Stand by. Spencer's working on that." Then Thane radioed to Spencer. "Hey Spencer, I need a sitrep, *quick*."

On the eastern side of the airfield, Spencer was already inside the cramped cockpit of the C-123. The MRAP with four of Pacenza's men had dropped him off on the run, then swung away from the hangar to draw off fire. He was hunkered down in the pilot's seat, firing up the electricals, but the controls looked like the last time they'd been serviced might have been in Vietnam.

"Man, this old bird is jacked," he said to Thane. "That's probably why they left it here. She's only got a quarter load of fuel. I don't know how far we'll get."

"See if you can crank it up."

"What do you think I'm doing, Thane?"

Spencer finished adjusting the fuel mixture, held his breath, and punched the starter for the starboard turboprop. The engine coughed like a pneumonia patient, black smoke burst from the exhaust, and the propellers started to slowly turn.

"Well, damn!" Spencer said with a crazy grin. "Thane, start moving our people over here . . . fast!"

Jason and Neveah jogged up to Thane with Sadaf in tow.

"Let's go," Kali said to Thane. With Thane wounded, it was protocol for Kali to take over as assault lead.

Jason and Neveah pulled Thane to his feet. He slung an arm around Jason's shoulders. The MRAPs started to turn, but their turrets swung so they'd maintain suppressive fire on Khalid's fighters. The entire Black Box team and Package started moving toward the C-123 on the other side of the field. But as they withdrew, Khalid and his men realized they were going to try to escape. They surged forward, jumping from burning wreck to concrete barrier and firing as even more of them poured through the west gate. Another Hellfire came streaking in and wiped out their point element, but still they came on.

Kali called over to Sumo as they all surged toward the airplane. He couldn't see Sumo, but he knew he was working the SOFLAM somewhere.

"Sumo, how many missiles do we have left?"

"We only got one more, then we're Winchestered," Sumo said, using the military code for "out of ammo." There was only one Hellfire left on the Predator's pod, and then there'd be nothing to hold off Khalid's men.

"All right, hold that Hellfire in reserve. We're going to need it."

"Acknowledged," Sumo said.

Inside the C-123's cockpit, as both turboprops started to whine and turn faster, Spencer roared like an NBA player who'd just hit the game-winning shot. He pushed a console button for the rear cargo ramp, and it shuddered and stuck for a moment, but then descended and dropped on the hangar floor with a clang. Package operators started flowing aboard.

Kali walked up the ramp with Jare and gently laid him down on the floor. A medic hustled over, bent next to Jare, examined his chest wound, and applied an Asherman Chest Seal, but he looked up at Kali and shook his head. More Package men arrived, carrying the corpses of three of their teammates. There was nothing the medics could do for them.

Thane limped onto the aircraft with Jason, Neveah, and Sadaf. He turned as he realized that Sadaf had stopped on the ramp, and then Ali—her partner Aberration agent—appeared from the darkness of the hangar and joined her.

"It is time for us to get out of here, Thane," Ali said.

"I know," Thane said. "Get on the plane."

"No." Sadaf smiled at Thane. "Ali means off this field and back undercover. Our work is done here, but not out there."

"Are you sure?" Thane said. He knew that if Spencer managed to get the plane off the ground, Ali and Sadaf would be left there in a hornet's nest.

"We're sure," Ali said with a smile. "We've been in much worse . . . Hopefully, we will see you again."

They both shook Thane's hand, and then disappeared out a small back fire exit.

Kali had Thane sit down on the floor and lean against the fuselage, then he took Jason and Neveah and went forward into the cockpit.

"Good to see you again," Kali said to Spencer.

Without turning his gaze from the windshield, Spencer replied, "Likewise."

"Can you get us out of here?" Kali asked Spencer.

"Yeah, but I've got to turn this thing around, and hope I can get it over those mountains."

"As soon as we lift off," Jason said to Kali, "they're gonna try to take us down with all they've got."

Kali nodded and spoke to Pacenza over comms.

"Pac, we're going to leave the ramp open when we taxi onto the strip, but we'll have our ass to those guys. Shoot everything you've got at them and maybe we'll make it out of here."

"Roger," Pac said, but they both knew the odds were slim.

The engines roared, causing the C-123 to vibrate like an old pickup truck. The rear cargo area was now packed with operators, and the last few, including Sumo, had just made it on board. The plane nosed out of the hangar and started a painfully slow turn to the right. Three operators lying prone on the cargo ramp started spewing covering fire with their M249s, but they were getting low on ammo and had to use controlled bursts against murderous automatic fire. Bullets whanged off the ramp and ricocheted up through the fuselage, missing fuel and control lines by fractions of an inch.

Kali ran back from the cockpit, grabbed Sumo with his SOFLAM, and they both went prone beside the SAW gunners. Kali pointed over to the left at a large fuel truck, hoping it was at least still half full.

"See that truck, Sumo?" he said. "Give me a lase on it and let's call in that last missile. Maybe we can give ourselves a wall of fire."

Sumo triggered the SOFLAM and painted the truck with a laser dot, but he reminded Kali, "Roger, but that's gonna be the last one."

"Do it," Kali said.

Sumo called over comms to an air force controller.

"Sumo for Spike, lasing my last target now. Fire when ready."

"Roger," the female controller returned. "Hellfire dropped."

The missile dived down at the strip like a raven with its wings tucked back, then it pierced the top of the fuel truck. The ear-splitting bang was horrendous, but a gout of flame burst from its ravaged steel belly and coursed across the field, creating a raging wall of orange fire.

"Winchester, Winchester," the air force controller stated. She had nothing left to give.

"That should hold them for a while," Kali said.

Four men had jumped from a truck and sprinted forward to Khalid with a large wooden crate. It had US stamped on the cover, clearly another piece of weaponry left behind. They yanked it open. There was a Stinger antiaircraft missile inside.

In the C-123 cockpit, Spencer had the engines cranked to full throttle. He'd wound the flaps down so he could execute the shortest takeoff possible, and he started raising the ramp as he released the brake pedals. The big airplane began to roll down the strip, but the engines sputtered, and they weren't hitting full RPMs. He doubted the old bird would make it. He turned his head to Jason and Neveah.

"You'd better get back there and assume the position," he called above the roaring engines.

"We're staying right here with you, Spence," Jason said, and Neveah looked at him with an affirming nod, "but punch this thing and get it off the damn ground!"

Khalid had four of Van Groot's Selous Scouts assembling the Stinger missile system. They were moving as fast as they could, and one of them was already down on one knee on the tarmac, waiting for his mates to lock and load. Six of Khalid's armored Humvees drove up on his flanks, the drivers and men inside ready to brave the wall of fire, but Khalid called out to them and waved them off.

"Even if that airplane leaves the field," he shouted as he pointed down at his Stinger crew, "we can blow it out of the sky from here!"

Spencer was racing the C-123 as fast as the engines would take him. They were nearly at the old contractor huts at the end of the field, where just beyond that the mountains loomed.

"You two better strap in," he yelled above the engine roar. Jason slid into the copilot's seat, Neveah jumped into the navigator's perch, and they both buckled in as Spencer pulled a mic module off the instrument panel and his voice blared from a speaker in the back. "Everybody brace for takeoff. I'm gonna rotate this bird!"

"We have to keep laying down fire!" Sumo called to Pacenza.

"Just do what Spencer says," Pacenza returned. "It's up to him now. We've done all that we can. Now grab something and *brace*."

Sumo and all the rest of the operators gripped fuselage ribs and hung on. Kali made sure that Thane was secure, then he moved over to Jare and sat down behind his head. He spread his feet, locked his boot tips under two cargo rings in the floor, pulled Jare into his lap, and held on tight.

In the cockpit, Spencer held his breath and pulled back on the yoke. Bullets were still pinging off the back of the airplane as the nose wheel left the runway, and the fat bird thundered off the airstrip.

Back on the tarmac, behind the wall of flame, the Selous Scout operating the Stinger looked over at Khalid and shot him a thumbs-up. The system was ready to kill.

Just then, a large convoy of armored vehicles rushed through the old US Air Force headquarters area and sped onto the field. There were dozens of trucks, all bristling with guns and warriors. In the lead vehicle sat Bilad and Shafik, the late Ziar Baradar's most trusted lieutenants. They skirted the wall of aircraft fuel fire, cut across the field, raced up to Khalid's position, and stopped.

Bilad and Shafik got out, both looking furiously at the hail of gunfire that was still lancing out at the lumbering airplane. They ran toward Khalid as Bilad shouted, "Stop!"

Khalid knew who they were—two of the most trusted and legendary mujahideen warriors. "What do you want?" he shouted back.

"We want you to stop this, Khalid," Bilad said as he halted in front of him. "In the name of peace, *cease fire*."

"Peace?" Khalid said sarcastically. "We can have peace when all those Americans are dead! Look at what they did. Look at all this carnage!"

"Khalid, listen to me carefully, and think," Bilad said. "If you bring that aircraft down, within one month the Americans will be here in full force. We will have another twenty years of warfare and this time our country will be destroyed. Do you want that, Khalid?"

"Yes! Let them come back, and *we* will destroy *them* as we did before, even if it takes another twenty years!" Khalid was still under the spell of Amir's influence, even though his warrior mentor was dead. "This is what Amir would have wanted." He pointed across the burning field at Amir's corpse, lying askew near the old control tower.

"Amir is the one who is responsible for all of this!" Bilad shouted into Khalid's face. "*He* killed his own father. *He* killed Ziar Baradar!"

"What do you mean?" Khalid said. "Ziar's not dead. He went to Kunduz . . ."

"No, Khalid," Bilad said. "He's dead. We watched Amir kill him, with our own eyes."

Shafik jumped in and calmly said, "Bilad is right. Our leader has been taken from us, and that South African, Van Groot, helped Amir cover it up."

Khalid stood there stunned. His eyes filled up as Bilad went on.

"Amir brought these foreign fighters here to our land—Van Groot, Nabuto, and all the others who have no business being here!"

Bilad swept a hand at Van Groot's surviving Selous Scouts, who stared back at him, wondering what was going on, because they didn't understand the language. They returned their focus to the Stinger and prepared it to fire.

Then Bilad spun and shot his fingers at the rattling old cargo plane that was struggling up toward the mountains beyond.

"That airplane, and those men that you are about to shoot out of the sky, Khalid. They came to right Amir's wrongs and restore Ziar's hope. Ziar did not want this. You *know* that. You know the man that Ziar was. You respected him. Amir was brainwashed, and he was twisted to do this, and he betrayed his own people. And if *you* do this you will further betray Ziar's vision."

"And what is that vision, Bilad?" Khalid said. "Since you know so much."

"Sovereignty and peace," Bilad said, and he quieted and extended an offering hand. "Let's rule this land together. Let's do what they said could not be done. Let's turn the other cheek. Let us not seek revenge right now. And then you and I, together, and Shafik, we will rule the way Ziar wanted to."

The Selous Scout Stinger team had locked onto the C-123. The missile's warhead emitted its fully armed warning: *beep, beep, beep . . .*

"Holy crap!" Spencer yelled as a warning indicator blared from his instrument panel. "We've got a freakin' missile lock!" He yanked the microphone to his mouth again. "Missile inbound! Brace, brace, brace for evasive maneuvers!" He tried to bank the big airplane hard to the left, but in a steep-angle climb it was nearly impossible.

"Damn!" Sumo said as he plugged his face between his knees and all his teammates did the same. "We shoulda kept on letting them have it!"

As the thundering commotion continued, Jare's eyes fluttered open. He looked up at Kali's face, upside down.

"What is going on?" he managed to say as a slight smirk crossed his face. "Did you bring me back onto an airplane to kill me now?"

"No, Jare," Kali said as he gripped his friend's shoulders to hold him down. "We're taking you home."

Khalid's Stinger operator started squeezing the trigger. "Launching in three . . . two . . . one . . ."

"Stop!" Khalid suddenly shouted to the Stinger team in English. Then he turned on his men who were still firing at the plane. "All of you! Cease fire!"

The scouts looked at him, shut down the missile, and lowered the weapon. At that moment, all the gunfire from the strip fell silent. No bullets or missiles leaped out at the plane. Khalid gestured to two of his sergeants and ordered them to detain Van Groot's men. Then he turned back to Bilad and Shafik.

"We will let the Americans go," he said. "In honor of Ziar Baradar, and for the sake of Afghanistan . . ."

Bilad stepped forward and firmly shook Khalid's hand.

Spencer looked down at the missile warning system on the instrument panel. It had stopped blaring and the blinking red light was off. He tapped it hard, thinking it was some sort of short circuit, but its silent message was clear. He swiped the sweat from his forehead and keyed the loudspeaker mic.

"Stand down from that warning," he called. "Don't know what's going on back there on the ground, but no missile's inbound."

Nobody cheered in the back, but they all raised their heads from their knees and hoped he was right.

In the cockpit, Neveah had pumped up the navigator's screen. "Give me 156 degrees south-southeast, toward Nawabad on the Paki border," she said to Spencer. "There are no antiaircraft batteries, and there's a big, fat highway on the other side. I think we might make it."

"Roger," Spencer said.

The big plane banked gently to the right, then lifted into the blue sky over the mountains.

Ando's voice suddenly crackled inside everyone's bone mics and headsets.

"This is Dark Horse Actual. I'm relaying a live feed from the air force over the Caspian Sea. Our squadrons have intercepted enemy fighters and the assault has commenced. Good work, people. Dark Horse Actual, out."

Pacenza and all his operators perked up as they heard the fruits of their labor.

"This is Phantom Five, I just splashed a Tango. Check your six, Phantom Four, his wingman is trailing you." It was the calm voice of an F-22 pilot. Then came another. "I see him! Peeling right! Who's got me?!" Then a female pilot's voice came over comms. "Phantom Seven here. I got you, Phantom Four. Peel out now . . . Missiles away." Two seconds later, "Wingman is down, Phantom Seven. Good kill. I repeat, good kill."

The operators in the back of the plane exchanged subtle nods and soft handshakes. To them it was just business as usual, but business that they knew hadn't been finished yet, as they were still in the air with their fully armed enemies on the ground.

Kali relaxed his protective grip on Jare as the aircraft settled into a lumbering cruise. Jare looked up at Kali and tried to smile.

"I . . . I think I beat your score, my brother," he whispered.

Kali nodded. It was over. He didn't need to disguise himself anymore, and he dropped his Nigerian accent.

"Yes, you did, my brother," he said to Jare. "Yes, you did."

Then Jare closed his eyes and died.

Kali was still holding Jare's hand. His shoulders slumped as he sat on the rumbling steel floor, and hung his head . . .

FIFTY-TWO

SITUATION ROOM, THE WHITE HOUSE

ON THE LARGE FLAT-SCREEN BEHIND PRESIDENT Turner's head, American jet fighters were knocking the Bagram squadrons out of the sky.

The screen was split into six big rectangles, each displaying a pilot's point of view in the cockpit. The clear blue skies over the western shore of the Caspian Sea were crisscrossed with afterburner and missile contrails, cannon tracers, and enemy aircraft flipping and spinning as they tried to escape but failed. At the bottom of each rectangle, each pilot's real-time vitals were also displayed—heart rate, blood pressure, oxygen percentage—but they seemed no more elevated than if the US fighter jockeys were playing an intensive volleyball match. Along with the visuals, which looked very similar to a wild video game, a low-volume soundtrack of their radio transmissions could be heard.

"This is Phantom Eight, it looks like we've got another cargo plane that wants to masquerade as a suicide missile. Are we clear to take it out?"

"Phantom Commander here. That sounds like a threat to me. Take it out."

"Phantom Eight. Good copy. Missiles away . . . Target hit. Cargo plane four down."

Almost all of the faces inside the Situation Room were turned toward the big screen, mesmerized by the life-and-death struggle in the air. The president's commanders of all the armed services were there along with their executive officers, including the chairman of the Joint Chiefs, navy admirals, and generals from the army, air force, and marines. Many of them were issuing urgent orders, using secure telephones to talk to their commanders in the field, but everyone had one eye locked on the unfolding drama.

President Turner, however, was turned to one side in his executive chair, head down in a low-voiced discussion with Ando, Frank Gibson, and a mysterious Caucasian man in a tailored sharp gray suit who didn't look too happy.

The mysterious man whispered aggressively at Ando, "We've been trying to identify Zero for years, and Van Groot just revealed he was our only link to him or her. Dammit, Ando! What part of 'capture him alive' did Dark Horse not understand?!"

Ando whispered back in a tone that matched the mysterious man's, "You saw what they were up against, and despite it, they did their very best to capture him! It just wasn't possible under the circumstances."

Sensing the tension between the two men who seemed to be of the same rank, the president chimed in to pacify the standoff: "We just had a big win, so let's take it easy on each other, shall we?" Then he looked at Ando. "Y'all did a very fine job. It's just I wish we would've captured that Van Groot fella alive. Did that satellite thingamajig intercept anyone else on target who may have made comms with Zero?"

"No, Mr. President. But don't worry," Ando said. "Our people are the very best. We'll figure it out."

"I'll second that, Mr. President," Gibson said as he stared angrily at the mysterious man. "They'll get the job done. That I promise."

"All right, gentlemen," Turner said as he turned back around to the big screen. The mysterious man switched his gaze from Gibson to Ando for a beat, then turned and slipped quietly out of the room.

The six display rectangles now appeared to be showing a cleared battle environment. There were no more enemy planes, and the American fighters were forming up near one another, wingtips close. One pilot pulled his mask down and could be seen grinning from a cockpit while jutting a thumbs-up. The president spoke over his shoulder to the commander of the air force.

"What are we looking at now, Maggie?"

"They've taken down all of their targets, Mr. President," she said from her perch down the right side of the big conference table. "That includes all refuelers, helicopters, and cargo planes. They gave our pilots no choice."

Then the voice of an air mission commander downrange came through the flat-screen's audio field. "Requesting permission to RTB, General Caufield." He meant Maggie, the air force commander.

"What's RTB?" the president asked her.

"Return to base, sir."

The president thought about that for a moment, then he said over his shoulder to the general, "No one's returning to base just yet. How much fuel do our eagles have?"

The general raised an eyebrow, then passed the inquiry to her air mission commander, who relayed it to his squadrons. After a moment, he answered. "We're low across the board, ma'am. But we've got air refuelers in trail. Once we link up, we can go wherever you order. Over."

A pilot's voice broke over comms. He was talking to his wingman.

"Where we goin' now, Chuck?"

"Damned if I know, boss."

Frank Gibson got up and leaned his head down next to the president's. Everyone else in the room was exchanging curious looks.

"What are you thinking, Mr. President?" Gibson asked quietly.

"I'm thinking I've been kind of a bitch the last three and a half years. I let politics get in the way of doing the right thing. But not anymore, Frank. Not anymore."

Gibson wasn't sure he was hearing right.

"Are you saying . . . ?"

"I'm saying we're gonna do what we should have done long ago," the president said with conviction. "I want all those Russian armored columns bombed, every one of 'em that's headed for Hungary and Poland. And then we're going to do the same damn thing in Ukraine, until that country's territory is back to where it was before Russia crossed the line."

"Attaboy!" Gibson squeezed the president's shoulder, then withdrew his hand and said, "I mean, very good, sir."

"Ando, get over here," the president said. Ando got up and came to him. "What's the intel saying right now? What are your Aberration folks saying about those armored columns, missile positions, targets, and all that?"

Ando picked up his secure tablet, where he had a carbon copy of his area-of-operations analysis from the big screen in his Black Box headquarters ship. He showed it to the president, pointing out targets of opportunity, all circled in red.

"These Russian targets are all strategic, sir," he said. "If we can take them out, it's endgame for the New Russia borderlines."

"Give that thing over to Maggie, Ando."

The president shot a thumb at his air force commander. Ando leaned across the big table and handed the tablet to the general as he clicked on an access button so she could download the digital map.

"That work for you, General?" the president asked her.

"It's perfect, Mr. President," she said.

"Good. Relay that to your squadrons right now. You got tank busters in the area?"

"We've got two squadrons of A-10s, sir. One in Ramstein and one outside Warsaw."

"Launch 'em," Turner said. Then he turned around from the screen, spread his big palms on the table, and looked at all of his "guests."

"People, we are going to push back the Russian offensive line. Whatever this fella Van Groot was trying to do can't ever be done again. This is the last time Moscow's ever going to make this play. It's over. I'm ordering a full assault on the Ukrainian territory they stole."

All the generals, executive officers, and uniformed adjutants stared at Turner. Then the chairman of the Joint Chiefs grinned and slowly started to clap. In a moment, they were all applauding with a roar of slapping palms.

The president nodded in appreciation. Then he turned to his Secret Service agent, who, as always, was standing nearby.

"Sean," he said. "Go get the steward. We're not going anywhere tonight. It's going to be a takeout evening for us."

EPILOGUE

LAGOS, NIGERIA

AT THE IKOYI CEMETERY IN LAGOS, KALI STOOD ON a small hill in the shadows of the Moringa trees. In the distance, among the ordered rows of lush palms and above-ground granite tombs, he watched as Jare was lowered into his grave.

Kali had arranged for Jare's body to be flown from Islamabad, Pakistan, to Lagos, but he couldn't accompany his friend, so he'd said his goodbyes as they loaded the metal transport coffin onto a commercial flight.

In Lagos, the body had been received by an Aberration agent, who had put Jare on ice. Jare's mother was then informed—by Kali himself, using a Nigerian Chameleon disguise—that Jare had been taken from his jungle mansion by a warlord's gang. He gave her only three hours to gather a ransom—such kidnappings were common practice in Nigeria—but to avoid any guilt from falling on her, Kali called back thirty minutes later with the news that Jare had resisted and had therefore been executed. She was then told where she could find Jare's body, in one of Lagos's sprawling parks. A call to the police had brought him home.

Though it may have seemed cruel, such extreme deception was necessary to keep Black Box and the international operation that Jare had been involved in completely hidden from the public eye. If anyone found out about Black Box, the unit could be dissolved, and even worse, there was the potential a discovery could lead to a copycat scenario. Ironically, in order to potentially save lives, Jare's mother could never know the hero he had become and the scores of innocent lives he had saved.

However, in an attempt to make up for such horrendous measures, Kali had the CIA deposit $10 million in restitution into a bank account in Houston. Both Jare's and his mother's names were on the account, and in similar fashion to his death cover-up, Jare's mom would be notified by the bank that she was now the sole benefactor and led to believe that the account had been started years earlier by Jare.

Choosing a bank in Houston wasn't an accident. Kali went a step further, ensuring that Jare's mom would be contacted by the number-one cancer treatment center in America—MD Anderson Cancer Center, located in Houston—and invited to partake in specialized treatment. A permanent green card would come along with the invite. Good luck wouldn't bring her son back, but it would certainly make living out the rest of her years a bit easier.

Now, watching the proceedings left Kali with a hollow and empty feeling. He could not participate in the final farewell for his best friend, but that was the way of Black Box, where personal connections and relationships were shunned in favor of duty. The Ikoyi Cemetery was famous for grand interments of state officials and media stars, but there were also graves reserved for lesser mortals, on the fringes. There, in one remote corner, a modest group of mourners with heads bowed were saying prayers as the white-shrouded body disappeared inside a granite encasement, soon to be covered in bright white gravel, and later, a modest headstone.

Jare's mother was there, aged and hunched in black mourning garb. She kept herself steady with a cane, and Kali could see some sort of medical device that was strapped across her shoulders. An older man in a suit was gently holding her elbow as she wept. Kali squinted, recognizing the man as Chibundu, the same policeman who'd betrayed his father and family. It was clear that across the years, the Lagos government had kept their claws in Jare, and then Van Groot had come along and made Jare wealthy, while doubling his torment.

Time had not been kind to Chibundu. He was gray and bulging in his suit. Kali would not be kind to him either, but that could wait.

His cell phone buzzed in his pocket. He took it out and said, "Kent."

"Where are you, Kali?" It was Neveah.

"I'm in Lagos, observing Jare's funeral," he said. "From a distance, of course."

There was silence for a moment. Then Neveah said, "Interesting. I've never known you to attend the funeral of an asset before, Kali." She continued with a hint of sarcasm. "You do know we have a whole unit that does that."

"Yeah . . . I figured I'd handle the follow-up surveillance to make up for the Van Groot fumble," he replied. "Somebody might show up who's connected to Van Groot, or this Zero character, and I'm sure I'll have a better sense than Shadow Four," Kali elaborated, referring to the Black Box unit that clandestinely gathered post-op intel on surviving family and friends of assets or KIA enemy combatants. Shadow Four also surreptitiously collected intel from battlegrounds such as Van Groot's island, the Bagram air base, and the Comando Vermelho takedown site in Brazil.

"Uh-huh." She wasn't quite buying it.

"How did Spencer's delivery go?" he asked, changing the subject.

"Jason and I just left their house. It went great. The girls were elated to see him, but of course asked about his bumps and bruises. I wish you could've seen Janie." Neveah chuckled. "Without hesitation she jumped straight into a cover story and explained it away. Let's just say, no other questions were asked after that."

Kali let out his own light chuckle. "Sounds like Janie's still got it," he said.

"She does . . . but to be honest"—Neveah sighed before continuing—"we think Spencer's pretty jacked up after this, and I don't mean physically. He got his deck shuffled pretty hard the last few weeks, and if my instinct's on point, I think he might be toying with the idea of leaving Black Box."

"What's Jason's assessment?" Kali said.

"Neveah and I are on the same page," Jason said—Neveah's cell was on speaker. "Once we landed back in the States and he came down from the high, he had that thousand-yard stare . . . Not good, brother."

"All right. I'll make sure to check on him when I get back. And if anything comes of this," Kali said, referring to his surveillance op, "I'll be in touch."

Neveah and Jason both said in unison, "Bye, Kali."

Kali looked at his cell for a moment as he raised an eyebrow. There was something about the way Jason and Neveah answered as one—an intimacy he couldn't put his finger on. But he dismissed it and put the cell back in his pocket.

In the distance, a priest was saying last rites over Jare's grave. Two men now were supporting Jare's mother so she wouldn't collapse. It reminded Kali of Chibundu and Reki handling Yvonne at his father's execution. Two gravediggers were starting to shovel the white gravel into Jare's open tomb.

Jare's death weighed heavily on Kali's heart, but keeping the facts of their friendship from Black Box—and especially from Thane, Jason, and Neveah—was now even harder to bear. The unit's stiff regulations about such personal relationships were sacrosanct, but it was more than that—it was the trust he'd broken with his teammates. He found himself regretting his tactical decision, wishing he'd done everything by the book. Yes, he told himself, ultimately Spencer was rescued, Van Groot was stopped, and his plot with the Russians and Amir had failed. But if Kali hadn't reacted emotionally to Van Groot shooting Jare, he might have been able to take Van Groot alive. They would now be closer to identifying this phantom individual, Zero, who might in fact turn out to be more deadly than a South African ex-commando running a Hostage Inc. The president himself had thought it important enough to get on the horn with Black Box in the field. Yet because of Kali, they were back to square one.

But the past was the past. He couldn't repair what he'd done. However, from now on, his adherence to the regulations would be ironclad; no exceptions. *I will never do this again*, he thought as he watched Jare's mother laying flowers onto her son's grave with her trembling old hands. Then he whispered, "Never again," to himself, before turning and walking away.

Kali got into his rental car and started driving south toward Victoria Island. He drove through slums, where many of the poor pedestrians hauled baskets of groceries on their heads, and if they had vehicles, the small motorbikes and beat-up cars coughed grimy black exhaust into the air. He drove through enclaves of mansions, where nobody walked, except to get into their Range Rovers or Mercedes. It made him recall his father's dream for Nigeria, where the corrupt would finally fall and the downtrodden would be up-lifted. Lagos was now a modern, bustling city, but it hadn't even touched the fringes of George's dream yet.

Kali parked the car on Victoria Island, pulled a canvas satchel from the trunk, and took the white-hulled ferry across the bay from Victoria Island to the beach at Tarkwa.

Walking past the throngs of tourists and locals sunning them-selves in their lounge chairs, he set the satchel down in the sand and stripped down to only a pair of short tan swimmer's trunks. Placing his waterproof cell in one pocket, he pulled a pair of IST Rubber Rocket fins from the satchel and walked down into the surf.

Kali swam like a man who'd been born in the water. It hadn't always been that way, but he'd been trained at the Farm by a US Navy SEAL instructor whose mantra was "solutions over excuses." It was a bright, cloudless day with a hard sun rising behind him, and he didn't need a wrist compass because he knew exactly where he was going—due west to Pearland. It was two nautical miles, first through a hundred meters of riptides, then indigo blue, white-tipped waves for the rest, but it was nothing to him. He'd swum through much worse before, at night and in the freezing cold. This was a warm, lush, summertime cruise.

Halfway there, the island appeared before him, like some Afri-can version of Atlantis or Brigadoon, rising out of the cobalt waters, with its completed structures of stone, glass, and steel gleaming in the sunlight through his watery vision. It was his father's island.

At two hundred yards from the island, Kali stopped swimming

and treaded water, staring at the jewel of his family's legacy. It was not the first time he'd made this trek, but the sixth in the past five years, and he always stopped at the same spot. He'd sworn that he would never set foot on Pearland until once again it belonged to the Adeyemis.

Maybe that wouldn't happen, or maybe it would. Either way, the outcome would have to wait . . .

His cell phone buzzed in his pocket again. He took it out, slowly kicking his fins beneath him as he answered. This time it was Thane.

"You're supposed to be on leave," Thane said.

"I am," Kali answered.

"I just heard from Neveah. She told me you're working."

"Just trying to tie up some loose ends," Kali said.

"It sounds like you're in a bathtub," Thane said.

"Something like that," Kali replied. "How's the leg?"

"It's all good," Thane said. "I'll sport a limp for a few weeks, then be back up to speed shortly after . . . Got some good news."

"What is it?" Kali asked.

"We got a lead on a link to this Zero target. Could be significant, but first Black Box seniors want to get us fully read in to what we're dealing with."

"Got it," Kali said. "I guess that's your polite way of saying get back to HQ."

Thane chuckled. "It is. See you soon, Kali."

Kali slipped the cell phone under the waves and back into his pocket. He treaded water for another minute under the bright sunlight, inhaling the sweet scents of brine and squinting at the vision of his father's dream. Of all the things he had learned as a Black Box agent, the first, and most important, was the ability to control his emotions, and the second was patience.

"Not yet," he whispered above the sound of the rolling waves. "Not yet."

And he turned around and started the long swim back, as the sun began to set behind him, reflecting its glory onto Pearland.

ABOUT THE AUTHOR

REMI ADELEKE was born into riches in Nigeria, but following the death of his father and the unjust seizing of his family's wealth by the Nigerian government, Remi, his mother, and his brother permanently relocated to the Bronx, New York, in 1987. After years of making regrettable decisions, Remi enlisted in the US Navy in 2002, serving as a corpsman with the First Marine Division, and later joined the Navy SEALs, where he specialized in combat medicine and human intelligence.

Ending his successful naval career in 2016, he was led to pursue opportunities in film and television consulting, directing, writing, and acting, including the 2017 franchise film *Transformers: The Last Knight*; the CBS television series *SEAL Team*; the Universal thriller *Ambulance*, directed by Michael Bay; and the Lionsgate blockbuster *Plane*. Remi can also be seen in Amazon's TV adaptation of Jack Carr's *New York Times* bestseller *The Terminal List*.

As a consultant, Remi worked on Netflix's *6 Underground*, the Apple+ TV series *Invasion*, and Netflix's *Here Comes the Flood*. Remi is the host and co-executive producer of the *Down Range* narrative podcast, which is distributed via Tenderfoot TV. Additionally, Remi is one of the hosts of the UK series *SAS: Who Dares Wins* and its US derivative, *Special Forces: World's Toughest Test*, which airs on Fox.

As a filmmaker, Remi wrote and directed *The Unexpected*, a thirty-two-minute short film that uncovers an international organ-harvesting ring. In addition, he has written and will be directing the feature-length version of the short, titled *Unexpected Redemption*.

As a screenwriter, Remi copenned the adapted teleplay for *Slave Stealers*, which highlights the abolitionist Harriet Jacobs. He also wrote the screenplays *The Chameleon* and *The Last Shall Be First*, the latter of which tells the untold true story of the first group of African Americans to serve in the US Army Special Forces and the integral but forgotten role they played in the retaking of South Korea from Communist forces.

Remi holds a bachelor's degree in organizational leadership and a master's in organizational strategy, both from the University of Charleston. Remi's incredible story can be found in his bestselling autobiography, *Transformed: A Navy SEAL's Unlikely Journey from the Throne of Africa, to the Streets of the Bronx, to Defying All Odds.*